LITTLE BOY WILD

Little Boy Wild was a small boy who did not have permission to be alive, and this is his epic real-life journey as an abused child in search of himself. It is fearless, hauntingly beautiful, and sometimes disturbing. This is complicated by his other personalities and the hilarious adventures they encounter as he lives semi-wild with the animals. His life is one of incredible discoveries, survival, growth and elevated states of consciousness!

DEREK KURTIS

TRAFFORD

USA ▪ Canada ▪ UK ▪ Ireland

Our web site is www.littleboywild.com

Note for Librarians: A cataloguing record for this book is available from Library and Archives Canada at www.collectionscanada.ca/amicus/index-e.html
ISBN 1-4120-7920-9

Printed in Victoria, BC, Canada. Printed on paper with minimum 30% recycled fibre. Trafford's print shop runs on "green energy" from solar, wind and other environmentally-friendly power sources.

Offices in Canada, USA, Ireland and UK
This book was published *on-demand* in cooperation with Trafford Publishing. On-demand publishing is a unique process and service of making a book available for retail sale to the public taking advantage of on-demand manufacturing and Internet marketing. On-demand publishing includes promotions, retail sales, manufacturing, order fulfilment, accounting and collecting royalties on behalf of the author.

This book is co-published by Tarkatu Ventures and Trafford Publishing. Sales enquiries may be directed to either www.trafford.com or to www.littleboywild.com

Book sales for North America and international:
Trafford Publishing, 6E–2333 Government St.,
Victoria, BC V8T 4P4 CANADA
phone 250 383 6864 (toll-free 1 888 232 4444)
fax 250 383 6804; email to orders@trafford.com
Book sales in Europe:
Trafford Publishing (UK) Limited, 9 Park End Street, 2nd Floor
Oxford, UK OX1 1HH UNITED KINGDOM
phone 44 (0)1865 722 113 (local rate 0845 230 9601)
facsimile 44 (0)1865 722 868; info.uk@trafford.com
Order online at:
trafford.com/05-2818

10 9 8 7 6 5 4 3 2

Acknowledgements

We feel so grateful at the launching of this work to be able to thank some of the many people who over the years gave *us* the courage to start, and to continue with this adventure into *"oneness,"* wherever it may have led. They were intrigued by *our* personas, and all the weird things that happened to *us*, but above all, they got a huge laugh at the humorous situations that arose. Tears, hurt, and laughter, were all a part of growth as we journeyed from a state of being highly dysfunctional and a danger to others – into a reasonable facsimile of "normalcy" today! Thank you all for joining us on this journey.

Our heart-felt thanks to Dr. Arthur Janov for his "The Primal Scream" and "The Primal Revolution," for *us*, both landmarks in the field of psychiatry. I have quoted or paraphrased Dr.Janov from time to time, as he was, and is, a beacon and guiding light through our hurt and confusion.

Thanks to Shendra and Collin Hanney for the many suggestions they contributed during the early days, and especially to Shendra for her critique and ideas at the finale. Thanks however, cannot do justice to their support during some of *our* more difficult psychiatric struggles during the LSD incident.

A special thanks to David Flumerfelt – a friend of many years, whose input got the ball rolling, and to Jon Taylor for his astute insight and observations. It goes without saying that this book was written despite my deepest misgivings! We also thank the many whose support and encouragement helped us continue to the surprise conclusion of the whole story.

Our cover design and artistry were produced by Julia Berschley of Pristine Graphics. She created a portal of trust for Little Boy Wild; and in a rare and emotional moment, he smiled, and shyly took her by the hand to lead her far within, to the ***"meadows of his mind,"*** – his sanctuary from the traumas that he could no longer endure.

The real work-horse assignment of critique and adjudication in the matter of structure, time lines and tenses throughout our story, were a work of love by Susan Wiebe and Rebecca Honigman. We are so thankful for their dedication to these fine details, and to the insights that they produced.

I do not have to thank ***all*** my furry wilderness friends, because they already "know" of their part in the healing process. We gifted our acceptance of each other in that timeless "Eden," and became as one.

Finally – a loving "thank you" to all other abused, and stuttering fellow sufferers, some of whom shared their own current insight and pain with us. Be assured – as we all grow beyond our fragmented selves to wholeness, one truth stands out – ***we are never alone!***

The Adventure Map!

Introduction

*L*ittle Boy Wild is an epic totally non-fiction work, and is a fascinating psychiatric journey toward whatever *"Normalcy"* is, to one who has survived extreme child abuse. It has taken a number of years for *us* to understand what the book was really all about, apart from the fact that people wanted to share in the laughter at all the strange adventures that *"We"* lived. *"We," being primarily "Little Boy Wild," also known as "Wild Boy,"* and *"Me," – I'm Derek, usually referred to as "I."* These are of course two aspects of a single self. One day Wild Boy put it to me this way quite succinctly!

> I am not He
> And He is not I
> He is not We
> And neither am I!

It has also been almost impossible until quite recently to gain meaningful insight into *our* fragmented personality; for example, who *is* in control? And what prompts Wild Boy to take over? Which one of us got married? And – which of us was baptized? Derek has always tried to go with the flow – doing what the Humans normally do within their value system, but Little Boy Wild runs powerful interference when Derek has wandered too far into Human territory and their false values.

So just what is this book all about? It seems to defy categorization the way my life has always defied the norm. But in the library would one find it under adventure? It *is* a series of intriguing explorations into a questionable life pattern, but it is also extremely funny. However, one would more probably find it under psychiatry and disorders of the mind! This might be closer, as it does track a journey through the labyrinths of a mind hiding from

1

the Human race that spawned it; a psyche in search of itself. It records the life of one with a deeply split and fragmented personality; plus some additional psychic variations. It may also more aptly come across as the reading of a psychiatrist's highly confidential doctor-patient journal of record, all wrapped up in hilarious humor and rollicking adventures. Although hurtful upon occasion, it is always very humorous. It is a record of turbulent graduation from the status of an unwanted and brutally abused child, to young manhood, and beyond—to a dubious split level of maturity.

My behavior throughout this odyssey was such that *we* alienated most Humans who entered our sphere, or *we* theirs. To make matters worse, *We*, that is *Little Boy Wild*, and *Me*, and let's not forget the *Preacher,* and that master mind, the *Movie Director,* all formed part of this personality fragmentation. They made me feel somewhat less than Human—if human at all! Each of these personalities took turns at the wheel of my life, charting courses of impossible predicaments and consternation to others, as well as to *ourselves* wherever *we* went. On top of that, they always left *me—Derek,* to face the music after these fiascos; to live with the irrevocable decisions that were made, and to pay the bills! During these writings I reveled in much uproarious laughter. I also shed many tears; they flowed from secret places previously hidden from understanding, and from a time when self esteem had yet to be born. I dedicate this entire story to all those persons who fall outside the pale of humanity; who dwell perhaps between several worlds of reality, and who endure the traumas of life from that position. At times it may touch your own psychic wounds, but I trust you will have the courage, albeit through tears upon occasion, to continue the journey; for where there is loss, there are tears, and tears are indeed the elixir of recovery.

Before we dip into our first chapter – it will help to be briefly acquainted with some of the relatively simple psychological terms you will come across! We'll be meeting *"neurotic behavior"* which is *defense against excessive psychological pain;* its purpose is to hide the tragedy of one's early life. The body continues to live at any cost—and that cost is *"Neurosis."* A person suffering as such is called *"Neurotic."*

Little Boy Wild views life from within the prison of time, and is not yet aware that *neither of us can go forward in life, until our past has been fully dealt with.* *"We"* have lived our lives apart, but running parallel to each other. I now feel it is time for us to become *ONE*. Little Boy Wild will share his explorations and feelings with you, as he attempts to grow into emotional maturity – if indeed he ever really does.

We are dealing here with *Dissociative Identity Disorder* (DID), which was previously known as Multiple Personality Disorder, usually the result of extreme repeated physical, sexual, and emotional abuse. (It's okay! It's not that deep!) When we refer to *"Dissociation,"* it's simply like "opting out," Little Boy Wild disappears *"Inside"* himself, and comes back later to check out the damage. His psyche separates and he puts psychological distance between himself and the pain he cannot handle. The traumas experienced by Wild Boy created a *splitting of the self.* It would appear that Little Boy Wild and I are *"completely split,"* and that is why so often, one part of us is able to watch the other go through the motions of life. These paranoid personalities talk with each other.

Some questions have been raised in relation to the *sexual focus* of the book. It is a recurring theme, but it is far from the essential core of what occurs, which is something of great beauty. Little Boy Wild is somewhat unwilling to explore his sexual orientation because as a youngster his focus and contact were primarily male, and he fears the stigma of being labeled as "gay," if indeed he really is. He was painfully forced into fellatio at age five through the rails of his crib, resulting in a traumatic and hurtful drama the next morning, when he was disciplined for his vomiting and usual bed wetting. He has no idea of what was done to him. But these days with increasing frequency, he *dissociates,* and flees to *"the meadows of his mind"* – where there is warm sunshine, lush green meadows, a profusion of wild flowers, and a number of rabbits, who are his very best friends. *Dissociation* is becoming his well worn path to happiness and survival. Best of all, it's safe – *he cannot be reached.*

So just what is a homosexual anyway? I paraphrase Arthur Janov of "Primal Scream" fame:

"It is a person who has sex with members of his own gender, or at least wants to. It is not a sexual deviation. It is what a human being does who was not allowed to be himself early in his life. *The gay act is NOT a sexual one.* It is based on denial of real sexuality, and the acting out symbolically through sex – the need for love. *Sex is not the goal – love is."* Recently I observed this in most of Little Boy Wild's unconscious revelations about himself.

From the age of six, Little Boy Wild was at the mercy of friendly, softly spoken words. These contacts with him are inviting, and he comes "partially out," with a half smile of acceptance. *It is a start toward confirmation that he exists, that he really IS, and "ISness" is essential for life to continue. It is as though recognition will create him, and cause him to appear in real live form.* He will risk *ALL* for that pearl of great price, the warm loving touch of human hands. A love-starved kid is easily identified, a smile and a gentle touch will expose his raw need and he'll open like a summer flower. *All he really needs is love.* No cost is too high. His body language is an eloquent request to have his pain level reduced. His silent scream is *"Stop My Hurt!"* while in his heart he hears himself say; "If only you will love me for what I am, and by loving me give me the gift of myself, a small boy, real and growing into the sunlight of a loving "NOW." Oh! Let it be that I may never again need to hide so deep inside myself to escape the hurt and hatred, that one day I may not be able to find my way back to the world I ran away from." Little Boy Wild is referring to what he calls his *"River of No Return,"* – a state of self-loss, which were he to abandon himself to it, he would float into a void beyond reach, perhaps forever.

Throughout his adventures, many of his actions could be classed as "socially unacceptable," and may well be outside of the "comfort zones" of those among us who tend to avoid the realities of life. In your tender forbearance, remember that Little Boy Wild is mentally unstable, lost, and unloved. Even his silent screams can never dissipate the hurt and neglect that modeled his psyche and behavior. *He is simply a product of his upbringing – for what has been sown – will surely be reaped.*

A number of interesting questions are often posed by readers, which if handled now, increases the fun and enjoyment of the escapades coming up! Number one is in regard to the switch in personalities.

"Well, what do you, he, or whoever, do, when HE takes over?"

I'll endeavor to explain. We feel it as a type of swirling agitation in the mind, and I know that Little Boy Wild is taking over and will control *where* we go, and *what* we do. I feel this change taking place as through an hypnotic fog. There is an overriding urge to get away from where I am, regardless of any need to handle current affairs and financial matters, no matter how important they may be. We need to be free! We literally head for the mountains, the forests, lakes and rivers to be "with the animals." In our childhood days we fled to the woodland to be with the foxes, rabbits and squirrels, but now, we flee to the wilderness to be with the grizzlies, the cougars, wolves, and a myriad of other furry forest creatures, and surely, best of all – the "Humans" rarely intrude here. Wild Boy is almost as ghostly as a black bear among the alder shadows and as wily as a deer when hunting season arrives. We soak up the summer sun "au naturel,"– the warmth of sunshine on his body is the only caring touch that Little Boy Wild has ever received. There is just wind song, flower song, creek song, and all of these are in his life flow. When eventually he escapes the ecstasy of sun, dream, and cosmic infusion, he *returns control* to me, and I then have to attend the mundane matters that the "Humans" require of us.

These are the struggles between our *"Real"* and *"Unreal"* selves where we switch personas. The *"Real Derek"* is *"Little Boy Wild"* as he was at birth – before he found that it was unacceptable to be alive; and the *"Unreal"* personalities are those who were created within his psyche – in order for life to carry on – a matter of survival. *This includes the "Unreal Derek" who takes care of the day to day matters in the Human world.* And this is surely what has made *our* lives so different – or, so wonderful in its amazing diversity of survival strategies.

Questions often arise on Wild Boy's unplanned venture into a massive LSD overdose, where he opened up the gating mechanism in to his cerebral cortex, creating an immediate disaster of unprecedented proportions. Again the critics say, *"Why ever would you do that? You know it is wrong!"*

But they cannot meet Little Boy Wild *where he is at,* and they have no concept of *unrelenting psychic pain.* There is little doubt that this adventure should have been performed under clinical conditions with qualified staff, and not under an October moon with a lone wolf howling! This was a landmark in catharsis. In the unleashed fury of psychic turbulence that followed, all the protective elements to preserve a level of normality that could, with some reasonable form of sanity, allow us to operate in the every day world were deleted. All that remained was naked, undefended consciousness. But the real coalescing of Little Boy Wild and me into one mature being could only come about over a period of many years. The powerful truths and terror that arise out of the depths of the unconscious mind have to be *re-lived* without threat to one's life, *and then integrated* into acceptance by the stronger, now more mature self.

Wild Boy has often proclaimed, "There is just *ME* in here and no one can reach me!" It was his recurring thought whenever he fled from unbearable reality. He was isolated, frozen, locked in and shut down. But as he discovered much later, this was not his escape to freedom, but rather a type of protective environment to shield him from the outside world, *and also to protect him from himself.* Wild Boy and I, in our self-searching for personal identity, get into deep discussions at times. I recently asked him:

"What is our biggest problem? What I mean is – how do we get together and be as *ONE* –whole and real all of the time? I know you've been gazing at the "River of no Return" as you call it, for a long time now – perhaps too long." He looked up at me; his young eyes tearing, and serious.

"Surely you must know" – he sounded somewhat incredulous. "I know pain—it's all I've ever known; but what *is* love? Maybe, love is mostly about being touched –differently, and I know it sounds weird, *but also, actually being able to feel, really feel.* Like being held and hugged if such were ever possible. *But, and this I don't understand – love destroys me!* Know what I mean? *I cannot accept love – nor can I trust, or give love!"* His voice began to break up, *"It destroys me! Why does that which I need most have to KILL me? Kind words stab me, and when I'm touched – I freeze.* It's like I'm a block of ice, and if I do have to touch or hug, which happens on rare occasions when saying Good Byes – I do, but I lock up, turn very white and disappear inside of me. *Love or personal attention disconnects me from the outside world! Is this where my silent screams come from?* It seemed that he had wrenched these words from the very depths of his somewhat frail being. At the same time a wild, hunted and desperate look possessed his face. He curled up tight and small into what *he* refers to as his *"fatal"* position. Then, in a pathetic voice, he said, "No one can *ever* hold me, hug me or love me, because if they do – *I won't be here to know about it – or to feel it! Because I'll be "inside" where it's safe!* Why am I so hated? And why does SHE want to kill me?" he wailed. Then uttering several short hoarse screams, he fell among the daisies into

6

the long grass, rolling over and over with loud anguished cries. After some minutes, he broke his trance to say quite forcefully, "I can't join you, because you distrust love too. You know this is true! We are identical, we *ARE* together, but we remain apart." This direct charge, more like an accusation, almost overcame me. Little Boy Wild continued to hug his knees as he leaned back against a fallen tree. It was a typical daisy strewn meadow complete with rabbits. Sadly he rocked rhythmically back and forth, allowing only low moans to escape his lips. Finally he rose, stretched and walked toward his playmates. But then he surprised me as he started to sing a little song that he quite often hummed in perfect key. "Somewhere, over the rainbow, where bluebirds fly,* somewhere, over the rainbow, that's where I'm going to die."

"You're *not* going to die," I exclaimed. "You're *not* going to die!"

Again his voice rose in a clear and magical way, "Somewhere, over the rainbow, where bunnies play...."

His voice trailed off and silence came upon him. He had dismissed me. Lightly he skipped away through the clover, and as he stooped to caress the silken ears of his bunnykin friends, I saw that his face was a study in tranquility. I reached out futilely to embrace his aura of innocence, to share the purity of his being; but apart from the fierce love that I felt for him, I could do nothing but dissolve his image with my tears.

Another question that comes up quite often about Little Boy Wild is: *"Doesn't this kid have a caregiver? His mother or father for example?"*

Dad is usually away, and Wild Boy likes him a lot. But, as you will shortly see, Wild Boy's mother is his *primary enemy,* and has been so since birth, and quite possibly before birth. As a result, in his unsupervised wanderings this love-starved kid unwittingly invited molestation and extreme trauma. Wild Boy sees his mother as hatred in motion with pain to follow. SHE, is to be avoided at all costs. Little Boy Wild knows – deep within him, that it *is* only a matter of time before she causes his death in some "blame free" way during a demonic rampage. Even dissociating will not dissolve this hurt, and this unsolvable problem gives birth to his silent screams.

---

*   Original lyrics by E.H. Harwood. Music by Harold Arlen. Wizard of Oz. 1939.

"Come now!" they say, "There must be someone you can talk to?"
Little Boy Wild: "I can't talk. I'm seven, but I cannot talk without stuttering. I lock up and stammer so badly, and contort my face to such a degree that only weird broken sounds come out, and it's even worse with strangers. In addition I now drool while this is going on; and if I were able to talk, how could I explain that for which I have no words?

By this time I may also have wet myself with fright, a common occurrence. *All Humans are my enemies.* None can be trusted, least of all, she who gave birth to me. Is it only the number of fingers on one hand, the times she has attempted to kill me? Or is my right hand now involved in the counting? I'm alone in here. SHE can't reach me and she knows this, which makes matters worse. It is not just my body she wants to kill. She wants to kill *ME,* the *REAL ME,*" in my eyes. When will she next try to kill me?"

Some publishers and printers say that these types of revelations involving child abuse, sodomy and psychological degradation have too much offensive content. No one should acknowledge that they ever occur, unless it happens to a woman, and even then, certainly not in print! And in any case, boys should quit their sniveling and "Act like men." I quote briefly from the preface in Mic Hunter's timely book, "Abused Boys." He states:

"This year, as in every year, tens of thousands of boys will be sexually abused. They will be damaged physically, emotionally, mentally and spiritually. Every aspect of their lives will be affected. When they become adults they will be plagued with sexual dysfunctions, troubled relationships, a poor sense of self worth and intimacy difficulties. Many will become drug addicts. Some will destroy themselves. It is time to notice their pain."

One of the more common reactions to what I have recorded in Little Boy Wild is, "*But why dwell on the past?* It's behind you, forget it! Life carries on, so think about the future, after all, to forgive is to forget!" Indeed, but how can one *NOT* be reminded of the past? Suffice it to say, all persons involved in this lengthy tragedy of abuse were forgiven long ago, for indeed, *they knew not what they did.* Their *actions* were really *symptoms,* born out of their own deep rooted *problems.* One can forgive Auschwitz and the other death camps in Germany, or the Japanese prison camps that were once a part of those atrocities, but one could never forget them.

I also frequently hear, "Well, we're all neurotic in this day and age, and we all go around with that little wounded child inside of us. Ha! Ha!"

It seems that they have no, "out of control" reverberating circuits of pain superimposed on their lives. *How could we ever explain those silent screams?* Will they ever stop? These screams carry at every pitch, the haunting tones of hopelessness, which once heard can never be erased. *They are part of the pain continuum, and that pain has a life of its own, driven by tension, and born out of deprivation.*

Little Boy Wild was denied access to drinking water and other fluids during his childhood, which resulted in desperate levels of thirst, and day by day strategies for survival. At one point this fluids shortage was poisoning his system and leading to kidney failure. One can live without food for an extended period of time – but not without water. Fluids were withheld because his mother equated water with bed wetting, and never understood that if the unrelenting abuse were stopped – maybe the bed wetting would clear up too.

Still other people say, "Surely you made most of this up, it can't all be true, I have trouble believing it, or do you just get your jollies from being so graphic in the portrayal of the grosser aspects of life?"

To which I reply that I do paint word pictures of pain, but I also do this with great love. Any child who has experienced heavy-duty, brutal, continuous trauma from birth to around age fifteen, does not need to fabricate stories. *When one is truly lost, and all connections with love are severed, one has lost identity.* On the "outside" people see what they think is just another human being, but in reality, Little Boy Wild is a living, seething body of emotional agony. He *IS* a living pool of Primal hurt. *Be warned! Make no mistake! Little Boy Wild is not normal – he is highly dysfunctional, and undoubtedly sick, mentally, psycho-sexually and emotionally.* He could hardly be otherwise with his upbringing. He was also fired from one job for being a *"Psycho,"* and from another for being *"Dangerously deranged."*

When trauma is this real, one is imprinted for life. Pain is triggered from unknown sources when one least expects it. These are not one-time mild incidents say, of not getting the family car for an evening of gallivanting around, or perhaps the financial stress of not being able to buy a new outfit for the prom.

These exposures are of every day, ruthless, unrelenting physical and psychological abuse. This is dead end, extreme *"Cornered Rat Trauma"* – where life and limb are on the line. There *IS no way out*. It leaves its indelible marks, and imprints circuits and reactions for life. It also deadens facial expressions and kills feelings. A lifetime of defense strategies and maneuvers is launched, superbly designed and maintained by the body in order to survive. Abuse also retards intelligence. Self esteem and confidence may never be born, or at the very least be many years into the future. In my own case I did not acquire self esteem until the age of twenty seven.

Let us take a look at this spaced out "Rat." Little Boy Wild was just an ordinary innocent young being. But now when he meets your eyes it is with a hunted expression, openly fearful. His shadowed face is haunted with ghosts of unspeakable experiences, and those ghosts may wreak havoc with his physical system for a lifetime. Because this "rat" hides so far back inside of himself he is labeled as a "retard," or stupid, and this tends to generate a self-fulfilling prophesy.

He cannot establish that he *"IS,"* and *until he IS, he cannot grow emotionally*. He is locked away in time. It is no wonder that from time to time he sadly insists, "I have to live with the animals whenever I can! Animals are my very best friends, especially rabbits. We scamper along the woodland trails, we inhale the damp woodsy earth smells, and when the red tailed hawk cries from on high, in my heart it feels like I'm being touched to the essence of my cosmic core with love magic! The warm soft caresses of the summer breeze tell me I'm here—somewhere. But, too soon I have to return to the darkness of HER domain. It will trap me, fear will grip me, and once again I'll know the bitter truth—*I HURT—therefore I AM."*

Little Boy Wild found solace and inspiration in two beautiful songs of his young years –they gave him hope, and something beyond himself in which to believe. One of them – *"Somewhere over the rainbow,"* he sometimes sang before and during his bouts of dissociation, in the *"meadows of his mind."* The other song, *"When You Wish Upon a Star,"** for him, was

---

* When you wish upon a star. Writer: Leigh Harline. Lyrics: Ned Washington.

pure hope. He would look out of his window on a starlit night and softly whisper his innermost belief –"When you wish upon a star, makes no difference who you are! Anything your heart desires will come to you!" He believed it. Even more so, because *Jiminy Cricket* sang it, and Wild Boy knew his animals would never lie – they were simply truth and beauty in motion. By now dear friend! You've probably had it up to your proverbial "Yin Yang," weaving through the matrix of psychic trauma and drama with Little Boy Wild! So let us start our adventures and have some rollicking laughter too! We'll meet you at the other end in the epilogue. Wild Boy – you stay with me!!

Chapter One

The boy stood tall beneath the pines, his slim form silhouetted against the night sky. Far off he could hear the sheep and lambs calling from the upper meadows. He was just above the mill pond which was brilliant with star reflections. Almost any night when the skies were cloudless he came to view the million lights reaching out to him from the other more distant worlds. It was almost as though he could touch them – like having his own star map, and as always his mind traveled across the water in dreamy quest, for what, he knew not. Many nights he would shed his light clothing to swim among the galaxies.

But tonight it was a water vole that rippled his star map, while an owl hooted from deep in the woodland behind him. He hooted in reply. He always talked with the owls as well as the animals, because they were as much a part of him as they were of themselves. Most thrilling of all was when he spoke to them in the intimate silence of their individual being. He felt as though he had become the bird or animal he was communicating with, as if he, and they, were one entity.

When he left the farm house for his nightly ramble down to the estuary – he was Derek, a human among the humans, but the farther he walked from the farm into the night woods, the more he became a wild creature in "Human" form. He skipped lightly down the trail, once stopping to view the Big Dipper, and only minutes later he was at the shoreline. I spoke to him – I'm also Derek.

"So why are you so sad and pensive tonight?" I enquired. "After all, you're nineteen, you're far away from HER – your mother and enemy from birth; you even survived the devastation of London, and what is more, you're even free of the "Humans," as you call them." For answer, Wild One sat on a large flat rock at the water's edge and gazed at the early moonlight silvering the estuary.

"I have this yearning for a friend of my own kind, and as you well know I'm always striving for *meaning and identity.* The Humans don't understand that I'm not always *ME.* Things happen; frightening things –and afterwards I discover that I'm me again. I explore within my mind, has this really occurred? And reality always assures me that it has. So where am I for those moments or minutes when I'm not here? And who is the Preacher? He is always in the background somewhere, and there is no doubt that things would be better if I didn't stutter so badly."

Moments later his moonlit form entered the water, and he swam almost silently from the shallows to the deeper coolness. Night birds called, and an otter called for his mate from quite close by. For a moment he thought it might be his little otter friend he'd named "Tarkatu." He whistled back, but there was no reply, so he just floated and watched the stars.

"Hey!" I warned him, "There's a heavy bank of cloud coming ashore, so *We* had better head for home, in fact *We* should *All* turn in for the night."

"Yes! I'm with you!" he enthused, flaring his nostrils to capture the scent of the echoing sea. Then, light as a deer, his naked form crossed the creek and was lost in the dying moon shadows. He didn't speak to me the next day. This was not uncommon, for when he was busy with the farm work, milking the South Devon cows, working with the tractor and shearing sheep, he was too preoccupied to discuss anything.

Early summer sunlight laden with warmth and golden promise after the cold damp Devon winter, flooded across the grey stone floor of the aging farmhouse. It was an idyllic setting. Two hundred years old, perhaps older and no longer a monastery, the ancient building yielded scary shadows to my imagination of a still earlier era, when pirates occupied it as a base for their smuggling operations, or so it was said. With the estuary a scant quarter mile away, and the English Channel just beyond, the tales had certain credibility. Even the cobble stoned walkway and a hidden tunnel could still be traced beyond the courtyard.

I had just lunched on freshly baked brown bread with slabs of cheddar cheese, a typical farm laborer's lunch, when Barry, alias Shiddyface, my orphaned white-faced lamb, called impatiently from the doorway. Oh! By the way—I'm Derek. I'm the one *"they"* talk to, the one who does things that shouldn't be done. I am *he* who faces the music afterwards when *"they"* are gone, and wonders who or what he is.

Barry stepped in with dainty muddy little hoofs softly clicking against the grey stone floor. His alert head held inquiringly high, just cleared the underside of the huge kitchen tabletop as he peered with bright eyes from under the hanging tablecloth, his usual place in the past few weeks despite disapproving looks from those in authority. Quickly glancing around to see if all was clear of Humans, I dipped a dirty finger into the cream jug as Barry moistly nuzzled my thigh. He eagerly sucked on my finger dripping with rich Devon cream, and his woolly tail flipped with excitement. The farmer, his wife and the other hired man had not yet come in for lunch, so the cream dipping process was repeated a number of times.

"What the eye doesn't see, the heart doesn't grieve," I quoted from somewhere in my past. I noticed how clean the sucked finger had become, pink and moist, smelling of lambs. Barry was my little woolly shadow, a true friend, one with whom I could discuss life's problems without reservation. His nickname "Shiddyface" had come about because as an orphan he had been forced to plunder his ewe from the rear as her own lambs occupied the regular suckling stations on each side. As a result his face was usually discolored, for the ewe would excrete under the pressure of his vigorous suckling attempts. Barry's mother was a snooty sort with a kind of superior expression. Indeed how could I forget her? It was to her that I had come from my warm bed at three o'clock one gusty spring lambing morn.

"Derek lad," the sheep herder had said, "She needs your help. See what you can do. I have to go up to the other lambing pens."

Without waiting for acknowledgement of his order he disappeared in a gust of dark wind across the meadow, his hurricane lantern casting feeble, eerie flickering shadows. Then I was alone. With racing heart and sick stomach, I surveyed the mess before me by the light of my own dim lantern, already low on fuel. I peered closer trying to make sense of what I saw. There lay Snooty, sides heaving, and obviously—even to my inexperienced eyes—giving birth, or trying to.

I had seen Bert the sheep herder, pulling something, but what to pull? How hard does one pull? And how does one know when to stop or for that matter when to start? Kneeling among the sheep dung and straw I pulled and sweated with slippery apprehension. My inexperience ruled the night. Surely there should be a tiny nose and a small head? So why was only one little hoof showing? It was all sort of mixed up, so a half hour later in desperation I left her to her destiny.

"You'll probably die before morning, and I'll get shit from the boss!" I shouted at her. Fierce wailing and whistling noises from the high winds whipped past the drafty door creating a desolate kind of feeling. The whites of her eyes gleamed and shiny mucous snorting sounds punctuated her twitching. Then I went out quickly closing the barn door behind me and stumbled across the yard, making it to the house just as the lantern's light gave way to the darkness. I felt my way through the entrance hall, and removing dung clad boots, crept through the kitchen where a faint glow marked the dying fire.

"YYYEEOOWW!"

I had stepped on the calico cat's tail, and she split the darkness with feline hurt. "Fuck you, cat!" I hissed back at her with fright and venom. Then I stepped up the spiral slate stairway leading to my dark room. Electric power did not exist here, and matches had a habit of never keeping company with candles. I still had sticky blood between my fingers, but too tired to seek icy water in the china bowl I let fitful sleep take over.

Later that morning, Snooty greeted us with twins, but a week later she died. One of her lambs died also, so Barry the survivor adopted me, or I him—I was never too clear on that point—but he was uniquely mine. After a few weeks Barry was expelled from the kitchen and had to wait for me outside the door.

When the grisly docking and castrating time came around, I hid him in a small rarely visited old machine shed in the west pasture. Shrubs had grown up around it camouflaging its presence. Barry didn't take too well to our parting and bleated desperately, but the thought of having to collect up all the lamb's tails and skin them to make a big vat of lamb's tail soup haunted me. Not knowing which might be his was too much to stomach. It was akin to cannibalism.

As for castrating the piglets, I empathized with them.

"Why dd-d-d-do they sq-sqsq-squeal so much? an' how do you ststst-stand this k-k-k-kind of n-n-noise every day?" I stammered, trying to establish some rapport with the grey-whiskered men who had come to do the job. I should have known however that talk was next to impossible with them, they just grunted. The farmer had given me the job of selecting the screaming victims and holding them upside down very firmly by the back legs, while the intruders committed that ultimate atrocity with deft surgery amidst the bedlam. At my question, the "surgeons" paused a moment with a significant exchange of glances between each other, and squirted brown juice from whiskered mouths while I prepared to capture another struggling pink porker.

"Why do they squeal? How would you feel at your age, what are you, seventeen? if we was to hold you upside down an' cut your balls out?" I had my answer. I realized that the piglets would have no monopoly on squealing if our positions were reversed. Occasionally one of the castrators would deftly pop a warm slippery little pork testicle into his mouth to chew on.

"It's good for you," declared one of them.

"A great delicacy," said the other, pressing the shiny little organ to my lips with bloody hands. I turned my head to avoid the pressure, and he promptly transferred it to his own mouth, sliding it around before biting into the still living tissue. When they were through for the day, each man wrapped up a bunch of these little delicacies in the Evening News for the Missus to fry up for supper with a lacing of onions.

"Barbaric," I told myself, "Indecent!" So Barry kept his tail and his ability to sire.

"You'll be making a danged fool out of that lamb, pettin' him like that," warned the sheep herder. It was only on the most strenuous objections by the farmer and his wife that I would lift him bodily outside the house each night before going to bed, or he would have followed me up the spiral stairway to my room.

Sometimes Barry's plaintive calls came to me with such heartfelt loneliness through my rose-trellised window that I would sneak out to sleep with him in the soft oat straw in the barn. He would run joyously toward me, bleating and snuffling as I called softly across the courtyard, "Shiddyface! Shiddyface!" What wild tail-flipping delight, we so desperately needed each other, and the ultimate bliss prior to our falling asleep was the warm snuggling companionship. Neither the rustling of the straw nor the quick scurry of tiny delicate mouse feet running over us, or the bright summer moon, beaming shafts of light through the myriad chinks and cracks above disturbed us.

Barry followed me everywhere, traipsing behind the smoking blue tractor in the early bird chorus of dawn, as we traveled to the work site in the hills. He nibbled clover and other vegetation selectively for the greater part of each day joining me only for lunch. Indeed the old shepherd's prediction had come true: I had made a fool out of Barry, or he had made a fool out of me, but I really didn't care. He filled my lonely days with love.

Chapter Two

I was almost *sixteen years* old when I fled permanently from what was known as "home," and sought a job as a farm laborer working on different farms, until a few years later when I landed a job in the West Country of England in my beautiful Devonshire. It had always been my choice of all the counties in which to earn a living.

That is if work were to be considered at all. *Now at nineteen*, my wish had come to fruition. Its lush hills with miles of enchanting woodland, natural bubbling springs and patchwork green meadows—as well as the blue glittering English Channel beyond; all of these had drawn me to Devon. But the Channel's space and distance also inspired in me a quest for the unknown beyond, and increased my restlessness. While plowing with the Fordson Major tractor, I never tired of seeing the three dark earth furrows turning behind me, and felt a wild kinship with the screaming gulls as they fed on worms behind the plow. But their cries served only to increase my yearning and unnamed desire.

It was a superb color photograph in a weekly magazine that tipped the scales to action and adventure. I gazed in rapture at the dancing rainbows that embraced the most majestic waterfalls I'd ever seen—the Angel falls in South America. I could just about feel the rainbow mists, see the dense rain forests, hear the pounding waters, and feel the skin prickling roar. This I decided I must see and experience. But how could I get there?

This problem occupied my mind through sheep shearing time, and on through the busy harvest summer. I posed the question to Barry on several occasions, but although he gave the impression of being thoughtful, his mind was on nibbling the choice vegetation. On my lonely woodland walks I even asked the huge fuzzy bumble bees among the hedgerow flowers and soliloquized at some length with the shy kingfishers down by the

19

mill house alongside the estuary, but they spoke only the language of silver fish and water shadows. Even the otters in the estuary of the River Exe only whistled at my problem. My playful Tarkatu, a young male otter that I had discovered while swimming there, came up the sandy bank to greet me.

"Hi Tarkatu!" I cried. "How can I get to South America?" He raised his sleek intelligent head and our eyes met, then he turned to re-enter the water.

"You mean I have to swim?" I questioned with a laugh, and I stripped off my clothes to join him. We played in the shallow salt water until he was joined by another of his family who was too shy to approach us. I say 'played' but that was in my imagination, he would never let me touch him, or approach too closely, but he was not frightened. I never knew why Tarkatu was so tame; perhaps he had been raised by the Humans and released. I had named him after Henry Williamson's famous book "Tarka the Otter." Tarka—meaning 'Little Water Wanderer'—and that's how my own Tarka became Tarka II—Tarkatu! Sometimes I would find him, but more often he found me, and it seemed he enjoyed swimming in circles around me.

"Tarkatu," I said, standing on a sand bar to address him, "The time will shortly come when I must leave and our ways will never cross again. There is a time to meet and a time to part, a time to swim together and a time to dry off." I stepped up onto the mossy bank where I had left my clothes. Only a faint ripple replied.

It was not only the magnificent waterfalls in the jungle that had to be experienced, I explained to myself, there was a whole new life of adventure beckoning us. It was while returning through the lower woods and moonlit meadows that the solution came to me.

We would work country by country, till we came to the dream falls, and settle finally in New Zealand or Australia! The most logical first step was Canada, land of giant timber and wilderness, and endless uninhabited territory. There were networks of fish-filled lakes awaiting us, mammoth rivers with their origins in gigantic mountain ranges, the Canadian Rockies, all waiting to be explored. I would see the racing turbulent river waters of British Columbia and finally I would arrive at the Pacific Ocean. The excitement never left me. The die was cast.

Anxiously I awaited the Weekly Farm Journal, for I recalled seeing a Canadian National Railways advertisement nestled among the fine print in the classified section which said, in effect, that if you are experienced in farm work and can pay your passage, we'll guarantee you a job. That was it. That was my ticket to adventure and freedom. The express train fairly flew from Devon to London. In no time at all I had found my way into the office complex of the Canadian National Railways and was speaking to an agent.

"Just select whichever province you'd like to work in, and we'll do the rest." He went on to speak of the vast Canadian west, of Alberta and Saskatchewan.

"How about Saskatchewan?" he asked. Images of advanced farm mechanization –ten combine harvesters, brilliantly red against the blue sky, approaching with purring perfection like some inexorable wave of harvest triumph, danced before my mind's eye.

"Y-Y-Yes, We'll go to Sask-sk-sk-sk-sk-skatchewan," I finally blurted out with a staccato stammer, making that province's name longer by a half dozen syllables.

"You'll have to be prepared to live at least a hundred and fifty to two hundred miles from the nearest settlement or trading post," my interviewer broke in on my disjointed images. He was preparing me for the worst.

"That's j j j jjust l-l-l-lovely," I stammered in high excitement. "We don't mind solitude, w-w-wwilderness, bl-bl-black b-b-b-bbears, m-mm-mmooses and Indians! And huge l-l-lakes and ..."

I was being viewed—no, scrutinized—by the agent as though he had landed some strange specimen from the deeps.

"We?" he queried at last, his huge moustache quivering. "Are you married?"

I blushed. "Oh no! *I always say 'we' when I mean I*, that is m-mme…" I trailed off into silence at the prospect of explaining how WE did things. No comment was made on my stuttering. Somewhere deep inside I could hear my normal voice calmly and flawlessly answering his questions, but outside me I had to watch him reacting as did all the people whom I subjected to my painful mode of address. It was all there inside me. WE could talk to each other but not to an outsider, not to THEM –the Humans.

When buoyant enough in spirit to do so, I resorted to play acting a character with an Oxford accent, for I had found that as long as I was not myself, I was almost word perfect. On the farm I continually play acted in speech, and this often relaxed me enough that I would find myself speaking as my true self, only to be promptly challenged and questioned as to why I put on airs. So around the farm yards in working clothes, I was one person and spoke as myself whenever coherence blessed me with its presence. In city clothes I became another person entirely, with different bearing, poise and speech.

By the time the interview with the CNR agent was over I had been approved. Apart from my stuttering I was considered quite normal and well qualified, even though I had defrauded railroads, murdered cats, stampeded cattle, siphoned gas from British military vehicles during the war, stolen government property, and generally raised hell on the farms where I had worked. So it was all settled. I would embark from Liverpool on the Ascania, a troopship partially converted to peace time use, and it would drop me off in Montreal, Quebec, on 19 May 1948. There! It was done! Step number one to Angel falls in South America, via Lemberg, Saskatchewan.

All that had to be done was the matter of settling personal affairs and bidding farewell to family and a few friends, including former employers with whom I had felt a relationship; although on mature reflection, I realize I had failed to observe their lack of reciprocity. Indeed, some employers genuinely expressed the notion that the "Colonies" would be a good place for me. I vaguely associated their remarks with criminals or remittance men, but neither of these categories gave me a feeling of identification. After all, we had been taught in school that all the criminals were sent to Australia! And I was going to Canada!

"Devon I love you!" I announced on my return from London. "Hello, ferrets!" I poked a finger through the wire of their cage. Missy and Kissy came to the front with red eyes blinking. Both ferrets were a dirty off-white color – or maybe they were just dirty! They would have to be sold before I left for Canada, but first one more rabbiting expedition. Missy and Kissy greeted the decision with head-weaving anticipation for the kill. So in high spirits away to the alluring woodland we went. The world was a mist of bluebells and yellow lamb's tails flipping in the wind among the trees.

Rabbiting was fun. We would carefully place the nets over the burrows, peg them firmly down, slip a ferret into the dark tunnel and stand back for action. One or more terrified rabbits would sound the alarm, I would hear them thumping powerfully deep within the burrow. If all the holes had been covered by nets, two or more of those bunnies would rocket into the nets and we would have rabbit pie! Sometimes a hungry ferret would fasten onto a rabbit deep in the burrow and stay there. Then I would use an iron rod or sometimes a sharp stick to probe the winding passages of the burrow as they went deeper and deeper. When a few hairs or a tiny bit of fur turned up on the end of the rod, I would get to work digging out both ferret and rabbit. The odd ferret got lost this way, especially when the burrows were very deep. And that is exactly what happened when Kissy went missing on that final rabbiting expedition. Next day a poacher acquaintance of mine bought Missy for half a crown. He was a loner who poached on the larger private estates where they put out grain for the local pheasants to fatten them up.

On more than one occasion, the head gamekeeper of the nearest estate had visited our farmyard and looked into my ferret cage, where he was greeted by Kissy and Missy tussling over fresh and bloody pheasant heads, still bright with their chestnut and green feathers. Although I explained I had shot them nowhere near the estate, I was not believed, and of course I never confessed to prowling at other times with a stick and gunny sack at dusk. The pheasants were there for the taking. In the moonlight or very late dusk one could see the dark shapes at roost in the low tree branches. So we often dined well on roast pheasant, and my ferrets gorged on the guts. Yes, I would miss the poaching and the rabbiting, and I would certainly miss my ferrets.

There was time for one last dash down to the estuary to see my furry otter friend, my little Tarkatu. The fern scented woodland trail merged with the shoreline and light as a fox and almost as quick, I arrived at our trysting rock. Dusk had fallen but the near full moon was rising. The stars seemed less distant tonight and twinkled with new understanding. While I skipped in high anticipation down the trail, I softly sang Jiminy Cricket's song – When you wish upon a star." It had come true at last! "Anything your heart desires will come to you!" For me it had! At last, I was starting my journey.

How did that song go? Something about "Like a bolt out of the blue, fate steps in, and sees you through?" Wow!

For a while I sat on the flat rock and whistled my high Tarkatu call across the water. I watched the silver moon ripples. An owl called. The water spoke softly to me, and moments later, the moon eddies widened as I gave myself to the current. Several times I rose to whistle, the notes carried far across the estuary and seemed to curve to meet the moon and vanish into its light. The chill of the night and the water reached me and struggling against the tide I returned to the rock. Dressing with a slight shiver I yielded one last whistle. It was high, long and sweet, only to be lost in the remoteness of the sea beyond.

"Our otter friend is upstream" I told myself, and with a mixture of joy and sadness I called out "Farewell Tarkatu! Farewell my bright eyed little friend!"

In the meantime Barry had refused to join the main flock. He stayed around as a pet on the farmstead, and lost his ramhood just before I left for London.

"So long, Shiddyface," I called. Ahead of me was adventure across the Atlantic. No longer would I have the chore of milking the fifteen south Devon cows twice daily by hand. Saskatchewan here I come!

Liverpool, like London or any other large city seemed prison-like to me, and like a startled deer I frequently reacted to situations with panic. Tall dirty brick buildings and blackened walls of alien structures crowded in as I sought the "Ascania" at her berth.

"What are we doing here," I asked myself, scanning a window reflection, "You long-haired, blushing youth with a stutter and a wild, hunted look in your eyes?"

Scurrying people in drab clothes—threats from a hundred directions—were everywhere. A trapped feeling engulfed me. I would have fled, but there was no secret woodland dell to flee to, there were no friendly trees or green beckoning fern fronds in which to hide; and I was so unaccustomed to walking on a flat surfaced sidewalk that I frequently blundered into people or kicked them or unwittingly tripped them, to their annoyance and my horror.

But then, before me as if I had conjured her up, laid the "Ascania" at her berth. Luggage, people, tickets, flurries of activity, and suddenly I was aboard. Slowly we moved from the port through the cold green seas into a bank of fog that stayed with us for two days. Then one morning I went on deck and was thrilled to see the distant icebergs drifting south in the icy water. The sea had an incredible dark blue richness contrasting with the white caps; whales spouted silver water fountains into the crisp sunlight and cold winds, while deep inside, I was surging with excitement. In several days we crossed the Atlantic. Unfortunately, during a lot of that time the dreaded sea-sickness engulfed me, but I survived. Coming up the St. Lawrence River in the early evening, the "Ascania" became stranded on a sand bank and leaned over –a little lop sided. We were destined to stay there till morning when high tide and tugs would get us underway again. When we grounded in the sand bank everyone rushed up on deck to see what was wrong, but I rushed downstairs because the showers would be free of people, indeed deserted. For the first time on the trip I was all alone. Grabbing my towel I enjoyed a long hot luxurious shower. Afterwards, below the tilting deck in my angled bunk, I relaxed in the luxury of solitude, a fitting preparation for adventure—to lie and to dream, or better still, to go back into the circle of time in search of my identity.

Chapter Three

Just who are you – O youthful fragment of consciousness? I asked myself as I reviewed the past few weeks of farewells and recollections – starting with my first employer; and then my life with Tim as we had our brief adventures and the million or so other fragmented, strangely distorted, elusively kaleidoscopic views that others had *of Me, and I of Me, and they of US, and I of We!*

The gentleman farmer who had been my first employer was not overjoyed to see me again. This was the location of my first farm job in a picturesque village in Buckinghamshire; where I faced for the first time hard work with little pay. I was barely sixteen at that time. Upon seeing me he looked somewhat apprehensive, and only brightened up when I grandly announced my imminent departure to another country. Then he explained his apprehension by telling me that one of his prize-winning shorthorns was still of a nervous disposition, never having completely recovered from its arrest in full flight from the dairy yard in what I had imagined to be true western cowboy style. But I doubted that her milk production had been affected for more than a day. I well remember her mad dash to escape from the cowshed that morning. She had gone into the wrong stall and I had yelled at her and whacked her with a pitch fork putting her to flight. Anyway, the particular reason for pursuit and capture as I raced alongside her on that occasion eludes me. Only the incomparable feeling of power remained. In a full burst of speed just before she reached the main gate I grabbed her by the horns.

"Son of a bitch!" I had yelled. Then throwing my weight with flair and skill, I twisted her silken neck to the give-up point, and she lurched heavily onto her side out of control, hitting the ground in a dusty skid cloud outside the dairy door, where at that precise moment the surprised farmer had come to stand. The heaving mound of bovine insubordination breathed heavily.

"Just what in Hell's name is going on here?" he screamed, his voice rising higher with each angry word. The shorthorn scrambled to her feet. With a side glance at me she bolted for the pasture. I was breathless and red faced with guilt but I managed to stammer, "She ... sh-sh-sh-she trying to esc-c-cape!"

"Escape from what?" he demanded. I gave him some excuse about her not being chained in her stall. He was quite upset. He gripped his rosewood pipe firmly between his even white teeth and stalked off with a thunder-cloud face to his house. Of course having graduated from throwing calves down in record time, this cow had been but one of a series that I practiced on. It was the satisfaction of mastering the big beasts, the powerful feeling of gripping their sliming noses with finger and thumb while they rolled their eyes back in what appeared to be extreme fright. Some of them could make their eyes almost disappear!

Such goings-on did not help milk production, and quite predictably on the day that a particular cow was wrestled to the ground, it was a number of pounds short on milk yield. I knew because it was my job to record all the production data. With wicked tail lashings they would kick the milker out or place a high-stepping hoof in the milk pail. On one occasion I delivered a bucket of this shadowy dirty hoof milk to the Big House for the family's consumption, having filtered the mud and dung out by hand. I passed the pail to the boss. He looked carefully at it, then exploded with a flushed angry face.

"I might give shit," he yelled. "I might take shit, but I will not drink shit!"

Before my surprised and fear-filled eyes, he splashed the entire con-tents of the pail over the marigolds in the flower bed. In frozen heart-stop-ping fear I watched the milky beads slipping down the orange petals as if it were all happening in slow motion. Then he passed the pail back to me, and as I stood there, slammed the door shut in my face. I returned to the dairy to wash the scum and sediment from the inside of the pail.

One day my gentleman farmer boss gave me instruction on driving the dairy cows out to the pasture with a willow stick. It was explained that I didn't have to whip the beasts to make them move up the lane, the whining swishing sound of my willow stick being more effective than physical application. Of course this had to be tested. About a week later when the cows were turned out after milking, I swished my trusty little willow switch and instantly had the whole herd galloping up the lane to the pasture gate. Success! Well almost, except for the Movie Director.

It was at the red brick bridge which arched steeply and narrowly over the canal that the trouble began. Unbeknownst to me as yet, the boss was coming toward us up the other side of the bridge in his new black Mercedes-Benz he was breaking in, having only driven it for about three weeks. The car was almost hidden by cows at the crown of the little bridge, and right then I had a sudden brief flash of the car, and also of the Movie Director's genius. Knowing what had slowed them down I poured on the pressure with the willow stick. Big beefy bodies pushed by the Mercedes, jamming that pristine vehicle against the brickwork, and making exit impossible from any door—cows on one side and the rough brick wall on the other and more cows surging up the slope! One of them, panicking to get by, reared up and came down with both front hooves on the gleaming hood of the Mercedes.

"Oh cows! Stop, stop!" I shouted. As I came to the top of the bridge, I realized that not only the Mercedes, but I too had reached a crucial point in the breaking-in process. The scene that followed may best be left to the imagination.

But there was an even more disturbing element than the juicy screaming and anger raising itself like a specter in my mind: *I knew what I was doing!* I had gotten a glimpse of the Mercedes and had deliberately pushed the cows into a panic. It was as though I were *standing outside of myself feeling and watching* the scene destructively unfold like a movie! *Maybe that was my problem*—I was an artist! A real artist who created live scenes and worked with real elements rather than mere oils and canvas. Perhaps I would make a good movie director.

But the fuse that finally lit my firing from the job was ignited at 4:30 on a cold dark, blustery January morning. Having despaired of persuading the cows to come into the barn through the deep mud morning after morning, I had devised a solution. The previous evening I had concocted a potent batch of gunpowder, the kind we had made at school with sulphur, charcoal and saltpeter. This particular formula was quite spectacular. I knew, because I had last used it during an air raid on a very dark night in the blackout somewhat close to London. On that occasion it had been ignited accidentally, turning our area into a prime target for the German bombers, and so terrifying my friends and myself that I'd sworn never to make it again. However, this was to be a special application and had the tacit approval of the Film Director part of myself who took fiendish delight in setting things in motion, but who was always missing when we had to face the music. After shouting and prodding the cows to no avail, I placed the large coffee can of grey powder carefully on a muddy hummock of turf. Swiftly I applied a match. A great scarlet sheet of flame and sparks shot thirty feet up into the cold dark air, illuminating the reluctant bovine forms. Then I saw this skinny sixteen year old kid leaping around like a berserk demon. He screamed with high pitched exultant abandon; his ghostly red form struck terror into the whole herd, and they were spooked in a grand way – out of sight. In the distance I heard shouting and turmoil that surged excitement in me. *I came back into myself again* and trudged up the lane through the destruction of gates and fences. Suddenly I was *ME*, and a cold tremor of fear ran through me. What had the Movie Director done?

In the yard I found the chief herdsman and others lifting the smashed and splintered yard gates to one side, while the herd swirled in agitated confusion around the milking sheds. The bellowing of cows, the milling around, the wavering light of flickering hurricane lamps and the shouting and cursing of frustrated men... What a picture! I loved it because I was on the cutting edge of being alive – *It enabled me to FEEL?*

"They came in a mite fast this morning Derek lad?" The herdsman's face was a grim, taut, lined mask. "You must've put some gunpowder behind 'em or somethin'," he said, tentatively wanting to get to the bottom of things.

"How did you know?" I asked in naive amazement, knowing the pasture could not be seen from the yard, but not realizing that the noise and great scarlet sheet of flame must have appeared like an incendiary bomb above the barn roofs.

"You mean... you don't mean..." His voice broke with incredulity.

"You do! You bastard! You really did! I heard you talk about it, but I never figured you'd ..." He shook his head grimly.

Striding from the shed toward the other men who looked curiously on, he yelled, "Know what that young fucker done? He done threw a gun powder bomb at them! No wonder they is so upset. Jesus!"

"I was wundrin' what that big red flash were," said Big John in his slow drawl. "Boss is gonna be real upset when he hears about his. I'll bet he don't know he hired a "psycho" kid to herd his cows. Hope he ain't carryin' his shot gun." My heart sank and my knees went weak. What had I done? The cows looked okay – but the destruction was terrible. It was just like a movie of a cattle stampede through a frontier village – devastation all over.

He fixed me with a blue eyed stare that said he wouldn't want to be in my shoes come eight o'clock. This was the end of my first job. I was fired, and during my firing, my boss explained that I was unpredictable, a liability, and dangerous to both man and beast. But the chief herdsman didn't mince any words. He put it quite simply. "Hit the road you psycho bastard!" Then I saw this lonely kid pick up his gunny sack of belongings, and as dawn broke, I watched him tramp down the muddy lane to the main highway.

I would not miss the house where I boarded. It was run by two old girls who were cat lovers—cat freaks of the worst type. The house smelled and was damp. The back yard always had a puddle that oozed from the over-flowing septic tank. Even my meager education told me that typhoid fever was possible, especially with cats running in and out of the house with germs on their feet. The old ladies were nice enough and they tried to keep things running smoothly, but those cats were another matter. They were al-lowed to walk on the table during meal times and sit in front of our plates. They even preened themselves with their tails dragging in the butter, and actively scratched their mangy ears with sharp distended claws, so that the tiny scales of dandruff or whatever could be seen sifting down through the shafts of sunlight onto the bread and potatoes. But it was when those mangy critters suddenly sneezed onto our plates that it was really revolting.

I used to bat those cats around on every occasion that presented itself, particularly in the early morning when the old girls were still asleep and I had to rise with the dawn. I would chase them round and round the dining room, faster and faster and faster, beating them with the newspaper. There were never fewer than seven to eleven cats present at any one time, so it was a merry sight. They leapt up the drapes, jumped on the table and climbed the walls. They yowled, howled, spat, swore and growled with enthusiasm and the flowing multicolor of escaping fur was pretty to see. When finally the room was boiling with cats, I'd open the back door and watch them flee to safety in the garden, rain or not. Yes, maybe I was fired at the right time. Maybe I *was* dangerous to the beasts.

Farm work was a winter occupation for me, because as soon as the late spring sun flooded its golden warmth across the countryside with the trees and bushes bursting with new buds, I had to be off in quest for the unknown. Especially, I loved the woodland when it became a mist of dancing bluebells, and in the orchards the apple blossoms smiled into the newness of life. I thought back to the sixty miles I had cycled for the interview to gain the employment I was now leaving; and how I had been too tired and hungry to cycle the sixty miles back through that hilly country, and had slept overnight in a rat infested barn. I had snuggled down among some hay and fell into a very deep sleep. Now, mice are friendly, one can feel their tickly whiskers and tiny exploring feet, and their high pitched squeaking and secret rustlings are enjoyable and good companionship. But rats are another matter. They would keep their distance while I was awake, but when sleep finally took me, the rats closed in and stole my only remaining food—two horsemeat and tomato sandwiches—from right under the crude gunnysack pillow I'd made. I awoke the next morning, rested but ravenous.

However, being of a resourceful nature with survival instincts as tough as any rat's, I was not hungry for any lengthy period. First, I reconnoitered a farm yard and finding a clean jam jar filled it and my pockets, with rolled oats from the calf bins. Next I mixed some of the oats with milk from one of the cows. This was a risky undertaking and took longer than usual as I was a stranger to the animal. Two eggs, warm and fresh from the henhouse were added to this raw meal. The whole concoction was tasty and satisfying, and it was the kind of diet that allowed me to travel without food money. Most farms I discovered had milk and eggs for the taking, as well as oats, maize, bean meal and calf feed by the sack full. These could be supplemented with carrots and turnips from the gardens and occasionally with hot, cooked potatoes from the hog houses.

My choice of places to sleep over the next few years was based on a situation I encountered during one of my "foraging and finding shelter" adventures. I usually traveled penniless around the countryside, exploring, thinking, dreaming and questing, and on this particular night, I ran into trouble. It was very frosty, with an almost full moon, and being extremely tired, cold, and shivering uncontrollably, I entered a warm cow barn and quickly buried myself under some fine soft hay in an empty stall. I fell heavily asleep amid the friendly cow noises of munching and rustling. Around 5:30 in the morning, the noise of milking pails and running water made me instantly alert. A cowman came by the stall, a tall heavily built individual, swinging his hurricane lamp. He hung it up on a nail as he went by, and in that same moment with barely a rustle I slipped through the door, just twenty paces from him.

The moon was low in the sky, and the icy morning air hit me. I could see my breath, and shivering, I turned to check what was occurring behind me in the shed. I saw the cowman come to the empty stall where I had lain, and plunge his gleaming two-tined pitch fork deep into the fodder. It was in the exact spot that had been my bed only moments before. I fled. The vision of those bright tines glinting in the lantern light, and the thought of where they would have been just twenty-five seconds earlier, changed my whole mode of survival. That was the last time I trusted the haunts of man for shelter. From that day forward I bedded down on the hillsides deep in the ferns. In the wet weather I pulled hay from under the thatched hay stacks until I had enough overhang to shed the rain and keep me dry. Somehow I survived. Was I just a weird half-human animal? Certainly I was a vagrant, wishing on a star in search of something unnamed.

On my travels I always carried my favorite book with me. It was entitled "The Story of My Heart" by Richard Jeffries. I knew the text intimately. It reflected everything I knew and felt about my strange quest. Like me, Jeffries had his remote "thinking places," moments in space where he could recharge his inner being with a more live reality than that which was recognized in normal circles. Like mine, his spirit hungered for those unseen elements that gave growth and strength. My whole search sprang from involuntary urges within me, from a dimension of thought that entered my physical form in such a way that I experienced life on two planes in delightful co-existence.

I had saved up enough money from my farm wages to buy a sixty-power three-inch Broadhurst Clarkson telescope. It was a little heavy, leather bound, but quite portable, and it kept me in touch with my immediate surroundings. It opened onto ever new worlds of color... yellow wagtails catching insects along the stream banks, fuzzy bees among the blossoms in the trees, as well as distant birds or rabbits across the glens. It was in this manner that I first discovered the wild red deer of Exmoor Forest. I found them quite accidentally late one evening as they bedded down for the night, while I was engaged in the same task. I fell in love with their timid beauty and graceful motion. In the days that followed I drifted with them, and they became quite used to me tagging along not too far behind. They led me through little hidden valleys, secret game trails, deep gorges and deserted tracts of utterly beautiful woodland. I found that although their trails wound through the hills and crossed moor and woodland, they never strayed very far, allowing me to return each night to my base camp. In addition the pattern of the trails enabled me, most of the time to know their approximate location. Until dusk and beyond when the cautious deer bedded down for the night, the air was filled with the calls and music of songbirds. The deer were aware of me as a foreign element in their world, almost to the point of being inquisitive in those weeks of ramblings, but they never took flight from me. I felt they knew of my need for their company and sleek red beauty.

Sometimes I studied the Humans through my scope when they were striding across the downs and wondered what they talked about. I was curious as to why, and what they laughed about, for I too laughed at times, usually out of the sheer joy of the life feelings that coursed through me. But I regarded the Humans with fear, for although we were alike in appearance, they were aliens, and I was not sure what I was. One afternoon I ventured into a nearby village on a little exploring trip, with the underlying motive of perhaps finding a friend, or at least to see people doing whatever people do, and there was always the possibility that maybe I'd find some money someone had accidentally dropped. Then quite by chance I spotted a young couple whom that morning I had seen through my scope on the downs. I remembered their happy looks and their laughter as they walked hand in hand. They looked at me at the same time that my features fired with recognition. She smiled.

"Hello," I said, blushing. "I too was up on the downs today! I saw you both in the hills through my scope."

He turned red and angry. "Spying on us, were you?" he charged.

"N-n-no. I j j j just s-s-s-saw you w-w-when I was s-s-scanning ...." I patted the scope. She intervened, "Oh James! Let's go. He wasn't spying!" But James would not be put off. I was baffled and uncomprehending of his anger. The village sidewalks were crowded. People looked.

He shouted at me, "I'll break that scope you spy, I'll teach you, you pervert! Give me that scope." He made a dash toward me as if to rip it from my grasp, but I eluded him and ran. His shouts followed as he chased me.

"Dirty bugger! Pervert! I'll break that glass!" People wanted to stop me as though I had stolen something. The chase ended. He gave up. Tears escaped me as I turned down a quiet lane and headed back for the deer country. The Humans hated me. This brush with them was enough to cure me of human contact, for a while anyway. It hurt too much.

Time was suspended during those endless hot summer days. Two months went by. It seemed like forever. I shed every vestige of clothing except for the rabbit skin moccasins I had made for myself. They were fastened to my eager and adventurous feet with strong twine and served their purpose well—which is more than I can say for my rabbit skin loin cloth. It never did become comfortable as the skins were not soft and cured, but rather scratchy and stiff. The rare Human who did show up on the fringe of my wild territory could be avoided with ease. In any case, these Humans were controlled by times and destinations, whereas I seemed to dwell in a timeless realm.

In the heat of noon I would find a deep pool to lie in, or I would stretch out in the bracken gazing up through the dark pines to the lark-trilled sky. I could watch rabbits playing; revel in the calls of chaffinches and blue tits, and sing unwritten soul music into the sighing wind. My midday meal was a salad of dandelion leaves and clover served up with water from the brook. Once in a while my trusty willow stick with line, hook, and worm would catch a perch in the deeper creeks, and rabbits, of course, were abundant. I always carried a batch of little copper wire snares—a life line for me. And oh, the satisfaction of appeasing genuine hunger with slices of half raw, half burnt rabbit legs liberally laced with wood ash. This would be followed by rabbit livers, hearts and tongues baked on the red hot, crackling rocks. New life coursed through me!

There is a time-stopping wonder that occurs while walking barefoot through flower carpeted woodland glades; or running in the first cool of evening through huge fields of purple clover when the dew is forming. The pockets of warm scented air are never to be forgotten. Later, tired and spent I would return to my fern-woven lair under the trees to dress and to sleep. I longed for companionship. Often I spoke with the owls, and I loved to take almost physical flight, wing to flittering wing tip with the flitter mice. Those bats swept so low over the grassy hummocks at times it seemed that we could dance together, touch the evening sky, and embrace the red glow of a day disappearing into starlight. To crown the night world, the ecstasy of dreams would carry us into the swirling solar light mists of the Milky Way, and as I snuggled down deep into the bracken I knew my red deer friends were not far away.

I have Human form, but, I am not one of them! In the mystery of star light, and even in the vast forest areas where I now rested, *I was just a wild boy – Little Boy Wild!*

Chapter Four

When the first vibrant colors of fall splashed their red and yellow leaves across the cool autumnal landscape, Little Boy Wild knew that we would have to find a farm job for the winter, or we would freeze or starve to death, so we usually came to agreement on a place of work that made us *both* comfortable and reasonably happy. At milking times he loved to snuggle up to the warm cows, and when the first "Ting-Ting" sounds of milk hit the pail – he could count on his many cat friends to show up for a feed. But, on one of these farms tucked away in the hills, in addition to our regular chores, *I* played the role of cat catcher—or as one of the other workers so aptly put it, "You ain't nothin' but a fuckin' cat killer. Bloody murder that's what I call it!"

In vain I protested that I was merely carrying out orders, and this was true. Indeed it was the most distasteful job I'd ever been called upon to perform in all my eighteen years.

"And you," the boss had pointed his finger at me; "You can round up them jeazilly cats and drown the bastards in the pond. Start with the kittens! Damn! We got more damn cats than hogs on this place."

I hated killing things unless hunger demanded it, and then it came naturally—but this roundup of kittens created all kinds of mental blocks and arguments. I placed them, warm and furry with cute faces and trusting eyes into a wheat sack, weighed it with bricks tied the top and sank it in the pond exactly as I'd been told to do."...an' make sure you bring that wheat sack back!" had been his final words.

Just how long does it take for a kitten to drown? I raised them after about five minutes and tipped them out onto the turf along with the bricks. They greeted me with glazed eyes, wet squirminess and pitiful, gurgling, mewing sounds—a sad, watery, wheezing orchestration. I was scared. I put them back into the sack, added the bricks and sent them down for the second time. Ten minutes later I brought them up again for inspection. As I tipped them out for the second time, I could still detect movement! They were not dead! Feeling quite sick about the whole affair, I fetched a short steel bar from the machine shop, and returning to the scene, methodically placed each kitten's head on a brick and split its skull. Out of fear I hit the first one too hard causing the brains and bloody mush to splash on my face. A squishy blob of matter lingered on my lips and wiping it off with the back of my hand and seeing the mess, I promptly lost my breakfast. Thereafter cats and kittens were always killed with a steel bar, and I used a longer bar for the fully grown critters to ensure quick dispatch.

However, disposing of the bodies was awkward at times. Following one big roundup, my victims were a red tom, a white female, and four or five others of assorted colors including a tabby, and a black demon known as Mooly. There was also in this batch a calico; it had one blue eye and the other brown. I had a special liking for her, but I was specifically ordered to include her in the round up, as she used to climb through the upper windows in the house, and raid the kitchen down below. They said she was too cunning, but I thought of her as being rather clever. Feeling tired after the extensive pursuit in the roundup, I decided it was too much trouble to dig the usual deep burial hole, so I left them all in a sack which I hid in the barn until the next day.

In the morning I took them on the hearse—the tractor that is, up to where I was plowing that day. There I laid them out all in a neat row. Each cat was pulled out of the sack by its stiff tail and laid individually in the furrow. The idea was that with the next ploughed furrow as it turned it would neatly cover them up, or so I thought. The farmer was quite disturbed a few days later when he went out to inspect the field. I returned to the yard for the milking chores.

"And YOU, you lazy son of a bitch, get up to that field tonight and give them damn cats a decent burial!" He roared.

"How did you f-f-f-find them?" I asked with my usual wide eyed guileless expression, amazed that this minor discrepancy had come to light.

"How did I f-f-f-find them?" he mimicked with a sneer. "Couldn't fuckin' miss'em with all them damn tails standin' up and wavin' in the east wind!"

Sure enough when I went up to investigate, there were their tails showing red, white, tabby, mottled, calico and black. As the icy east winds blew, their tails stood up, and then relaxed after each fierce gust. I had just not had the plough set deep enough to do a proper job. I contemplated cutting their tails off, but lacking a sharp instrument, had to set about burying them deeper; shuddering as I viewed each shrunken face with lips drawn back in a shriveled snarl, I decided I'd sooner leave this job than be told to go through another cat round-up.

Luckily I would not be called upon to perform this task of rounding up the cats again, as I was fired from that job. They told me to 'fuck off,' and never return, because I was a *dangerously deranged* bastard. They were not very friendly at all.

Here's how it happened. It really wasn't my fault – or was it? It was because of the rats, and well, it had been one of those days.

I had gone to collect the eggs from the rat infested henhouse. There were never many eggs for almost as soon as the chicken laid an egg a rat would snatch it, or face you, daring you to take it from under the chicken before he did. It was a little unnerving, because they were big rats, over a foot long. So I decided it would be a good day—it being Sunday and all—to go "ratting." Behind the barns were large earth banks riddled with holes. Earlier they had been rabbit warrens, but now they were one giant rat's nest.

It was a lovely sunny day when almost anything could happen, and where *WE* were, usually did. Across the hills and dales of the surrounding countryside, church bells were tolling hymns of welcome. I picked up about ten gallons of gasoline, which was massive over-kill, and a few matches.

"Rats! Rats! Rats!" I exclaimed excitedly to the farm terriers. Two of them got the message and in yapping anticipation followed me. Behind the barn I poured gas in copious quantities into the rat holes till all ten gallons had been used. This was the standard method of performing this operation because the gas vapor travels deep through the runways and burrows and can be ignited with a single match. The results are truly astonishing! The rats would leap out of their holes, some escaping, while others were caught by the canine ratters. The dogs flip them with lightning speed, snapping bones and puncturing the rat's insides till the victims are dazed and then they deliver the death crunch. On this occasion, the yapping of the terriers brought the farmer to the back of the barn to see what the terriers were doing digging around a rat hole. Although I could see him, he could not see me behind the thick brush and so he was not aware of the ongoing process. Going down on his knees beside the terriers I watched as he peered into the hole.

Simultaneously, *I saw myself* ignite a match and flick it into the burrow nearest to me. *It was a deliberate act and quite beyond my control.*

There was a deep, thundering, booming, earth-ripping explosion. It shook the whole area and spurted blue and yellow flames several feet out of the holes. The farmer was either partially blown back, or had hurled himself back from the hole. I was really scared. I watched him as he groped on the ground for what I learned later, were his eye glasses and an upper dental plate, but he failed to find them. In the explosion his arms were singed as was his hair. In fact the area around him smelled like we had been touching up chicken carcasses with the blow torch. Following his first shout of surprise and fear, the air was blue with wrath and swearing, and he looked kind of freaked, and I wondered why he had not smelled the gasoline.

"Is that you, Fuckin"Orace?" he yelled. "'Orace? Fuckin"Orace, where are you?" he shouted. Here, I must digress for a moment. You see, on this farm I was called "Fuckin"Orace" by everyone. It had all come about because of my frequent inability to speak because of the stuttering problem. On the first morning I'd reported for work in the big shed where the plans for the day were laid out, they had asked me my name. I was tongue tied.

"Tell us your name!" they demanded. I smiled and looked mysterious or so I thought, and tried to act a part, having found that I didn't stutter if I could be someone other than myself. But even then with all eyes on me, I couldn't for the life of me say, "My name is Derek," without contorting my facial features and turning somewhat purple for lack of air while trying to utter that which refused to be uttered.

So I said, "Maybe it's Horace."

"Horace?" they yelled with gleeful incredulity. "Orace, Fuckin"Orace!" they shouted with loud laughter.

"No, no!" I protested. "I was just kidding. My real name is Derek." There, I had said it, realizing that things had gone too far.

"No, you said your name is Orace!" they insisted.

So that's how I became known to one and all as "Fuckin' Orace" and that is how my boss came to be standing behind the barn that Sunday morning shouting, "Fuckin"Orace, is that you? Orace! Is you in there?"

Having dashed back about twenty paces or so at the time of the big blast, I shouted from the bushes, "Someone calling me? Who's there?" and in a superb act of innocence I burst forth from the undergrowth.

"You knew all the time I was here you bastard! You was tryin' to kill me wasn't you?" Icy cold prickles and ripples of damp shock went through me as I analyzed his accusation. White faced, dirty and scared, I faced the livid fury before me. Was it really true? Had I tried to kill him? No, I decided. If that were true he would already be dead. *No, I had just wanted to—to what? Why, on seeing him, did I knowingly flick that match?*

It just seemed that the movie director impulse had come over me, and I had been as usual, *outside of myself, looking at myself* acting in the movie. Anyway the farmer was alive. He was badly shaken up and his hair looked kind of weird, and I don't think his moustache looked quite the same either. Dave, the farm foreman was on the scene by this time, and he was in a belligerent mood. He was going to protect the farmer from weird types like me, once and for all.

"Fuckin"Orace!" he yelled with righteous indignation, "I'm giving you five minutes to get your ass off this place, or I'll beat your fuckin' face in! You fuckin' psycho." However, he cooled down eventually, because with the labor shortage – they still needed *me*, but not the psycho part; but I couldn't separate them – we were all in one package so to speak.

Now, here we are again, several weeks later, and I have another run-in with Dave, who already bore me grudge because of the "big blast." We were digging with a crew in the orchard, when nature called him and he'd gone to relieve himself, and... Well, before I continue with this story –I must digress a moment or two more, because first I have to explain about old Jack, a kind of bum or tramp who hung around the place.

He was unshaven and scruffy with filthy clothes, and I never did know where he disappeared to at night. Like anyone else, Jack used to relieve himself now and then, but he never went in the bushes like the rest of the farm hands. No, he had his peculiar trademark which he left around the headlands of the fields. When Jack performed his craft, even from a distance you could see his rear end wiggle, almost like a bee telling the others in the hive where the nectar is. But his would not be in a pile or lay decently like a normal "log." Jack would deposit his gift to the land in the form of a "D" shackle, like the ones we used to hook the implements up to the tractors. In fact I almost picked one up the previous day, thinking it was a rusty shackle. They were always the same design; an elongated "U" with a strip across the end like an open bolt. I knew, because I checked them in passing.

So, when Dave the foreman on this particular day had gone to relieve himself, I had been seized with an inspiration. Deftly I took up Dave's round-nose shovel with its D-handle, ran to the edge of the field, and there maneuvered one of Jack's specials exactly across the horizontal bar of the handle, allowing the ends of the "special" to sag over the ends of the bar. Then I sprinkled a little dust on top so as to hide the fresh ginger brown fresh color and thereby not attract attention, and finally I placed the spade carefully back into the ground, standing it up exactly as he had left it.

Dave came out of the bush, his face easy and unclouded as befits a man who feels light and refreshed. The other men had seen what I'd done, and had shaken their heads and advised against it. But I was powerless to do anything but obey, because when the Movie Director in me said, "Lights, camera, action", that was it! *I had to obey.* In spite of their misgivings, they kept Dave talking and his mind occupied, so that without glancing at his shovel handle, he bore heavily down with a strong grip and revoltingly squishy results. I could imagine the stench.

He looked at the others and then at me.

"Fuckin'"Orace!" he bellowed, and charged me like a mad bull. Fury contorted his face and his hands were thickly brown and shining. I ran for my life. He was in good shape and a powerful runner, but I was younger and my feet were swift with fear. If he ever caught up with me... I could taste it! It lent wings to my feet.

At last he desisted and went back to clean himself up; and then in a surprise ambush attacked me later in the day after work, when unsuspectingly,

I walked into the barn. He confronted me in a fury while I just stood there frozen with fear. First I got a knuckle in the nose, and then he grappled with me until my shirt disintegrated into strips, and *all the while I was outside of myself,* watching this young kid writhe in both psychic and physical pain. Little Boy Wild rolled on the floor among the oat straw, and when Dave quit punching him, he curled up into his fetal position and between his sobbing and tears; he rocked back and forth wailing "Keelematu! Keelematu!"

Dave – who was really quite a nice guy of about thirty years old was quite taken aback at the turn of events. Wild Boy struggled to his feet; his shirt hung in twisted bloody disarray from his thin frame, and as he looked at Dave, things took a turn for the worse. Dave approached him and put his warm strong arm around his shoulders; but this sudden, kind touching, with such closeness and feeling, stabbed Little Wild Boy with a great surge of pain. He knew this would lead to blackness and dissociation, so he broke free, picked up his little bag of tools and ran for the doorway. As the evening air hit him he gave several loud cries of anguish and disappeared into the gathering fog.

He heard Dave call out in a friendly voice, "I'm sorry Horace, you dumb kid," but this only increased his pain level. As Wild Boy quickly ran into fog, he sensed the general direction across country where he could intersect with the railroad, and then all he had to do was to follow the tracks home, a distance of about five miles.

He slept among the hay in the barn with the rats during the week, and on week-ends he visited the family home for a one night stay. There he would have a hot bath and wash some clothes before taking off again. But, tonight he was far off his mark and came to the river, he knew now that all he had to do was to follow the river upstream till it was crossed by the railroad bridge, and from there all he had to do was to follow the tracks into town. When he did arrive at this house of horrors – called "home," it was very late. He was met with the usual hostility from his mother, and he assured her that he would leave in the morning, and not inconvenience her by having breakfast. He was told it couldn't be too soon for her, as she retreated into her sewing room. Reviewing the day while soaking in a hot tub of soapy water, Wild Boy felt that he probably deserved the scene with Dave, and there was no point in going back to the farm as his fate had been sealed, and he doubted very much that they would mail him the balance due on his pay cheque.

In any case, it was summer time now. Time to take off for the hills, live wild, and look for whatever it was **WE** used to seek or expected to find on these ventures. But this was the land of the Humans, and we knew that in order to survive physically and mentally we had to flee quickly to melt into the countryside, to live our passion for the summer flowers, to **become** the squirrels, the deer, the otters and the foxes; and to project our being into the Morning Star. So we took off on our quest, behaving rather like the red foxes do in their travels, keeping a low profile, hiding when necessary and eating where we could.

Following his most recent trauma, Little Boy Wild was **driven** to "look for himself." He needed to be held, to be loved, and ultimately, soothed with sexual release, so that his world could come back once more into focus. But no one knew of him – or cared about him in any way. So that night he resorted to seeking a deep lonely pond, which he found between a cow pasture and a clover meadow. He left his clothing by a Hawthorne tree along with his small rucksack, and wandered "au naturel" into the warm clover scented night. No one was ever going to comfort him, only the rabbits saw him, and only the stars touched him. He slowly floated out into the sun warmed water. He felt a frog swim by – it was a friendly contact, and he glowed at its touch. Indeed, as always, he had his wild friends all round him in the woodland, and as the ecstasy of the night kissed him, he murmured, *"Is this not what life is all about? Swimming among the stars and being all creation?"*

Chapter Five

Two weeks later I returned to the family home in Middlesex long enough to pack my rucksack with my one and only freshly washed wool blanket, a ground sheet, two mole traps, and two dozen snares along with waterproof matches and sundry items including my precious copy of Jeffries' "Story of My Heart"* That same day I traveled to an area of several square miles of sandpits that existed in the midst of a farming district. They had been abandoned long ago. It was the sort of place where few people had any reason to go; a maze of little valleys, sand caves and rocky outcroppings, but best of all it contained small narrow lakes of water warmed by the summer sun.

As usual a feeling of freedom descended on me the moment I entered the first valley. Traveling to a little sand cave which I'd used on a previous expedition, I quickly made it comfortable. It was small but I could stretch out full length, even though I was by this time just over six foot one inches in my bare feet. It was so much better than the hollow tree I had slept in one night. That had been cramped but dry; my only complaint had been the hooting of the owls which used the upper branches. Owl pellets had fallen on me, and examining them by morning light, I saw they contained mouse fur and the iridescent shells of beetles. Having discarded all clothing as usual, I ran through the hot sand to wash up and swim in the pools. I was at peace in my world. Distant tractors hummed in the hills and crows cawed. Big honey bees worked on the sweet scented honeysuckle blossoms around the edge of the pits. I was my usual lonely self. Would I ever find someone to adventure with and share the beauty and excitement of each day?

In the late afternoon I returned to the caves to pick up the mole traps

---

* The Story of My Heart –Richard Jeffries 1883.

and a few snares and ventured into a farm orchard about half a mile away. There, finding mole runs, I set the traps. It would take a pile of those silky black moleskins to make pants, a jacket and a cap for the coming winter. I scouted the farm and through the scope saw a herd of shorthorns, some Wessex saddleback pigs, many chickens and a couple of dogs. I made a mental note that I'd have to be careful when foraging here for food. I always moved slowly on these little farmstead explorations, particularly when I came to a clearing or open area. Moving slowly and cautiously I would watch for the wind direction, and appear or melt into the bush as imperceptibly as the red foxes. Watching the woodland animals had taught me well.

Humans were to be avoided at all costs. Often I had observed them even at very close range without being discovered. They had cold eyes and hostile expressions, and the aggressive vibrations which emanated from them gave me a sinking feeling. With the first chill breezes of evening, I would put on my only clothing, a shirt and cord shorts, which I had crudely cut down from long pants with my knife. Ragged and comfortable, they kept me warm on cool rainy days, and were essential at night. One day when my snares were empty, hunger drove me on a food search, and I decided that a farm would have to vanquish the empty growling in my stomach. I saw a red fox loping through the dusk, nose to ground, bushy tail flowing. He was hunting too. Bats were out squeaking at the first stars. The Humans were in the farm house talking loudly. Music floated across the yard and a calf bawled from one of the sheds. The hen house was tightly shut.

"The dogs must be in the house," I told myself, as I opened the cowshed door. Only one cow remained in the barn and she had just calved the day before. Finding a large can, I fashioned a crude handle with baling wire and having fastened it securely, took it outside to the horse trough and washed it thoroughly. On my way back to the barn I checked the house for activity. All was well. The cow was nervous being in strange hands, but I had a way with livestock now, and a good half gallon of milk had flowed into the can without difficulty when one of the dogs barked in the house. Quickly I vanished through the orchard into the darkness of the friendly sand pits. Although there was no moon that night, there was enough star-light to return to base with my prize.

Shivering with cold I lit a small fire, balanced the can of milk on the rocks to heat, and set off to find more firewood. When I got back the milk had set like solid creamy custard with a thick heavy skin on top. Of course, I should have known if left too long, the milk from the freshly calved cow would turn to "beestings" as they called it, because it contained so many rich elements to get the calf off to a good start in life.

"Well, Derek," I said, "If it's good for the calves in the liquid form, it should stick to your ribs in the solid form." I spooned it out of the can with a little dipper I had carved that afternoon. It was hot and rich and very satisfying, and feeling drowsy I let the fire die down and curled up in my blanket with a very full belly, and fell into a deep sleep.

When I arose refreshed, the sun was already high in the sky. After a quick dip and a swim in the cool water I set off to check the traps. One rabbit glazed of eye and wet with dew had been snared overnight. He was quickly gutted, one back foot spliced into the other for carrying and I was on my way. One mole had been trapped, I extricated her, smoothed the dark fur, and having reset the traps in a different place prepared to leave.

A scream of pain, hoarse with hurt and protest came from some place in the group of farm buildings. Twice it was repeated. There was shouting and cursing. I melted into the woods. Those screams held a ring that reached back into the fear and darkness of my childhood. After skinning and dressing the rabbit, I washed him in the pool, stuck a stick through him like a spit and roasted him over a small hot fire for the main meal of the day. While the rabbit cooked I skinned the mole. In the afternoon sun I lay by a glinting pool browsing through "The Story of My Heart." Jeffries had been drawn to his favorite thinking places as had I. This was my pilgrimage too – and I read from his book:*

"To get away from the endless and nameless circumstances of everyday existence, which by degrees build a wall around the mind, so that it travels in a constantly narrowing circle. Remain! Be content, go around and round in one barren path, a little money, a little food and sleep, some ancient fables, old age and death."

"Yes! That is exactly how I see the Humans existing!" I sighed in agreement, and jumping up I grabbed my roasting rabbit by the ears and rotated

---

* The Story of My Heart –Richard Jeffries. 1883.

him a bit. He had a cute furry face, but from there down he was naked and brown. But why did he look at me that way? A dialog followed.

"He's not looking at you Derek, you're looking at him."

"Okay, but next time I'll cut his damn head right off, then he'll just be meat!"

"Suit yourself!"

"Other people have homes! They have food ..."

A higher pitched voice cut in: "But the idle have nothing! Go see the ant, thou sluggard! He works mightily and fills his belly and stores food for the winter!"

"Fuck off, preacher!" I yelled. "See what Jeffries says."

"I deny altogether that idleness is an evil, or that it produces evil, and I am well aware why the interested are so bitter against idleness, namely because it gives time for thought."

"That is what it is all about," I exclaimed. "Don't give them time to think or they might see the truth!"

"The truth shall make you free!" interjected the Preacher.

I returned to the pond and lay by the water's edge listening to the giant blue dragon flies that skimmed the surface. A small brown water vole swimming across created scintillating light patterns and tiny ripples, then disappeared as a furry wet brown blob of fur into a hole in the bank. Was this the real life? Or was the real life in the smoking stink and noisy darkness of factories and tall brick chimney's spewing their black filth into the pure blue heaven? There was the crowding, the quiet resignation on the faces of the older people, the mask of despair and resignation distorting the features of the younger ones. Earning money on the treadmill and missing the tranquil enchantment that now surrounded me. There beneath a tree lay a broken chrysalis, the split shell cast aside. I marveled at what it had contained and pondered on the shell of human youth and its incredible potential. "Derek! The unseen thought forms that guide you in the invisible are more real than the illusions that the human world projects!" I concluded.

After a week of living like some imagined South Sea Islander day after day between the hot sand and the sun, I had collected four rabbit skins and nine moleskins in my cave and had stashed a sack of rolled oats away to enrich my diet. Late that night the moon was almost full, it bathed the whole countryside in silver light with darker shadows. I was on a milk raid with the billy can. Softly I followed the tree shadows bordering the orchards and kept to the darker shadows of the barns. The farmstead was asleep, no lights were visible. Imperceptibly I eased open the cowshed door and slipped inside. After a few moments I was able to make out the outlines of several cows, two of which had recently calved or they would have been out with the main herd in the pasture. Then just as I was preparing to select one for milking, smoothing her with my hand and talking very softly, a slight sound at the far end of the shed caused me to look up sharply. The small door opened and someone stepped inside with a quick light movement. With no time to escape I shrank back into the piles of hay.

The visitor knew his way around. He moved to my end of the shed with barely a sound. Breathing softly, he came close to where I lay in the hay. A shaft of moonlight pierced the shadows and I saw he was a young man of about my own age—some sixteen or seventeen summers. He was not as tall as I— about five foot seven I estimated—but as lean, though some-what more muscular. Momentarily, he wore only shorts and runners, then he tossed his shorts into the hay – quite close to me, and in the dim light it quickly became obvious that he was athletically engaged in a bovine liaison. This situation was not uncommon for me as I had run into it on several of the farms where I had worked –and not just with young guys like us. A few minutes later, I thought I'd try for an escape. But, just then the wire handle of the milk can fell with a tinny clang against its side. It was an alien alarm among the rustling cow noises, and the boy leapt back, staggering slightly, and asked in a fierce whisper, "Who's there?"

"Name is D-D-D-Derek!" I almost said, 'It's Fuckin'"Orace!'" I came to my feet.

"Holy cripes!" he exclaimed, now catching a full view of me. We both stood there with little shivers of shock coursing through us from the en-counter. He looked vulnerable in his nakedness, and as he quickly groped for his shorts he said, "I'm Tim – and just what the fuck are you doing in here?" I explained that I was in a milk raid, and where I was hanging out. Of course I had seen him several times before on the tractor and around the yard. He came back with, "Fuck! You scared the livin' Jesus out of me! Thought you were my old man. He'd beat me to death if he caught me in here like this!" He laughed with relief. "Derek – I just gotta have it, or I can't think, work or do anything, are you like that?" I nodded in agreement. He then went on to tell me of his foster parents and how he was going to leave them in the next year or so and go on his own. We grinned at one another, enjoying the discovery of mutual comradeship. Of course, we had to have a sex discussion – *IT* was the number one subject on our minds – like any teen aged male kid. Tim said that if the farm was not so distant from the nearest village – things would be different, and I believed him. Indeed, I was the deranged one here; he surely couldn't be as badly screwed as me! Outside an owl hooted twice, it was a sad note, but friendly, and it utterly relaxed us.

"Tell me more about yourself Tim. Hey, let's get comfortable and talk awhile." We leaned back into the pile of hay which was fine textured and soft.

"What a way to meet!" exclaimed Tim. Then he fished around in his pockets and came up with a chocolate bar which he shared with me. Oh! The luxury of chocolate after a diet of roast rabbits! To my surprise he told me he had seen me on several occasions collecting firewood. I decided I'd have to bring up my wood craft a few notches for sure.

We talked of our hopes and experiences far into the early hours. Finally, after being quiet and thoughtful for some moments, he said, "Hey, why don't we team up and become blood brothers. Let's go adventuring together!"

My heart pounded with agreement. "Nothing I'd like better! I've been looking for someone to explore with," I said in an excited whisper.

"I'm ready to leave here anytime, the way they treat me." he said. Tim had already spoken of the many troubles in his home life, and we found that we shared a somewhat common ground—abuse by parents in my case and similar treatment by foster parents in his.

"Let's become Blood Brothers" I enthused as I placed my arm around him. He flinched and then I dimly discerned some huge raised welts and darker markings on his back.

"It's my foster father, he beats me up when he gets these temper tantrums, maybe it's the booze. He's got one fuck of a temper..." He swallowed. This then explained the pained cries I'd heard the previous week.

"My folks are about the same way," I commiserated. "The old man's okay, he's an easy going type, but SHE is another matter. I suppose that's why I'm out here wandering around..." I trailed off into silence. Our shared background of abuse deepened our understanding and closeness, and we found a new joy of togetherness and caring flowing between us. We both looked up, wide of eye, to listen to a fox bark in the copse not far away.

"How do you get out at night without them knowing?" I asked, visions of creaking stairs and a host of similar complications crowding in from the past.

"Oh, I climb out back through the window then they never know when I'm out, especially when it's real late like now."

Silence fell between us for some moments. I wondered what he was thinking. Just then he turned to me. He smelled of clean hay, the nectar of fresh apples tinged with chocolate was on his breath. I could see the whiteness of his teeth as he smiled warmly. It caused a warm glow to envelop me. Perhaps I actually meant something to someone! I looked at him shyly and in some way it sealed our bond of friendship. Tim sniffed and then we laughed, first softly, and then louder as mingled pain and happiness encompassed us. We lay back in the soft hay which our combined weight had hollowed into a deep warm bed of comfort—deluxe accommodation compared to my sand cave. A feeling of great sadness fell over me, and as I leaned further back into the hay, I felt it would not take much to fall asleep.

"Well here we are, Tim. Are we really going adventuring together?" this, after talking for about an hour.

"Sure thing," he replied huskily. "There's nothing here for me. What've I got to lose?

"That's great and the sooner the better." I replied. We both laughed and rising we knew we had to get some sleep. Milking time always comes too early.

In parting he said, "Derek let's see each other on Sunday. I don't have to work then. I'll meet you on the far side of the orchard, by that real old walnut tree early, about seven."

"Why not meet me Saturday night and we can have more time together," I suggested.

"Okay, let's do that!" he exclaimed in high excitement. Then retreating behind what seemed to be a mask of fear he took off, skipping rather like a hare with grace and precision of footing toward the rear of the house and was lost from sight. He would shortly be called for the milking chores and wanted to be in his room.

One of the yard dogs barked loudly and I too took swiftly to my feet to merge into the anonymity of the sand hills. A tireless energy possessed me as I ran down the first narrow valley to branch off toward my base. I seemed to float, my feet barely touching the surface, nor was I winded as I ran to dissipate the warm surges of joy that sprang up within me. At last the old caution took over as I approached the sand cave. I tested the wind for scent like an animal, as the wild part of my survival techniques came into play. I knew that continuous observation of the terrain, plant life, trees, the actions and sounds of animals, birds and insects, including their flight modes and calls would tell me of any danger. Dawn was breaking, and hunger pained my stomach upon safe arrival at base. My few belongings were dry and secure, including my precious small sack of rolled oats. I planned to mix them with water because oats can be quite dry on the tongue, but they were delicious and filling. While chewing on my oats, I let my mind recount the night's adventures, reliving the intimate moments. Questions arose about Tim. Just how long would he go adventuring with me? Would he really meet me as we had arranged? My anticipation of our next meeting could hardly be contained. Those two days were almost an age. I went fishing without success. I trapped two more moles and I found a hare lying in a snare, the thin coppery line was deeply embedded in the ruffled fur around the neck. He must be saved for a feast of feasts. Yes. I must have a banquet prepared for when Tim arrives. We would celebrate the beginning of a great friendship.

Chapter Six

Before the up-coming weekend I had time to leave my base and go exploring. I wanted to find a wooded secluded base, and chose to explore a wild fringe of woodland about one mile to the north. Skylarks sang endlessly, their songs rising and falling in the great blue expanse above. Here I would commune with the whole wild world. Keeping to the hedgerows, following the deeper ditches, and shadowing through the trees as I'd seen the red foxes do, I arrived without incident unobserved by any other than two grey squirrels who accepted me without scolding They watched me with bright eyes and flicking tails as I silently passed. Just ahead in a patch of bright sunlight lay a shallow woodland pool bordered with a haze of blue forget-me-nots. I savored the moment. Chiffchaffs called in the bushes, chickadees hunted food and chizzied one to another.

I threw my rucksack on a grassy bank. It was time for a dip so I stripped off and lay in the shallow pool just under the surface and turning to one side in the fluid coolness, I studied some tiny flowers at the water's edge. Suddenly near my left foot, something moved in the water, and with swift movements amid a swirl of diamond water droplets I was able to catch a handsome king newt with a brilliant orange under-belly. I held him high and he wriggled as I smoothed a wet finger over his shining black back. He was much larger than the salamanders being almost nine inches long. I christened him "Nooty." He would be my companion for the day. Leaving the water I rigged him a little harness and lying down placed him flat on my wet belly. It was a friendly feeling to experience his tiny clawed feet scrambling around as he endeavored to escape. I tied him up to a tree with access to the water, spoke softly to him and stroked his dark head while he looks uncomprehendingly at me.

As the sun rose higher in the sky, I turned to Richard Jeffries "The Story of My Heart," and quoted him aloud.

"It is eternity now, and I am in the midst of it. It is about me in the sunshine. I am in it like the butterfly floating in the light laden air. Nothing has to come; it is *NOW*. Now *is* eternity. When all the stars have revolved, they only produce NOW again."

"Oh Richard," I exclaimed, startling Nooty into the water, "I feel you are right here with me now, and that you understand!" His next words paralleled my own thoughts.

"It would not surprise me in the least if a circumstance outside physical experience occurred"

"Nor I Richard!" I cried. "I feel the other dimensions around me too." A distant crow cawed out a warning somewhere and time stood still. Nooty glistened jet black at the water's edge. I gazed in rapture at the woodland scene, the silver birches in spring green and silver, the serenity and the magic of "NOW" all contained therein. Placing a small red fern as a marker in the book, I flicked a long legged speckled bug off into the grass and closed "The Story of My Heart" with a snap that caused the wood pigeons in the elms to clap their wings in wild alarm and take flight across the meadow.

"Why am I not like other people? What do you think Nooty?"

Nooty blinked, and at that moment I knew he was part of "NOW," and that in some way I was not quite contained in my own "NOW," but looking in from outside.

"Nooty when I'm with you I don't stutter. It's only when I'm in contact with the Humans that I'm so incapacitated. They mimic me. *I see myself outside myself*—red- faced, a flaming anguish of frozen words unuttered.

I'm five years old – early memories come to me from my parent's farmhouse with the shiny ivy climbing high to the eaves, where the red tile roof joins the great brick walls. I'm in the attic at the top of the stairs that I dread to climb. This is my bedroom, and for me it is filled with terror. Something happens every other night or so, that makes my heart sink with fear. Right now the door is open with light—friendly light—shining from the hallway. I lie in a small wooden crib with railings all round. I hear footsteps, quick businesslike footsteps and the door to my room is closed. The sound of foot steps fade down a flight of stairs. For a while a small light shows under the door, then, it too is extinguished. There is nothing but silence. Sometimes though, the winds blow at night battering the old house and making weird noises. There is a small casement window at the far end of the attic where the ceiling slopes steeply to the walls. A faint light, a star glow of illumination tells me where the window is. I lie sleepless but warm under my blankets. It is friendly in the crib. I am me, Derek. *I'm safe until "they" come – safe until SHE comes. SHE is my mother.* I'm safe because I'm alone. I cannot face her hatred. What have I done or not done? Forget it. You're warm and safe right now. Safe? No! I move in my crib and it's happening again. *They* have arrived. The ivy rustles by the little window. It's the wind, yes, just the wind. Plop! A light weight drops to the floor from the window sill. Plop! Another one has dropped to the floor. There is squeaking and I hear their feet scampering. *The rats have arrived.* Plop! It's really dark. I'll try to sleep, maybe they'll go away. I close my eyes and hardly breathe. My body retains the tension that my closed eyes can't relieve. There is movement, and I know they are reconnoitering the perimeters of the attic. I sense one climbing the leg of the crib and freeze. I feel one walking over my tummy onto my chest. My arm is on the outside of the cover and when I poke at it, I feel its fur. It makes a throaty squeak and sits there. Its eyes glow. It is quite bold. I scream and thrash my legs around making it disappear through the railings. There is scurrying. I scream again and again. I cry. I call. Light bursts into the room with my mother. I'm ordered to stop making a racket. I'm too frightened and too incoherent to explain what the problem is, other than to point to… it isn't there anymore. THEY are not here. SHE is here –one living nightmare exchanged for another.

Light reveals nothing and I'm harshly told to shut up. I feel the physical slaps of disapproval. I promptly wet my bed. SHE doesn't believe in my terror. SHE hates me anyway, but at least I think I know the parameters of the pain she inflicts. It is predictable. It is *them* I don't know about. Finally I fall asleep, but I'm awakened several times in the night and I scare them from my blanket. But, they always come back. What do they want? Once there were two rats, one by my head and one lower down. I seem to sense that they realize I am too large to attack. But I cannot sleep –and I must not scream. *So I do what I always do – disappear inside myself.* If the rats should bite and attack me, I'll have to come back and fight. If **SHE** shows up, I'll just get slapped around –that I can handle. Over an unknown period of time, for me, this scenario repeats itself again and again.

Once I heard HER conversing with someone on the rat possibility as I lay there. It was discussed in my presence as though I was uninvolved, an uncomprehending inanimate object put into the attic for storage. Later I recognized the dawn of faint understanding illuminating her face, and thereafter the window was closed at night. The rats had been climbing up the ivy into my room. Several times SHE closed the window without latching it, and the dread night foragers returned. My screams of terror were rewarded with the usual slapping and a cuffing about the ears. Sometimes she checks the window and latches it. That distinctive click rolls a weight off my mind and relaxes me into a deep sleep. At other times she forgets, and I know I may have visitors. This leaves me exhausted, and I'm sure to wet my bed again anyway.

More early memories from the tender age of five:

Wet beds and the thrashings that follow always leave me frightened and defensive. I also know she will viciously pinch me on the slightest pretext and I always flinch as she passes me, and try to keep out of her way. One day I escaped to the vegetable garden; the hot sun felt so good that I scattered my clothing among the carrots and tall runner beans and sat naked in the loose soil. Next I collected a lot of black and yellow striped caterpillars off the tall runner beans. They crawled on me with friendly sticky feet and I loved their touch. I also like to eat them. Sometimes I eat several of them in a morning while I'm wandering around the garden. I eat the peas too because they take some of the bitter taste of the caterpillars away. This particular morning a high pitched scream rent the air, and then another scream! I've been discovered by an Aunt.

"Come here!" She calls to mother, "He's eating those awful things!" More screaming, then I'm swiftly captured and dragged away. So mother gathers up my clothes. She thrashes me again and again. Then it's all over till next time.

Some days are good. My father smiles at me on the rare occasions that he is home, and I feel warm all over.

"Go away!" Mother snarls, as she sees my face light up at the attention I'm receiving.

"O-o-oh-h," says Dad, "he's all right!"

"I can't stand him!" She screams vehemently.

With trembling lower lip I flee guiltily to some haven of safety. I like the rains though. If it really rains hard for several hours I know that water will come in under the door and creep across the red tile floor, and with it will come earth worms and baby frogs, yellow and friendly. I am unafraid for with the rains I become a hero. Mother's voice softens with admiration when she asks me to collect up the offending creatures and dispose of them. I am the centre of attention! SHE smiles. Once she touched me —differently. I love the rains. The frogs scare her but I have long talks with them. They know much. Then there is my older brother. He is seven now and my arch enemy supreme. He can do no wrong. He schemes, manipulating HER, and plotting the situations which will result in extra beatings for me. Once when a snake came under the door I picked it up fearlessly. Even BROTHER was scared. I waved it at him while he cringed back frightened and angry. It ended in the usual beating and I was not a hero that night.

Brother stole a large chunk of butter out of a little yellow enamel cup one day and SHE wanted to know why the cup was empty. Brother lies and says he saw me eating it. She is so furious she picks me up, pulls down my pants, and too blind with fury to beat me effectively, sinks her teeth viciously into my tender posterior. I scream and roll off her lap. I hit the hard slate floor. Pain shoots through my body. SHE gets the stick and the blows rain on me. As always I shield myself from them with my forearm. I'm dragged to my attic room and thrown in. I glow with the red welts. I turn and peer at the purple tooth marks on my rear where the skin is broken. Sleep takes me. Later I awaken. It's time to eat and it's dinner time. SHE calls me; I leap in fear and carefully walk down stairs. She looks at me with distaste. Brother eats supper nicely. I feel sick and do not want to eat.

"You'll eat!" SHE snarls. Leaping up and springing around the table, she stuffs a whole small potato in my mouth with a spoon that has sharp edges; it cuts my lower lip and gums. It is bright red with blood when she throws it on the table. She then holds my jaws shut and pinches my nose so tightly that I cannot breathe, and while I thrash around she screams, "Swallow! Swallow! Swallow it you swine!" This scene is a somewhat common routine. I have to swallow or black out. Today I can't breathe or chew. It's too big a lump, but it goes down anyway. It hurts. It hurts terribly. Brother looks on with a sly grin. She returns to her place at the table opposite me. My eyes are large with tears. The pain, the pain, the lump; suddenly I vomit across the damask table cloth. The still whole potato hits my plate and skids off from the force of the eruption, scattering vomit droplets with saliva and blood over their plates and the table cloth. I burp loudly and choke. My throat slimes up and my nose runs as I gasp for air. I see HER leap up through my blurred vision. The chair is knocked out from under me. I hit the slate floor hard. My ears feel the ringing impact of heavy hands. I'm dragged to the doorway, kicked into the passageway and I flee to my room. My small legs can only take one stair at a time, but SHE takes the stairs one after another. The blows from her fists rain on me. I cannot get away. Only when I disappear into my attic room does she go downstairs. I crawl under my blanket shivering with cold shock, fright, and a hopelessness that is dissolved into sleep. Later I awake with shock. Oh God, I'm wet again! I know the results already. Sleep, sleep, blessed sleep until the next onslaught.

Today there is a fire brightly burning in the living room fireplace. The maid has a day off, so it's going to be a rougher day than usual. We had maids in those days. They gave me a kind smiles and I glowed when I smiled back. SHE was not quite so cruel when they were around. But there is BROTHER to reckon with. He is rocking my high chair and struggling to push it, and me, into the fire. There is murderous intent set in his face. I'm trying to block his efforts, but not too successfully. The chair is going to tip. I am screaming in fright, and as I stand up, making it top heavy, he succeeds, and over I go. I scream as I fall past the fire irons, and my nose is cut as it catches on a wrought iron hook. Flames, blackness and heat engulf me. SHE comes into the room, and somehow I'm rescued. He explains that he was trying to keep me *in* the chair, when quite the opposite was true. Of course I got a good shaking up, and later a doctor stitches my nose. Life carries on.

Suddenly I find myself back by the forget-me-not pool with my big black and orange newt; at the same time I heard rapid wing movements, unnatural fluttering and shrill bird cries. I had came back into the sunlight

ROOT

from the darkness of childhood to see a sparrow hawk, talons sunk into a wood pigeon, his fierce hooked beak slashing at the breast as feathers flew. Poor Nooty was flipping about on the edge of the pool so I released him and told him to return to his own realm, which he achieved in a single "Plop," as he broke the surface of the water. I watched his point of disappearance, as the widening ripples reached out to the flowers at the edge.

I also noticed that my own thought patterns flowed much the same way, ever wider, and some times two sets of circular ripples interfered with each other creating two worlds simultaneously. I toyed with the idea of living in both dimensions at the same time; (which in truth I suppose I was already doing, if I could but analyze the fragmentation of my psyche.)

"Yes, you *are* different Derek because... Anyway Tim, I hope you'll be as understanding of my pain, as I will be about your welts and scars. We both have to rise above the hell the Humans have created. I like to feel your closeness; I already have your smile etched into my memory, and I really need you as a friend and fellow adventurer.

As I left the forget-me-not pool to make my way through the deep brush, I discovered an old woodcutter's hut—a very small one room crude log cabin about eight feet by ten feet with a rotted thatch roof and no window or door, but covered in honeysuckle vines. It leaned at an angle but was quite firm. This was a thrilling find. No Human tracks led to it. It must have been abandoned long ago.

"What do you think of it, Derek?"

"It's just super!"

"Yes. You and Tim will have a place to stay."

"Do you think he'll really come with me?"

"Why shouldn't he? He says he will."

"But you know he may change his mind ..."

"You should get things ready. He'll come, even if only for a day ..."

"I want him to stay with me for a week or a month or a whole year!" I threw my arms out as if to embrace all the days of friendship in one instant bundle.

It was time to make a change, anyway. I made it a rule never to stay in an area for more than a few days, lest habit and footprints lead the Humans to my hidden sanctuaries; where they would surely desecrate my altars of solitude and quest with their dull minds of condemnation. Quickly I scraped the bird droppings from the floor of the hut, inspected the swallow's nests, and said hello to a few surprised field mice that scampered around in the corners.

"You're welcome to stay little friends," I invited. I then left my pack and traveled a quarter mile to the east where I had spotted a stack of oat straw bales. Two of these I lugged back to the cabin in two separate journeys, being careful not to leave straw tailings behind, but this was hard to do, so I had to go back and pick up any tell-tale wisps of straw that I'd dropped. On arrival I broke open the bales to form a soft dry bed for the night. When my task was completed, I knew I had to stay awhile longer to enjoy the honey-suckle scent. This is a real adventure –to be able to capture in one's mind, moments that can last forever. It is not a matter of just scenting a flower as one goes by. This is a scene so special that it has to be absorbed. It is dominated by the flowers, their color and shape, by scent, the movement of leaves and the magic of the solitude. The relaxation of seeing the old cabin surrounded by such dense bush yielded a warm feeling of security, protection from the rain or cold wind, and the friendship of mice or nesting swallows up on the beams. I loved to hear the swallow families softly "talking" at night. In dark times, were they to occur –one could escape by recalling the beauty and step right into the scene! It is, in its essence – going back in time, and I have yet to plan some experiments to achieve this. I need to determine a method whereby I can access time travel through a change in my mental frequencies or levels of consciousness.

Cuckoo! Cuckoo! Cuckoo! With startling clarity a cuckoo called from close by. At first I was afraid of the attention it might create if Humans were nearby, and then remembered that cuckoos called from all over the dells and hills at any time so I relaxed once more. Before leaving the hut I took the prize hare from my pack and hung it from a beam, it having previously been gutted. All was set in our new home. It was the best yet, and Tim was on my mind as I set out for my old base.

Chapter Seven

I had to return to the sand cave for my ground sheet, the blanket and the sack of oats. The fiery red late evening sun wooed the first star, and ushered the furry flitter mice into squeaking arrival before I returned to my base.

On arrival I paused. Something was different. There was a dark shape by the cave and it moved. Now I was intensely alert and foot by foot moved closer, slow as a moon shadow along the base of the cliff. Closer still I saw that someone was sitting at the mouth of the cave, and there was a darker hump nearby that did not move. I was almost there, a matter of a mere thirty feet when the shape moved and sprinted away with lithe grace into night flight.

"Tim!" I called softly. "Tim!" I called, my voice edged with urgency for I knew instinctively that it was he. In a moment he trotted back, puffing, and we ran toward each other. I knew he was smiling as we hugged a warm welcome. Then standing back a pace, "What are you doing here? I asked. "We're supposed to meet tomorrow night. How did you find me?"

"Hey! I've known this area for a long time so I figured you must be holed up hereabouts," he replied.

"Yes, but what...?" I looked at his pack, then back at him, all questions.

"I'm running away!" Resignation and apprehension were in his voice. "I just can't take it any longer. I said fuck it! The old man doesn't know I'm gone yet. I'd like to see his face when he calls me in the morning for the milking chores!"

Grabbing his hands, I danced up and down. "You're here! I'm here! We're free! Together!" Tim firmed his grip and we danced around in the soft sand. Fiercely I claimed, "We can do anything, we can over-come anything, 0 my blood brother!" I stopped. "S-s-s-say! Guess what! I f-f-found a real old cabin about a mile from here where we can stay for a night or two. It's all r-r-r-ready. L-1-let's go!"

"Oh great!" There was relief in Tim's voice. "I have to get away from here or I'll hear my old man shouting and ..."

"We're on our way! Grab your pack and let's go!" A partially hidden moon showed the way and we said hardly a word till we'd covered quite a distance.

"Derek! I can't believe its happening!" Tim gave a little shiver; he was still feeling the tentacles of routine, rule and pain clinging to him.

"Believe it Tim. We're both here and going places – hope I can find our cabin."

Once when the moon came from behind the cloud cover we saw a badger on his nightly prowl. Owls hooted notes of intrigue to the misty wisps in the hollows. In the distant hills around us lights showed from farm houses and the farther habitats of the Humans. Sooner than I thought we arrived at the forget-me-not pool where we both drank thirstily. It was easy to find the old log structure from the scent of the honeysuckle that grew thickly around it. We entered the rustling blackness. I risked a match. The brief illuminating flare gave Tim the picture. My chest suddenly ached as I saw his strong face in the dying flicker; and just to feel and hear his presence put my loneliness on the run. My need for his company pained me, for I had always roamed alone and I was glad the darkness mercifully hid my emotions. Tim dumped his pack and opened it to take out blankets.

"It's perfect Derek. No one will find us here."

"We might be able to stay for a few days," I told him, "but we should move further west to be as far as possible from your folks." Tim explained that he had an aunt in Plymouth and suggested that we could stay with her for a while.

"We'll do all that and more," I announced with a confidence I somehow didn't feel.

"Tell you what," said Tim, "we can stop off somewhere for a few days, or a week or so, and then go to my aunt's place. It'll give us a holiday, and we'll have some real adventures." On this we agreed. We slept in our clothes that night for extra warmth, snuggling up close together under our blankets in the deep straw. Feeling secure, we floated away in a sea of warm dreams, and I wondered whether Tim would care for me as I already did for him; and whether he felt the same emotion which fleetingly held me when I looked upon him. We slept.

The bird chorus of dawn stirred us, but we turned and slept on till the sun had risen. Lying there I realized suddenly that we had never seen each other by daylight. How different we might find each other! Neither of us had much to go on other than a moonlight meeting in a barn. But the details quickly filled themselves in. My unruly mop of wispy brown hair was interlaced with straw, while Tim's wavy gold locks flowed neatly. The oat straw in mine must have looked alien, but it looked quite natural on him.

"I reckon you have a wild sort of look about you Derek –like you shouldn't walk through the village or they'll stare at you!"

We laughed. With a pang, I observed the light on his brows in the early sunlight and the smile lines that creased teasingly from his expressive mouth.

Tim was clean and orderly in his habits. He had a toothbrush, some soap and even two towels in his kit. I'd not been able to swipe a towel before leaving and seeing my interested gaze he passed one to me. We went to the pool on a soft leaf moldy trail and in doing so found the small stream that fed it and kept it so fresh. At the main pool we soaped ourselves and each other, splashing with carefree laughter.

Once when Tim stood up, shielding his eyes from the sun to look distantly away from me I caught him by surprise. In sheer devilment I reached high between his legs from behind with a soapy hand, and grasped his low hanging silhouette in a firm but gentle grip. He started and then froze.

"Just like the wild d-d-d-dogs on the African veldt," I announced like a film documentary. "This is how they bring the T-t-t-tthompson G-g-ga-zelles down. When seized they cease to run, and suddenly it's all over, they can't move" I released him with a slow slippery movement.

"We'll see who the wild dogs will get!" he yelled.

Then he chased me with swiftness and power, and we scattered diamond clouds of water among the blue mists of forget-me-nots. He was gaining on me. We came out on the far side of a little woodland strip into a clover field. Winded, I slowed up. We were both laughing. Tim grabbed me and we wrestled among the pink clover blossoms rolling over and over, scaring the big fuzzy brown bees into taking low-winged flights out of reach. We lay there panting spreading our arms and legs, while we watched the little filmy wisps of white clouds accompany the skylarks as they wove their songs into morning sky magic. In the distance we heard a farm tractor start up, and we arose as one to return to our little cabin among the honeysuckle blossoms.

"What's to eat?" I asked. "I'm starved."

"Me, too," said Tim, turning his pack upside down and letting everything tumble into a heap, including a couple of sexy magazines. "I got extra pants and shirts, too ..."

I felt inadequate and inferior, thinking of my mole and rabbit skins and the clothing I had yet to make.

"That's what I d-d-d-don't have. When I d-d-dress, this is it." My tone was apologetic. Tim tossed me spare pants and a shirt as I emptied my rucksack next to his. I had several pairs of socks and Tim had none, so we reallocated these.

"We could have a small fire and stew my h-h-hare," I stammered, pointing to the corner of the hut where some flies were exploring the glazed eyes of that soft-eared snare victim. It hung, moving very slightly in the doorway air currents on a snare wire I'd strung from the beam.

"I have a billy can," said Tim.

"And I have my old milk can." I enthused, holding it up for his inspection with some pride.

"Looks like we'll make out," he murmured. Then he produced a whole long loaf of honey brown bread, fresh and home-baked, and a tiny pack of butter. My eyes widening with hunger watched his amusement.

"We're going to feed you Wild One," he said huskily, squatting before the loaf. Drawing his sheath knife he hacked a chunk off, slapped a pat of butter on it and threw it to me. I was ravenous.

"Wait Tim, wait. Let's do it properly. I'll get the hare ready; you get some cans of water." I eyed the bread.

"Eat it," he commanded. "You'll never last till that hare is cooked!" My salivary glands ached with anticipation. It was pure heaven. Oh what a taste. Real bread! Real butter! Then I saw in Tim's eyes how hungry I was, and blushing self-consciously wolfed down another slice. Tim lit the fire and fetched the water while I prepared the hare, cutting it up and then scraping the skin to later stretch and dry it. In no time at all it was gently simmering and we lay back smiling at each other in mutual appreciation. Tim seemed impressed with my snaring skills. I already knew we would not lack meat, and salads grew wild in healthful abundance.

He reached for my "The Story of My Heart," and I watched his face as he opened it and scanned the pages.

"Do you read much?" I asked.

For answer he passed me one of his erotic sex magazines, and I quickly became intrigued with pictures of half-naked busty females in poses that made my heart rate increase. We repacked our rucksacks in case we should have to leave in a hurry, and then lying on our backs, we watched whiffs of steam from the stewing hare rise among the drifting wood smoke. I told Tim about my book.

"It's all there," I urged. "Look..." and I quoted:

"We live, that is, we snatch an existence, and our world becomes nothing. The piling up of fortunes, the building of cities, and the establishment of immense commerce ends in a cipher. These objects are so far outside my idea that I cannot understand them, and look upon the struggle with amazement."

I rolled onto my stomach and glanced at Tim. Tiny frown lines of conflict chased lightly over his face. Silence fell, punctuated only by chaffinches calling from the bushes. Tim didn't comment on the passage that I'd read, and we both watched a large beetle make tiny leaf-rustling noises with his busy feet.

"You know at times you stutter an awful lot," he said suddenly, rising on one arm and turning to me, "And then you read something and scarcely miss a word, even tough consonants. Did you always stutter like that?" A cold shock wave of rejection hit me, and I flushed deeply.

"Yes," I said, swallowing hard, but I was stabbed by the caring tone of his voice. Acceptance and kindness invariably incapacitated me; it split me in two and pained my chest.

"Better look at that stew," I croaked and stumbled a little blindly towards the blue wood smoke and flickering orange of the fire. I stirred the contents of the billy can, and dabbed a few tears with a smoky hand. There was smoke enough to alibi the situation if it had come up. The hare was simmering slowly with no danger of burning, and seeing that Tim had become absorbed in my book, so I took off down the little leaf-moldy trail. Breaking into a trot to clear my head of self-pity and uncontrolled emotions, in a few moments I reached the clover patch, and lying there, studied the overhanging hawthorn boughs heavy with pink and white blossoms.

"Why can't you stand a simple gesture of kindness Derek?"

"I don't know ..." I replied to myself.

"When you're accepted it blows your mind apart, doesn't it? It's like being sabotaged deep inside, I disintegrate. It's a wholesale destruction of my ability to think or act –and among blushing and extreme embarrassment, an attempt to disappear physically, which being an impossibility gives me the alternative of dissociating – which I do. But when I come back almost immediately, *I'm still here!* And that creates an "in-out, in-out sequence that leaves me shaking and weak. I then try to physically remove myself from the situation.

Again Wild Boy sighed as he lay there inert and tense. "Derek – Why don't we go in that anti-clock wise direction *and drop down the dark spiral of memory*.

My life is in a room at the end of a dark passageway, close to the servant's stairway. My room is dark. They store unwanted furniture and junk here... and me... There is a window, and beyond I can see buildings. In the distance a bright red neon light flashes with monotonous regularity; HORLICKS, HORLICKS. I've been told that's what it says. When people ask me where I live, I say "At Horlicks."

This is not the farm where we used to live. There is no longer the strange panic and anger when it rains, because SHE has to put on a raincoat to bring in the one and only cow in case it catches a cold! Nor do I have to endure her fury because I cannot direct the cow into its stall; because when it comes toward me, I run and hide behind the door.

This is a new place, a club of sorts, it's ivy-covered too, and there are tennis courts as well as short green lawns and manicured bushes. Baby brother has arrived, all brand new. SHE looks after him. SHE and my nemesis, BROTHER, inhabit the warm well-lit rooms on the other side of darkness. They have color, music, and things are happening. I am banned by the day, week by week to my room. When dusk falls I get into bed. I cannot reach the light switch as it is high above me on the wall by the door. Once I climbed on a chair to turn it on. SHE came in unexpectedly, and I can still feel where my hair was almost uprooted from my scalp, as well as the stinging of the red welt on my face. It is bad to have light. The room is cold. The only warmth is in bed under the covers whether by day or by night. SHE must not find me under the covers dressed by day. It is forbidden. I've been thrashed for this. If I hear her coming, I sit on the edge of the bed looking at a book. After she is gone, I snuggle up under the still warm covers.

One time I thought to capture her pity, so she would take me into the warmth and light of the area where THEY live. Knowing SHE will eventually come like a jailor to bring a small tray of food, I lay my hands on the marble slab of the washstand by the window. I raise the window slightly to increase the chill, and watch my hands turn from red to blue. They are numb. I push the window down. SHE is coming. Now perhaps I'll be taken into the warmth where there is music and color.

I flinch as she enters. I'm four and flinching is a built-in reflex. She passes the tray wordlessly to me. I try to explain that my hands are too cold. Indeed even as I reach for the tray they refuse to respond. I'm in trouble and words won't come to my rescue. I need the food, and SHE wants to get back to do whatever she was doing. But I am an object, an object that can't hold a tray. I fumble and it falls. There is confusion, and the force of the slap on my face jolts my head, felling me. SHE picks up the wreckage, snaps out the light, and her indignant footsteps click out of hearing behind the slammed door. I imagine her entering the world of warmth that I need so much.

I have no supper today, and I rub my hands to restore circulation and curl up on the bed. Actually, it's safe to undress now for she will not return until tomorrow. It is unsafe to undress by day as the pain of a thrashing will be greater on my bare skin. I'll sleep, but first I must use my chamber pot. They have emptied it, and left a little water in it to keep it fresh. I'm always thirsty because I'm not allowed to drink anything after mid-day. She says if I don't drink, I won't be able to wet my bed. I quench my thirst by drinking every drop of water from my chamber pot. Once, on a dark evening before supper in my white nightgown—the one with the yellow bunny on it sniffing a blue flower—I lifted the heavy chamber pot to my lips like a huge china bowl to quench that terrible thirst. The pot has ornate designs on it. I study them in slow motion as I raise it to drink, trying to adjust the thick china edge to my mouth so I can gulp that tepid off-tasting water. The pot is too heavy and the edge rattles against my teeth as I tremble with the effort of holding it. I slurp up the water and feel some of it dribbling down my chin and dripping onto my nightshirt. I hear her accusations echoing in my mind, they ring in my head... "You!" she will snarl with narrowed eyes, as she is about to empty the pot, "No one else does this thick, dark yellow syrupy filth except you! Look how you're staining the pot!"

I flinch. It's my fault my urine is so dark. With disgust she takes it for disposal, and as usual brings it back with a little water in the bottom. I make sure to drink the water before using my pot. It's about the only moisture I receive apart from a glass or two of milk each day. A number of times I forgot and used the pot before drinking and later had to quench that awful thirst with my own diluted urine. I hear footsteps. Clumsily I drop the pot. It makes a dull thudding noise as I shove it under the bed and dash under the covers in a panic.

The light hurts my eyes. She is standing there holding the tray.

"What were you doing?" she demands with imperial ferocity. "What was that noise you little swine?" Her face is dark with suspicion.

"N-n-n-noise?" I stammer, feigning innocence.

"You know very well what I'm talking about," she says and places the tray in front of me. I drop my knees flat to make room for it, and expose my sopping wet front. Even the yellow rabbit is wet. He probably won't mind. I'll explain it to him later. He's a friend.

"You've been stealing water from your pot!" she charges with red-faced anger.

The tray is banged on to the marble washstand. I am pulled out of bed and dropped onto the hard oak floor. Then she takes her shoe to me. When she is through, in a livid fury she grabs the tray, and the light is snapped out. Again the door is slammed and I have the security of darkness again. The red neon Horlicks sign flashes on, off, on, off, on, off. Horlicks, Horlicks, Horlicks, it is hypnotic, and I watch it transfixed, ignoring the comfort demands of my body. The Horlicks' light is friendly but distant. I stop crying and crawl into bed to achieve forgetfulness. I dream of a glass of cold clear water. From then on, no more water appears in my pot. She knows I drink it. Now I will know thirst as never before. But my pot is getting more stained. Now I'm ruining her pot. She is furious because she knows it must have water in it to prevent the stains, but she also knows if water goes in it, I will DRINK it! These brushes with her frustration result in more cuffing and beatings.

Once beyond the dark passage I was caught dragging a chair up to the kitchen sink, so that I could climb up and get some water. SHE heard, and I was knocked off the chair. In the screaming hair-pulling sequence that ensued, I wet myself. I must have been getting some moisture! SHE sees the tell-tale patch. I am beaten. I'm in my room again. I hear the birds chirping outside my window. I make a conscious effort to enter my dreams. I am safe there. They have color, and the sun is warm on the green fields.

Many nights I can't sleep because of the TERROR. There are creaks and cracking sounds among the stored junk. The tall door opens a fraction, then widens to about a foot. I can see a shadow. Sometimes I can discern a vague white face in the passageway beyond; it usually disappears when I have screamed long enough. Once in a sheer desperation do or die mode, I approached this indistinct apparition, and it receded down the passageway. I have a vague feeling that this thing in my mother, but I have no explanation for her actions.

But there is another very scary thing. About a foot and a half high, IT sits or stands on the top outer edge of the door and watches me. Its eyes are dark ringed. Its hooded head turns from side to side or round and round and round. It makes no sound. My heart pounds and my mouth is dry with fright, and there's no water in the pot. I watch the thing and it watches me. Some nights it doesn't move at all. There are times when I call and call and call for help, my voice shrill with terror. No one comes. When I ask her about this "thing," SHE says it's nothing but a bad dream. But IT still moves its head and fixes me with a stern unforgiving stare. IT will stop me from screaming one night. IT will land on my bed and its silent stare will absorb me. I am larger than IT, but the real me is small, and I will disappear. Only my terror-frozen body will remain. Once someone came in to see me, a maid I think. She turned on the light and said something nice; she even put her arm around me. I tried to explain IT, but my stuttering incoherence made no sense, and her touch... her warm touch caused me to cry uncontrollably. She left, confused. IT returned as soon as she had gone. Many years later I identified IT as the revolving metal cowling on a roof, projected through my window!

One day SHE brings in my usual breakfast tray with porridge and milk, along with a slice of toast. It's my birthday! I'm five years old. There is a card on the tray. It is gold and has gaily dressed teddy bears in costumes of blue, red and green, a thing of detailed beauty. It is for ME. Someone knows about ME! I glow inside.

"W-w-where d-d-d-did it c-c-c-come from?" I ask.

"It's a birthday card from your cousin in New Zealand," she snaps. "Although why they'd send you a card, I don't know!"

I reach for the card again as SHE passes it to me, but the moment I lean forward, the milk from the porridge bowl spills onto the tray.

"Look out you bloody swine!" she screams. The card is snatched up and torn into small pieces before my eyes. "Just for that, you shan't have it!"

The pieces are thrown into the trash container. I cried. But today the tray stays with me. It's my birthday. She says I'm five years old, whatever that means. I've heard about birthday parties but I have no idea what they are about. After eating I crawl softly out of bed and retrieve the pieces from the trash can. Just the touch of the card in small bits gives me a warm feeling. I know! I'll put it together like a puzzle. SHE bursts into the room; she is wearing soft slippers, so I had not heard her coming.

"I thought you'd do that! Give that to me you cunning little beast!"

She wrenches it from my hand crushing the last hopes of my birthday card into her apron pocket. My warm glow recedes, disappearing like my shadow when clouds obscure the sun. I'm alone again. It's been a rough night, and a sad start to my birthday. I get very drowsy and sleep. IT will return ... SHE may come back.

There is one exciting break in my day that keeps me in touch with life. Just above my pillow where the oak paneling joins the corner of the room is a small rectangular hole, about five inches by three, which allows me to see into the next room.

It is occupied by a waiter at the Club. His name is Stewart. He is of medium height slim and dark haired. When he comes to bed at night I relax. If "it" decides to attack me I can get help. I watch him undress every night that I happen to be awake when he comes to his room. He lies on his bed smoking, looking at the ceiling, or he walks around the room. Sometimes I am very concerned for him. He throws off his bed covers and sits up naked. At the same time he appears to be seriously ill; he grasps and shakes a rigid part of himself between his powerful legs and gasps for air. His normally pleasant face is contorted and flushed with pain. Then the movements cease. His face is normal again, and after he mops up the stuff that has leaped all over him, he lights a cigarette or reads for a while before turning out the light and sleeping.

At other times the nice maid goes to bed with him. They play games and laugh. I laugh too, as he holds her down and wrestles with her pretending to eat her, biting at her big breasts. She moans and cries out. I giggle and feel warm all over. Once they even paused to look in my direction.

This game they play is fierce at times—and sometimes they play it three times in one night—but they are never angry. Afterwards, he climbs off her, and they both kiss and make up, afterwards just talking quietly or blowing smoke to the ceiling. Sometimes the nice maid starts the game. She holds his long soft appendage until it grows bigger and
bigger until her two small hands let it go. Then he has his revenge with the breast biting game and she even bites his shoulders. Once they wrestle in daylight before he goes to work, but he never lets her up until they both stop struggling.

Stewart is nice to me. Sometimes I leave my door open so I can see him.

He smiles and says, "Hello there!" He has nice even white teeth, and one day he dropped into my room to see me and have a chat.

"Have you been sick?" he asks.

"N-n-n-no," I say. "I'm not s-s-sick."

'Then why do they keep you here in this room most of the time? He asks with concern in his voice. I can't tell him. "Why does she beat you like that? Is she your mother?"

"Ye-e-e-es."

"Are you hungry?" I smile at him.

He shakes his head, his face dark and shadowed.

Next day he brings me a large blue tin crammed with biscuits, chocolates and candies. He gives me strict instructions to eat only when I am hungry, and shows me a hiding place behind the junk where we can hide our secret cache of food.

"Don't tell HER," he warns, "under any circumstances."

I nod in agreement and just before he leaves he opens the magic food tin and offers me some. I am unable to take a single one. I just look up at him smiling, and despite his best efforts, no matter how he coaxes me I cannot accept one. Fear holds my hand back. Stewart's gift is connected with the warmth, light, color and happy sounds on the other side of the dark passageway; therefore for me it is taboo. For BROTHER yes, but not for me! Several times in the next few weeks, Stewart checks on the tin and sees that I have been nibbling like a shy animal.

"I got them all for you," he urges. "They're all yours. Eat them. I can always get more." What he fails to understand is that everything in that tin creates thirst, and although sometimes they forget and put water in my chamber pot, many times they do not. There is no solution to this problem. I never think to ask Stewart for a bottle of water, and I cannot tell him where I drink from, or the humiliating occasions when I am forced to sip at my own urine and give up in disgust as the smell and taste are repulsive.

After the last session with Stewart, I feel quite encouraged and eventually become careless. I still have a chocolate in my mouth when SHE appears with the tray. It is stuck to my teeth and saliva is running down my chin.

"What are you eating?" she demands.

I flush and tears start rolling, "A chocolate" I reply.

"Who gave it to you? Come on; tell me who gave it to you, you swine! Don't lie to me! Don't you dare! Answer me! Who gave it to you?" Her voice reaches a screaming pitch and she stamps her foot. "Do you have any more?" Tearfully I face her wrath. "Where are they? You hid them, didn't you?" Like a black dragon of doom she bears down on me with ear twisting, hair pulling pressure. My tell tale eyes are riveted on the hiding place. Following my gaze, she pulls the junk back finds the tin and looks inside. Then with anger she confiscates it and my food tray, but not before thrashing me and leaving darkness and the ruin of a betrayed friendship in her wake. Stewart cares and I have let him down. Several days later he drops in to check on my supply. The fearful look I give him tells the story before he reaches our secret hiding place. He looks disgusted and tells me it was my own fault. I am tearful then and relate the whole story in stuttering incoherence, and the more he puts his warm strong arm around me the harder I cry. He strokes my head and tries to mop up the tears with his handkerchief. He says he will get me some more goodies. But I am not crying over lost candies. It is his warm caring touch and the way he holds me that causes me to cry uncontrollably.

Sniffling, I look shyly up at him. "I see you every night," I confide in a whisper. "You're my friend."

He drops to crouch before me. His grey eyes look into mine.

"How do you mean you see me every night?" he asks kindly. I lead him to my bed and pointing with a small finger, show him the hole in the paneling. He lies on my bed and peeks through. Several times he whistles softly. Then turning, he grips the front of my tunic almost roughly.

"Have you told anyone about this?" he questions. There is threat in every line of his body. The kindness has fled from his face. "What have you seen? How long have you been watching?"

"Oh a long time," I reply truthfully and explain what I have seen. I ask him where the stuff comes from that splashes over his chest and tummy. His mouth opens as if to say something, but I continue before he can speak.

"You like to wrestle with the nice lady don't you? I know because you always win, but I'm glad you don't hurt her too bad when you bite her. I don't think she's angry with you because you always kiss and make up afterwards, and she plays with your..." I look down almost expecting to see it, wondering how there is room enough for it. Stewart rolls his eyes, rises to his feet and sighs. He ruffles my hair and leaves, closing the door softly behind him. Later he brings me a whole tin of nuts and chocolates and we

73

find a new hiding place. Quietly he tells me that these things are a present from the nice maid lady in the doorway.

"Thank you," I murmur, beaming.

"But," warns Stewart, "you must never, never tell any of our secrets, right?" "Yes," I say.

"No," he replies.

"I m-m-mean yes I'll keep our s-s-s-secrets," I smile. They leave talking softly to each other. That night there is blackness over my peep hole. I push my longest finger in the hole. It just touches hard unyielding wood. I can only hear their light laughter as they play their favorite game. I feel hurt and left out, cut off from a world that smiles and makes friends.

Meantime back in the reality of NOW, a cuckoo called out close by. Only minutes had passed in the relativity of time, but an age in memory had been scanned and relived. I felt good but light headed. I leapt up and ran back to where I had left Tim, stopping at the stream to refresh my tear stained face in the burbling spring water. Returning to the fire I inspected the hare stew. It was cooked and piping hot.

"Delicious," I exclaimed loudly.

"Oh, you're back," said Tim with welcome resonance.

"It's ready. Let's eat," I called.

In one effortless liquid flow of motion Tim came to his feet. As he crossed the clearing toward me I studied his tanned body in wrinkled blue cord shorts, then dropped my glance to his straight, well-muscled legs, fuzzed with a darker hair than his gold mop, and finally to his unlaced running shoes.

"One back leg for you, one back leg for me!" he piped in sing-song fashion. He dipped into the blackened pot with a sharp green stick and ladled the meat onto the plates he had brought with him.

"I get the tongue!" I chanted in tones childish enough to match his and I jumped up and down on my toes.

"You can have the whole damn head! Here!" And he dropped it onto my tin plate in a puddle of thin gravy. We shared out the other parts and then with chunks of his heavy brown bread to soak up the gravy we sat down to a memorable feast. I met the gaze of the hare from the follow of its empty eye sockets as I picked out the cheek meat. Next I pried its jaws open to retrieve the little pale white tongue. The dark yellow teeth still had some grass wedged between them. I looked again into the accusing eye sockets staring vacantly before me as I chewed the liver Then I rolled the heart around my mouth before puncturing its flavor. Finally I picked the skull up from my plate and with a light shiver tossed it into the bush. The ants would give it a final cleaning. Tim was biting into a back leg, a piece of brown meat disappearing into his mouth, trailing brown gravy down his chin.

"He out stared you—got the better of you, didn't he?" he teased. We cleaned up every last drop of gravy and every crumb of bread. Now we had nothing to eat at all. We lay back to enjoy the full hot feeling.

"Tomorrow's another day," I said.

"Let's head west tomorrow as far as we can." Tim burped noisily. "Why don't we take a train to Plymouth where my aunt lives?" "It takes money" I gestured hopelessly.

"Don't you have any money at all?" Tim asked.

"Some ..." I counted one shilling and sixpence in my leather purse and a ten shilling note. "And of course I have my telescope, I could sell it if need be." Tim picked up the shiny leather-covered scope. I'd kept it waterproofed with repeated applications of shoe polish and Dubbin over the years. It now possessed a slightly worn but greatly loved and cared for look. Tim was surprised at its weight, as he extended it to look over the downs and scan the slopes below us.

"Boy, can you ever see things with this!" he exclaimed, adjusting it to scrutinize different objects.

"I use it for watching birds and the Humans mainly, and it's valuable when I'm scouting new territory."

"It's a super instrument," Tim enthused.

"How well off are you for cash, Tim?" Putting the leather lens cap back on the scope he passed it back to me and delved into his back pocket.

"I've got Ten pounds. I've been putting it aside just in case"

"Ten pounds?" I shrieked. "You're r-r-rich! We can buy bread, cheese, beer, matches, and railroad tickets, see some flicks! Hell, you can even afford a woman, a real whore ..." My eyes shone as I sprinted in circles spending Tim's money. I could see huge chunks of mellow cheddar cheese, frothing tankards of beer!

Tim held up his hand as if to ward off the spending spree. Then looking serious, he said, "The first thing we've got to do is get far away from here! Let's catch the early train there's one about 5:30. I think it stops at most stations."

"Your aunt lives in Plymouth doesn't she?"

"Yeah, but we can stop off someplace for a while before we get there. She's the sister of my real mother. She was always a good sort, she told me no matter what happened if ever I needed her to look her up." I'd not heard much from him about his background, and didn't care to pry too deeply unless he volunteered.

"It's a real mix up," he said. "Mother died and father remarried and then he was killed in a train bombing outside London a few years ago. Then my step mother remarried. They don't need me around for anything except for the work they can get out of me." He looked as though he was close to tears.

"Well, I'll contribute the eleven and sixpence and I'll sell the scope. That'll even things up a bit."

"You give me five shillings and I'll get the rail tickets," Tim announced. "And let's keep the scope." He spoke with a boldness and maturity I'd not thought him capable of.

"Okay, Blood Brother, it's a deal. We can leave at first bird call. You've been missing for a whole day, so we'd better approach the rail station with caution," I added. That night, lying in our honeysuckle cabin, we talked softly. Not a lot of luxury, but a roof over our heads. We were clean and well fed, and we were setting out for adventures tomorrow. As the first star glinted low in the western sky, Tim turned toward me, rustling in the oat straw. His face glowed palely.

"You know, you're a wild woodsy sort of animal Derek, but I'm sure glad you're here. I feel I can trust you to be you... know what I mean?" From Tim this was pure eloquence, and for me the most heart-rending flower of acceptance I'd ever been privileged to hold.

"Yeah." I swallowed. "I guess we're both on a kind of spiritual trip, like Jeffries I suppose. Smiling in the darkness, I put my arm around Tim and he relaxed with a heavy sigh moving closer, his soft hair against my cheek. A long silence caressed our twilight communion. Only the friendly sounds of mice and owls intervened. After a while Tim slept, but I lay awake and I wondered if this feeling that had overtaken me with such sweet power existed only because of its newness to me in contrast with my life so far. Do the Humans feel this way all the time? Impossible! There is usually a darkness in their souls that shows in their eyes. They have not yet awakened and may die, asleep, without even knowing or feeling the dim dawn of spiritual unfolding. Then I too slept. In the early hours of morning I awoke, not knowing why. The air was cold. Tim stirred.

"What is it?" he whispered.

"Don't know yet. Something woke me up, not a threatening sound, but..."

We listened intently, but there was only silence. Then moments later the lilting song of a nightingale cut the approaching dawn in two, so loud it must have been perched in our own thicket just outside the cabin.

"Nightingale," breathed Tim and relaxed into sleep again. I fell asleep also, mounting the wings of dream to blend that haunting melody with honeysuckle scent, the softer colors of sound radiating paths to the other side of consciousness. How many people I wondered, could mount a nightingale's song and travel in search of themselves? And what might happen if a note of that song were missing and I were to fall into the missing space.

Chapter Eight

By dawn the rains had come and we needed no urging to rise. Great sheets of wetness battered the snug cabin and we wrapped all our belongings in our rubberized ground sheets before stuffing them into the packs. It was a skin soaking trek over the wet miles to the railroad station. With slight shivers and water running down his neck in tiny rivulets, Tim checked out details with the ticket agent. Afterwards in the dingy cafeteria we gulped red hot tea. The waitress was cheery and chatted with her tired-looking patrons.

Minutes later we boarded the train and hoisted our packs into the net luggage racks from where they rained droplets on those who cowered below. But when we subsided opposite each other on the warm plush seats in the packed compartment, the frozen faced people on either side of us shifted slightly so as not to be contaminated; their shoulders twitched and their averted heads spoke of our undeclared offences. There was just the clicking rhythm of wheels on steel and the gentle power of swaying speed while the scenery clicked by on a huge screen framed by black window edges. Black and white cows turned red and red to black; sometimes they multiplied into vast bunches of black-faced sheep or multi-colored farmsteads and the villages flashed by us. Sometimes our screen revealed miles of waterlogged meadows and dreary farm buildings.

In the railroad carriage, as our body heat built up and the temperature rose, the natural smells of wood smoke, rabbit gravy and dried perspiration wafted from our damp clothing. We had taken the train to drop us off at some distance from Plymouth, and planned to catch a bus for the rest of the way in a few days. When we disembarked we rested for quite a while on the station platform seat, for with train long gone we were waiting for the ticket collector to go for tea, thus allowing us to leave the station without question as Tim had not purchased any tickets. This was nothing new to me—I'd done it many times previously. We found a quaint tea house and stopped there for coffee and cakes.

"Let's dump our packs someplace," I suggested after we'd eaten. "It'll leave us free to explore."

"That's a good idea." replied Tim. "Let's find a hiding place for them."

We found the ideal place beside a high wooden railway trestle and were able after about fifteen minutes work, to hide our belongings atop a massive wooden pylon among the heavy timbers. Then we were ready for adventures—if that is what they could be called—like gathering rocks and hefting them at the ducks on the village pond. We scored hits of thudding satisfaction and worked the ducks into such a frenzy of raucous quacking, wing beating and water thrashing that the local blacksmith came out of his shop to investigate the ruckus.

"Bugger off or I'll call the cops!" he yelled.

We'd already seen that beefy red faced symbol of law and order on his bicycle, so we left to take a nap under the elms in the park both being tired from our early rising. That evening on the edge of town we came across a poster claiming superb music and dancing in the local hall that night. Tim was enthusiastic.

"Let's dance Derek! We'll pick up some girls, and get into something hot tonight."

I could see he was set on going and nothing I could say or do would dissuade him.

"Can we afford it?" I asked.

"I can! You can't!" he teased. Then seeing my wounded expression and downcast eyes, he threw a warm arm over my shoulder and said seriously.

"Let's both go and if either or both of us get involved we'll meet back at the railroad bridge later on or whatever." We retraced our steps to the village.

"You'll have to comb your hair a bit," Tim said. "Here, give me your comb." He parted my hair with care and concentration. I looked into his serious eyes; feeling the warmth and proximity of his body and aching at the attention he bestowed upon me. Then he stood back to admire his handiwork after straightening my shirt, but doubt and amusement chased in ripples all over his mobile face.

"You still look like some wild critter out of the swamp. Maybe they won't let you in!" The thought convulsed him into spasms of laughter. Then becoming serious again, he said, "You'll be all right, just be yourself." So he bought tickets.

"What do you think of the girls?" I asked.

We scanned the line up of girls; they were short, tall, skinny, fat, dumpy or just plain, and the same could well be said of the crude scruffy looking males standing around. Some of the girls had cute dresses that almost exposed their breasts, but the gloomy sad faces pale with the cares of civilization and lined with paint and powder left us cold. Their tired eyes and assumed mannerisms failed to inspire us, and we, both being a green seventeen had much to learn.

Tim asked one to dance. She blew a cloud of smoke into his face, looked him up and down and announced she was waiting for her friend. Then she turned and giggled with her girl companion. Tim returned and sat down.

"What a bunch of dogs," he mumbled.

Later on he did get in several dances, but I was not so successful. I asked one girl but gave up on the d-d-d-dance portion when she recoiled from me and said, "May you have this dance with me? No, I'm sorry. I'm waiting for a friend." With a relieved red face I returned to my seat. After a while Tim and I looked at each other.

"We're not happy here," I said.

"You're right," said Tim. "It's not our type of world yet and maybe it never will be."

We left the hall and passed into the night, walking slowly down the village sidewalks in the cloudy starlight. When we arrived at the bridge we checked our packs. They were still safe and intact exactly as we had left them. The night was warm and neither of us tired so we walked the railroad tracks, catching glimmers of reflected starlight on the shining steel. We sat on the heavy timbers with the bank of the river beneath us we lapsed into silence and listened to the ripples of the eddying water as the current flowed by.

Then there were footsteps below and we discerned by the light of the matches that lit their cigarettes an army corporal and his woman on the footpath. They leaned against the wooden pylons unaware of our presence, whispering quietly and kissing with low moans and murmurings. Tim looked at me pointing to the sounds below and to the glow of their cigarettes. His jaws were working; he was gathering saliva in his mouth. I knew what he had in mind and joined in so we could drip it down through the gaps in the timbers on to the couple below.

Missed," I whispered.

It was just then that we heard the sound of a barge, its echoing engine noises chugging along the river banks, announcing its arrival long before it fully appeared. Tim had a sudden inspiration. With pointing and grimacing he indicated with his hands what he had in mind. I almost laughed out loud, but without hesitation loosed my belt whilst that stirring member needed little kindling into rigid action. Tim did likewise but with a grunt that made me shush him with a finger to my lips. We were shaking with suppressed laughter. The couple, some twenty or so feet below was unaware of us. If there was a snicker or faint noise it would be muffled by the sound of the approaching barge, which had heralded its coming with low twinkling illumination.

What we had in mind was a sort of seminal christening, to drip our semen on the lovers below us; and just as I reached the point of no return Tim dropped his hand to his thigh momentarily listening with head on one side indicating he'd heard a sound as yet unidentified. A moment or two later we had collected enough fluid to proceed. Silent laughter shook us and threatened to become loud and noisy. We could see the barge was approaching as we slithered the fluid with careful aim and watched it fall. It hit their hair and faces as they kissed, and the woman touched the wetness in her hair looking upward with alarm.

"Hey! What's going on here?" A deep male voice boomed.

Now they both looked up. We screamed with laughter. The soldier roared threats of beating our heads in as they both walked away without further ado along the bridge path to the village. We were safe and out of their reach high up on the trestle bridge. In the next moment, almost imperceptibly at first and then gaining rapid momentum, we heard a sound louder than the chug of the barge now approaching below us. At the same time we felt heavy vibration, and then the noise became a roar.

"It's the fuckin' train!" Tim yelled.

"Which track?" I yelled back at him in breathless haste struggling to stand up.

"Fuck knows!" Tim was ready to run in some direction when the express train to London roared onto the bridge. Huge and terrifying, it was a new high speed diesel electric locomotive. With monkey like agility Tim leaped to the opposite side of the trestle and disappeared from sight.

At the same moment I slipped over the edge and clung to a heavy creosoted timber gathering slivers in my belly. I heard the deafening roar of the high speed steel rushing through the night air, felt the cool diesel wind, and then as I looked down I felt my pants drop to my ankles held on only by my shoes. The binder twine that acted as a belt had loosened as I had clambered over the edge. I saw the water flowing far below and the barge was upon us. Rhythmically the train clicked itself into the distance with diminishing sound.

"You all right?" shouted Tim.

"Fine!" I shouted back. "But I can't get back up! My pants fell down!"

Tim scrambled nimbly to my side of the trestle and peered over the edge.

"Help! Help!" I squeaked as my arms weakened.

Tim jumped up screaming with laughter throwing his head to the sky; then as he knelt to grab an arm for the big pull, the barge crew below the trestle shone their beams up at us. A woman on the barge cackled shrilly, "He's gonna get some slivers in 'is balls before 'e gets back up!" She cackled on in a cracked distorted kind of voice.

A deep voice from the barge deck yelled, "You all right mates?"

To me it was not so funny, but Tim was strong and helped haul me to safety, and only then could I unlock my legs from the restricting pants.

"You know Tim wearing pants can be downright dangerous at times!"

Still shaking with mirth, Tim released me.

"With you Derek I can believe it! Why don't you throw all your pants away?" We started back along the tracks. "Anyway it's about time to shut her down for the night," he said. Shouldering our packs from among the pylons we went our way, re-telling and re-living each part of the evening over and over again, until we found a straw stack in a meadow adjoining the churchyard.

Under our blankets in the straw we gained warmth side by side, and a short time later, Tim's steady breathing told me sleep had come to him. I stayed awake for awhile thinking of the night's incredible adventures and wondering how come I had been in the middle of it—with my pants down –as usual!

Chapter Nine

Before joining Tim in dreamland I listened to the skittering of little mice feet among the straw and fell into recollection. I'm attending college. *I'm six years old* and not a child protégé, nor am I brilliant, on the contrary I am perhaps somewhat mentally and emotionally retarded; factors which were environmental and not a birth defect; it's just that I don't usually understand what is expected of me. This is Tower House College. We all wear blue black and yellow blazers and caps, with neat light grey short pants. I board here now. I live here. This is a boarding school. THEY finally got rid of me, out of the Club that is, you know, HORLICKS, where I used to be penned up down the dark passageway.

Just before I left for college I was doing my ABC's and trying to learn my numbers. I have a pencil and paper and go to my room. I close the door to keep from being observed by BROTHER. If he sees me he will destroy the pencil and the paper. I sit thoughtfully at the edge of my bed. A slight noise comes to my attention. I look up, and there high above me where the junk furniture is stored, there is an animal.

It is large, real, live and about three feet tall. It's looking at itself in the mirror up there and smacking its big lips. I scream and scream again. It has reddish brown hair from top to bottom. It's an ape or a baboon. It swings from the mirror onto my bed to look at me. Its eyes are big and bright and I can see I see its yellow fangs and mobile lips. I drop the pencil and paper, leap off the bed and tear at the door knob to get the door open and escape. I then flee down the passageway to my parent's room gasping with panic and fright. This area of the house is OFF LIMITS for me. This is forbidden. SHE dwells here. This is her domain. It's early morning but SHE is up already as I burst into the room.

"What are you doing here?" she yells. "Get out!"

Father opens his eyes and looks at me. "What's going on here? Something wrong?" he asks gently.

"Get OUT!" she shouts for the second time. "You're disturbing your father!"

'There's an animal in my room! A kind of monkey, a big one! And it's after me!" I scream.

"It's probably a kitten that walked in there," she says disgustedly. "That thing wouldn't know the difference anyway."

"Go down and look," says father. "The boy is obviously scared out of his wits. Look at his eyes." I feel a huge glow of warmth for Dad. He is kind. He talks to me. He touches me. I stay with Dad in his bedroom till SHE returns.

"There's nothing there," she states. "Get OUT! Its just pulling a stunt so it can be down this end."

"Well, what's wrong with that?" Dad questions reasonably with a smile.

"Bha-a-a! You wouldn't understand anyway!" she snarls. But Dad does nothing. I'm pulled out by the hair, screaming. When am I not screaming? I'm tearful and banned to my room now. The window is still open. I close it and look under the bed. But it may appear up there again by the mirror where I first saw it. I scream and in a panic bolt down the passageway like a pursued rat. I now have nowhere to go. Dad is shaving. I stay with him and follow him from room to room like a shadow. I sneak into all the rooms and close the windows and doors. I ask Dad if it's possible for an ape to come down a chimney. He thinks not. I try to figure out how to block the fireplaces up.

SHE comes in. "What is THAT doing in here?" she demands pointing at me. I have not been "He" for some time. It has long been confirmed that I am an *"IT"* or *"THAT THING"* an **OBJECT** to be removed, dismissed, and thrashed or whatever. Dad intervenes for me and I shadow him till he leaves for work. Then I am at HER mercy again. The void of hopelessness sucks at me.

I escape to the servant's quarters. I visit the kitchen which is strictly off limits where they look at me with pity. They wonder why I am here... I hear them saying things like "poor little chap" and "always beating him" and I look around to see the little chap they are referring to. He must have gone. I don't see him. There is only me here and I'm an IT and not a chap. The servants are talking about a baboon that has escaped from the wild animal show that has rented the grounds next to the Club. They sit around the table sipping tea, or noisily sucking it up with big protruding lips from their steaming saucers. I explain the baboon was in my room this morning. They don't believe me, but they don't beat me. One of them offers me a warm sausage roll. I'm hungry and my mouth waters but I refuse it. SHE might see. SHE can appear at any time; and I know that sausage roll is attached to a severe beating if I take it. Why? It's simply because I smile and show normal emotions when I like something. The servants can see from my eyes that I want it, they try to coax me, but I cry and run outside. I cannot go back to the servant's quarters or the kitchen; kindness and sausage rolls are my enemies too. I shouldn't really go outside; the baboon may be in the bushes anywhere.

When I join HER and BROTHER for meals, they allow me to eat meat and vegetables, but when dessert is served—dishes that I find irresistible—my face gets bright ...and it's my downfall.

SHE smiles sweetly. "Will you have some cake Derek?"

I soften, she has used my name, and so I smile and glow. BROTHER has a queer look on his face. I reach for the sponge cake and as I'm about to grasp a piece, SHE hits my hand away and withdraws the plate.

"Get that smirk off your face," she snarls. "This is not for you! You would like some wouldn't you? Well just for that you're not getting any." One day it is BROTHER who passes the dessert to me, the next day SHE. They wheedle and sweet talk me and always at the last moment, they withdraw it from my reach, and share it among themselves laughing at my tears.

"See how the hand goes out, see how the hand reaches." (She runs a commentary.) "IT thinks it's going to get some, see that?" And they look at each other and laugh as my face collapses into tears. I will not reach for the dessert or accept dessert no matter how they coax me. Now they are furious because I will not extend my hand to reach for it.

SHE is insulted. She is deprived of her pleasure. She drags me from the table, and I get beaten and banished to my room. Its dessert time again.

Oh, no! What will they do today? If I reach out my hand I will get beaten. If I don't reach out she will beat me. I will run from the table. We haven't finished even the first course yet. I'm not hungry anymore. I hurtle down the passageway to my room. SHE hauls me back. My hair is pulled. I'm screaming. (What's new?)

"Its bad manners to leave the table before the others are finished, AND we haven't had our dessert yet, have we?" She smiles with cruel gaiety. Once when a maid was left in charge because SHE had gone shopping, we have supper and the maid is confused that the others may have dessert but I must not. They assure her that there is no medical reason for it. I'm given a piece of cake; I eat it and enjoy it. All eyes are on me, the others say they will tell HER when she comes in they did. My beating came late that day. My terror the baboon is recaptured the next day while climbing the ivy on the side of the Club house where we lived. Talk drifts by me, maybe IT did see that thing in its room... SHE denies it.

"No, IT just imagines things. By the way, what is IT doing in here?" I physically leave. *I can now leave when I want to – I mean ME, inside* – whether I'm here or not, and I escape more often these days to where SHE can't find me. *I hide inside myself*—so far inside that sometimes I cannot find ME—and yet, I mustn't disappear completely or I'd never get back to visit my rabbit friends among the primroses, for these are treasured moments of acceptance. Often I lie among the wild purple violets on the creek bank, and we play together without a single shadow of rejection to mar a whole quiescent summer afternoon... *(that is—in the meadows of my mind).* But there are other times when I don't come back, because things are going on that I don't want to know about... or feel. Somehow I seem to understand that HER anger is often refuelled because she can't reach me—and I know she must connect with ME (not just my body) to satisfy her hunger to inflict pain. Sometimes I have not had time to return from far inside and have only come halfway out, and my slow reaction has infuriated her so much that I go all the way back in... to nothingness. SHE won't return for hours... it's very peaceful.

Meantime in the "NOW" of tonight's reality in the straw stack, Tim stirred slightly and I came out of my painful recollections. Turning on my side I moulded myself to him, my left arm across his downy stomach. I held him closely, scenting his sweet youth and oat straw smell, and loved him for not rejecting my hunger for his closeness. *Once more I travelled back into my thought world and went to college again to delve into the behavioural enigma I had become.*

It is night time and twelve of we six and seven year old boys are in a dormitory. Two have flashlights that they shine to make shadow fingers that reach down the wall for me. I scream. I always scream. I've had lots of practice. This is fun for them. I'm hoarse from screaming. I hide under the covers and vomit with fright. In the cold of the morning we all get up. I'm pasted sticky with sour cold vomit. I stand and shiver. A SHE comes in. I'm dragged to the cold washstand, washed, threatened and slapped. She helps me dress and her face is dark with anger and disapproval. I escape just as she turns the sheets fully back. The bed is wet too. I get lost easily and I never have known the difference between right and left! One of the masters ties a blue ribbon to my left wrist and a red to my right. The other boys laugh and titter. I glow in naive innocence; I'm the centre of attention. I whirl the blue and red ribbons round with a delighted smile. I know the colours by name, but I forget which colour represents left or right, and they never call out, "Turn red! Turn blue!" along with the about face commands and so forth! Often in gym drills I face or turn the wrong way and the boys laugh. Dark disapproving looks from the instructor and frequent canings do not help me. I confuse his left and right with my left and right as I face him. Now I dread instructions to turn in any direction; and my mind freezes and I panic whenever I hear "left" or "right". *Even when the master crouches in front of me and explains carefully and slowly, I don't hear a word he says.* He is being kind to me, and my mind is rapt in studying him and *trying to cope with the emotions brought on by his closeness;* of coping with being worthy of his attention. I'm overwhelmed and confused. As he leaves I hear only his parting words and cannot remotely recall anything else he has said.

Now we are doing stationary drill, jumping with arms and legs extended. I am not coordinated and lack the synchronization that the master calls for. His face is flushed, he is angry with me, and the boys cast their approving and delighted smiles at me. I grasp at retaining the radiating warmth of their attention. I deliberately flop around like a wounded chicken. Now they titter and laugh aloud. The master shouts for me to behave, but to behave for me means to be re-frozen in my ice block. Again I do the wounded bird routine, and fail to see what sudden cloud hides my classmate's sunny approval. I only feel the cutting stings of a willow stick applied to my welting legs and thighs. The Head Master had approached our group from the rear, and now the wounded chicken, truly hurt, performs with precision but has been returned to his ice block.

Now we run. One two! One two! One two! But I cannot keep up. Breathless I slow down to rescue a brown woolly caterpillar on the pathway. We talk, touch and understand one another in a weird cosmic sort of way; meantime my classmates have disappeared around a curve in the pine needled trail. Carefully I placed the fuzzy chocolate caterpillar on a tall green plant and wonder what to do next. Fear pains grip me for I am lost, and I know the consequences and how they translate into pain when I'm found. By now my classmates are quite out of sight and sound. I'm left with just my tears, the birds, the breeze and my friend the caterpillar. There are sudden sounds as another group of boys runs by and I tag along behind them. They must be much older for they are far taller than me, and they have powerful hairy legs and deep voices. We arrive in front of an ivy covered building to do gym drill. They know I don't belong to their group but they are very kind and acquiesce to my staying with them. I cannot tell them where I come from because my voice is stricken silent by the kindness of their concern. Vaguely I point to a group of beech trees and indicate that it is the direction I came from. Slowly they shake their heads and smile. I am allowed to stay with the group presumably till they finish drill and then they'll relocate me to my own class.

Suddenly we're in the left and right hand turn routines again. Oh no! Which is which? I glance in desperation at the red and blue ribbons on my wrists. I turn the wrong way and bump into a tall curly headed senior boy. He reaches out and turns me around. His warm smile and equally warm touch on my shoulder that I feel through my shirt reactivates my panicked brain. The drill continues but first the youthful angel who guards me, stops, bends down and releases my wrists from the confusing coloured ribbons. For the rest of that brief drill routine all is well until I again turn incorrectly. This time my angel looks at me with disbelief and rejection. I meet his cold blue eyes and recoil, while simultaneously my body leaps with rejoicing at his firm touch.

I see a white light as I split in two and flee with wet vision to the shelter of the trees where maybe I'll join up and become one again. There is a brief pursuit, but I curl up small as a rabbit and hide motionless in the green shrubs just off the path-way. Masters in flowing black robes and mortars go by. I hear them talking and calling and my fear deepens. Then I spy my friend; he still has my ribbons hanging from a pocket in his silky white gym shorts. He stops. I can hear him breathing. I study his tall powerful young form as he shades his eyes. One half of me wants to leap up in the shrubbery to be captured, in order to feel his warm touch and hear his soft voice; the other half crouches closer to the sweet smelling earth as I see his cold lofty blue eyes, and again feel the pang of rejection. He trots lightly down the trail to disappear. But for me he is not really gone, I still retain my vision of him; and I can still feel his beautiful touch and smile somewhere deep inside me like a real live thing. I have found a friend... perhaps.

Gradually the sounds of pursuit fade away, and I tune into the world of crawling creatures and watch them with wonderment. *Silently I scream, and silently I cry... See me... Touch me... Hold me.... Love me... for in return you will see who I truly am.* I rise to stretch my cramped legs and brush off an earwig among the clinging earth particles. I push through shrubs to the pathway and then run to hide under the huge beech trees where I join the day boys as they go home for lunch. Hunger assails me. I ask one of the boys for food. He points to a horse-drawn bakery cart.

"I dare you!" they say. "Take a loaf from that wagon!"

"Yeah!" several of the boys pipe up and gather round me. One says, "I dare you to steal a loaf and kick it along the gutter like a football!"

I do just that. I select a large crusty brown loaf, and being torn between physical hunger and the hunger for acceptance I take a huge bite from it. It tastes good. I take several huge bites from it. Then I play football with it in the gutter. My peripheral vision picks up a shadow, and as I look around I feel the horsewhip descending on me again and again. I dance a tragic dance with welted scarlet legs.

"I don't mind you stealing to eat if you're hungry, but I'll not see good food wasted," the baker man shouts. Of course I'm wet after the whipping.

I don't have light grey pants now, they are dark grey pants. My shoes and socks are squishy where it has run down my legs. In the afternoon I'm re-captured and returned to college where news of my escapades has reached everyone.

One day I collect slugs in the garden and fill my pockets with them. They are the kind that slimes a silver trail behind them. I show the other boys and they are excited. I'm a hero again surrounded by approving smiles and laughter. As we enter class I pop a small black slug into a number of the little china inkwells recessed into the desk tops. We get our books out. At least ten or twelve inkwells are blowing fine sprays of ink like tiny volca-noes or baby whales spouting in the dark blue sea. There is pandemonium. All fingers and white smiles point to me.

"Empty your pockets," the Master demands, red faced and furious.

Inkwells are overflowing. Slime is bubbling up and oozing onto paper and books, some of the boys have ink running down their desks onto their clothes. I place a heaping handful of slugs onto the Master's blotter.

"Get them outside!" he yells. The class is in an uproar. I unload them in the bean patch whispering assurances of my return after class. They were fine pets. Later, all the ink wells had to be washed out and pen nibs re-placed, because slug slime and ink will simply not write on paper!

On my way back from the bean patch I need to relieve myself before it's too late. I'm scared now and rush to the toilets where I've been harassed and tortured in the past. They appear to be deserted. I'm too small to climb up and sit on the white seat and in any case my classmates have caught me in this position before, and bending me in two, have pushed me into the toilet and tried to flush me, and this even before what I have already "done" was flushed. I exercised my screamer to fullest ear splitting volume, but to no avail. I was in a real mess and they leave me this way. So now I squat in front of the white china monstrosity and lay a five inch log. Wiping myself, I'm just about to pick it up and plop it in for flushing when a group of boys pour in and see what I'm doing. They call a master and I'm dragged by the ear to the Head Master's office. They always pull me by the ear, while at the same time they twist it. The pain is quite excruciating, and I squeal loudly. Maybe I'll grow up with pointy ears like a wolf.

The Head Master demands an explanation, which for me in such a situation is a stuttering, incoherent babble of distorted sound. Nothing is explained to me. Their only answer is to cane me, and the blows fall on my hands again and again. This treatment hurts my small hands so much that they swell and curl up so that I have no control over them. This is deadly for me today as we have a writing class after lunch. I cannot do my writing assignments and for disobedience I'm sent back to the Head Master. The vicious cycle closes over me. But he understands why I cannot write, after all he did inflict this damage but just a short time earlier, and that punishment was for toilet infractions. It's a wonder that I don't have to write 100 lines that read; "I must not crap on the floor." Punishment is a perpetual rote for me. My entire life is comprised of pain inflicted because I don't do what I'm supposed to do, largely because I simply do not know how. I solved the toilet problem once and for all by frequenting a little hidden gully among the beech trees. Only the grey squirrels saw me, and my ears returned somewhat to their former shape.

Some weeks later I have my revenge in the most unplanned way on the baker man and his horse—if indeed it has anything to do with revenge at all. It is lunchtime. I walk up the road to explore. The sun is hot and high in the sky. Seeing the baker's horse pulling the cart loaded with bread I stop to watch the baker man making deliveries.

Then I watch his horse with his nose bag on, eating oats. I stare in fascination as that horse unfolds his penis—giant, black and pink with heavy veins. It becomes engorged and rigid, twitching as the odd fly lands there. Then I see myself take a willow stick from the hedge and sneaking up close, I suddenly whap that horse's penis with the willow stick. His head comes up. He jumps. I whap him twice more, hard, right where it is pink and tender. He rears up with a neighing scream before bolting down the road. What a sight! Bread exploded off the wagon scattering everywhere across the street. White loaves, brown loaves, and crispy rolls dancing away like tennis balls. The horse's mane was flying and his hooves rhythmically dancing. What a sight! I am very helpful. I pickup a lot of bread and help that baker man when he comes running from a nearby house. I still even have my trusty little willow stick under my arm.

Returning to the school grounds I feel good. I hear no more of the incident, except when some old ladies talk with me one day, and tell me with horrified expressions that they had seen what I did. I bear no ill will or grudge against the horse, the baker man or the bread. That horse penis just looked like it should be whipped with a willow stick, and it was. I have no idea why.

I'm still six years old and still in college. I need private tutoring. I cannot keep up with my class. Arithmetic does not make sense. The numerals are pretty in shape and each has a name. That's nice. I give them my own names; but the reason for their being, and their relationship to quantities eludes me. I greatly fear the math teacher. I'm ordered not to leave at recess, so I cannot relieve myself until all the numbers make sense. The other boys all leave, even the master leaves. I draw birds, caterpillars and bunnies on my math pages. Lots of happy bunnies with silky ears and long whiskers are scampering over my text book and math papers. They are so friendly in this hostile situation and I can talk to them.

The boys and the teacher have returned from recess. The handsome youngster who sits beside me has the fresh scent of leaves and wind on him. He flashes his white teeth at me in a friendly smile and looks at my math pages as if to help me. Involuntarily he laughs out loud, and as the Master seeks an explanation the boy says, "Sir! Sir! He's drawing rabbits! He's not doing his arithmetic sir! Just rabbits sir!" The class titters and they all turn to face the drama. The math teacher approaches. He has failed to get any reply from me to his questions and his face freezes my speech mechanisms. His black robes flow among the desks and he stands over me.

"They're not r-r-r-rrabbits sir! They're b-b-b-bunnies and some caterpillars," I explain with scarlet face. The class roars with laughter. The master becomes a dragon with eyes aglitter. My eyes tear up as I meet his fierce countenance, and I wet myself creating a huge steaming puddle under my chair. I'm told to go and change. My shame increases as

I walk from the rear corner of the room all the way to the front, and right across to the far exit door. They are all pointing, tittering and murmuring. A boy is assigned to see that I return shortly.

A week or so later a senior boy is assigned to give me private lessons in order to catch up. We are assigned to a small room. The boy finds in short order that I'm a hopeless case and gives up after a few days. My mind freezes in response to anything to do with numbers, so he tells me stories instead. Day after day he tells me stories of murder, horror, sex and fun. One of these tales is very exciting. Robbers are chopping up people and stashing them in a cave on giant meat hooks. Just coincidentally this morning I have an erection. The senior boy has observed this before when he tells me stories. Today he takes me to the storage room. He has asked me in there before, but now he pretends it is the robber's cave.

He is smiling. I glow at his friendly face and warm touch. But when we're inside he becomes very rough. He is strong and his eyes are glittery and strange as are his facial expressions. I think he is turning into a robber too. He smiles now only to make me do his bidding. I'm scared of what I see. He places my two small hands around it, but it is longer than I can grasp. His face looks wild as he holds my head as he tries to push it into my mouth. It hurts my jaws and as it touches my throat I retch. He is annoyed and turns me around from him; he unbuttons my grey shorts and tries to force it into me. I complain that he is hurting me. I feel his powerful grip and his saliva is all over my neck. His hot breath comes in rapid gasps.

Just then we hear the door open and the Head Master comes in. There is utter confusion. The senior boy is angrily dismissed. He is very red-faced. I hope he is not angry with me. Despite all the questions I can't tell them what happened or why. They are quite concerned. I'm not. I'd do anything for him although I do wish he had been a little gentler. My private tutoring lessons are over. From now on I join the regular class with the other boys.

The highlight of my college weekends as a boarder is playing sausages and macaroni with Benny. Teachers and pupils are mostly gone, and only a few staff members remain to look after us on the week end. Benny is a red haired freckle faced kid with green eyes and a deliciously devilish grin. We play in the deserted vegetable garden by an old storage shed under towering trees where the bees whisper tales of faraway fields to the white blossoms. Benny and I have nothing to do until supper time, and this sets the atmosphere for the afternoon.

We take the old mossy wheelbarrow into the hot sun as it will be our frying pan. Then we dig with bare hands for mounds of juicy, cool earthworms. The moist soil and freshly pulled grass roots fill our nostrils with delightful earth scents. Next we strip, flinging our clothes in wild disarray. We squeal with sensuous pleasure as the hot sun falls on our cool skins and we race for the frying pan. Benny is the cook and I am a sausage. A fresh clump of macaroni worms writhe beside me. I lie in the barrow sizzling while he pokes me with a stick to see if I'm "done", and between giggling, sizzling and stirring macaroni, we alternate till we're both a golden brown of greasy boredom and go to raid the apple orchard. At the last big skinless sausage fry, we packed the wiggling worms around our full two inch erections. This tickled ecstatically, and surrounded by squirming macaroni we sizzle and cook beautifully. Benny climbs into the pan with me and we tickle and touch till Benny says, "Let's not be just sausages! Let's be dogs! Hot dogs!"

"Hot dogs?" I query. "No I want to be sausages! What's playing hot dogs anyway?"

For answer, Benny who is lying on my back barks twice.

"Woof! Woof! You know, like real dogs," he pants, pushing his stubby little prong against me. Rejecting him I lie sideways in the pan squashing macaroni, while Benny clings to me complaining about not having any fun. Then as a grand finale, we both lie back in the pan pissing yellow sunlit arcs of relief from our stiff little fountains, thus refurbishing the earthworm macaroni with much needed moisture. The cascade sprays over us and we squeal with loud delight until the wheelbarrow tips us into the long cool grass.

"What is going on here?" a doomsday matron type voice rends the air. Benny grabs his clothes and runs. I latch onto my shirt and follow. My pants are nowhere in sight. Thus it was that we arrived back at the ivied halls of torture in time for supper with me wearing only a shirt which is not even long enough to cover my cold shriveled privates. In my left hand, encrusted with earth are two fat earthworms that lie somewhat dormant. I scratch an insect bite on my thigh and stare at the boys all neatly eating their evening meal. My eyes are round with hunger and I wish I had found my pants somewhere.

Before the early shouts of laughter fade from the dining tables, authority bears down on me in swirling black robes, my left ear stretches to match that of a wolf's ear, and my howl matches that ear's heritage. The fearsome white gurgling monstrosity swallows my friendly earthworms in short order and seems to eye me too. The cane warms my cool rump. Water removes the earthy markings and grass stains from my body, and once again restricting cloth encloses me but keeps me warm.

"Just what were you two doing?" the forbidding individual asks.

"We was playin' sausages. We was jus' playin' sausages, sir!" says Benny hopefully.

It is difficult to explain to a dead adult, the beauty of naked bodies side by side, or live wriggling earthworms moving over your tummy; or of tingling gigglement in a cool mossy wheelbarrow on a hot afternoon. How could he see the fuzzy bees on the white flowers, the blue sky, Benny's wide grin, or know the nice feel of his body and our carefree squeals of pleasure?

"One of us gets into the frying pan, an' the other keeps pokin' him with a stick to see if he's done," offers Benny, trying to give the Master some understanding.

"But why were you in a state of undress?" the Master demands.

I sigh heavily. "Ww-w-w-w-w-w-we're sk-sk-sk-sk-skinless s-s-s-s-sausages," I explain. "'cept for when Benny turned into a hot dog." I give Benny a look of disapproval.

"What do you mean? Just what did Benny do?"

I cast a peek at Benny's flushed face. "He just t-t-ttested me with his p-p-p-prong, his st-st-st-stick ..."

"Yes, yes! But what exactly did Benny do?" Exasperation at my crossed up explanation dominates his impatient tone.

"Oh," I say, realizing I am on dangerous ground, "He s-ss-spreads the macaroni around real good!" I grin at Benny and our eyes meet.

"Macaroni?"

"The w-w-w-worms," I explain warmly, my eyes shining with feeling for my moist friends. The Master eyes us and then his gold pocket watch. He sighs and pronounces judgement.

"You may leave, but you are not to go to the vegetable garden again, ever! Nor may you two play together on the weekends. Is that clear?"

"Yes, s-s-s-sir." I hang my head.

"Yes, sir," whispers red faced Benny.

Later we dine alone on weak vegetable soup, roast beef and turnips. "Eat your turnips," a voice commands saturated with authority. I shudder with revulsion as I view the pile of mashed turnips on my plate. I eat them but I have to force them down. They stay down for about seven minutes, and deign not to walk upstairs with me to the dormitory, preferring to leap out of me as I turn my head about halfway up the oaken stairway. The yucky turnips, carrots and lumps of beef sprayed and slithered rather mushily to the lower level. Those following me needed no encouragement to join in as they watch the steaming lumps sliding past and the sickly stench assailed their nostrils. We slip and slither in all the turnip beef vomit amid cries of alarm and consternation.

"What the bloody hell? Who did this? What's going on?

A finger points towards me. "You!" the voice identifies me as the culprit supreme. A steel trap snaps onto my right ear pressuring me up to the bathrooms. Matrons and caretakers arrive to exclaim in horror and disgust, while my insides tighten and writhe. The clean-up begins.

I sneak a peek into a mirror as I am hauled past; I half expect fur and pointed ear shapes, but my ears are still even and rounded. That night as I fall asleep in exhaustion and sick feelings, I wonder what happened to my socks back in the vegetable garden, and why my pants were missing at such a crucial time.

Once more I returned to my "NOW" with Tim. The straw stack made dry rustling sounds as I turned over to my other side. Far off the owls hooted mournful notes. I dismissed all memories of the past from my conscious mind as Tim rolled over with me, and breathing deeply, he reached out and drew me close into his sleeping embrace. I fell asleep in his arms loving the feel of their firm pressure, yet sensing for the first time his need for me also. We slept.

Chapter Ten

The musical clang of church bells tolled across the dells, rousing us both at the same time. We pushed our straw bedecked hair into the morning sunlight and looked at each other. Since the dance had been on Saturday, this noise today was to bring people to their knees for forgiveness.

"Do you think we need saving Tim?" I asked. I was feeling quite bubbly and exuberant.

"No!" he replied decisively, shaking the straw from his wavy mane.

"What do we need then?" I asked.

"First a good leak! Then let's scrounge something to eat."

"You think in far too basic terms," I heard myself saying in the preacher's voice "Seek ye first the Kingdom of God, and all of these things shall be added unto you!"*

"That's enough out of you Preacher—be gone to your Sabbath rituals," Tim retorted, as I jumped down from the straw stack.

"Let's get cleaned up and catch a bus to the seaside with your money. We'll run like wild stallions across the sandy beaches, maybe find some innocent country girls?"

"There's a stream down there. Let's wash up!" said Tim. We carried our packs to the lower end of the meadow near the church, where we'd heard water flowing the night before. Here we stripped, and carrying soap, stepped into the water causing the water boatmen to skate away in alarm. We were only about three hundred paces from the church and in full view of the congregation as they ambled up to the heavy oak doors to be swallowed in groups of twos and threes.

---

* King James Bible –Matthew 7. 33

"Maybe they'll forgive us or pray for us," I said as Tim soaped his hair.

"What's to forgive?" he asked. "But if they want to they could pray for us and bring us some grub." Two different worlds side by side, I reflected, while laying in the shallow water watching the light edges of the burbling water smooth the dark hairs down my stomach. Jeffries had written:

"Most injurious of all is the continuous circling on the same path, and it is from this that I wish to free my mind."

"You're so right, Richard," I thought. The churchgoers do their thing and we do ours–what's the difference. I allowed myself to be moved slowly downstream with the current over the fine gravel bed. A water vole climbed the bank and merged into the darkness of his hole and a watercress plant loomed up at eye level. The difference I perceived, was that they appeared to do one thing all their lives, as though they lived on a horizontal line, whereas I skirted the horizontal and did numerous and different things each year, and so experienced growth in a vertical dimension. Some people lived even narrower lives than the horizontal people, repeating one year's experiences twenty or thirty times over, instead of living each year separately and uniquely in richness of experience and growth.

I nibbled on the leaves of the watercress plants; they were dark green, hot and cleansing to the taste. The church tower loomed into view above the bank where I drifted. Thoughts floated with me from Jeffries' observations:

"The complacency with which the mass of people go about their daily tasks ... is appalling in its concentrated stolidity. . . If the whole of the dead in a hillside cemetery were called up alive from their tombs and walked forth down the valley, it would not rouse the mass of people from the dense pyramid of stolidity which presses on them ..."

Any more I thought, than those churchgoers who would just continue walking through those oak doors without a glance at the miracle!

"We've been spotted!" I called as I ran toward him.

"So what?" he challenged, and for the benefit of our audience he modeled his lithe body, shining like a wet bronze statue by the stream. There were crystal water droplets on his eyelashes. Just then the ponderous notes of the holy organ reverberated with the first hymn, spilling out through

the still open doors of the church. Holy, holy, holy, Lord God Almighty…
Early in the morning, our song shall rise to Thee.

"Better watch out for the preacher!" Tim teased. "He'll have us in church in two shakes of a lamb's tail!

I shook my head with slow deliberation. "Not a chance!" After we'd dressed we looked each other over appraisingly. I knew I was woolly looking. My brown hair was always unruly after drying off; in fact I'd had to make myself a headband by interweaving hair from horse's tails and manes with a blue ribbon I had found. It tied at the back.

"We need meat," Tim said. "A good leg of lamb, a roast deer, or a suckling pig…" He thumped his belly.

"Will you settle for a chicken?" I asked.

"Anything, I'm damned hungry." He turned to me, sensing a plan behind the question.

"Well," I said, "the local farmers are in church, some of them anyway. The farmyards are unprotected and chickens are wandering around …" Tim looked doubtful.

"Follow me 0h thou lover of roast chicken over a wood fire!"

"Don't forget the dogs!" warned Tim. "They ain't in church."

I'd forgotten the dog menace, but I decided that I'd cross that bridge when I came to it. Before setting off I cut a stick of about one inch circumference. Then I carved a small notch about three inches from the bottom end, and in the notch I tied one end of a heavy piece of white string about four feet long.

"A fishing pole for chickens?" Tim asked, looking at my engineering marvel and shaking his head in disbelief.

"A chicken pole," I countered. Going down to the water, I thoroughly soaked the string and afterward, I whirled it back and forth whistling over my head.

"I know," said Tim, "You're going to beat them to death!"

"Hold on there chicken lover, there's a farm down there about a quarter of a mile away." I pointed to a cluster of red brick buildings. I unfolded the scope and scanned the yard and buildings with studious care.

"Damn! People are coming out of the house. Oh, good, they're getting into the truck. There'll probably be only one person at the house. Let's go!"

"What the hell are you going to do with that string!" asked Tim.

"Come along and see the Master Chicken Catcher in action!" I announced with exaggerated confidence. When we reached the yard we saw the usual Rhode Island reds, barred rocks and other mottled colors, all scratching in their careful unruffled farmyard style.

"Whatever happens," I told Tim, "We'll meet in the woods about a half mile upstream. I'll just go upstream till I meet you."

Casually I wet my string in the horse trough, while eyeing the house and yard. Tim's eyebrows were raised in question as I strolled through the chickens in the yard. They were undisturbed. Slowly I bent low with the stick in my right hand, then lower still I crouched, until with a lightning blur of wrist action, I whipped out the wet string so that it wrapped around the legs of the chicken nearest me. I dragged it toward me in one swift motion. It squawked loudly, but I grabbed its beating wings and leaving my whirly stick behind, ran back to where Tim waited by the brick wall. He didn't know whether to bust a gut laughing or congratulate me on the capture.

"Hold the wings," I commanded, then laying her head over a rock, I whacked it cleanly off with my heavy sheath knife. Tim held it while it struggled with its last life spasms. No alarm had been raised. Everything was normal and peaceful. After all, it was Sunday and broad daylight; foxes and thieves only come by night.

"How about another one?" I asked Tim. "We'll need at least one apiece."

"Okay," he agreed. He passed the headless one to me. It was still struggling. "But I got an easier way. You stay here." He slid with liquid menace directly into the hen house. Afterwards he told me he had just gone up to a laying hen, pulled her off the nest and broke her neck. He came quickly to the wall without bleeding her.

"Let's get out of here," he rasped. We followed the hedgerow, keeping to the stream and holding low profiles, and making sure that we left no blood and feather trail. At last we reached the shelter of a copse that ran down to meet the creek bank.

"Cut her head off," I said. This little task was quickly completed, and we looked at each other a little guiltily.

"Not one, but two!" breathed Tim, his eyes wide. "Wow!"

Fearing possible pursuit, we took to the stream bank for another quarter of a mile, then still wearing our runners we stepped into the shallow water and went easily upstream with little noise. It might also put the hounds off our trail in the event of pursuit. Minnows and brilliant crimson throated sticklebacks darted away from our feet as we waded through the sunlit shadow dappled water. We decided to travel another mile or so to a piece of heavily wooded country we could see distantly through the scope, and there feast and rest up before going west to the sea.

"Looks wild enough, I think we'll be okay there." I said. So the die was cast and away we went.

"What if they find your whirly stick chicken catcher?" Tim laughed. "Like to see their faces as they try to figure how come it's there, much less what the hell it is! Say, you ought to patent it, and have a whirly stick factory!"

Shock hit me. "We left the chicken head behind! They'll see it!"

"So what? We'll be far away by the time they get home. Hey, tell me how you thought up the whirly stick," Tim urged. "Oh, that ... Well, years ago BROTHER and I were sent away for a couple of weeks to a farm near Tunbridge Wells in Kent. I got the idea one day when I was playing in the chicken pen, and when I found it worked, I went there every day and practiced. They were all white chickens—leghorns, I guess—but not for long. I'd whirl them around and around high over my head, and the string didn't come unwound till I'd put them through five or six revolutions. Then they would land with this wet heavy Wump! in the mud, and stagger around the pen, while the next unsuspecting victim was captured and rotated. I guess it was bad for egg production. I always went after the ones without any dried mud on them, so as to be sure they all had their fair share of the excitement! I was caught by the farmer one day. He heard all the commotion and thinking there was a weasel in his hen house, he came charging down with a shotgun. He just stood there dumbfounded. He'd never seen a chicken so swiftly captured, rotated, and 'whumped'! You know, even when he came running up to me, I was quite unperturbed, just as if he'd caught me innocently flying a kite on a windy day. I had this bright open smile on my face! Then of course, he wrenched the stick out of my hand and applied it to my seat and legs.

"I wus wundrin' 'ow come they chickens looked so danged dirty!" he quavered. Tim shrieked and threw himself on the grass. He just couldn't believe it.

"You an' your whirly weasel rod!" he chortled again and again.

We reached the friendly shelter of the woods. There were large oak and beech trees and some dense bush. Before we reconnoitered the area, we followed my usual procedure of hiding the rucksacks and on this occasion our feathered loot too. We seemed to be quite far from the nearest farmsteads; grasslands surrounded us and black Aberdeen Angus grazed on the slopes to the south. We returned to the packs.

"Let's find a good dry place in case it rains like hell," I suggested, eyeing the distant cloud formations on the hills.

"You find the staying place and I'll pluck the chickens," said Tim.

"Okay," I agreed and disappeared down the trail. The full scent of woodland gave me deep peace.

"Oh Richard!" I whispered, quoting from his book out loud;

"They shall not work for bread alone, but for their souls ..."

It was the preacher's voice that cut into the soliloquy. "They shall not live by bread alone, but by every word that proceedeth out of the mouth of God!"

I stopped him by announcing loudly, "Today they shall eat stolen chickens and afterwards they're going to read some of Tim's sexy magazines."

I had arrived in a small grove of conifers where the branches drooped low to the ground. I crawled under them and came up close to the trunk. It was darkish but a dry and cozy place to bed down even if it poured with rain.

"This makes me truly myself!" I exclaimed, as I walked back.

"Who're you talking with?" asked Tim, although he knew full well that I talked to myself most of the time, asking questions and getting answers.

"Oh, we were talking about the feeling of freedom in the woods. I found a real dry place to bed down,"

At this stage of my life I spoke quite naturally of *me* as *WE,* and although this seemed to mystify most people, Tim seemed to understand quite easily. After all, were we not WE? *There was ME—in the flesh that I could see walking down the trail —and there was the ME who looked at and talked with me, thus making us WE.* WE lived in harmony. Of course there was also the **Preacher** who would join us now and then, mainly to raise hell, but WE usually shut him up. But the **Movie Director** would not be denied when he wanted his cameras to roll; he seemed to live for the opportunity of saying, "Lights, camera – action!" and we had to perform.

Tim was surrounded by feathers which the wind had caught and was blowing hither and thither. Quickly I gathered them up, added a few dry twigs, and lighting a match, released the anticipated horrible smell among the puffs of smoke. As the orange flames licked upward, we singed the chickens to clean off excess down and long hairs. We did the messy internal work with surgeon like precision, then cleaning off our knives we prepared the whirly-stick victim for roasting. Tim was somewhat annoyed that I had used up almost both of his sexy magazines to start our fires, because almost every sundown he used the pictures to escalate his releases, whereas I did not need erotic magazines – just watching Tim's contortions, as he gasped and writhed naked on his blanket in the twilight was enough to send me into a starlit explosion.

"Let's put this little fire out Tim, and locate our roasting fire in a more secluded spot by our camp," I suggested. So away we went. Tim was impressed with the layout and the dry areas under the conifers.

"Couldn't be better if we were hiding out," he said happily. A short distance away in a level clearing among the beech trees, we soon had a fierce red fire blazing. We were quite secluded here and the blue wood smoke dissipated among the tall trees. Tim set to work rigging up a spit and I went exploring for water with the billy can. I finally found water at the Black Angus drinking pond, but I was away so long that Tim had become concerned. He eyed the armful of kale I'd picked up.

"Salad?" he enquired.

"No Tim, kale, we'll cook it like cabbage."

Our stomachs growled and rumbled. We decided to cut up one chicken for stewing and mix the kale with it, while Tim put the other on the spit for roasting. Whichever was ready first we'd eat. Tim had rigged an impressive spit for the roasting chicken, and the way he slowly turned that future energy made my saliva run. Already it was turning brown, and our mouths watered as the first cooking odors teased our nostrils.

We gathered wood to feed the fire and then we had the rest of the afternoon to lounge or explore. The peace of well-being came upon me. The weather now looked undisturbed and little fleecy clouds floated high. What more could we wish for?

I ran these good feelings past Tim to see if he could add improvement. He could and he did. Crawling under the conifers to where our packs lay, he wriggled back out a moment later with two bottles of Guinness Ale. I was amazed.

"Where did you get them?" My eyes were huge with surprise. "Open them up!" I squeaked.

He grinned broadly. "This'll make the Wild Boy really wild, you'll see!"

We stood by the fire slowly gulping the dark fluid down our throats. We read the labels out loud, musing on the inscriptions from that other world.

"How many bottles did you get?" I asked, thinking about the almost empty one in my hand.

"Oh, several," he said slyly.

I cavorted around the fire waving the brown glass symbol of release. "Hey, let's be real red Indians and have a fire dance!" Tim ignited like dry tinder.

"Yeah let's!" We shed our clothing and runners at the edge of the clearing and dashed back to the fire where Tim squatted momentarily to turn the roasting bird. I stirred the kale and stewing chicken with a stick, poking the ends of the kale down into the boiling broth. When I straightened, I saw Tim returning with two more bottles uncapped with creamy froth around their narrow necks. "Yahoo!" I screamed. Trembling with recklessness and grabbing a bottle, I looked up into the skylark's domain and drank deeply of both. Then carefully placing our bottles on a level piece of turf, we danced around our ancient red fire, enveloping ourselves in the hungry worship of hot chicken smells and steam wafting skyward with the wood smoke.

The earth pushed our dancing feet skyward from the springy grass as we chanted in low pitched toneless sounds, translating ourselves into another realm where craggy faces peered from the darkness that encircled our fire-lit cave. Far off a mammoth screamed its trumpeting prelude to fight, and wild dogs with luminous green eyes circled, waiting to fall upon our kill. At last we settled by the fire grinning at each other in appreciation of the mood we had created.

"The sun shines as of old; the stars look down from heaven, the moon crescent, sails in the twilight..."— I quoted from somewhere and continued—"On bushy tops in the warm nights, naked, with mad dance and song, the earth children address themselves to love."* For some minutes I fell silent. Tim gazed into the coals, while I studied his lithe form. I broke the silence.

"This is the life Tim! We have each other, and the Humans can have the world beyond." Then I added softly, "I'd really miss you if you went off on your own ..."

Tim nodded then after a moment he said, "Well, you are sort of wild you know Derek." I shrugged and smiled, thinking he referred to my appearance, but he went on, "It's like I belong to the Humans as you call them, and I see you out there looking in at us. Somehow you just don't see yourself as one of us."

"I know. I'm an outcast. A misfit turned wild and ..."

"No, it's not that! It's just that you talk about observing 'The Humans' all the time. If I'm Human what are you?"

"I used to belong with the Humans perhaps far back, but if belonging brings so much pain and hurt, then... Tim; their civilization kills the spirit of man if he allows it to! I live in a different world. Besides, we're afraid of those two-legged animals. WE avoid them. If they got too close, if they loved us, we'd just disappear ..."

"How could you disappear? I care about you, Derek, and you're still here ..."

"You don't understand. This is different. With you I'm safe, but with

---

* Towards Democracy -Edward Carpenter.

them I'll disappear, evaporate... *because I can't be real unless I hide inside where they can't get me ..."*

"Come again? If they love you that will make you disappear? So what's left?"

"Just my body I suppose because I wouldn't be there... or anywhere." I felt sad.

He shook his head. "I think it's time to eat. I'm starved." He broke off a chicken leg and a chunk of white meat and laid them on a piece of bark which served as a plate.

"I think you're human all right, but there are times that I wonder..." He sank his teeth into the chicken leg and his smile lines disappeared behind a strip of chicken skin.

"Grab a leg," he said. "It's perfect!"

In mock battle stance like an animal I bared my fangs in challenge, and ripped off a chunk of white meat. Tim stopped stuffing his mouth in momentary amazement, and before he could recover himself I was on him, snarling. My teeth closed over the meat still protruding from his mouth, and I pulled it from between his teeth as he overbalanced and fell backwards in surprise. Crouching back with throaty growls I ate my prize, still shiny with his saliva. He sprang up.

"I'm right! I am right! You're nothin' but a fuckin' wild animal!" I threw myself down screaming with laughter; and the more I watched the expressions on his face the more I laughed.

"I say Tim old chap, let us continue with our repast. I do believe the beast has been fed."

Tim kept shaking his head, but he soon settled down to eat again. Once I was full something had to happen! I grabbed a handful of greasy chicken and rubbed the fat all over me wherever I could reach; then squatting, I gathered handfuls of the cooler ash and plastered it over the oily areas. Tim watched with an amused but somewhat wary smile.

"We is red Injuns. We do ceremonial dance!"

"Maybe you are, but I'm not ..."

Before he could get fully to his feet I had wiped two handfuls of the excess greasy ash on whatever parts of him I could reach as he struggled.

"Well," he said, surveying the damage after he had broken free, "Injuns it is then! He dashed away shouting, "I get firewater!" and returned with more ale.

"A tr-tr-tribute to the F-f-fire gods!" I raised my bottle.

"Cheers to the mighty chicken hunters!" Tim joined the toast.

A voice broke in: "You are children of the Devil. Evil is in you!" The Preacher had taken over. Tim lowered his bottle and looked at me strangely. "Shut up Preacher!" I commanded in my own voice. "Jesus loves the little children, even when they are smeared with chicken fat and ashes. So get lost!"

"You should get rid of him," Tim advised. "He don't know nothin' anyways!"

The Preacher departed. We hooted, waved our arms and pranced back to the fire, contorting our bodies in sensuous choreography, blood Brothers in search of destiny. When we tired a little, we dropped beside the fire to finish the last of the ale.

"I suppose w-w-we should g-get washed up," I said. "If you could see yourself ..."

"How do you think you look? I mean, even under normal conditions you're a little unusual." He smiled. "Yeah, that's it! You're unusual!"

I threatened to throw a bottle at him and he ducked. "Grab the soap, Tim."

Seconds later two naked ashy forms sped from the woods and out across the downs.

It was a large pond, and quite deep, probably fed by underground springs. First we drank before stirring up the water, and then set about the task of cleaning ourselves. It took quite some time. We had to work on each other in the inaccessible places. Finally we just swam around feeling good, clean, tired, and glowing all over. We walked back to our camp smelling of clean pond water and wood smoke.

"This is what I mean Derek, how is it possible for things like this to happen? How could you explain to anyone how come we were looking the way we did?"

"They must lead dull ordinary uninteresting lives. It's just that simple Tim, we have a joy in life and we express it. Oh! It might be misguided exuberance at times ..."

"Yes! But it only happens when you're around. I never got into things like this till I teamed up with the Wild One."

I then explained to Tim all about the fine art of staging real life dramas, like an artist working with oils. "But don't you see Tim, we don't need oils, for example –we use real cows in a stampede, just like a film, except this is even better than film, we have the smells, the feelings, the real action, and above all WE are the creators and directors."

"You mean that just about anything you can cook up in your screwed up mind can be made real?" he asked skeptically.

"Perhaps – because they say that whatever the human mind can conceive it can achieve. I'm not too clear on how it works. Let's just enjoy it." I replied.

I then noticed the tiny red marks on my stomach and some on Tim's too. We found they were slivers from the trestle bridge escapade, and we concentrated for the next little while on digging them out of each other. "Did you get any slivers in your balls like that old gal on the barge was screaming about?"

"No," I replied, "But it could have been a great deal worse. I could have dropped off the bridge smack into the river; and you could have been squished by the train! We are some crazy characters!"

"Speak for yourself," Tim replied. "I shudder to think how weird and reckless you will get when you're older, anything can, happen and probably will!"

After we had packed away some gear, we snuggled down into our bed of boughs and got comfortable. But this evening the Guinness ale hit my head with a dull ache. It was similar to the terrible headaches I had as a child – way back in the Club days when I was still seven years old. That was my first brush with alcohol. On the way to school, BROTHER and I would sneak into the lounge and bar on the main floor downstairs, and look for money that patrons had accidentally dropped on the floor. Sometimes we came up with the equivalent of about fifty cents. But the real attraction in the bar was draining the wine and sherry glasses still left on the tables from closing time – the odd one was nearly a quarter full. We would do this just before leaving through the back door. A couple of times I was too drunk to get up off the floor, and too terrified to crawl back upstairs, so we both staggered on shaky legs to school, arriving late, and reeking of liquor. One morning, BROTHER found a coin on the floor, put it into a slot machine –and hit the jack-pot. He had to run upstairs to get help from Dad, along with a container for all the money. But, this jack-pot, plus reports of us coming to school in a drunken state, all finally blew up, and from then on, the doors to the lounge and bar were locked.

Tim looked cozy, relaxed and innocent as he fell asleep, his sun-burnished locks fell carelessly across his tanned cheek, and his whole body had a lithe look of power even in repose. As I lay beside him in the gathering warmth, I felt good all over, just to have him as a friend – even for a short while. He was substantial, real, and live. I loved his laughter. Comparing him to my own picture of me – I came up pretty short on the asset side. I was just a scared ragged kid on the run, and I could not find anything attractive about me. My front teeth were a little crossed. My hair was tied up at the back with hair from horse's tails, but worst of all – I could not look into my own eyes – or even at my own face, at least not in a mirror. I looked a little better in a pond reflection – but what was it about my eyes that scared me? They were green, okay, but they projected to me a desolate, beaten, withdrawn creature, a young alien that had no hope. Tim was rescuing me – but for how long? I wanted him to melt all of his boyish good looks and smiles into me – I wanted to be HIM –I never wanted to be myself again. With difficulty I restrained myself from reaching out to embrace him, and instead, curled up separately, small and fetal, quietly crying, while surges of pain tortured my chest with silent screams. Will they ever leave me? I shook and heaved. Tim stirred; maybe I was a little too loud. I pretended to be deeply asleep, and he relaxed again.

However, I could not sleep. I just kept murmuring, "The Black Swan – the Black Swan….No! No! No!" Of course the Black Swan was the pub –the Club where we had lived. "What are you looking at?" I asked Derek –alias Little Boy Wild. I sat up – "I remember now. One day I was captured while exploring the passageways close to the bar. By captured I mean taken submissively by the hand and led to a janitor's night room. There are mops and pails along with a camp cot complete with a stained and smelly mattress. The whole place has the stench of beer and sour vomit. There are no windows to let fresh air in from the outside. I'm seven years old. My captor turns off the light and leaves me standing there. He says a nice man is coming to see me, and may tell me a story or even give me a penny. Minutes pass, and at last I hear foot steps. The door opens briefly allowing light to flood in, and darkness follows. Strong hands lift me onto the cot. "They tell me you like this," this guy grunts in a gravelly voice. He reeks of smoke and I can tell that he is already naked from waist down because he brushed me with his thing. Next, he strips me, and contorting my body to the right position, starts the painful process of penetration. (Many years later I wondered why so few of my perpetrators ever used a simple lubricant). My tears do not deter him and I cry out at every gasping thrust. Finally, it is too much to bear and I disappear inside myself. When I return from the rabbit meadow the door is closing and I'm alone. I roll off the cot and the slippery stuff runs down my legs into my socks as I struggle to find my clothes in the dark. I tell myself I'll go and hide in the garden when I'm free. But it is too late. Another man comes in, but he leaves the light on. I cry and struggle on the cot where he placed me. All his attempts to enter me are unsuccessful, for now I kick and struggle and try to defend myself. He gives up. He swears at me while he pulls up his pants and leaves. I hear gruff voices in the corridor, and then shouting as he asks for his money back. For some reason I feel I've let everyone down. As usual I'm the problem, that's what all the fierce arguing is about. It's entirely my fault, but I cannot stand the pain. Awhile later the door opens again. Oh! No! Terror strikes me again. I scream and scream. This man leaves the light on, and eyes the creamy mess on my legs. Next he drops my short pants to look at me. I'm trembling with terrible shakes; they rack my whole body and are entirely beyond my control. (Years later I recognized these shakes as classic shock symptoms).

"It's okay, it's okay," he says gently. "You poor little tyke, what have they been doing to you?" I look at him through a kind of fog and start to scream.

He said, "No, no, nothing more is going to happen to you, it's alright." He holds me for several minutes talking quietly to assure me, until the great heaving sobs subside. He is warm and he is holding me, so I'm able to calm down. Afterward, he fastened my shirt and shorts, wipes my tear stained face and releases me into the passageway.

I can tell no one. I vomit during the supper period. Food will not stay down, and this results in a cuffing about the ears, and my usual dismissal in the form of a vicious pinch. Is this the night SHE will come to kill me I wonder? How will she kill me? I've lost a lot of sleep waiting and listening for her stealthy approach, but sleep always wins over. I'm still here in the morning. Maybe it would be better for all if I did not wake up.

Back under our bushy tree with Tim – I collapsed onto my blanket, still quivering with silent screams and tears. I must have awaked Tim at some point, because he placed a blanket over me, and merged his bedding with mine. Then he put his warm firm arms around me as we lay there, and slowly I relaxed into a euphoric state of bliss. Awhile later we were snug and warm, but restless – very restless. I had calmed down completely after my Black Swan session, but sleep simply would not come to either of us. Finally, it was inevitable that we would resolve the problem by inviting sleep to come as only desperate male teens can – in a most delightful way. Shortly after, we sighed and faded into dreamland, while high above us, the wind swayed the great branches. Owls called, foxes barked, the moon rose, and the twinkling stars revolved on their courses as they had for eons – in total disregard for us.

Chapter Eleven

Today was one of those special long and beautiful days for me. It seemed that everything we did, even the way we lay in the sun under the beeches was meant to be.

"You said that most people lead dull lives," Tim said thoughtfully.

I sat up. "Thoreau said in his Walden something about the mass of men leading lives of quiet desperation. I don't want that kind of life." I leaned toward Tim, eager to make my point. "But that means we have to depart from all established recognized values and goals. We have to direct ourselves vertically in other categories of thought and feeling toward the real world which is higher and far more beautiful than this."

Tim smiled. "You didn't stutter once when you said that. Was that you or the preacher?"

"It's not the Preacher. It's the wild me that distrusts all mankind. The one that knows what is meant by man's inhumanity to man."

Tim rested his chin on his knees and gazed over the rolling countryside. He looked sad and introspective.*

"You ought to read Walden, Tim," then I quoted from memory.

"It would be well perhaps, if we were to spend more of our days and nights without any obstruction between us and the celestial bodies. And he says that most men stay poor all their lives because they think that they must have a house just like their neighbours, and he talks about the bondage of the people out there in the towns and villages."

"Your Jeffries says that too," Tim commented.

We fell into a thoughtful silence. A stag beetle hurried by. Chaffinches and yellowhammers called their distinctive notes from the beech trees. The

---

* Walden –Henry Thoreau. 1947.

fire died down and we flicked ants into the red coals watching them shrivel and blacken.

"See Tim, they're like the fleeting enlightenment of men before they turn to embrace the grave again." We lay and talked about books, sharing our nearness. I had always read a lot, only dimly sensing the simple truths between the lines that would make me free forever.

"There's more here than I really understand Tim. It's powerful stuff. We truly understand with the vision of the spirit, and we grow in direct relationship to our ability to read between the lines of blindness in the affairs of men."

Tim turned to look at me. "I don't follow you."

At that moment I saw what I was trying to explain. "Like right now Tim, we are spiritually awake, so our eyes are open, but we're just baby spirits sucking milk from our books and the exchange of ideas, and like real babies any moment now we'll fall asleep and when we wake up we'll be ready for more food; more spiritual food!"

"Yeah," said Tim, "that sort of makes sense." He smiled.

"Well I was going to say that in normal development, our periods of wakefulness, of being in possession of spiritual consciousness lengthen all the time; so that some day up ahead, we'll be spiritually mature and stay awake all day, all twenty four hours maybe. Then time won't exist for us."

I could see that Tim was puzzled. "You don't know you've been asleep spiritually Tim, till you wake up again. It's like you don't know that you've been away in sleep till you wake up in the morning ..."

"Are you sure Derek?"

"Wait Tim!" I said excitedly, "I have to get this idea out while I still have it. We have to bring the body and the spirit into one unit because only then will we become mature men, real men... when spiritual consciousness is with us all day long in everything we do and think!" I threw my arms up in mock triumph. "So there you have it! I've solved the riddle of the universe!"

There was a long silence between us.

Then Tim said slowly, "You know, it's pretty tough to relate all this spiritual stuff you're handing out, with all that other stuff about letting the cameras roll with real physical things; and running around naked and plundering farmyards ..."

"You'll just have to grow up Tim – it's that simple." I said, teasing him.

Then he chased me with boundless energy through the woodland pathways until almost out of breath, we collapsed into a clover field with him on top, trying to stuff a squished grasshopper between my clenched lips. He tossed its crushed body aside, and for a fleeting moment I met his disturbed gaze. Our touching was needful, magnetic and magical. I searched his glazed eyes – and just then, a boyish tenderness captured us, and in its closeness we celebrated the reckless joy of youth. Time absorbed us in the scent of clover and the bleating of distant sheep – while slowly, the lust ebbed from us, and calmness returned. Tim spread-eagled his supple naked form among the purple blossoms, and breathed in deep relaxation.

"You know Tim... it's like what happens in Africa," I started to explain.

"Oh no Derek! Not your fuckin' wild dogs again ..."

"No Tim, it's like the male elephants when they get afflicted with "Must"... you know, they must!" I gesticulated with my hands to convey a fatalistic sequence of destiny. "They get dangerously excited, in a sort of frenzy. It grips them—I think it's when an elephant get so sexed up it hits his brain. There's no female elephant ready to mate with, so he runs around killing people and destroying huts and trees and..."

"Derek," said Tim his voice cut into my pseudo rationalization with a tone of calm clarity and common sense. "I've heard and read about the 'must' you're talking about. But this was not must, it was just raw plain lust, same type of thing that hits all the male animals, an' they just, must, lust." He chortled at his unintended alliteration.

"Yes," I agreed. "It's better than running amok in the village below. They just don't know how lucky they are, with two young mustang bull elephants under control—for the moment at least."

A soft breeze dappled silver sheens across the clover, and we lay watching the fluffy white clouds as they broke apart, reformed and swirled about in the blue.

"Hey! There's a horse with a long tail," I exclaimed, pointing. "Do you see it?"

"Yeh! And there's a dragon—see the white smoke coming from his nostrils?"

"Where?

"There! Quick! His tail is disappearing."

"Yes I see it now, and look there Tim—two rabbits humping! Wow!"

"Sounds to me, you still got a touch of the "must" on you Derek!"

We lay peacefully, our imaginations forming animals, people, and a host of creation out of the swirling cosmos.

Finally Tim said, "Let's go for a swim and then come back to our camp."

We arose as one and leapt before the wind across the downs. Our speed was effortless; it seemed as if we became part of the wind… it had a mystical quality of swift winged flight. I turned my head once to glance at Tim. His face was a study of eager flight and his form floated with the careless grace of those who care to touch the earth but once in a while.

Back in camp again we both lay fully back in the grass. If we opened our eyes we could scan the country for miles. *I allowed myself to go back,* exploring the labyrinths of my mind and *memories of not so long ago.* Do I belong to the Human race, or have I been translated into the current situation through a particular warp in some wavelength of time? Would I become more normal if I stepped a little further into Tim's world… since he is a pioneer on the horizon of where *our* two worlds meet?

I have a sister now. I have left college. We have moved. I have a small room. Life moves on to strange things, both by day and by night in my eight year old life. For at night the cats come. They wait till the house is still and all the lights are out. I can reach the light switch if I wish, but the cats can always come back, and they do. An endless procession of black cats walking the perimeter of my bed, almost nose to tail, whispering by my pillow; they stare at me with unfriendly yellow eyes. I reach out and touch them. Their soft fur and tails are as real as any I've touched in all my eight years of life. They do not like to be touched; they lay their ears back and threaten me with bared fangs. I hide under the covers and then peek out. They are always there, and I don't know what they want. I hear the whispering feline sounds of their passing and it's as scary as if I had accidentally intruded into their dimension, or have they intruded into mine? I don't scream anymore. I'm silent. Quiet tears are my only outlet for fear. The cats won't leave me. I struck out at them one night, and got scratched on the back of my hand. We do not own a cat so I know beyond any doubt that in some way, two dimensions are occupying the same time frame. I show HER the scratches in the morning.

"It's just a nightmare," she states with impatience; but I don't think so. Even in the light of morning those red scratches are very real, and I know I have not accidentally scratched myself on something.

One morning I peered over the bottom of my bed in broad daylight to retrieve a book from where it had fallen; and I came face to face with a most diabolical countenance. It is huge, all head and face. No body. It's a fiery red and orange face, with ghastly leering yellow features that seem to simmer as they contort into a face of evil incarnate. I sit up and tell myself I'm dreaming. I look over the edge of the bed again. It is still there. It knew I would come back to see it. Its smile is deeper, even more knowing and terrible. It is a face of a bottomless nameless terror that wants to draw my mind... ME... into it, out through my eyes. I will die if I weaken. I must fight it! It draws me closer. Now I can feel the red heat. I tear myself away again. I check my room. It is daylight. I am not dreaming. Again I look, and larger that ever it is there, silent and terrible. The power is strong. The expression is unbelievable. I will touch it with my hand. I reach out, my face getting closer and closer. Stop! I grip the wooden board of the bed frame and push myself up. Twice I scream then tears take over my retreat under the covers to watch the bottom of my bed for hours... and hours... and hours.

Again, I experience life in two or more dimensions in some way. The creatures of some lower world intrude onto my plane, or do I intrude into theirs? These are two real worlds to me but just nonsense to HER.

"Your imagination is running away with you! You always were a queer little swine anyway!" she states.

Early one morning before I got up I am playing with a pencil in bed. It is against the wall and vertical between the bed and the wall. I am idly moving the pencil back and forth like an inverted pendulum. Now I'm not touching the pencil at all, but it continues to move all by itself! I stare at it in fascination. It has a life of its own! It keeps moving back and forth and doesn't want to stop. I put a finger in the way but the pencil pushes it to one side and continues its motion. With a fright almost bordering on terror I recognise things in my world are getting out of hand; I shout and grab at the pencil, I feel the power in it like something alive with a mind of its own. I dare not pick it up again.

Several times I've seen a white being on the stairs or in my room, or around the house. She is a ghost. She carries a candlestick in her left hand. She wears a veil. Even SHE admits to having seen her. The ghost means us no harm, and never communicates with me, so I ignore her when she passes through. But then one day a small white being of a different kind comes to me. The significance of its visit is unclear. As I look at it I feel I'm falling, falling….And spinning dizzily with great speed; I am sinking, slipping through a bottomless kaleidoscopic pattern of whirling color and revolving movement on such a grand scale that I cannot believe it. I grip the bed. This is not a dream. It is early morning, but it's quite light.

Maybe I'm dying, or is this the gap between the two dimensions where my worlds are mixed up? I'm dizzy with the sinking, spinning, falling, timeless feeling. It's like I've fallen out of my body! I don't want to die yet. I've not even lived! Lord Jesus, don't let me die! Slowly the great drop ceases. It was like a fast elevator coming to a sudden stop!

I almost forgot the earlier morning scare, when just before it is really light; I wake up to a noise by the window. Something is trying to get in. The window is partially open. The creature is large and reptilian and as I watch, the window suddenly bursts open and this black, very heavy creature lands on the floor with a huge noise and a force which shakes the house. It moves my bed as I scream and dive under the covers. This thing is lying on the rug besides the bed – a shapeless reptilian type of blob. It doesn't move.

I wait for a while then dash into my dad's room and wake him up. He hasn't heard anything and tells me to go back to bed for a while. I peer into my room and the "Blob" creature is still there, but there are shadows moving around it. I went downstairs until I heard the household arousing. Then I felt it was safe enough to recheck my room. I tell my brothers and Dad again; but when they look there is nothing there and nothing is disturbed in any way. They say I must have had a nightmare.

If my present world of reality in this house with my family is as hurtful as my experiences tell me; and my parallel dimensions have black hostile cats, an evil face, a ghost that roams the house, a pencil with a life of its own, and the terrible blob creature, among other phenomenon, what next? I'm not sure that I want either of these worlds.

I see myself outside of myself while I think about the multiple dimensions; I feel scared and disoriented. I see that I have to choose my own reality, perhaps on a different frequency inside myself. Only then will I feel safe. This is where I usually go when I'm attacked by HER, and now I also have to opt out for the evil scary dimensions too? I know of HER horrors, but what future terrors might these other weird dimensions reveal to me?

Suddenly crows called loudly in alarm, and *I returned to my "NOW"* to hear someone say; "The Lord cannot be bribed or bargained with!" It was the Preacher interjecting again. I must have been thinking of Jesus and the Holy Spirit; not that I knew very much about either of them, but it was a safer than the other mixed up stuff.

"Shut up you damn hypocrite! I was not bargaining, I was just thinking of my own safety!" I replied angrily; although exactly what he was referring to I don't know.

Coming into the present I realized from the look on Tim's face that I'd been talking and thinking out loud; I had run the total sequence past him. He raised himself on one elbow and was staring at me, and placing his whole hand squarely on my face he said, "It seems to me that you were dropped on a concrete floor sometime, head first and from a height!" He chuckled. "And your brain is sort of scrambled and screwed up!"

Then, feeling that his hand placed so firmly on my face would represent rejection to me, he removed it and passed it over my hair in a ruffling motion, creating a flow of acceptance again.

"You were driven into those other worlds Derek," he said gently. "You know, to escape. That's the way you found a sort of peace."

"Perhaps" I replied, feeling a great sadness cloud over me. "I know I found fear."

"Didn't they ever stop beating the piss out of you?" he asked. "It's a wonder she didn't kill you."

"She almost did." I winced at the memories as they crowded in.

"I don't know why it didn't scramble your brains quite a bit more, by God!" Tim chewed on a piece of grass. "It seems to me that you've always been in the middle of an impossible situation," he said thoughtfully, "and you haven't changed much. Things will just get worse on a bigger scale unless you change somehow."

"I know Tim, but how can I change? I'm simply compelled to do what I do. I respond physically and mentally to the way I've been programmed to react in my brain."

"But there must be a way. You're not stuttering too badly right now are you? So something is different, some kind of change is taking place ..."

Evening came on suddenly. The fire dropped away to dead ash, and sleepily we crawled under the conifer tree into our den and snuggled down warm and dry for the night. Over the next day or so, having eaten both of the chickens and all the kale, I taught Tim how to set snares in the woodland. The weather held beautifully. We had a lot of time to rest and think when we were not swimming in the Angus pond.

When we had our afternoon siestas I had time to go into our past, it was something I had to do on this great quest for myself. On this occasion it landed me up at a cousin's place for a few days. I'm about nine years old. We are in our pyjamas just before bedtime, when our cousin brings out a monkey puppet. BROTHER puts it on his hand like a glove, and creeping into the bedroom makes it appear over the bottom of my bed. He turns its head and contorts its face. I scream. It holds me with its bright eyes, and I scream even louder. For me this is no longer my cousin's place; it has turned into the prison home of torture from a few years earlier. Distinctly I see the baboon leap from high up by the mirror down to my bed. Like a movie scene flashing from the live baboon to the monkey puppet, it alternates with no escape.

It is beside me, I see its fangs again and its bright eyes. It seems to be as big as I am. I scream a terrible high-pitched scream of terror. BROTHER and cousin haven't had so much fun in a long time. The whole bizarre sequence ends with Brother and cousin being told to go to bed, while I am thrashed soundly for screaming and creating a disturbance. Needless to say by this time I am soaking wet and remain so till the morning when the next thrashing is administered for just that reason.

We go to the seaside. I've never been before. It's for the weekend only. I'm frightened. The beach slopes to the flowing white-capped water. The waves are tall, cold looking and grey green in color. I fear drowning and hold back. SHE takes one arm and BROTHER takes the other; and in this manner I'm pulled screaming down the beach. People look as I'm cuffed about the ears and face to shut me up. We are getting close to the water. I scream the loudest fear screams I'm humanly capable of.

"You're going to kill me! You're going to drown me!" I scream.

I am fighting for my life. Strong hands block my mouth from screaming and I can barely breathe so I dig my feet in the sand. I try to fall down or to lie down. But they just drag me and I'm kicked from behind with cutting force. The people around us look, they talk and they point, but they do not come to my rescue. The grey-green waves are closer now and they foam with giant drowning menace. The roar of the water is terrible. I can't hear my screams now and the world is getting shadowy... We arrive at the water's edge.

"Just for that you can go into the water!" she yells.

They push me forward, and I fall onto the wet stones. The great green wave hits me. I scream and suck in salt water. I'm pulled out of the water and both punched and pinched for being in it. I'm wet. It's not just sea water but they'll never know the difference. It is a mad scene, but it is lost in the hustle of the afternoon. The people on the beach are angry at me for screaming.

"Just for that you shan't go to the beach again!"

I hope not, but I guard the happiness of my expression lest it be seen and revenge taken. I must never forget that anything that I like is not for me, so I must pretend to dislike that which I would enjoy. My unguarded expressions are usually my downfall. Water is dangerous. They want to drown me. I'm sure of it.

I love my grandmother. A great feeling of well being overtakes me at her place in the country. She is the kindest woman I have met in my life so far and I feel her love and her disagreement with HER over me. There are chickens and ducks at grandmother's house; and a lily pool where I go to clean my teeth and talk with the friendly frogs.

SHE often yells at me, "Get out of here you swine, cut yourself a twig off the willow tree and clean your disgusting teeth, I'm sick of looking at your green and orange fangs!"

So I made this a teeth cleaning routine; sometimes my tooth brush comes off the apple trees and I eat an apple afterwards to polish them. They must look better; SHE has not cuffed me about the ears or pinched me for about a week over my ugly teeth.

The tall grandfather clock with the Roman numerals on its gold face ticks slowly, and is a great comfort to me. It slows my world down. Time is smoothed out, and I don't have to look for an escape or be wary every moment. There is love and safety here with my grandmother.

BROTHER asks me into the meadow one afternoon. He has that "queer" look in his eyes. I must beware. I go with him, and as we walk toward the deep end of the pond where the cattle drink BROTHER'S queer look strengthens. It has purpose and resolve now. He is trying to get me to the edge to look for tadpoles. I love tadpoles. He is trying to bait me toward the deeper end in our search, and finds a spot where he claims he sees them swimming all over the place. It is extra deep here.

"Here, take a look at them!" he says.

But I don't trust his eyes. I will not take one step further. He sees I will not come and jumps for me swiftly but I elude his grasp.

"You're going to drown me!" I scream in panic. I run. As I struggle under the barbed wire fence my shirt catches in the barbs. HE is almost upon me. He can still drag me and throw me in. I leave the barbed wire fence with a piece of my shirt and run for my life back to the house.

Scratched and bleeding with tears coursing down my grubby face, I run faster to the house. I tell HER. HE comes in and denies it, and tells a different version entirely. I get

thrashed for being near the pond and get extra strokes for tearing my shirt. Also my hair is pulled for disobedience. BROTHER sits in the kitchen with a cookie and milk a sly smile on his face.

Granny disapproves. "You're too hard on the little fellow," I hear her say. "You watch; he'll turn out to be the best of the bunch…"

"Can you believe that Tim? Me – the best of the bunch? No, I'm just me, whoever WE are."

Sometimes SHE goes shopping in the heart of London, and in her absence we go really wild. In the semi-detached house where we live, we have covers covering the covers that cover the upholstery in the off limits, unused icy dining and drawing rooms. One day when SHE was away, we kids were on the upstairs floor chasing each other in and out of the windows of the larger bedroom. We leave one window; cling to the narrow ledge past the large fixed center window pane, all the while squealing with fright and delight to come in through the other window. Then BROTHER, who is twelve and quite strong, closes both windows leaving me on the ledge, and having failed to pry my fingers from the window casing, which would drop me some twenty feet to the ground, he drops a rope down the side of the house. I don't know where the rope came from; maybe he had previously asked our sister to fetch it. Holding the window closed against the rope, he instructs our younger brother to fasten it to the wire incinerator, a mesh affair about four feet high. It is filled with paper and cardboard. Then while I plead for admittance, BROTHER issues orders for the trash to be ignited. Rex lights it.

The flames burst brightly upwards. Brother hauls the flaming mess up the side of the house with the rope. I see what is shaping up; he plans to burn me off the ledge, or I will leap to my death below. I battle to get in. The flames are coming up to meet me and I can feel the searing smoke. But HE cannot haul with both hands and at the same time hold the window closed and our sister refuses to help him, thank God. So the whole affair is a see-saw of flames rising and falling against the side of the house leaving black smoke marks, and me screaming and wrenching at the windows to get in. The neighbours are concerned. They should be. Brother thumbs his nose at them from the upper window. Finally with my sister's aid I get inside, and we all go outside to see how we can hide the burn and smoke marks on the exterior of the house which is beige stucco. SHE will probably not notice anyway. Then we play hide and seek in forbidden places, like the wardrobe where HER full length grey squirrel coat hangs in moth balls preserved for great occasions that never arise.

I sighed. "You know Tim, I was rarely allowed in the living room for more than a few hours a year? The only warm spot in the house was the big fire in that room, the heat radiates and it's bright and cheery. The others read or play games by the fire. Whenever Dad is home he sits beside it reading. She lives in its warmth each evening sucking on Fox's Glacier Mints and chomping Kit Kat bars. It's her sacred supply which we children are never allowed to taste. I live in my cold bedroom and am rarely allowed to hear the radio. I walk into the warm living room. They all look up as if I'm a stranger. Trouble is brewing. Like desserts, this room is off limits. This fact is emblazoned on every face except Dad's if he is home. My face lights up seeing the fire and the color and the wonderful music on the radio. It's beautiful. All of this is reflected in my face and is therefore my downfall.

"What's that thing doing in here?" SHE demands. "Get up to your room where you belong!"

"Why?" I ask, standing enrapt with the music.

SHE turns the radio off so that I cannot hear it. No one else can hear it either. The others clamour. It is MY fault that they are deprived for a few minutes. Dad intercedes trying to be reasonable.

"Why can't he stay?" He asks reasonably.

"If *IT* stays I leave!" she yells fiercely. This endless campaign of hatred is accepted by my siblings as "normal." It is habitual, or as SHE says –"it's the way things are!"

My staying in the room creates other triangles with pressures and repercussions that I can sense as they bounce around the family. It's all my fault like everything is, always has been, and always will be, for ever and ever, amen!

"Look at ITS face!" SHE exclaims venomously.

"What's wrong with his face?" Dad asks.

"Bhaa! You wouldn't understand. Go back to your book!" she commands. The others are yelling to have the radio on. It won't go on if I stay. I stay anyway meaning to push the limits of this situation. SHE leaves the room. Dad has said enough so that she is reluctant to beat me in front of him for entering the room. But almost immediately SHE returns in desperation, her face is distorted with hatred and fury. SHE grabs me.

"I told you to get out! Now get out! So we can hear the radio and have some peace!"

My ears are pulled and my hair strains to stay rooted. I am pinched punched and banned to the cold loneliness of my room, leaving behind the warm friendly family chatter and music. SHE returns to her knitting alongside the Fox's Glacier Mints. They want no part of me—ever. Like a ritual this same drama of banishment is re-enacted year after year. One day an old friend of HER's comes for a visit. She talks with my siblings and there is laughter and a bit of showing off because we rarely have company.

"Where's the other boy, what's his name – Derek?" She asks.

"Oh! *IT* stays in its room," She says lightly. The truth is SHE carries the key to my prison is her apron pocket. I am locked in day by day, all through the holidays of summer too. One weekend leads to another. My young sister and brother often head out on adventures and I imagine them running through the scented meadow sedge or catching scarlet sticklebacks in the creek. Summer magic is in full bloom. SHE empties my chamber pot every day or so, and I get meals of their left overs on a tray. Sometimes I don't eat, even though I'm quite hungry. I often have the feeling that maybe the food is poisoned; it depends on how she looks at me. Any hint of a smile or being nice could equate with a painful death for me. I feel deep down inside of me, that some day, in some way, she will kill me if she can; *after all* she *is* my mother, and that is strange logic, but somehow acceptable. I only hope that I can survive the traumas of life till I'm old enough or big enough to leave forever – if I do indeed survive.

Suddenly I hear the rattle of a key, the lock turns and the door is pushed open. SHE stands there fiddling with her key; and her guest is beside her.

"Why do you keep him locked up?" She frowns as she asks the question, and looks at me.

SHE laughs and shrugs it off with; "Oh! That's the way it is around here, that's all. IT just stays in its room." I get the feeling that the visitor may be the key to my escape. My face lights up.

"Hello Derek!" She says softly. But her tone is as kind as the way one would try to put a scared rabbit at ease; it is just too kind and too caring. She scans me with some uncertainty. This scene is deadly for me. I freeze and blink, and I'm only *'half way out,'* I open my mouth to say something. She looks at me and all I can do is drool.

"Are you not going to say hello?" She asks. Wide eyed with fear of

HER and paralyzed with emotions that I cannot handle brought on by the visitor's concern for me I manage a weak "Hello." I'm out of control now and trembling all over. SHE is watching me and her eyes carry a killing threat. I go back inside myself, deep back inside where it is safe and begin to wet myself.

SHE says, "Let's go down now." The key clicks and the lock turns. Their voices fade. Now is the time to fully flee to the *'meadows of my mind'* because when the visitor leaves SHE will return. First she will cane me for being wet, but I will stay that way.

Secondly she will thrash me if she checks my chamber pot and sees that I have not used it, and the little bit of water she left in it is missing. I cannot even drink from my pot any more. I think she puts water in it, knowing that I will drink it, and that validates her righteous rage and my beating. She deprives me of anything that will quench my thirst because she thinks this is what makes me wet my bed.

Eventually this fluids shortage took a bizarre turn. Man can live without food for 30 or 40 days but he must have water. One day I am not at all well and run a very high temperature; I feel as though I have to "let go" in some way. I do not care anymore. I become worse and SHE finally calls in a doctor. He checks me out and can't quite figure out what is wrong. He wants to take my temperature in the usual way under the tongue, but SHE intervenes and says that I will probably chew on it and to find an alternative method. This means that I lie naked with the thermometer in my groin, and at nine years old, I feel uncomfortable and embarrassed at both of them watching the thermometer. While we are waiting for the temperature to register, the doctor sees my chamber pot. It has not been emptied for about two days, and he says, "Is his urine always this dark?" It is not light yellow or even dark yellow, but is a brownish color.

"Oh yes" she replies he's always done stuff like that. The doctor frowns and says she must try to get me to take in more water. For just a moment I saw a demonic flash of conflict cross her features. The doctor was there of course as I realized many years later, because my system was so overloaded with poisons, that my kidneys were just about to shut down for lack of moisture. This meant that I would have died of infection and kidney malfunction. If she gives me water I may wet the bed; if she does not give me water she will have the cost of the doctor. In either case I deserve a thrashing. Both ways interfere with her absolute control over my life and death. Somehow I just know that this doctor visit will result in an extra beating. It's my fault as always that my urine is so dark. Thereafter she brings me a mug of water once a day, and as she does so, she looks at me in a peculiar way, and I know I will have to taste the water carefully before I drink it. She may know of a poison that has no taste if such is possible. Thirst is ever an on going problem. When it rains, little pockets of water collect in the outside window grooves on the windowsill frame. I stick my head out in the rain and suck up any water I can reach. I do this whenever it rains, especially at night and early morning when SHE is not around. I must be very sure that my hair does not get wet though, or she will figure out what I have been doing. I have little doubt that she will nail the window shut from the outside if she finds out.

Sometimes when rocking back and forth on my bed, I bang my head against the wall. I almost expect something to happen. When circular repetitive hopelessness sucks at me I bang my head even harder because the physical pain detracts from my mental pain. My head aches and I can only cry softly, or SHE will come up with the bamboo cane. Eventually I sleep to escape.

On odd occasions I am trapped to go on a shopping trip to the village. I serve no useful function on these trips other than to be a prisoner under constant watch. We are walking and there are passers-by. However, I am instructed to walk on the opposite side of the street or a little way ahead or behind, but not with THEM. When I ask why, SHE explains that it's my looks and my face. They don't want to be seen with me, but they won't leave me at home, so they insist on taking me to keep me under their cruel control at all times. Years of this treatment burn into my brain. It affects the way I try to talk, the way I walk and certainly my facial expressions because I must never laugh, and when I do have a bout of involuntary suppressed laughter, I get told, "And take that smirk of your face before I smash it for you!"

Reading had always been a great escape for me. One day SHE came upstairs to the room I have been banished to. I'm reading a book. These are my early reading days. I'm eight years old.

"What are you doing?" She demands, upon entering.

"Reading." I reply.

"You can't read you swine! All you can do is look at the pictures!"

"I AM reading." I reply defensively. So she put me through a number of words and sentences in the book. She is amazed and goes downstairs to the others and says to them including my father, "Did you know that swine can read now?" This does not bode well for me. I am here upstairs, segregated from the family for reasons of eternal punishment. I believe my crime is that I am alive and I'm not supposed to be.

From this day forward all books are banned from the room. She knows I like reading and this irks her in the worst way. She is losing her power of infliction and I'm not being punished for being alive. I read and enjoy myself and this is not allowed. But what she has overlooked is a little bookcase mounted on the wall between the two beds that contains about ten books by William Shakespeare. They have blue covers and the pages are gold at the edges. I find these difficult to read and to understand as I'm only eight years old, but I do get their drift and I study them.

Oh horrors! One day SHE catches me with "A Midsummer Night's Dream" and she explodes. She rips the book from my hand and seizes all the other books off the bookshelf. They disappeared and I never found them again! When I'm allowed out of the room or escape because she is in the garden, I searched for them to no avail.

So I resort to writing. Both SHE, and my older Brother who has always been innocently involved in this campaign against me, seize my writing. They ridicule it and tear it up or just take it away. So I designed a code, for example "A" = "K" "B" = L and etcetera. I write in code and become quite adept at reading what I have written, although it is a much slower process. When they seize it from me now, they cannot read it or understand it, and it infuriates them, especially HER. So she withdraws all paper and pencils of any sort.

Now as I stay in my room I can neither read nor write. I never let her catch me looking out of the open window as I watch and listen to the thrushes, blackbirds and robins in the garden. How will she prevent me from doing this? Will she attempt to blind me? I believe she is capable of doing even this so great is her hatred of me. It is unrelenting. The question of why I'm treated this way is never questioned by anyone at any time. It just IS. The only recourse I have is to go *'Inside'* where it is friendly. I have all my friendly animals inside, and it is from these internal adventures that I draw my life source. Of course I am allowed to go to school, but my pathetic progress there is derived from my conditioning.

Back in the world with Tim and our adventures, I trotted off along the deer trails among the tall oaks, then picking up speed I ran flat out for a while, leaping over small bushes and fallen trees, then slowing as I caught sight of a red fox. He wheeled to the west and I paused for breath and lay in the grass watching him disappear. Yes – foxes are my friends too, I feel that I'm almost a part of their family. I had seen a red fox the morning I'd first run away from home. I had scanned the deserted streets and later the farms – strange –I will not be in school today. They will miss me and it will create quite a stir I suppose, but for a ten-year old this is a daring and necessary departure.

There is screaming and yelling in the kitchen. Indeed, when is there not? I am refusing to do something. SHE is livid with fury. If she tires of beating me up she sets BROTHER on me, but I'm getting bigger now and harder to handle. Today I sneer at her and rebel. SHE is exasperated. It is not uncommon for her to be drinking tea, see me looking at her speculatively, and throw the whole cupful of hot tea into my face.

"Now look what you made me do!" she says, and I am beaten because the table cloth is tea stained. "It's all your fault!" she screams.

Today is a bad day. BROTHER has attacked me with a plate in his hand. I throw up an arm to protect my head. We connect and the plate breaks in two and crashes to the floor.

"What did that swine do now?" SHE asks HIM, and then makes a dash for me.

"Smash one of my plates will you?" She sticks her thumbs inside my mouth for grip—currently this is her favourite mode of attack. She's wrenching my mouth and cheeks apart while she faces me snarling, her face contorted.

She screams. "I'll spiflicate you—you bloody swine"... *slow motion*—is this spiflication?... Maybe I'll grow up with an extra big mouth and look like a giant cod or shark. Visions of natives with artificially stretched features and Chinese babies with bound heads and feet float by. Her nails have caused my gums to bleed. She shakes my head as I fall back against the kitchen sink. Sister screams. Young brother starts crying. HE just looks on. Then I bite her thumbs, hard, as I should have done before now, and she withdraws her hands as I vomit on her and all over the kitchen floor. She whirls to the table, grabs a kitchen knife, and strikes me again and again in the chest. It is good that it is blunt and round ended and doesn't pierce me. Again and again she stabs and hacks at me, tearing at my chest. I have knife marks on my arms and wrists and my hands are cut as I ward off the blows and protect my chest. Finally, I am thrown in the corner. Brother and Sister are crying. HE is silent, just watching with that peculiar look in his eyes. She whips me as I slip up on the floor in my lumpy vomit. She then wheels on brother and sister.

"What are *you* crying about?" The bamboo cane descends on them too. We all scream and cry. I escape only because she is exhausted.

Today as I leave the house in the dewy dawn I examine the stab marks on my chest made with the knife. I run swiftly towards the place where the meadows come into view and where the beautiful serene woods start their rolling protective world. I feel a wonderful kinship with the little red fox as he flows across the ploughed field beside me. I slow down and look again at the purple and blue bruises on my scratched chest. It still hurts. If the knife had been pointed, I may not have made it through to breathe the cool morning air of today. I know, I will live with the foxes and hide out in the woods; make some kind of a home for myself and learn to live with the wild animals. The bushy red blur of flowing motion sees me. He stops to look. I call out, "Wait! I'll run with you!" He gives a friendly little toss of his sleek head—I believe he smiled at me, panting, his pink tongue lolling—before his red brush flowed to melt among the oaks. I think SHE is a fox killer – she has this dead fox fur wrap around her shoulders when she goes out. I sometimes find it lying on her bed, and for long periods I look into the fox's eyes. They plead with me. I stroke his fur – why did they have to kill you? He just looks so sad, and I visit him whenever she is not around. SHE likes to kill things.

I'm alone again. I can't go back. The sun is already high in the sky. With pencil and paper I lie under a large oak and compose poetry. Noises of the busy world of man reach me as I explore, keeping to the trees. For music I have the seasonal birds, most of which I can name. Rabbits and squirrels are everywhere and they accept me. In the whole wild scenic woodland of color and birdsong I am not rejected. I feel love from the trees as I talk with them. I caress the tiny wild flowers and they smile back at me in perfection. I talk with a myriad of insects. They all accept me without question. I too am a wild creature among them. Only the Humans reject me. Everywhere people are far more kind to stray dogs and cats than they are to me.

Hunger assails me and weakness follows, but of food I have none, and at this tender age I do not know how to find it in the woods. I write, I dream and rest in the sun. Finally when the sun is low and cold winds whip across the commons, and I rise from the base of the oak where I've been sitting dejected and miserable, to trudge wearily back over some five miles to what I know as home.

On arrival there is silence. SHE ignores me totally and carries on knitting while I go to my small room weak and hungry; coming back home has not solved that problem. Then I get thrashed. At least that warms me up. I go to bed hungry and defeated. But a tiny flicker of hope has risen in me; the little red fox understands. I have friends out there in the woodland along with acceptance and mental tranquility. I hold it tenaciously like a precious gem in the centre of my mind. Next time I must plan, find food—steal food and take clothing.

I sleep in the deep, deep sleep of utter exhaustion. I hurt while I'm sleeping. Then more hurt, stinging hurt. I start and slowly wake. I'm in the middle of the floor. The light is on. BROTHER is standing in the doorway. SHE is standing over me, red-faced and furious, the cane swishing and descending on me again and again. SHE is asking a question, but I cannot absorb the meaning in coherent form with my brain. I writhe around on the floor under the lashes of welting pain. My mind will not work. All I can see through the stinging fog of pain is the little red fox smiling from beneath the oaks. I emerge more and more from the haze of sleep and hunger as the pain bites into me, and the screaming interrogation continues.

I shout, "No! No! No! No! I don't know!" It wouldn't have made any difference if the answer to the unknown question had been "yes" or "no."

The light is snapped out. The door is slammed and I'm left on the cold floor, wet with urine. I'm not even safe in my sleep now. I try to plan how to escape for good. I sleep soaking wet. I stink of steamy urine, the welts are burning, and my ears are ringing. It feels like I must have been pulled bodily out of bed by my hair. Later, sleeping with my mouth partially open, my face becomes wet, and I become dimly aware of something unnatural in my mouth. I reject the taste. My eyes open a fraction. SHE is standing by the open door, convulsed with laughter; the scene is illuminated by the light from the passageway. BROTHER is attempting to urinate into my open mouth. I wake with a start. Quickly they leave and close the door as though they were never there. I hear HIM laughing. Then normal voices as he prepares for a bath. I wipe my mouth and re-enter sleep where I dream of food in a lush green meadow, where I'm surrounded by families of rabbits. They skip, hop and play freely in a warm aura of care and love.

In the summer the wasps stream in through the open kitchen window at jam making time. SHE grabs the swatter, and leaning across the table to the window, she swishes the swatter left and right. If it connects, young brother or I will have that angry stinging black-and-yellow enemy down our shirt fronts somewhere or in our hair. We duck and scream in panic. She misses the wasp and I get swatted in the face for creating a disturbance. One day, long suffering little sister will not sit squarely in her chair. She claims with a pink teary face that there is a wasp there. SHE denies this.

"There's no wasp on your chair!" she screams. "Sit down!"

Then SHE forces poor sister's naked thigh flat onto the chair; where-upon she screams a peculiar high-pitched trilling note of mortal terror, dropping to lower screams of bloody blue murder. Her face is slapped for screaming. Her hair is pulled. Involuntarily she leaps out of her chair and there is the wasp in stinging good form, damaged but angrily buzzing and quivering his jet-black stinger. Sister's thigh is swelling already.

"Why didn't you tell me there was a wasp on your chair?" SHE yells.

"We did," I pipe up.

"I'm not asking you, you bloody swine!" She licks the bamboo cane across my face and neck raising conspicuous welts which are hard to ex-plain away to school companions after lunch. SHE is a wasp eater. Maybe that's where the venom comes from. She cooks the wasps along with the preserves when they fall in. It's her jam anyway. In the winter she crunches them when eating her bread and jam, pulling them from her mouth like cherry pits and placing their pathetic curling crisp bodies on the edge of her plate. I feel sorry for the wasps. I've looked at them through my little pocket microscope; they have jolly friendly faces.

Although I'm not locked in a room and fed there – which seems to be reserved for school holidays, I've been banned from the kitchen table at meal times. The table will only handle four persons and I am the natural fifth to be disinherited, although I am the second oldest. My table is a wooden box to one side and facing away from them. I eat the other's leavings or there is little food for me. They throw their "scrugs" off the main table to me. Often I have to pick them up off the dirty floor. BROTHER never eats the crusts on the outside of his bread; he eats only the soft insides and throws the crusts to me, gnawed and distorted like orange rinds. SHE throws her crusts for me to eat as well, so that my bread comprises mainly of what the others may or may not leave. The table scrapings are put on my plate too. They call me the "Scrug Merchant," but I eat and survive.

Usually I'm in such a foggy haze from beatings, avoiding HER and rejection misery, that frequently I rock back and forth on my little stool – moaning. Rocking and moaning maintains a partial blankness in my mind. But what I crave is *"OUT,"* or nothingness. I just don't want to be here. In the last little while as my despair deepens, my actions cause them to laugh and hoot in derision. SHE gets the biggest kick out of it. When I'm doing my moaning and rocking they say I'm like a chicken laying eggs, so they place a saucepan under my stool to catch them. This adds hugely to their merriment.

However there is a worse problem. It is when SHE shakes me like a terrier shaking a rat. I still can see her features contorted in hatred as she grips me. I am so violently shaken that the breath leaves my body. I cannot regain any air—and the saliva flies from my mouth along with strange sounds. Just before I pass out she releases me and I hit the floor—tossed aside like a discarded rag doll. She returns with the bamboo cane.

Several times I have thought of killing myself; I have banged my head against the wall till I'm stunned and bruised. I've tried not breathing and tried to strangle myself, but nature in her wisdom takes care of these little situations. I live on. My death has to be planned in a better way. I shall have to hang myself properly, but first I have to find some good strong rope, and the right place, and even then I really don't know how to do it. Maybe SHE will do the killing job for me.

It was truly time to get back to Tim. I rolled onto my side scenting clover leaf and flower, just as the red fox reappeared scant yards away; shining bloom on his red fur, happy, loping, flowing and smiling. I laughed out loud for the joy of life and rose quickly to run back to camp. I loved the smooth flow of power and the springy movement of my limbs, the tireless breathing and effortless speed. I felt good as I panted up to Tim.

"Running it off makes you feel better, doesn't it?" he said.

"It clears the old hurt stuff out." I agreed.

I dropped to my knees beside him. "Right now, more than anything else, I'd love an ale," I said, knowing there were none left.

For answer he rose and sprinted into our den. Moments later he reappeared smiling broadly with two bottles of Guinness.

"Tim! You sneaky bastard!" I exclaimed. He passed a bottle to me.

"I've been holding onto a few bottles for just such an emergency as this. Right now we need it."

We stirred up the fire and settled down to drink. Tim began to sing in a fine tenor voice and I joined in after a moment. We began with old English country tunes, but by the time we each had a second bottle of ale underway we were into hymns. Early in the morning my song shall rise to thee... We finished up the verse, hooting like the proverbial drunken owls that we were. The words meant little but the tune was appropriately blasphemed among the empty ale bottles.

"Jesus, are we stewed!" slurred Tim.

"Blasphemy!" screamed the Preacher out loud. "They shall not hold him guiltless who takes the name of the Lord in vain ..."

"But being good Christians," I mocked, "They'll forgive him!"

"God will not be mocked," screamed the Preacher.

"A toast! A toast!" Tim had raised his bottle. "Fuck the preacher, fuck 'im, I say, right in the fuckin' ear!"

"I'll drink to that!" I laughed, although it occurred to me that the preacher would probably enjoy it.

"Let's throw that son of a bitch out once and for all!" Tim roared. "He's always buttin' in!"

"Reckon he'd like a drink?"

Our laughter echoed across the clearing and into the quiet evening.

"Hey, I know a song…" and once more Tim began to sing. Just then the sun dipped beyond the hills from sight. I cut some fresh pine boughs for our bedding, and checked our gear making it ready for darkness. Everything was set up for bedtime or for leaving at a moment's notice if need be. Tim piled up the wood supply for the night. I slipped down the trail out of the trees and across the downs to the Angus pond to get a can of water. On the way back I chipped some salt off the cattle licks to flavour our stew. Back in camp I eased the billy of rabbit stew to one side of the fire. Tim emerged from the shadows with more wood and the flames leapt a little higher. We slopped our rabbit stew out onto plates.

"How come it's so salty!" enquired Tim, looking at the rib cage on his plate.

"Oh, it's a chunk off the iodized cattle lick. I may have added a touch too much, but if it puts beef on them, think what it'll do for us!"

Tim laughed. "Derek we ought to do some planning. I thought we'd stay around here for just a little while longer and then take off for my Aunt's place in Plymouth."

"Sounds okay to me," I agreed, and yawned widely. I sensed he really wanted to be on his way back to some kind of job. Maybe he was right.

We listened to the partridges calling among the dells. Bats skimmed across the first stars. It was another timeless evening. For a while I read some Richard Jeffries by firelight, while Tim dreamed out loud about naked women – the very last thing he needed was lustful urging before we retired for the night. Afterward we headed for the conifer grove and our bed under the low sweeping boughs. It was quite dark with almost a chill in the air. With ground sheets down and the soft pine boughs forming a scented mattress, we shared our blankets and wriggled around for comfort lying side by side to share body heat.

"Tim," I said, "I keep meaning to ask you. Where did that ale come from?"

"Ah, you really want to know, don't you?"

"Quit stalling!"

"Well while you were so peacefully napping in that park by the bridge

I went exploring. And when I passed the blacksmith's shop I saw this ale in the back of his truck, so I whipped it. I even used his gunny sack to put it in."

"You mean the guy that came to rescue the ducks?

"That's the one!" said Tim. "I thought it would make a nice surprise ..."

"We'd better be careful as we go through the village when we head for the railroad station," I warned.

"No one saw me" he said and yawned with satiated luxury. "Oh, am I gonna sleep tonight!"

"You know what Tim – you're a fuckin' thievin' rat!" I charged. I snuggled my left arm around him and we relaxed with alcoholic stupor into warm closeness. I'm sure the guardian angels of God watched over us with a forgiving smile, while the other part of *We – prayed for ME and US.*

Chapter Twelve

A morning or two later Tim came running up the slope to our camp, and when he was within earshot he shouted, "Hey Derek! Look what I caught!" I was cleaning up our camp site and saw that Tim had just returned from his snare sets, and held up a beautiful hare. His tanned face was radiant. This was his very first catch. From then on it seemed he became even more adept than I, so we had our meat supply well in hand. We interspersed our rabbit feasts with occasional raids on distant farmsteads for bags of oats, and bean meal, eggs and the occasional chicken. Vegetables were easy to come by and what little we took would never be missed from the rows of abundance. We became familiar with the wild life in our small world and we studied numerous birds with the telescope. We shunned man whenever he infringed on our territory.

Our days were almost complete except for when the boiling pressures of youth asserted their urgent rights—as natural as starlight, and as demanding as the strong current of a young river.

"I'm all for a good woman, someone who can take care of all seven and a half." Tim declared as we had a sex discussion. Tim was rather well endowed much to my envy, and he did look like a young stallion at stud. He had just achieved an overdue release and had splatted our latest rabbit that we had not yet hung up. So I strung his love bunny from a branch; it was glazed of eye and its brown fur and silky reddish ears were creamed and wet with unfulfilled dreams.

"What makes us so different?" Tim asked one evening. "It seems there're US here and THEM out there."

"I laughed. "Welcome Tim! I've been waiting for you!" He looked puzzled. "Don't you remember saying that you were looking out at me, and

I was looking in towards the Humans? Well it looks like you've joined me, and now we're both looking at the world you came from—at a distance."

"You mean I've become like you?" He seemed incredulous.

"Oh no!" I said, "You're a guest in my space. Where we stand is a merging place for our different worlds. When this happens to me it seems that time stops and all the past present and future become now. That's the NOW feeling I told you about."

"You're losing me." Tim complained.

"I don't mean to. Look, just think in terms of many different worlds occupying the same space at the same time ..."

"Now I am lost."

"You're not lost – you're just falling asleep." I accused him.

"I am not! All I'm asking is why we seem to be not like THEM!"

"Well for starters Tim," I replied. "I believe it's because I think man *has* a body, and not that man *is* his body."

"You mean they think that their body is all there is?" said Tim.

"Right! Think of all the grave yards and the fuss they make over memorials and grave stones. They really think that their loved one is in that box below ground. They even lay them in satin with soft pillows as if they could feel."

"If a man is not where his body is; then where is he? Sounds like riddles to me." Tim looked like he didn't want to discuss the matter further.

"Tim," I said patiently, "it's just that I think we inhabit our bodies from another space. It's in our heads, and yet in another world."

"Well I don't want to be split up. I'm gonna stay in one piece." He stared up into the reddening sky. The next morning the clean scented air of dawn half woke us, and shortly after the bird life orchestrated sunrise. We leapt up. The drama of another day had begun. Today we would break camp and head west. All the gear was dragged out; blankets and groundsheets were spread on low branches to dry off in the early sunlight. It was time to take our last dip in the Angus pond.

"I'll race you!" I challenged.

Tying on our runners we sped out of the woods feeling the wet grasses whip our bare legs. Rabbits feeding at the edge of the wood scattered in alarm. The cold water hit us with a stimulating shock, and then enveloped us in a tingling embrace as we swam. Several frogs fled into deeper water. While we swam around, the full beauty of life, blue skies, youth and friendship came to me. Afterwards, we picked up our sealed jar of leftovers from among the reeds at the water's edge where it kept our food cool; and then we raced back to camp drying off in the morning air.

"What's for breakfast?" I wanted to know.

"Bean meal with cold rabbit jelly, and there's a head and tongue you can nibble on, and I'll finish the leg."

We sat by the rotting oak to nibble the leftover rabbit. At least Tim did. I got a little meat off the head and decided I didn't want to eat rabbit again for a while.

"Tim, let's have coffee in the village today before we catch a bus to your aunt's place," I said. In the village we learned the bus was not due for three and a half hours, so keeping a low profile we went for coffee. Oh! What delicious brew and what thick warm brown toast with marmalade, and what delightfully quiet, attentive bustling around of those who served us. Afterwards we took a short exploring trip on the outskirts of the hamlet, down narrow lanes with high hedges where bullfinches splashed crimson breasts in the sun.

"We should take my aunt a small gift or somethin'," Tim said hesitatingly.

"Why not take her a nice fat hen?" I asked.

"Oh, no!" exclaimed Tim in mock fright. "You'll make another whirly weasel-stick."

"No!" I cut him off. "I'll do the same as you did, just walk into the chicken house and grab one."

"I dare you!"

"You're on!"

We left the roadway and walked along the hedgerows to come up at the back of a scattered group of farm buildings.

"There's the chicken house," I pointed, "and there's a bloody dog! Damn, damn, damn!"

It came charging out of the yard, through the fence and rushed up to us barking furiously. Tim squatted against a low brick wall; put his hand out to the hound as if it had been his pet since it was a pup. It wagged its tail.

He reached into his pack and fished out a piece of cold rabbit meat, he'd made a friend for life. This left me free, and without hesitation I stepped into the dim chicken house where several hens were laying, selected what looked like a plump one and grabbed her. I wrung her neck, the wings beat a bit and then she went limp. I stuffed the Rhode Islander into the gunny sack and we took off. The dog followed for a while and then turned back to continue its guard duty.

"You are one cool bastard," Tim said.

"Well, your aunt deserves the best." I smiled at him guilelessly. A little further along the road, we stopped to crouch in the ditch and pluck the hen, then hustled off to the bus stop, with the naked chicken on top of my pack under a gunny sack.

Eventually our bus arrived and in a matter of minutes we were looking at the green hedgerows flashing smoothly by and thinking of a civilized night in a bed. Tim sat next to the window and I had the aisle seat, my pack on its side by my feet. It was hugely enjoyable—the quiet ride, the speed, and the interesting passengers.

On leaving the bus we headed for a phone booth for a telephone directory to find out where Tim's aunt lived; and when we did find it neither of us had enough change to make the call.

"Well we have her address let's just go over and drop in!" I said. Despite several false starts and misdirection from passers by, in about an hour we came to a section of semi-detached homes with brick walls and divided gardens, where tall hollyhocks swayed gently among the other blooms. He then found his aunt's place. He opened the neat white gate and we walked together up the flagstones to the front door. It was shiny brown wood with a brightly polished brass knocker, one of those where a lion holds the knocker between his fangs. We squirmed, probably because we both needed a good leak, and we must have looked quite a sight. Tim let the brass knocker fall heavily.

It made a hollow sound. We could hear footsteps within and moments later a pleasant-faced refined looking woman was looking us up and down. She had blue eyes, her hair was greying and she possessed a mouth that smiled often.

"Yes?" she inquired. Her voice was low and at the same time had a musical quality about it. "What can I do for you?"

I had of course retreated into my "hunted look" and was on the verge of bolting. I saw that Tim was blushing and I think it was only the second or third time since I had known him that this had occurred. He toyed with the piece of paper with the address on it, shifted his feet uncomfortably, and then finally looked up to meet her eyes said, "It's Tim! And... and this is my friend Derek. We... we... came to visit you."

"Tim!" she shrilled. "Tim!" Her eyes were suddenly large with recognition. "But you've grown so much. Oh, do come in! Have you come far? When did you arrive? You should have called me and I'd have had someone pick you up!" She ushered us into a small, tastefully furnished spotless parlour.

"Put your things here. I will get organized in a minute. My, you must be famished you growing boys," she gushed, and then bustled about filling a copper kettle and stoking the cheery fire.

Tim sprawled in a flower covered chair his hands hanging loosely over the sides.

"Oh, Tim dear how did you cut your hand?" she asked solicitously. Tim looked, as did I and we saw the chicken blood.

"Oh yes, I should wash up," he said, rising.

"Yes, why don't you both wash up? I have a spare room. You won't mind sharing a room, will you?" she addressed us with warmth that left me feeling inadequate. We cleaned up and afterwards had tea and cakes in the parlour while Tim filled her in on our recent adventures.

"Aunt Julie, Derek's all right. He may look a little wild, and sometimes he can't get a word out straight, especially when he's in the city around people or in confined spaces, but he straightens out a lot when he's in the forest. Isn't that right, Derek?"

I nodded trying to look civilized, rather than risk the "yes" that was called for. I felt that if I did reply, the word "yes" would be the longest in the English Language. Aunt Julie beamed on Tim. Now and then she cast me a guarded look as if I were a stray dog to be tolerated for Tim's sake, as long as I were deloused and didn't jump on the furniture. I suppose I was somewhat extra scruffy with my long hair and my trapped look. Like a hunted animal my eyes checked the doors and windows for avenues of escape.

After tea we were shown to our room. Aunt Julie led the way up the narrow staircase, and there off a small landing, was a pleasant room with a sloping ceiling, two small windows and a large double bed. On the uneven oak floor was a rug with a paisley design. I was dumbfounded at the luxury. Buckingham Palace had nothing on this after the places we had been sleeping. Above the carved headboard of the bed hung the portrait of what appeared to be a family ancestor. The work was good and Tim and I both stood gazing at it.

"That was your grandfather Tim, a very fine man," Julie volunteered, answering our unspoken questions. I thought his curling moustache made him look aggressive, and his fierce bright eyes seemed to follow us wherever we went in the room.

"Well I'll show you boys the bathroom and you can get cleaned up; and when you're changed I'll pop your things in the boiler and they'll be clean in no time."

Tim explained that we had no better clothing than that which we wore, our spares being equally in need of soap and water.

"Derek only has a few rabbit and mole skins that he hasn't made into clothes yet, and they smell because they haven't been cured."

Aunt Julie gave me a strange look. This new information apparently confirmed her original suspicions about me, but she took it all in her stride, bless her. She dug some old clothes out of a trunk and said, "Try these and round up all of that clothing. I can have it ready by morning." We thanked her warmly, the door closed and we were alone.

"What do you think?" asked Tim.

"I think she's terrific, a real good sort," I said with genuine feeling.

However I did have the feeling that Tim had explained me to Julie as though I were an escapee from an institution for the retarded or the semi-dangerous. I knew deep down that he didn't mean it that way, just as I knew that I looked out of place in the trappings of society. The bathroom smelled of scented soap.

"What's that?" I asked, pointing to a real toilet bowl with flushing mechanism. Tim chuckled.

"You bathe first Tim. I'll follow. Take your time."

He luxuriated for forty-five minutes in a tub full of hot soapy water and came out looking shiny and smelling scented; but I still preferred his previous odour of pond water and wood smoke; and of course when his clothes were washed he'd be just about unrecognizable. Then my turn came. I washed the dirty ring around the tub that Tim had left, then allowed the hot luxury to flow in, even sneaking in some bath salts as I suspect Tim had done. I too revelled in the soap scent until I was squeaky clean. Wrapping a towel around my middle I dropped my smoky clothing in the general heap, just as Julie arrived with a basket to haul them away. We donned the ill-fitting garments she had found for us and descended to the parlour.

"I know you boys need a good feed," Julie said, smiling sweetly, "So I'm cooking something very special for dinner this evening. Something I'll bet you haven't had in a long time."

"It's ch-ch-ch-chicken, r-r-r-roast ch-ch-chicken, isn't it?" I smiled, pretending pure delight. Tim jabbed me in the ribs, flushing a little.

"Why yes, how did you guess?" she replied brightly.

"Well we sort of had ch-ch-chicken on our m-m-minds for a very special reason, Aunt... May I c-c-call you Aunt J-J-J-J-Julie?" I stuttered with deepening colour.

"Why, yes, that would be fine." And her smile seemed now to include me rather than leave me in the periphery of acceptance.

"I'll be right b-b-b-back," I said, springing up the stairs two at a time to reappear before Tim and his aunt in seconds flat, holding up our mute naked "Gift."

"We haven't cleaned her yet," explained Tim. "Just needs a touch up on the kitchen table.

"Well, what a lovely surprise, Thank you! I suppose I shouldn't ask where it came from!" She took the dubious looking gift from me and disappeared into the kitchen area, while we relaxed in the parlour; and after a short while I excused myself and went upstairs to allow Tim the opportunity of discussing more intimate family matters with his aunt. I looked at myself in the mirror wondering why I looked the way I did, and feeling it would be nice to look like anyone else but me. Sleep must have taken me while I lay back contemplating, because I was awakened by Tim looking me over as he gently roused me.

"Supper's ready," he announced. We went down together. The parlour was warm and the fire threw a friendly heat. On the dining table was roast brown chicken with stuffing, loads of beautiful vegetables, sprouts, carrots and even little baking powder biscuits. We ate off real china, patterned with tiny red roses, which set on an embroidered table cloth.

The quality of the surroundings made me blush with confusion. I felt awkward and was clumsy; Aunt Julie's kind words of acceptance only further sabotaged my mental apparatus. Oh, I enjoyed the comfort of velvety chairs, plush furniture and trappings as these the very things that had been denied me in my family's home—but sitting on a stump by a wood fire listening to the owls, or seeing the branches move with the wind would have given me that special peace of mind.

Tim darted the odd look at me during dinner. Now that he was cleaned up he was very handsome. When Julie commented on my vegetable appetite, he said, laughing, "Oh, he eats almost anything—clover, dandelions, nettles, kale, turnips, and he loves chicken."

There it was again. As though I were some sort of harmless mutation that Tim had found in the woods, something that liked to be petted once in a while. I felt odd, as if I were devastatingly close to the truth.

"W-w-w-well, w-w-when you're hungry, y-y-yes, you eat what you can g-g-get..." I trailed off stuffing more carrots into my mouth. Desserts were served; a mouth watering trifle with gobs of homemade raspberry jam, creamy custard and real Devonshire clotted cream. We ate all the trifle, then Julie served coffee and suggested that we go to the cinema.

"I have your clothes ready. They just need a touch-up with the iron," she said. "There's a good show on starting around seven. Why don't you both go? Catch a bus at the end of the block. It'll take you right there," and so it was that we saw "My Friend Flicka" with Roddy McDowell.

We returned to the house just after ten, after scouting the local girls unsuccessfully. Then saying good night we went upstairs to bed. Undressed and lying between clean cool sheets was strange indeed. We heard faint traffic noises outside on the street, and a dim yellow shaft of light from the hazy moon glowed through the small paned window. It was all so alien and comfortable that after we'd turned the light out and chatted for a while we could not sleep. We didn't have to wriggle and adjust our hips to hollows in the ground or huddle together for heat. We stared up at the ceiling. Time passed and eventually we both fell into a deep sleep without even talking about erotica –and that was quite a change!

Morning came with bright sunlight and the smell of fresh coffee mingling with that of bacon. Downstairs we heard Aunt Julie busy with breakfast. Washed up, we both looked pretty neat and presentable, except when I looked into the mirror to check myself and compared that image with how Tim looked; I was somewhat aghast.

I saw a wild type of animal in human form; it had a hunted look in its eyes, and was seeking to escape. It didn't belong. In contrast there was Tim looking very civilized with lovely gold wavy hair. He had an air of self esteem and confidence that I had never acquired, it was in the way he moved and also the way he conversed with Aunt Julie. I just wanted to flee for the shelter of the woodland and never see another Human again. It was just too painful. We descended the stairs to breakfast and set to on eggs, bacon and home baked toasted bread. Every slice was solid and overlaid with honey or thick raspberry jam.

"Well what plans do you two have?" Aunt Julie looked fondly at Tim, and then turned to address me. "I've told Tim that if he gets a job in town he can stay here." I knew she wanted Tim to stay and I also knew that I was not included job or no.

"Oh that'll be nice for Tim," I murmured gently with lowered eyes. I felt deserted, betrayed and alone again. I wanted to escape to the normalcy of flowers, foxes and my beloved rabbits. I almost wanted to opt out and go far back inside, but I didn't want to leave Tim.

"You're both welcome to stay for a few days to rest up, and when you make up your minds, well ... that's up to you..." She bustled away into the kitchen with the dirty dishes.

"Let's take a bus to the sea," I suggested. We both decided it to be a good idea. Julie packed us a lovely lunch, and gave each of us a ten shilling note. As we paused by the door to thank her, she said, "Away with you. See you tonight some time. Have fun!" We left the house but a serious mood had settled upon us. We didn't speak. The silence just seemed to continue under the small talk that came from us. Underneath, we both knew that real issues were at stake. After leaving the bus we took to the fields and across the woodland to the rocky shoreline and white-plumed waves. The smell and the crashing of the waves did wonderful things to every crevice of my mind. Tim was affected too; I could see it in his face. I also saw sadness and indecision. There were other factors to be considered too. We had both passed our British Army medicals in the conscription, first class, but we had not been called up because were already in "essential services." We walked for about a mile along the shoreline, and in a particularly deserted stretch of water, although the beach was somewhat rough even to our toughened feet we went for a swim. Afterwards we slipped on our runners and walked along the beach carrying our clothes while the sun dried us off. Then leaving the wave-lapped shore we walked inland finally settling on a grassy bank where we sat and gazed long at the distant sea, tuning into the windward gulls and nearby meadow pipits, delaying the inevitable conversation.

"Well Tim, are you going to stay," I asked, "or get a job or... or do we travel and adventure for a while yet?" I risked the last with a softer tone of voice. Tim lay back and looked up at me. I could see the conflicting emotions in his face, and came to his rescue recklessly.

"If you really want to stay, by all means stay. I'll be okay." I was unsuccessful in restraining the tremor in my voice. "I'll just knock around in the West Country, and we'll get together from time to time to see how things are working out" Time stood still. Silence reigned and wind songs caressed the waving grasses. Tim smiled.

"The Wild One will stay wild." He looked down and began plucking little blades of grass.

"Do you want to land up with some old hag?" I pursued, "A little brick council house, six kids, a dark job in a filthy factory belching death?"

"I might find work on a farm," he ventured.

"In which case you'd be staying on the farm and not with your aunt," I reasoned. "She knows of a job in the city for you, isn't that right?" I questioned with persistence.

Tim looked sideways at a ladybug on the rough grass stem beside him and teased it idly with a clover leaf till it flew away.

148

"She thinks I ought to settle down and be with her part of the family, what's left of it."

"What really counts is what you want." I ventured. "Of course we could bum around for a few more weeks and see if you still feel the same way?" I asked, but I could tell by the little shiver of loneliness that passed through me that shadows of decision had already clouded our companionship.

Conversation sparkled that evening. Aunt Julie was especially attentive to me, which made it difficult for me to speak. I loved her for the warmth she extended, but my stammer increased with the upcoming departure. I didn't blame Tim; this was a real home with real love and family warmth. I knew they had discussed plans already, and the next day after a hearty breakfast, Tim and I talked and silence settled between us. I cast long glances at this friend I'd come to know and to love as we walked across the meadow beyond the churchyard. His future was assured. He was excited about the new horizons opening up for him. I burned into my memory the sound of his voice, the essence of his spirit when he smiled, and the essential presence that made him uniquely Tim.

"What will you do?" he asked.

"Oh, live around in the hills, poach rabbits and pheasants, write poetry, and ..." I caught him looking directly at me with such concerned affection in his manner that it blurred my vision.

"Race you to the gate," I challenged. Tim was slightly ahead of me.

We tramped the lush meadows and explored the woodland that whole sun drenched golden buttercup afternoon, revealing thoughts to each other that we had never before expressed, and reached an understanding in our relationship, so that it became relaxed and beautiful in our shared tranquility. We alternated between sitting "au naturel" on a wide flat rock in the creek under the overhanging trees, and wading back and forth pursuing scarlet sticklebacks, and slowly the afternoon became a timeless kind of adventure. We ran through the blossoming meadowsweet to dry off and it showered us in a golden fog of pollen, which clung to our damp bodies like yellow talcum. The captivating scent permeated our magic flight, and as always, I glowed with elation as I studied Tim's lissom form in motion. Then – it being hot we returned to lie in the creek.

As usual, if we were fed and rested, we discussed sex – because sex was inevitably uppermost in our minds. Tim looked at me intimately, and in a lowered voice asked, "When did you first give any guy a "BJ" Derek?" I stepped off the flat rock into the water, while gold reflections from the wavelets chased intricate designs over my tanned wet skin.

"I'm not sure, maybe age seven, or thereabouts, there was this kid Jason, and I also clearly remember the occasion when I *wanted* to do it, but not for the reasons that you might suppose! It was at Tower House College, which was a boarding school, and I stay over, even on weekends, because "they" (my parents) don't want any part of me. I'm wandering around alone on the lower floor when shouts and laughter of the winning soccer team are heard as they come in to shower and change. I stand watching them through the partially open door, and almost magnetically I'm drawn in. I am intrigued with them. They see me standing, rooted there. One young fellow noting the direction of my gaze as he sits there on a low bench, points to his naked tool, and the gist of what he says is, "Hey Kid! You want it?" There is general laughter among the players who stand about me. Someone says, "Get that kid out of here, what's he doing in here anyway?" But I have already approached the young blond player who first spoke to me. He has such a nice smile and very white teeth. He makes me feel good and my eyes are riveted to his stirring member. "Hey kid!" he jests. "Want to get your mouth around it?" There are roars of laughter as the team watches me in disbelief as to what I may do next. Meantime, HE looks at me with such peculiar intensity, that I approach and kneel between his fuzzy golden legs with my hands on his thighs; ready for whatever he might want me to do.

"Cripes! I think he knows how to do it," exclaims the golden boy in amazement.

Yes – I do know what to do Tim – *it's not new to me;* and after all the writhing and moaning is over, *I hope he will hold me in his arms for a while, just hold me...hold me until. . . until what Tim?* By this time several of the players were seriously disgusted with me. I felt their disapproval as I'm bodily picked up and dropped a little roughly into the corridor. The door locks behind me. I even tried the door several times over a short period of time while I listen to their chatter, but it was quite unyielding. As I leave, I hear their ribald laughter. Tim, I kept picturing the golden boy, I wish it had been *he* who had picked me up; his warm touch was so good.

I like being touched Tim! It pumps new life into me, and I feel good. Of course they reported the whole matter to the Head Master, and from then on I was banned from the lower levels of the college." I sat next to Tim on the flat rock again.

Tim whistled. He'd been chuckling and throwing rocks across the water, and with a delighted smile he said, "Sounds to me like you really wanted it in a big way!"

"No Tim, it's not like that. Try to think of it this way –what does a little seven year old kid know? He can't have any idea of what he's involved in, or why they want him to do it! He has no idea about sexual touching, urges and pressures. That little kid is absolutely innocent! *His only need and greatest hunger – is to be held and loved, to be touched, comforted and caressed by someone who cares about him!* Not brutalized and sodomized."

We left it at that, and returned quietly to the house with the first star, and Aunt Julie served us cocoa in the kitchen. She asked few questions. Our faces told all, as they still held a touch of creek magic. At least Tim's did. But as the reality of man's values penetrated our world in these pleasant civilized surroundings, that magic slowly faded. We slept well that night aware of each other's presence, our togetherness and our separateness. Next morning Tim gifted me his own blanket so that I would be warmer at night. I kissed Aunt Julie goodbye and with the ten shilling note that she had given me, started for the bus with Tim. I avoided looking at him; maybe I was letting him down. Hurry, bus, hurry! I pleaded mentally.

"There's the bus now!" Tim said and we started to run. I turned, shook his hand, and thanked him. We grinned broadly at each other.

"Bye for now Tim, take care!" I panted. Inside the bus I walked the gauntlet of eyes all the way to the rear with blurred sight and wet cheeks.

I returned to my parent's home a little southwest of London, thinking to stay for a few days while I got reoriented. I'd not been back there for several months, and at mid-summer I'd already turned eighteen. I knocked and entered.

SHE looked up. "What do you want? And what train are you catching back to wherever it is you came from?"

"I'll be leaving tomorrow," I assured her.

"Well, it can't be too soon for me!" She spat out the words with some venom.

I rummaged around, packed up some poems I had written about seven years earlier, and a lengthy essay which I had entitled "The Illusion of civilization"; it described in a few pages my whole impression of life as it is lived on this planet, a stark tomorrow in a hostile land. The next morning I cashed my one and only National Savings bond, trudged to the railroad station and bought a ticket back to beautiful Devonshire. It was here that I found work on the lovely farm by the estuary only a mile from the sea. This became home; it was the farm where I had the lamb frolics with little Barry. I stayed for a whole year. It was the longest period that I had ever worked on one farm. Now—soon to be twenty—a whole new life beckoned in Canada.

It was some months later before I was able to take one last trip from the Devon farm to see Tim who was now in Gloucestershire. I arrived late and had to walk miles, until I was near dropping from exhaustion, I found a hay-stack alongside the road, and crept stealthily to the sleep of the deadly tired. At sun-up I made my way to Tim's address and learned he would be home from work about 5:00pm. I spent time exploring around town. and later, wanting to surprise him, I waited outside the brick walled factory where he worked. It belched its death fumes over the town. At five the factory work-ers poured out onto the streets, some walking or running, some pushing bicycles, talking in groups of twos and threes. My heart leapt—there was Tim. He saw me right away and walked over with his Raleigh bike. He was almost a stranger. Of course he was dirty from working all day, but it was more that that; his handsome face was white and thin, the golden glow had left him. We shook hands. He smiled but without any deep communication. There was a veil between us; and it quickly became evident that I provided a somewhat inconvenient situation as he had a special date that night with his girl – Susan, and was unwilling to change it. He said he would, but I would not hear of it and this made him happy. We moved in two different worlds. I felt childish beside him. He was a lot older, much more mature, and his worldliness baffled my simpler mind. This was a new Tim, a Tim captured by the killing web of man's values. Had my Blood Brother died, and who was this I spoke with? We went to his place and after we had both

152

cleaned up, he opened beer and we filled each other in on the intervening time span. Talk flowed and we joked around, finally planning to meet the following afternoon on his day off. Then we talked some more about his girl.

"I'm going to marry Susan sometime," he said seriously, and he seemed to express the warmth and love that he had for her, "She's fantastic, wait till you see her!" and then looking a little embarrassed at leaving me, we parted, with him giving me a smile that was almost like the Tim of old times. I gathered he was bringing her back to his room that night, so that left me with no other option, than to walk a couple of miles out into farm country and hole up with the rats in some barn. Nothing new there!

I had failed to locate a barn and had to sleep under a haystack. When I rose to the bright new day, I explored a strip of woodland and found a small pond where I completed my morning ablutions, and headed back into town. I idled time away by browsing in a few used book stores, had a steak and kidney pie for lunch, and then hustled over to Tim's place. There, I met Susan, dark eyed, beautiful, a wonderful girl with soft curling brown hair, and a laughing voice.

"Sue, I'd like you to meet Derek, I told you about him ..." She flashed me a warm smile.

"Hello! I've heard so much about you." she smiled. Then she was gone with a quick kiss on Tim's lips, and all that remained was a faint scent of lily of the valley. Tim and I took the bus for some miles, and then climbed high into the green hills till we could see the River Severn snaking across the country toward shadowed distant places. Larks trilled high in the blue. I talked. Tim spoke occasionally but the old feelings would not surface. There was no more soul magic. Tim was greatly preoccupied, but he attempted some enthusiasm, and even endeavoured to placate and humour me as I tried to reach him. Where are you, Tim? Have you fallen totally asleep in the stream of time... how can I wake you? We came to a pool in the hills that reminded me of the forget-me-not pool and others. "Hey Tim, let's have a dip!" I smiled up at him.

He felt the water with his hand. "Too cold Derek, we'll get pneumonia or something."

"No way!" I said, "Just watch this." And seconds later I was stripped and splashing about in the water, swimming in the deeper parts. Tim waited on the mossy bank watching me with the familiar grin on his face. I came ashore, flicking off water and sat beside him like a sleek wet otter. He grinned more broadly.

"Still nothin' but a wild critter! I don't reckon you're gonna change much. Maybe Canada will be big enough to tame your wildness."

"Either that," I replied, "or I'll go so completely wild that I'll disappear into the bush and they'll never see me again."

All at once I sensed he wanted to be rid of me. I had sabotaged his schedule; he was really pining for Susan. I was glad for him and I told him so as I dressed. He lit a cigarette, offered me one which I refused. This was a different Tim. Only once on the way back down the trail did he almost become the Tim of old. Like a sleeper aroused, he woke out of his living dream and for a few beautiful moments he was beside me. Then he disappeared into smoky maturity and worldly responsibility. The gulf had opened between us, our continents divided, and oceans flowed in. Farewell Tim.

And so where am *I*, where are *WE*, Derek? Well, I told myself, it's the 14th of May, 1948, and *I'm still lying on my bunk on the S.S. Ascania.* We continued to lean over on a sand bank in the St. Lawrence River waiting for the tide, the tugs, and time, to float us into this new wilderness world of our choice. At eventide we steamed away into dusky starlight. We had hoped to leave the Preacher on the sand bank, but he stayed—lurking in the shadows of consciousness.

"Hey Derek!" I spoke out loud. "What an outfit!—You, Me, the Preacher, the Movie Director and all of Canada. Maybe the new world will never be quite the same again!"

Chapter Thirteen

The Canadian National Railway's powerful steam locomotive chuffed its way across Canada day by day. We passed through portions of civilization but for the main part it was endless lake country, rocky barrens, green beautiful forests and eventually the flat plains of the endless prairie country of Saskatchewan. Never had I seen so few trees, nor had I quite envisioned the bare flat land that raced by. After a change of trains in Regina; it was the tall red grain elevators of Balcarras that announced the close of a great journey. Canadian National had done its part, now it was up to *US*.

As I left the train a slight tanned blue eyed man approached me and introduced himself as Harold. He was my new employer. We dropped into a restaurant on the dusty main street for a milkshake and a banana split, both of which were quite alien refreshment items and meant nothing to me. Later, due to the unaccustomed richness of the food, they were hurriedly splatted over the fleeing grasshoppers on the road to the farm. It was just too soon a change from wild rabbits to ice cream.

"H-h-how did you know it was me when the train came in?" I had stammered. Harold threw an amused look at the Chinese restaurateur. "Hey Charlie," he wants to know how I identified him at the railroad station!" –they both found the question highly amusing. On my part I had checked the highly polished mirror behind the counter and saw a long haired youth with a ruddy complexion attired in formal British Harris Tweed. Later Harold said, "You just looked like a bloody Englishman!"

The farm that was to be my new home stretched almost as far as the eye could see. I quickly learned that a section of land was 640 acres, and which farmers had several sections. I learned that the jogs in the road were meridian correction lines made necessary by the curvature of the earth's surface. There was much to learn in this new world. Down in the coulees among the mewing catbirds we had a tiny creek and about a mile further out a larger one with a small but deep swimming hole which would often accept my hot limbs with a cooling embrace under that burning Saskatchewan sky. The whole country was gloriously exciting, wildly beautiful and pulsating with life crying out to be lived to the hilt. Late spring and seeding time merged into equally busy harvest time. The typical farm year was made up of mending fences, rounding up the Angus cattle, and shooting the nests of giant black hornets off the low branches of the black poplars from a supposed safe distance and other dangerous pastimes. When I arrived, the weather being hot, mosquitoes were in biting good form and they raised huge lumps on me until some immunity set in.

Every dew-laden dawn filled Little Boy Wild with awe. As his body moved through time his consciousness floated on a sea of ecstasy. The Humans around us apparently did not feel this or if they did they never spoke of it. But for Wild Boy, these rainbows of rapture were surely a reflection of Eden! It was in the flight of the falcon, in the flash of the bluebird on the wing, in the lope of the coyotes, the frisk of gophers, and in the nodding of nestled yellow violets among the grasses.

However the dragon of stuttering was always lurking. I avoided speaking unless I was sure that something intelligible and free of stammering could be produced. Sometimes I would stare at the sugar across the table, half expecting it to be willed to me of its own accord. I would have felt a lot better if I could have yelled "Fuck the sugar!" because in angry articulation I was always word perfect. Hardly recommended by Emily Post in any circle, but it would have been better than "W-w-w-w-would you p-p-p-please p-p-pass the sh-sh-sh-sugar!"

In August I celebrated my twenty first birthday by using part of my one hundred dollars a month summer salary, for necessary work boots and clothing. If I were careful the balance would buy a radio. Often as I laboured around the farm I'd seen the dust trails from automobiles speeding along the distant highway to Regina, the capital city, and now at last, I too was really going there. It was a disappointingly tame day in that hot city, but I did acquire my very own portable radio! Now at last I'd have access to music, news, drama and information that had been denied me for so long. I bore my treasure lovingly back to the farm house and spent long periods of time lost in this new delight; lost in warm thrilling sounds of great musical works by masters I'd never heard of before.

One night in the spring of 1949, almost on the first anniversary of my arrival in Canada, I tuned into a drama from CJGX Yorkton, Saskatchewan, the local radio station some sixty miles distant. The play I tuned into was gripping, but the actor's intonations were not true. They sounded as if they were reading their lines from a book they had never seen before. At the conclusion the announcer asked the listeners to mail their comments and criticisms to the station. Not realizing that anything on radio could be other than professional, I immediately wrote to them saying that I could do a better job any day. After all, had I not been judged a good actor in a school drama festival not so very long ago? And was our play not adjudicated to be the best in the festival? Or was I really that good? The truth was that as long as I acted I was almost word perfect, but as myself I was a failure.

I went back to my school in England to review some of those school days in quest of some sort of truth. This is Class "C," above us in ranking are classes "B" and "A". We are the misfits in "C," and we just don't have it in us to move any higher. We are trapped in "C", and it seems they store us here season after season. For us class "C" means the "Culls," the ultimate write-offs.

Freddy Todd is a fellow "cull." He is a pigeon toed boy who also is hated and badly beaten by his parents. He sits off to the right and in front of me at school. Whenever he turns to catch my glance—I see his face so darkly shadowed with sadness and despair—that even I recoil from him. He wants to run away with me—to the north of England. He speaks of Sheffield and other heavily industrialized cities, but I shudder as I envision the mills, the belching filth and dirty smoke stacks, and I'm unable to persuade him in joining me to flee to the hills and forest land of the West Country. Also—I do not want to run away with one like myself. I need a laughing level headed friend who can indoctrinate me into normalcy—whatever that is. But this is not possible—as one such as this has no need to run away. I study these types of boys in my class, they are mostly average looking—but they have a quality I cannot quite grasp. That is, they appear to be real —they have substance, they are tangible—*whereas I am unreal. I'm not really here. I have no actual substance. It's as though I only think*

I'm here—although I can feel my body—I don't count, I'm simply not in existence in their world. Life goes by, but I'm not a part of it.

I long to share their carefree laughter but I know they have largely written me off. In gym class they all leap over the gym horse with ease—many with flowing grace —whereas I run up at full speed, and just when I am supposed to leap—I see myself standing by this tall leather contraption, grimacing in fear, pain, and frustration. I fully intend to leap over—but my body refuses to respond—the mark of the ultimate 'cull'. I retreat. Even when I'm told to repeat the performance again and again—I fail, and it only serves to reinforce the stigma of the reject. Freddy did finally flee northward and I never heard anything about him ever again.

There is also Audrey, a friend now, but she was not always so friendly. She's an epileptic and I used to put on a great show in the playground for the kids by imitating her. I'd stagger, roll my eyes wildly and foam saliva all down my chin while making weird hissing noises. Then I'd topple and fall while foaming at the mouth and thrashing my legs. My act draws crowds and if the turf is soft, I bang my head on the ground for an encore. I am famous for this and kids say "Hey Derek, pull a fit!" and I do my full repertoire of seizures while they scream with delight.

Everyone keeps an eye out for Audrey as a matter of common decency but one day she is present. When my performance is over she leaves, crying. Afterwards she talks to me about it. I believe she and her parents know that I am as sick in my psyche as she is unavoidably sick in her brain. I like her a lot after this chat, and we develop closeness. Once she had me give a command epileptic performance for her friend, but I have made a pact never to do it for the other kids anymore. When they ask, I just give a crazed look with my tongue out and eyes rolling just enough to capture their laughter and approval.

I love music, but not the teacher. Most of my classmates know what the music lesson is about, but I have difficulty. It is the bright students who raise their hands that get help. I fall farther and farther behind. I don't see how the notes relate to music. I look at them in different ways and suddenly they form the more familiar faces of my tadpoles, except their tails go straight up and down, and they seem to live in different levels in the water. Some of them are in clumps. They have names but I don't know which is which, and finally I head for the real tadpoles inside my head. We talk. They tell me about the water beetles and the dragon fly larvae, and other water mysteries.

"Derek, are you with us?" Sudden fright returns me to my desk.

"Y-y-y-yes, sir!"

"Tell us Derek, we'd like to know, just what were you thinking about? Music perchance?

"N-n-n-n-n-o sir. I was watching the t-t-t-tad-poles, sir." The class murmurs in merriment. This is going to be entertaining. It usually is when I'm around.

"And what makes you think of tadpoles Derek?"

"It's the n-n-notes, sir. They all have t-t-t-tails and they swim about, sir ..."

"Oh! Derek, so now we know," he comments with sarcasm, "You believe this to be a natural history lesson! Do you plan on joining us for the music lesson now?" The master is already somewhat annoyed, but the laughter of my class mates tempts his ire further. He turns on them glaring and then pounds on me again.

"Another thing Derek, why do you keep raising the lid of your desk?"

"It's to g-g-g-get air, sir."

"You need the air that is inside your desk?"

"N-n-n-no, sir," I mumble. "It's for my hedgehog."

"It's what?" He yells.

"He says it's for his hedgehog sir," pipes up the curly headed kid next to me. "Ee's got a fuckin' 'edge'og in 'is desk, 'e 'as!"

"Jesus!" says another.

Now the teacher is standing directly beside my desk, tapping a ruler in his hand.

"And how did a hedgehog get into your desk Derek?"

"H-h-h-he's a f-f-friend, sir." I now raise the lid top of my desk and there is little Hedgy. Immediately he curls up into a tight ball. I have just one quick flash of his black eyes and they tell me everything.

"Sir ... he's scared of you, sir. He's h-h-h-hiding."

"I can see that. And what is that lump in your mathematics book?" I get redder. Math has always been a write off subject for me.

"Open it up!" he demands. I open the book and there is a heap of muddy worms freshly caught that morning.

"It's his f-f-f-food, sir. H-h-h-he eats worms, sir."

"I'm sure he does ... Derek, I'm going to make an example of you. Come to the front. I'm waiting Derek."

"Yes sir." He stands with cane in hand, making little swishing noises with it and I hold out my left hand to receive the punishment. When lunchtime comes I carry Hedgy to the far end of the grounds, and place him deep into the underbrush. I tell him I'll return after class... but I already know he'll never wait for me.

It is my acting in our drama festival play, "The Patchwork Quilt" that makes me a firm part of the class, especially when we are adjudicated as the best in the festival over several competing schools and win the coveted drama cup. I play the part of a young bridegroom. Joyce, my bride, a stunning blond beauty, greatly contributes to the smoothing of my speech flow. It is the comfort and understanding in her eyes that pulls me through. *On stage I act and speak a part; off stage I'm Little Boy Wild, and I still stutter.*

My world is a study of animals, insects, birds, astronomy, earthquakes, reptiles and botany. I read everything on them that I can lay hands on in our library. My classmates now call me the "professor". They don't understand my marks in math—three to nine points out of a hundred—but they do know my knowledge of woodland and field lore is without parallel in our school.

Back in Canada, after mailing the fateful letter to the radio station, I thought nothing more of it. Certainly I did not anticipate a reply. Then on a bright day in August, right in the middle of the harvest, with stoking and combining running at full speed, I came in for supper to find a message awaiting me. I was to call a Mr. Bill Liska at CJGX Yorkton. I was baffled as I knew no one outside the Lemberg farming community, but with pounding heart I called the strange number.

"Derek," Liska said, "We have an opening at CJGX for an announcer. Would you consider auditioning?" I was too stunned to answer.

He continued, "I've got the letter here that you wrote us last spring. You say you've had acting experience ..."

"Yes," I said, my voice finally activated, "but I'm not a professional actor. I'm just an immigrant farm worker!"

"Well, you think about it," he said.

I ate supper greatly preoccupied, but the next day I was back at the harvest struggles. Several days later Liska called me again. Would I come to Yorkton for an audition? Again I refused on the grounds of my personal limitations, this despite that fact that I had read and re-read the Readers' Digest's condensed version of J. Clement Stone's TNT—The Power within You—how to "image" the desire of a reality and claim your wish. But

I had begun to speculate on whether it was possible for me to become a radio announcer. I, who could not even ask for the cr-cr-cr-cream for my c-c-c-coffee! A week later Liska called me a third time to ask if I had reconsidered his proposal. Opportunity was battering the door down!

"Yes, Bill," I heard myself say, "I'll come up on Saturday morning for an audition." There! It was arranged, even though I was badly needed on the farm to run the John Deere binder. I went out behind the barn to talk things over with the cat birds. A radio announcer in the big city! Maybe I'd have to shave, cut my hair and wear a tie? Oh, No!

With semi-permission I took the bus to Yorkton and showed up at the CJGX studios looking exactly like the long haired, frightened country kid right off the farm that I was.

Bill Liska was friendly and helpful. Apart from having a reassuring smile, he inspired confidence in a difficult situation.

"This is a microphone." He pointed to a shiny metal object in a stand on the table. "I want you to read these commercials, and this newscast," he said.

My eyes widened with fear, but evidently he put my stammering down to nervousness. He sat at the controls and the red "On Air" sign illuminated my last fear. His finger dropped to cue me.

"You're on," he mouthed silently from the control room behind the heavy glass.

Thinking of my drama days in school, I turned my attention to the gleaming inanimate microphone, and the news and commercials flowed smoothly out of me without any preparation or delay. Fifteen minutes later it was done.

161

Liska came out of the control room, smiling. "Great! You'll be all right Derek. When can you start?"

With scarcely a moment's hesitation I heard myself say conversationally, "How soon do you want me?"

"Monday morning," Liska said, "Monday will be fine."

"Okay," I replied, "I'll see you Monday."

I thought guiltily about leaving Harold and the farm in the lurch at the peak of the harvest season. Then I cast my mind over the upcoming winter. I remembered the last one, hauling hay from the haystacks for the Angus cattle across the frozen snow laden prairie at forty degrees below zero, keeping the narrow sled runners of the hay racks precisely in the same narrow snow packed trail on the return trip to the barns. The penalty for even a slight deviation, when the sled runner ran into the soft unpacked snow, was the tipping of the entire rack of hay all over the landscape, and then the reloading of the rack from square one, while breathing the billion twinkling silver ice crystals as they filtered down through the sub-zero air under that icy blue sky. I remembered the sun dogs casting their cold glare accompanying the sun in its futile rounds, and I smelled again the warm horses as they tossed their heads with impatience, anxious to get back to their cosy barn. "Oh by the way how much will I earn?" I asked as an afterthought.

"We'll start you off at one hundred a month," said Liska cheerfully.

"Fine," I answered without bothering to make financial calculations, which for some reason had always been mixed up with rabbits for me. But after I had arranged for room and board at seventy dollars a month, I realized I would be left with only thirty dollars a month for pocket money. Ah, but now I would have a nice warm studio and a new life with much to learn.

Then *we* –talked with each other. "But suppose you start stuttering on the air Derek? It is possible you know."

"I know." I sighed. "But according to the formula you have to do the thing you fear most"

"Yeah, but there are going to be thousands of people out there, you know, all the living dead you always talked about ..."

Returning to the farm at Lemberg was difficult. How could I simply announce my departure on the morrow, leaving the farm undermanned in the most crucial part of the year? Should loyalty come before opportunity? And would opportunity come again? The weekend was not pleasant. I was beset with fears, and on top of everything the farmer thought that my contract with CN Rail bound me to the job on the farm, like an indentured slave. I checked this out with the local government offices and learned that I was a free man in a free country. On Sunday I departed for Yorkton, but with deep misgivings.

Just before leaving there was time enough to visit the swimming hole and stroll the coulees. In saying goodbye to the horses I recalled following a piece of advice I'd read in a western novel. The cowboy said, "If you bite your horse on the left ear, you let him know who the boss is, and he'll never give you no more trouble."

I had come down to the horse barn one morning while the horses were feeding and picked on one that was a little cunning and rebellious. I had to harness him anyway. His head was down gathering wisps of soft hay. I leaned over him and grabbed a big firm silky ear. Without delay or comment my teeth chomped through hair, skin and all, but before I could unlatch my molars, he squealed and threw up his head with me still attached to his left ear. My one hundred and sixty pounds sailed toward the rafters like a bale of hay. I landed in the straw beside the offended animal, horse blood around my mouth. He showed the whites of his eyes, and laid his ears back. The left ear was cocked at a funny angle and as I left the stall he aimed a kick at me. A splitting headache attended me as I presided over the pre-breakfast chores and remained all day, and it seemed that my teeth were not as firm as before. I never did master that horse and he was quite leery of me from then on. It just goes to show that you can't believe all they say in the cowboy books. Farewell farm.

As the bus headed east, I cast a long look at the bustling little prairie town of Lemberg, where we used to do all our shopping. The town had its own newspaper—the LEMBERG STAR. How was it that the nice folks of Lemberg strongly suspected that it was me who snuck into the printing office last week, just before they did the final run for publication, and turned the word STAR around? That week our paper was called THE LEMBERG

RATS!* Now Derek, why in the world would they think that WE would do a thing like that?

The gophers squeaked and flipped their tails. Grain elevators came and went, farms dwindled and the great city of Yorkton appeared. The radio announcer stepped from the bus. "Well we're here!" I smiled. "Are we ready for all this new situation has to offer?" "The real question is, Derek – are they ready for *US?*"

---

* In actuality I had nothing to do with the newspaper incident.

164

Chapter Fourteen

There were very few dull moments at Radio Station CJGX, mainly due to my inexperience, but mostly because of my undeniable knack for creating difficult situations or at least being found in them; and the Movie Director had that artistic talent for painting small disasters with cutting realism. Who could forget the day when I crashed a Trans-Canada Airlines plane at the Yorkton airport? It was all done in perfect innocence with no malice aforethought or ill will intended. It happened on a typical sub-zero morning just before the eight o'clock news; the usual time for announcing the estimated times of arrival for the various transport systems.

"CPR #801 arriving on time at 9:15 a.m. Greyhound schedules are all on time even though we have blowing and drifting snow. TCA flight #701 arriving right on time at 7:55 a.m. which is right about now," I announced impersonally. "And here she comes!" At this moment to add a little excitement I brought up the sound effect disc of a plane engine droning normally on turntable #1. Then with an emotionally charged voice I said, "Is that plane all right?" And on turntable #2 up came the sound effect of a spluttering twin engine plane in deep trouble. With speed and fiendish delight, I flipped back to turntable #1 and phased in an old Heinkle 88 bomber in a power dive screaming into an irreversible crash.

"Wow!" I announced happily, "Look at that Trans-Canada Airlines plane drop in there folks! Right on her nose and right on time!" As the power dive sound effect ended, I cut back to turntable #2 with the sound of a terrible head-on auto collision between two autos with screaming rubber, rending metal, and smashing glass; there were even a few desperate human cries of pain. Then to top this whole production off—as if it needed topping—I picked up the huge Webster's Dictionary, stood on my chair and dropped the dictionary in front of the live microphone.

"Yes sir! TCA has arrived on time!"

Then thinking no more of this little stunt I proceeded with the eight o'clock news. The phones rang continuously for details of the TCA crash. Some local people who were to pick up passengers from Regina were quite emotionally overwrought, thinking the passengers had been killed. The local travel agent was somewhat upset, and in addition, TCA from Regina and Toronto checked in with us for explanations. The RCMP became involved—the start of a lengthy association, as their duties and my life seemed to run down the same track. When a Regina radio station called for details I knew I was in deep trouble.

Eleven passengers had been scheduled to catch that flight in Yorkton to fly to Winnipeg and Toronto, but only two of them would get on the plane. The others were spooked and refused to board the plane which, of course, had arrived on time, but was now in lengthy delay. Some passengers saw the affair as an ill omen and returned to their homes to reserve a flight for another day.

On top of all this, local and regional TCA officials had quite a conference with the management of CJGX, and there were rumours that the station would be sued for loss of business. Some of the spooked travellers had apparently suffered mental anguish. I never joked around in quite the same way again ..... until later that is –but that's another incident!

It was well known by then that although I was almost word perfect on the air, I still had difficulty speaking directly to the Humans whether with my own group around the radio station or people elsewhere. In the early days of my announcing career I would introduce a musical number on the air, then turn around to request a disc or some other item from a fellow announcer, and not be able to get a word out straight. I would be tied in such fits of stuttering, that it was easier and less painful for everyone—especially me—if I got up to fetch whatever I required myself.

At other times an announcer I'm working with would ask me to fetch a certain recording. He needs it right away because the platter he is playing is nearly finished. I can't locate the record in question. It isn't there. I Panic; it is an unreasoning panic and I dissolve into the mauve and green era of HER rule. *I flip out and find myself back in England.*

At age three, mauve and green are her banners of entrapment for me.

166

Our curtains, quilts and towels are the same colours. All her gowns are mauve and green too.

"Bring me the safety pins. They're on the dresser!" she calls from another room. I am trying to dress myself. It's cold. I'm tangled in my underwear. Time ticks by. The pins are not on the dresser or perhaps I just cannot see them from my height and angle. I can't see them anywhere.

"Have you got them yet? If I have to come myself..." I feel the "mauve nothing" feeling coming on. I know what is going to happen. I cannot think. Panic –I see only whirling nothingness. Do I run now?

"Where are those pins? God you're stupid! You can never find anything!" Now her voice appears in living form.

"Here they are, right on top all the time, you . . you..." she snarls. The pain arrives on time in the form of a vicious pinch that will be multi-coloured for many days. Why do I get trapped? I know I'll never find anything for anyone because as soon as they ask my mind switches to a circular track of nothingness. I can't find anything because even before I look, I feel the pressure of the trap from which only interrogation and hurt will spring. Worse still, what they ask for is never where they say it is, and it's then that the mauve dizzy feeling engulfs me.

As a small child I'm learning to disappear with regularity. It doesn't hurt when I'm not here; for this is when I run to the *"Meadows of my mind"* where they can't reach me. This is a land of beautiful color and of friends. No rabbit has ever made an unreasonable request of me, no mouse ever compressed time into pain, and no flower has ever blazed with fury. I feel only their warmth and love for me. They set me free, and I stay until I'm called forcefully back to the outside world of endurance. Perhaps it is because I retreat to my valleys of serenity so often to join my furry woodland friends that people think *"I'm not all here."*

Am I seven or eight years old? It matters little. I cross the bridge. Beneath I can see the fast green water. It frightens me. I'm out for a walk— perhaps for the whole day—alone as usual. The house with the flea-ridden bed is out of sight. This is not our regular house, I think it's a rented one and we're on holiday. I scratch. These fleas have given both my older brother and me a restless night of tossing, turning and scratching.

The sun is hot. Sparrows are chirruping. *I'm far away, deep inside myself.* Suddenly I strike an object and I gasp with hurt. I come out to see what has happened. I've walked into the radiator and gleaming grille of a parked car. I stare in fascination. Something about the polished chrome and gleaming dark hood arrests me. Two ladies are coming from the house, they chat gaily with each other and they acknowledge me. I stand rooted with a vague smile on my face. They have talked to me! They enter the car. I still cling to the shiny grille. They start the engine and I feel a paralyzing terror that I can see no way out of. The horn honks loudly and my heart pounds. If I step to the left a wheel will get me, and I can't go to the right because the other wheel awaits me. They are going to run me down. Ever so slightly the shiny grille pushes against me with an inexorable force. The ladies are no longer happy.

"Get away! Get Away!" they shout while waving their gloved hands. The engine stops. They get out.

"He's scared," says one.

"I do believe he's not all there," says the other in a disgusted tone.

"Come to the sidewalk dear." It's the tall one speaking, the one with the veil. They both smile but I am unable to move. I must be still far back inside. My legs refuse to respond. A woman reaches for me. I'm pulled to the sidewalk. I scream and run. Oh good! My legs are a part of me again. I run and run and run, till I have to stop for breath. That phrase comes back to me again and again. *"Not all there."* SHE has said it many, many times. *Not all there.... Is part of me missing?*

It's another day. I've crossed the deadly green water bridge. I've gone so far that nothing seems familiar anymore.

"W-w-where am I?" I ask a passer by. But I can't say my name. He walks on with a shrug of his shoulders. Just ahead is a bunch of kids who pick on me. This *is* my usual adventure trail.

"Hey stupid, my mum says you're weird!" a pushy youngster announces. They bar my way. I watch their antics with a vacant stare.

"Yeah," one titters, "You're Simple Simon!"

"He's a fuckin' retard! Look at him! He's bloody stupid!"

They surround me. "He's a fuckin' retard! He's a fuckin' retard!" Their chant is irritating, but maybe they are right. I'm not all here! Of course I'm not all here because part of me is someplace else where it's friendly. I'm in my rabbit place with my furry friends. We're in the green meadow lying in the long grass among the wild flowers. Their fur is soft and their ears silky to my touch.

"Rabbits just are!" I blurt out, "and ... and I just am too!"

"What the fuck is he talkin' about rabbits for?" says a kid with a North Country accent. I'm pushed. I fall and scrape a knee. All my parts are here now.

"You boys, you leave him alone. It isn't fair. You're not being very nice." The kind grownup rescues me. Voices drift by.

"They may be right. He really doesn't look all there but they don't have to be so cruel."

"Where do you live little boy?" a tall lady asks me. I come into focus from somewhere back inside my head.

"By the b-b-b-bridge with the green w-w-w-water that k-kkills you," I tell her. There are shouts of glee from the boys. She shakes her head. It's not quite the type of address she is used to dealing with. I follow the lady for safety. The trailing mobsters fall away.

They are like the crows trying to peck on a wounded one of their own tribe. I think about my poor little dead crow by the sycamore tree. First the maggots, then the beetles, and the rest of him just sort of blew away in the wind. He had fallen from a nest. We were friends for a while.

A little later I pass a house with a garden that I recognize. No, it's not the garden; it's the strange man that I recognize.

"Come with me, I've got something to show you." He smiles.

Previously he had pulled me roughly into his garden but I struggled, broke free and ran. He had that molten glittery look in his eyes just like my special tutor at college. Today I run by him. Ah, there is the bridge. Halfway across I stop to watch the gurgling green water beneath me through the metal decking. It swishes, little whirlpools form and whisper. Dirty white froth is sucked into the whirlpools to form eyes. The water's voice is low and rumbling. The eyes are smiling in a horrible way. I've drowned. My body is sucked under and borne away. That is why the eyes are smiling and the water hissing. I clear the bridge. The house is ahead. I flinch as I go by HER and run to my room and open my rabbit book. The fleas will have their supper before I have mine.

Indeed when did I not flinch? My built-in reflex is a raised left arm to ward off the blows, my head lowered to one side with rapid wincing and blinking—traits which do nothing to suggest I have normal intelligence. Any sudden movement in my vicinity will trigger this reaction. Sometimes my eyes stay closed and *I hide deep inside myself until it's all over.* This can take some time because after she has become physically tired from venting her fury, she says, "Oh you exhaust me you swine!" and turns to BROTHER with, "Here, you have a go at him! I'm tired!"

HE needs no encouragement. His punches are powerful and direct. It's useless to fight back. If I do, she forgets her exhaustion and pitches in again. I just curl up with my arms protecting my head and hide there. I have seen chickens gang up on a wounded one in this manner. The hurt one finally desists, and the aggressors pile in, pecking flesh and blood until the grey film drops over the victim's eyes. I suppose the attackers then feel they can feed without the inconvenience of resistance.

If I flinch whenever SHE passes by, and she says, "Oh, expect it, get it!" and she pinches my thin arm to the bone. "Can't have you disappointed, can we?" and she laughs at her own little joke.

"Expect it, get it! That's what I always say! In any case, I owe you one for the other day, you bloody swine!" And she pinches me again. I will have a large purple blotch on my upper arm. I maintain a collection of them in ripening sequence of colour, ranging from purple for today to the greens, yellows, and blotchy browns of previous days. As the years go by, the flinching syndrome does not leave me—nor do the bruises, they are in plentiful supply. One day in our scout troop meeting, two of the boys beckon me over to them. They are about two years older than I – about fourteen. They have observed my constant flinching. One of them suddenly moves his arm, and already I'm cowering with my arm raised defensively, while I rapidly blink and grimace in extreme fright. But I need not have feared for there was no aggression in their eyes or stance –only curiosity.

"It's okay, we're not going to hurt you," one of them says softly. They smile at me and look meaningfully at each other. They speak to me, drawing me out, and I actually managed a couple of sentences without stuttering. I emerged from my shell like the sun coming from behind a rain cloud. The scouts look at each other. "See! What did I tell you?" one said, and then I was discussed as if I were not even there. But they were kind, and whenever I met them after this, I glowed and felt accepted.

Another situation that disturbed me greatly was that while I was being taught how to tie certain knots by the scout master, he spoke to me with such patience and concern in the face of my ineptness that I shivered and shook uncontrollably. He asked if I was cold, and I truthfully answered him and said, "No." But the shakes became so violent, especially when he accidentally touched my arm, and I felt the warmth from his body, that he suggested that I lie down for a while, and that we do our knots training next week. By this time I was already dissociating and I became totally incoherent. I was red with embarrassment and shame when I went to lie on a small couch in another room of our scout hall. In the future I may have to dissociate whenever a training session come up.

At a medical examination, the doctor comments on my flinching. SHE explains that I am of a nervous disposition .... "It's his nerves, he's highly strung." A tonic is prescribed. It is called 'Parrish's Chemical Nerve Food.' SHE buys it under protest—I'm costing HER money. At times I forget to take this bright red metallic tasting compound, and SHE lays the cane about me.

"Take your nerve food you swine!" SWISH! She connects. "Take your nerve tonic now!" SWISH! I cannot pour it into the spoon under these circumstances. It spills on the floor.

"Watch it! You're wasting it—you bloody swine!" SWISH! SWISH! When the bottle is finally empty, SHE complains that I have been taking too much, and eventually decides after several bottles, that I no longer need it.

Meantime back in Yorkton at CJGX the radio announcing job was changing my life on an unprecedented rate. I was growing because people were accepting me, and fear no longer dominated my days. I even had friends—although they regarded me somewhat warily at times. When word got to England and some of my former workmates heard I was now in radio they were incredulous. I could picture them talking about me over after-noon tea .... "That Fuckin 'Orace what couldn't never say nothin' straight—'ees on the radio now!"

It took a good friend—a fellow announcer by the name of Earl LePage, a highly talented musical performer—to point out that since I was usually word perfect when speaking on the telephone or into a microphone; my hang-up had to be "people fear." This was quite a revelation to me and helped me to understand why I could talk clearly to inanimate objects and animals. The problem was, all the world was filled with people.

There were however, bad days or "down cycles"—rough days when due to pressure or emotional low spots my stuttering would creep onto the air. This was like having your familiar nightmare become a sweating, desperate reality. For a period of about a year, I resorted to Johnny Walker and a few of his friends to overcome the problem, but they only lowered my effectiveness, slurred my speech, and a number of times I had to be sobered up to hit the air waves.

The letter "C" as in "Your Community Station, CJGX Yorkton" raised trouble. That was our regular station break. It was particularly bad for me. If I ever started C-c-c-c-comm-m-munity Station, it would be the longest station break on record, so I gave the station breaks straight, just CJGX Yorkton, despite orders to the contrary. The front office didn't recognize my problem or didn't want to, and insisted on the "Community Station" terminology.

Now, according to all my positive thinking books, since the word "Community" was my nemesis, it had to be confronted or attacked sometime. *Do the thing you fear most!* I recalled that fearful command! But would I get stalled on the "C"? Or find myself high centered on the "M"? Or both? Here it comes. What makes it come? It's the inexorable big red sweep second hand of the studio clock. It pulls me forward on reluctant time wings. The hell of the next second is NOW. It screams at me, NOW! HERE! NOW!

"This is your C-cu-cu-cu-cu-m-mu-mu-mm-munity Station CJGX Yorkton!" All the cuckoos and moo-moos disported themselves on the air-waves, dancing friskily on a ruthless trail of shame, failure and pain. So great was the trauma in physical and psychic effort that time was suspended. In a flash I saw the Little Prince,* his willow slender form lying impressed in the soft desert sand—a wistful smile on his parted dead lips.

I screamed silently, "Send me your live golden anklet O Prince!" But

---

* The Little Prince – Antoine St.Exupery.

the tiny golden snake had already transmitted the Prince with deadly precision according to their pact. His liquid gold tail flicked a message of finality
–he would not ever return. Wait! Wait!! Send me too!!" But only the low
ancient stonewall remained, and it turned into a control console that demanded flawless speech. Now time was with me again, it moved forward.

"Well, you are tuned to CJGX Yorkton," I announced with ironic humour in the calm clarity of my tones, indicating that I'd not flipped out
completely during that station break. The usual shock waves followed, hot
and cold. The stabs of psychic pain were real and shocking. They left me
weak. It was almost the same kind of cold wave that sloshed over me later
on the street, when a friendly merchant laughingly asked, "Well Derek,
How is the c-c-c-ccom-m-munity Station today?" I smiled ruefully while
he slapped me on the shoulder in fun-filled healing acceptance.

*All those persons who have ever stuttered will recognise the agony
involved in these sequences!* Some days, "B" would be the real tripper.
Other days all the consonants in the alphabet were rough, particularly B C
D G K L M N P S T W. Help! What's left?

To cope with commercials I became a speed reader before speed reading was ever heard of. At a glance I would read the entire page photographi-
cally, and then scan the paragraphs and reword, re-design, and re-phrase
the entire commercial to avoid my specific consonant stumbling blocks. I
found three or four words in my vocabulary that I could unhesitatingly in-
terchange with the obstacle words. Interestingly, some of the inter-change
words began with the same obstacle consonants, but I discovered I could
deliver these perfectly because my mind was concentrating on the task at
hand—revamping the commercial—so I was not listening to myself. On
really bad days, I would deliberately block my hearing so as not to involve
myself with myself. It worked. And experience supplied expression and
tonal qualities to my voice so that it didn't sound too unnatural.

The continuity girls—copy writers, were not happy with me. All their
beautifully worded commercials would be gone like a puff of wind, as I
blithely adlibbed around the messages. Time and again they would insist
that I read exactly what they had written, but it was not always possible.

Some words like the name of a sponsor in a commercial just could not
be changed. You can't tell the listeners to buy it at Dongo's Drug Store when

it's sponsored by Baker's Drug Store! And you just don't have enough time in a thirty second station break to sell the drug store to a new owner who has a name you can say on that particular day. Baker's was a nightmare, because of the "B" and because it came in a station break between CBC's Campbell soup Mmm-Mmm-Good Show, and the Dick Haymes Show.

"Baker's Drug Store brings you the time. It's 6:15 p.m. The temperature is 35 below zero, courtesy of Baker's Drugs." There it was: twice within a few seconds, and then I'd have to give a station break—CJGX Your Community Station—flip the switch and bring in the Haymes show.

To one who stutters, to say a "B" when you have to say it, is one of the most exquisitely cruel forms of mental torture. Sometimes I'd stumble over it as (silent "B") aker's Drug Store. I even changed shifts to avoid that commercial, and several times had another announcer sit in for me on the pretext of having to go to the bathroom. To bridge the gaps and to hit certain consonants without a flaw, sometimes I would induce severe physical pain by pinching myself, or digging a small penknife into my wrist or hand. This caused hot and cold sweats, but the pain did divert my mind from the wording. With droplets of perspiration running into my eyes, and waves of trembling effort coursing through me, I would hear myself speak the words, but it was as though I were listening to someone else. Then waves of relief would wash over me when the perfect and powerful voice of the network announcer would come in on cue. And tomorrow would be another day.

Vowels were not exempt from the stuttering syndrome, with "E" at the start of a sentence possibly being the worst. Of course, there was also A, I, 0, and U left to trip over. One way that I discovered to eject these vowels—and the same went for problem consonants—was to start the sentence with very little air in my lungs, because I found I couldn't stutter if my air volume was limited. The stomach muscles have to be contracted to get enough air to commence speaking; once speech was underway, I could begin breathing normally.

Bill Walker, who was well known in radio and television circles in those days, was working with CKRM Regina, and while I briefly visited that station, he asked me to take part in a commercial they were producing. They wanted an English accent – and one walked in the door! It was a simple three line blurb that included the words "United States of America." Each time I hit it, I said USA. Four times Bill Walker, the other two announcers and I did that commercial, maybe it was five! But despite Walker's quite patient and specific instructions not to abbreviate United States of America to USA, each time I swerved aside at the last moment, like a horse refusing to jump the hurdle. It was not the "U" in United –it was the "N" that followed it. It would have come out as "U-n-n-n-nited States. The other two announcers gave me disbelieving looks each time this occurred. Bill Walker thanked me, and I'd sure they did that commercial the first time round as soon as I left the studio. How could I tell those nice fellow announcers that I couldn't say "United?" How could I ask one of them to stick a knife in me somewhere –not too deep please, but hurtful enough to divert my mind, so that I might speak calmly with perfection and clarity?

Several years later when I was a newscaster at CJOC Lethbridge, I met a very dear lady by the name of Bertha Biggs, who acted as consultant in elocution, announcing techniques and enunciation. I believe she worked with that group of affiliate stations. She interviewed the announcers individually, and asked each one to read a standard piece of prose, which she knew by heart from listening to hundreds of readings.

"Read this, will you?" she commanded with a gracious smile. I did, using my usual adlib word interchanging method.

She looked at me curiously. "Will you please read that again?" She had a lovely smile. I did her bidding. "And again, please."

Five times I read that same little piece. Each time, of course, it came out differently, but without any change in the meaning or intent or flow of the original. Miss Biggs' face was a study of discovery and amusement. Pointing a finger at me she said, "You stutter, don't you?"

I blushed deeply. This was developing into a compound situation. As long as discussion of my problem remained reasonably impersonal, devoid of specific kindness or attention, I was still on safe ground, but if she became more personal, or if she reached across and touched my hand in reassurance, it would destroy my speech ability on a grand scale.

"Y-Y-Yes!" I blurted. "D-d-d-does that mean I'm through? Am I to be f-f-f-fired?"

"Oh no, nothing like that. I think it is really marvellous that you have been able to adapt. Your vocabulary and reading ability are quite excep-

175

tional. To do what you do is unusual to say the least, but it'll remain our secret."

By this time I had become so accustomed to speaking normally on the air that it carried over into everyday life situation. Either that or I had become less scared of people. There was one thing I knew that would automatically eliminate my stuttering—anger—and it shouldn't be used on the air. I could swear flawlessly when furious. It would come out word perfect with superb enunciation, diction, inflection and intonation.

It is 11:45 a.m. It is a "Ladies Program" "Dad and the kids will be in for lunch shortly," I announce smoothly in my most mellifluous tones, "So here is some soft music to prepare lunch by, and the lovely tune—'Violetta'!"

In those days the turntables had both 78 and 33-1/3 RPMs, and as I changed the speed to 78 the clutch slipped, and the turntable began clicking at me... Teclick! Teclick! Teclick! Teclick! In a fury, I enunciated in perfect English:

"God bugger the fucking thing!"

Frantically I made efforts to get the speed of the turntable adjusted. Dead air was piling up, and dead air is a "no-no." The turntable clicked obstinately at me... Teclick!... Teclick! ...

"Fuck it!" I exploded. An announcer in the main studio, knowing that everything coming over his monitor was also going over the air, signalled frantically, pointing his finger in the direction of my microphone. Horrified, I saw that my mike switch was on. Teclick... Teclick...

"Jesus Christ!" I exclaimed, "My fuckin' mike is on!" And only then did I switch it off and finally got some soothing music flowing over the air waves on that relaxing program for ladies making lunch. This was a bad one. If the station was being monitored by the authorities at the time, it could lose its license to operate. My brain was reeling.

Later in the day, our chief engineer, a very fine fellow by the name of Dave Glass who ran a little radio repair shop below on the main street, relayed the story of a lady who had come in to pick up her radio just before lunch.

"Plug it in," she said. "I want to hear how it sounds now."

Dave plugged it into a socket. There was total silence and some strange clicking noises. They both listened intently. Then in flawless English a beautifully clear voice charged with anger announced: "Fuck it!"

The lady looked at Dave, not believing her ears.

Dave said, "Lady there's nothing wrong with that radio!" The lady turned back to the radio and stared in fascination.

"Jesus Christ! My fuckin' mike is on!" exclaimed the English accent. Dave unplugged the radio.

"Lady, it's working fine," he said. His customer looked incredulous and somewhat bewildered.

"I'm not sure about that," she told him. "What have you done to it?" She looked at the radio as if were a snake about to bite. Dave grinned, peering at her through his thick glasses.

"Take it home lady. If it swears tomorrow, bring it back in." She left with a sort of confused look in her eyes, clutching the obscene radio under her arm.

It was after pressure-type scenes like this that Little Boy Wild had to escape to the bushy areas of the surrounding prairie. He was driven to quest relief from his psychic pain, and to do this, he let the wind caress him as he ran "au naturel" among the gophers and golden orioles. This breathing would change, and his elation with life would transport him to other dimensions. For hours he would alternate between wandering among the brush, and lying beneath the trees absorbing the summer sun. Before Wild Boy returned to the Human routines, he would take a dip in a slough, talk with the frogs, and let the cool water return him to as near a "normal" reality as he was capable of. He would join the coyotes in their joyful evening chorus as the early stars appeared, and if the summer moon and warm breezes discovered him, he would lie on a grassy hill, reach up to touch the stars, and travel the galaxies in dreamy wonder.

Chapter Fifteen

My younger brother Rex arrived from England in 1950. He had been my great ally through thick and thin, and the hell of childhood. Oh! How marvellous it would be to see him again. I studied the shiny railway tracks shimmering in Melville's noon heat... soon the "King" would arrive.... *And I went back in time,* thinking about the number of times he and I had placed rocks on rails similar to these in attempts to derail the express trains from London to the West Country. We had nothing against the trains. We collected the numbers and names of the engines in our notebooks, and waved to the locomotive drivers as they raced by. It was the people in the carriages behind the engine that we wanted to shake up.

"We d-d-don't want to kill 'em, do we Rex?" Rex nodded in agreement.

"But a good d-d-d-derailing will fix 'em up!" I explain. "They shouldn't t-t-t-take t-t-t-trains for granted, anyway!"

"Maybe we should use bigger rocks," Rex suggests helpfully.

I had one of my sudden bright ideas. "Or maybe we can pull one of those levers and shunt it into that siding at seventy miles an hour! That'll fix 'em!" The levers unfortunately for our plans were locked and immovable. We pondered the problem and in the end had to be content with pelting the dining cars with rocks as they flashed by.

Now the Canadian National train was arriving. No young fiends have attacked it or tried to derail it on its long journey west. The Canadian National Rail train's brakes had become silent and the doors opened. A few people milled about, and then, there at last was Rex the King. He was still the same happy good-looking character I'd always known, and after some joyful greetings we drove through the clouds of dust to Yorkton in the car I had borrowed. Rex and I had developed a very close relationship over the

179

years. Four years younger than I, he had been the favoured son due to a car accident in which he almost lost his life; but I had in no way felt slighted by him due to the favouritism. It did not affect the depth of our friendship, Rex was just very special to us all.

Reflection on Rex and England triggered all kinds of memories, and seemed to be a part of my quest for self identity. I questioned as to why we did such destructive things to innocent people. Rex had surely always been a supportive and willing accomplice when I waged my vendettas against the highly polished doorsteps and the snooty people who took such pride in them – **but why?** One sunny day Rex and I found a sack of potatoes, they were so rotten that they were slimy to the touch. Wet and heavy, those potatoes were begging to be splatted somewhere. Our minds work as one. Right next door to where we were standing was a home where the red wax polish has produced a porch step shine of such exquisite perfection that it cries out for us to rescue it. Our eyes meet, and within seconds those spuds were pounding and mushing onto the step. We hurled about thirty of them, delighting in the squishy sounds as they splatted onto the windows and the whole front of that beautiful house, until the lady opens the front door. Then we pelt her and her hallway. But the unexpected occurs. She has two Great Danes—huge yellowish creatures with black jowls. She sets them on us. They leap the garden fence and we are captives before we have fled more than fifty paces. Amid threats and anger we are pulled by the ears onto her disgusting doorstep. The dogs growl and whine. She instructs them to guard us while she calls the police, our enemies supreme. We hear her dialling, then talking. Our world is falling apart. The end is upon us. I extend a hand to pet one of the monsters. Rex does the same. We talk to them softly. Then we edge slowly up the driveway, through the gate and walk with elaborate casualness to the tall wire fence opposite. Moments later the woman screams commands to her hounds, but we have already climbed the fence and are running across the field to the creek and beyond to safety. We have surely escaped whatever we so richly deserved! **What makes us do things like this?**

SHE, will not normally let Rex and I go out together as she thinks I'm a bad influence on him, and one day Rex let's something slip, and she knows we have been out together. All hell broke out and our Dad comes in to see what the problem is. He looks from HER to me.

"SHE won't let us go out together! That's what it's all about!"

"Who's SHE?" he demands, then answers his own question. "She is your mother and you'll call her mother!"

"I can't! SHE's S-H-E!" I scream between clenched teeth, my eyes blazing.

"You'll call her Mother!" he roars.

He picks me up like a rag doll and thrashes me. Rex is crying. Sister has disappeared. As usual the screaming and beatings will make her sick with acidosis attacks for days and days. Father drops me and I throw myself clear.

"SHE's S-HE!" I scream again and again in welted defiance. "SHE's S-H-E!" I cannot say 'mother'—the word won't form, my lips contort, and I'm as desperate as a cornered rat. Now I see the look in my father's eyes change, and I know he really means business. I am picked up and almost hurled down the passageway.

"Up to your room!" he shouts.

I disappear into my room and crawl under the covers on my bed. I reach for my favourite picture of the rabbits in their flowery meadow and walk right out of myself into their circle. I join them in morning rabbit talk and between nibbles of clover and playing games, the morning passes. Afternoon comes and goes, evening descends and I'm still with my friends. I may stay and never come back. It's the scent of wild roses that keeps me here. It's the delightful sense of play that my furry friends have, and best of all we don't fight! We live and let live. As darkness descends my rabbit friends disappear. I strain my eyes in the gloom to see them, and finally I find myself back on my bed, holding their picture.

To give Rex a job in Yorkton the two of us decided to go into the trucking business. In a most persuasive interview, we borrowed the down payment for a truck from Art Mills, the manager of CJGX. Mills was one of the true pioneers of Canadian radio and a fine gentleman. It took me several years to understand how we had been able to talk the money out of him. Only later did I realize that we hadn't. He had just wanted to help us out of the goodness of his heart. He knew what he was doing. We certainly did not. We bought a new Dodge one ton truck and built a box on it. It was decided that Rex would drive it and I would help as soon as I came off shift at the radio station each day, which really meant that trouble now had a wider range in which to operate. More things could go wrong in more places more often, and they did. We rented a very small office at the front of the York Hotel next to the Ball Taxi Company office in downtown Yorkton.

We had no place to stay so we rigged the office up with a hide-a-bed lounge which we "bought" from the Hudson's Bay Company. Wonderful people… Apart from a down payment of twenty dollars we never did pay for it. It was always something we were going to get around to and never did. On the quite infrequent occasions when we had cash, the Bay was far down on our list of priorities. We'd look at their big bustling department store and say to each other, "They can't really need our cash. They have more than enough of their own. We'll leave them for awhile." We added a telephone, a hot plate, an electric heater, and an old desk with two oak chairs. We also acquired a shiny new bucket which was placed behind the door in the corner in order that we might relieve ourselves. We were in business.

It was a wonder that we survived that first winter. We were just a couple of ignorant immigrant kids, who knew nothing about business or trucking. We were completely unprepared for the forty-five below zero weather, and we had no proper clothing, no gloves, no parkas or long-johns. Furthermore, we were also too dumb and too proud to accept the help that we so obviously needed. Dear Molly George who worked in the front office at CJGX offered us heavy overcoats, older ones in perfectly good condition which would have markedly reduced our forty-below shivering, but we were too young and immature to understand the love with which that help was proffered.

Hunger drove us to look for work. I was able to provide free commercials to Wing's Cafe around the corner in return for hot scrambled eggs, bacon, toast and coffee delivered right to the control booth of CJGX. The free commercials were of course given without station permission, but good natured Emil Yaholnitsky came through in fine style with the breakfasts as his part of the bargain.

Within two months we were in a terrible bind for a truck payment, the finance company was breathing the fires of repossession. "Pay or we will seize the unit," they said, and thus we became familiar with that mysterious figure from the world of finance—Julius Caesar – he who seizes! Whenever others were with us and we were catching up on the events of the day, Rex would say, "Julius called today. Wants us to drop in for a visit!" and I'd know it was time to get our heads together and raise some money. One day we heard that the Yorkton General Hospital was paying really good money for fresh blood—a whole twenty dollars a pint!

"That's exactly what we need!" I exclaimed to Rex. "One pint each and we'll have the truck payment!" I enthused. So we dashed to the Yorkton General to sell our life's blood, although in our weakened state, gaunt and hungry, we could ill afford to lose any. We lay back luxuriating in the big deep chairs as the attractive white-coated attendants swabbed our arms. The needle had entered my arm when Rex asked the nurse, "Is it twenty dollars or twenty-five dollars that you pay?"

"Oh," said the nurse gaily, "That was last week. That's been discontinued. It's purely on an unpaid voluntary basis now." We both jerked upright in horror. I snatched the needle out of my vein.

"Hold still!" the nurse hollered at Rex.

"No way!" I yelled, "Twenty dollars a pint or no blood!" To the utter astonishment of the nursing staff we fled the hospital and took off in the truck. I was still bleeding.

Suddenly it struck us as really funny so we stopped the truck and as was our way, hurled ourselves onto the grassy boulevard and screamed with laughter.

"No way!" Rex kept repeating as we went into fresh gales of laughter. But the dark hand of Julius was closing around our truck. In the tiny office with the heater on, we made soup over the hot plate. Most evenings, especially Friday night right up till the beer parlour closed, we'd hear the vigorous cascades of urine like small fire hoses playing on the steps leading up to our little office. Some would even climb the steps and arc their hot streams over our door. In the morning we'd slide on the yellow ice and have to chip it away with a spade. One night we opened the door, turned the light on three of them and heaved our own bucket of cold piss over them.

There was darn near a riot, what with the shouting, cursing, and fist waving by the staggering drunks.

There was a broken skylight at CJGX just above the control console and turntables. Often the heat would go off in the night for unknown reasons and I'd have to sweep snow off the console at six in the morning; and sit there in gloves and coat, trying to thaw out the frozen turntable so I could bring the station on the air with "0 Canada," on time. The anthem would come wowing in at about ten RPMs and then as the turntable thawed it ran at about sixteen RPMs, and finally it would achieve its full operating speed of 331/3 revs! No one ever complained that it sounded different.

One day I was supposed to do a special promotion for a local restaurant that was located in the Greyhound Bus Depot.

"Think up something for that deal, will you?" said management. How was that for planning? Think up something! The broadcast was due to start at 2:00 pm. and here it was 1:00 p.m. and I was still in the studio from the six o'clock morning shift.

Then an idea came to me. I had seen an egg promotion on the teletype. Some poultry farmer in eastern Canada had eaten eighteen raw eggs to promote his product, then a farmer in the Fraser Valley had eaten twenty-two, then the guy in the east had eaten twenty-seven... I would join the egg eating contest... unofficially of course. Away I dashed to the new eating establishment. At two o'clock with mike in hand I introduced the new restaurant describing its beautiful facilities and fine food. Then I announced my intention to beat the world egg eating record and began glopping down the raw eggs from a metal milk shake container with the crowd cheering.

"More! More! More!" they yelled, "You've only swallowed twenty-nine so far! More!" Glop, glop, glop...yuk! I downed thirty-eight Grade "A" large raw eggs in that nineteen minute broadcast and it became a new world record. Of course the promotion was a huge success. The station management beamed, the sponsor was thrilled. Hooray! But oh, my aching tummy! I felt thoroughly sick, and rushed off to consult the doctor across the hall from the studio. He probed with questions and cool fingers as he examined me. Finally he said, "Your stomach is somewhat distended. Do you think it is something you ate?"

"Well," I said thinking hard, "I did just eat thirty-eight Grade "A" Large raw eggs down at the bus depot ..."

He sat bolt upright. "You don't need a doctor," he exclaimed with horror. Rising swiftly he took my arm, led me to the door and pointing to the washroom at the end of the passage said, "Get in there. Put your finger down your throat and get rid of it!" The treatment worked. My egg eating escapade hit the newspapers around the world. My fame even spread to England, and I heard from a couple of the farmers I had worked for.

They were of course still wondering how Fuckin 'Orace had become an announcer, seein' as 'ow he never could get a word out straight.

A month or so after that, I was out for a walk in the early spring when ice still locked the lake in its grip, when I had a sudden urge to go for a dip. I rarely monitored sudden urges; I simply performed them since they were apparently a part of the script. I cracked a large hole in the ice and stripping in the cold wind, lowered myself into the icy depths to splash around. It felt really good, but after three or four minutes my bones begun to ache painfully. Quickly I climbed out, dressed, and headed down to the Broadway Cafe for some hot chocolate. I felt damp but good. I slid into the booth next to a couple of announcers who were down from the studio for their coffee break.

"Cripes! How come you're so wet?"

I slurped my hot chocolate. "I just had a swim or a dip anyway, in that lake at the edge of town."

"You did what?"

"I took a dip" I said. "After all spring is on the way."

They thought I was crazy of course, but they pounced upon it as a promotion. The Yorkton Enterprise reporter was called in, and despite my protests the whole group hustled me down to the lake for a repeat performance in the icy water, something I distinctly did not feel like doing at that point. Pictures were taken, and there I was grinning among the floating ice.

Of course it hit the news wires. The media headlined the story: "Zany Radio Announcer Does It Again!" and "Announcer Takes Dip in frozen lake," and so on. Once again it hit the British newspapers and confirmed the suspicions of family and friends that I was, to use the British term, a little "weird".

The guys at CJGX loved to do things on the spur of the moment. One morning Don Slade had a bright idea. "Let's interview the people on the sidewalk below. You know, real gut stuff, get the feeling of the public on the important issues of the day! Learn how they feel!"

"Great!" I said. And away I went with miles of mike cord trailing behind me. The street was almost deserted. Even at that early hour, a lone figure was approaching in a limping shuffle.

"And now for our on-the-spot broadcast in downtown Yorkton! I'll switch you over to Derek who is going to interview one of our local citizens. Derek!"

"Thanks, Don! It's a beautiful day in downtown Yorkton, only twenty below zero this morning. The sun is beginning to feel warm and even the sun dogs have disappeared today folks; and here's a fine gentleman coming toward our microphone. How are you this cool invigorating day, sir?" I passed the mike to the lips of the decrepit individual who had shuffled up to me. He raised his bleary blood-shot eyes with yellow globs of guck oozing from their corners, spat, and snarled through grizzled whiskers and yellow fangs, "Fuck off! Fuck off!"

"And that folks is the word from downtown Yorkton. Back to you Don!"

Poor Don sat frozen at the controls. Unfortunately for us, it was before the days of built-in delays and beep-beeps. Another time I interviewed a dog. Yes, a dog. It was the sole living thing on the street at that time. As it didn't say much we cranked up the volume so the listeners could hear its breathing. Then suddenly it barked twice—loudly jerking the VU meter needles on the control console so far into the red that the transmitter was nearly knocked off the air. Never a dull moment!

Lee was a good announcer dedicated to his job. I guess I was kind of envious of his professional sound and the way he approached his work. He sure tried to stage big productions like he was on Broadway. Above all he loved Pepsi. He drank Pepsi anytime, anywhere, all the time. This one evening, Lee had dressed in an immaculate white shirt, beautifully creased white pants, and his red hair was shining with a rich lustrous bloom. Seeing me enter the studio where his great news production was to take place, he greeted me warmly with accustomed exuberance.

"Greetings Gate – let's fornicate!" he rhymed with animation. We all had our silly pet sayings in those days. "Say friend," he grinned, "Run down and grab me a large Pepsi, I'm about to do the news." He flipped me a quarter, and then was lost in rapt enunciation of difficult names that he had to get his tongue around in the next fifteen minutes.

I ran down to get the Pepsi and ran straight back up without delay. In addition, with fiendish delight I shook that bottle really well. The red 'ON AIR' sign and Lee's authoritative news voice told me that all was on cue. Quietly slipping into his studio I held up the Pepsi. Lee made a sign for me to open it. With guileless countenance I questioned his request with sign language for confirmation. Again he nodded his head. So I tiptoed up to him and uncapped it. Oh! Help! Is this really happening? If I had intended to wreck this big news production, I could not have done a better job. Lee stood there before the big boom mike, while I gushed forth Pepsi like a fountain in a summer rain storm over everything. I tried to look appropriately surprised and shocked.

Had I really intended to go this far? Yes! For surely the Movie Director had achieved what he had in mind. Lee's furious face ran with Pepsi rivulets staining his immaculate whiteness. The news items he was trying to read became dark and unreadable as they blotched or simply went soggy in his hands. He attempted to correct his pace and hold composure, trying not to reveal the minor disaster via his voice to the radio audience. It was a gallant effort. I departed. Luckily it was my day off, and I escaped into the anonymity of the prairie trails far from his righteous wrath.

Some of the things that Rex and I got involved in caused ripples throughout the community and defied all our skill at explaining them away. We had taken an office over Carnduff Motors, the Mercury dealer, right next door to the Roxy Theatre, and on one extremely hot, close night, Rex and I lay naked on the floor close to the window that overlooked the street and sidewalk below. It was impossible to sleep, and we were flipping a heavy sofa seat cushion back and forth with our feet—a kind of catching, balancing game—when suddenly with a huge flip, the cushion sailed through the open window and disappeared to the street below. We lay there laughing trying to persuade each other to go down for it.

Gradually at first, and then rising in volume till it caught our attention, there came a great murmuring of disturbed voices from below. We peeked out and shock hit us. There below, surrounded by a crowd of people was a woman sitting on the sidewalk crying and holding her head. Faces were turned upward, and someone was picking up the offending seat cushion to place it on the hood of a parked car. Fingers were pointing up at our window.

"There they are!" someone shouted.

"I see them! They're up there!" roared a big farmer. All this took only a second or two. We ducked back inside.

"Where are my pants?" I whispered fiercely.

"I can't find mine either!" said Rex in a panic.

By this time fists were pounding on the door below. Shouting rose. Then Rex found his pants. The RCMP had arrived with a low wail of sirens. Their flashing red lights reflected off the dark ceiling and struck terror tremors into us.

"If they ask what happened, Rex, here's what we say; we came in late from a hauling job and were sweeping the office up. We had the seat cushions stacked on the windowsill, and the broom handle accidentally nudged one of them causing it to fall. Just stick to that story through thick and thin or they'll lynch us or something!"

Rex pulled on his pants and scampered downstairs, while I searched for my pants. I joined him about two minutes later. The Mounties were looking at the woman who was sobbing hysterically. People milled around making angry comments, despite our wide-eyed, apologetic looks of innocence.

"Get a doctor," instructed the RCMP officer.

"Yes sir." I dashed off in the truck after rescuing the offending cushion. At the doctor's house I rang the bell and waited. It was by now one o'clock in the morning. Eventually he appeared at the door, blinking at the light he had switched on for me.

"What's the problem?" he asked, hand to mouth to stifle a yawn.

"It's a woman. She's b-b-b-b-been h-h-h-hit outside the Roxy Theatre. She's crying real b-b-bad!" I was a little overcome with emotion at the whole affair.

"Hit by a car?" The doctor was wide awake now and reacting fast.

"N-n-n-n-no, sir. Ssh-sh-sh-sh-she was hit by a c-c-c-cushion! A s-s-sssofa s-s-s-s-seat fell on her from..." I looked skyward trying to estimate the vertical height from which she had received our direct hit. He got the picture.

"A cushion?" His face registered disbelief as I tried to tell him my version of the story. Finally he interrupted. "She doesn't sound too badly off, got a damn good scare probably. Tell her to take a few aspirins and see me in my office in the morning ..." Suddenly I was looking at a closed door.

I hurtled back to the scene. Only a few people remained now, grouped around the woman who still sat on the sidewalk where she had been felled. The two RCMP officers hovered over her. Chuck, the boss of the taxi company, had arrived to see if a taxi was needed; his blue eyes met mine and I got a whole raft of conversation in that one glance.

I blurted out, "The doctor ..."

"Is he coming?" asked one of the officers.

"N-n-no. He said for the lady to take an aspirin or two and see him in the m-m-m-morning." Whereupon the victim began howling once more about the pain in her neck, she was a sorry sight.

"Now," said one of the officers, turning to Rex and me, "Tell me exactly what really happened."

Rex went back over our story again with the Mounties—sticking to the plot I had made up for him—while I dashed off to get her husband. They lived behind the bakery that they operated. I hammered on the door finally getting his attention. He swung the door open.

"What is it? What do you want?"

"Oh good evening," I greeted him. "It's your wife! She g-g-g-got hh-hit..." There! It was out. The poor man was visibly shaken.

"Hit?" he yelled. "By a car or a truck?"

"Nn-n-n-nno! She got h-h-h-hit by a c-c-c- ..."

"A car?" he screamed.

"N-n-nno, a s-s-s-sofa s-s-s-eat on the h-h-head." There –I finally got it out. He regarded me without comprehension.

"Where is she?" he said at last. I told him and he dashed off in his car.

Except for the rumoured threats of us being sued for everything we didn't have, it was soon all over. The local taxi drivers insisted—knowing us—that we had deliberately bombed the woman just for the hell of it. They didn't buy our story any more than the RCMP did.

"Now tell us the real story," they said grinning. "Just how did it really happen?"

Rex and I called the victim up the next day after she'd seen the doctor and apologized, but she didn't buy our story either. The RCMP closed the book on the case in the end by telling us to keep the peace in future and patiently explaining that things like this were just not done. But of course it all depended on the Movie Director and what he wanted. *He* usually came on the scene without any advance warning.

Maybe it was the police uniforms that triggered it – but while in the middle of the current fiasco *I was flashed back to a farm scene in England* of not so long ago, where *he* had taken over. We are cleaning out the cattle stalls in the spare barns. We're a happy bunch; there is banter and light laughter as we tease each other to relieve the tedium of the job. The Italian prisoners of war who work with us speak of their women and of what they will do after the war. Outside—a buzz bomb is droning—we listen for its engine to stop, and try to calculate where it will hit. This is our favourite pastime these days. We tingle with apprehension. In my section of this barn, my fellow helper is getting carried away with a fantasy about his Rosa. He describes her dark laughing eyes, her firm breasts—his eyes are shining as though she were right here. He almost sees her approach as she greets him once again in his beloved Napoli.

At that moment for some unknown reason, I tease him beyond the accepted bounds for the situation, and the provocative things I say—absolutely appall me—*but it isn't me that is saying them.* Although it is my voice, it is in fact the Movie Director—and I retreat as he rolls his cameras. Rosa's lover throws his pitchfork down and chases me. I trip and fall in the straw—I am laughing uncontrollably—but he is not. He lies heavily on me pinning my arms in grips of steel. Now he kisses my face, eyes, my lips and neck. Next he bites my shoulders and for the first time I really feel his strength. I, a strong eighteen year old am held powerless. I stop laughing. This is no tender sweet experimentation of adolescent youth—this is very different. I cannot move. The shoulder straps of my overalls have already slipped off in the initial struggle, and now with one hand he rips my shirt right off—it's almost in two. I see the buttons fly and feel the material tearing like tissue paper. I push against him ineffectually and then desist —because I'm *disappearing...* His wiry chin stubble prickles as he bites my nipples and I'm slippery with his saliva. Now it's as though *I see myself* lying almost naked in the straw, my scared face is white beneath its tan. He turns me—and once again I feel my college tutor... and others, and I disappear inside myself.

There are muffled shouts—urgent commands. Faces come into focus as I'm hauled to my feet. One of the younger Prisoners of War brushes the straw from my body, and helps me tie my clothes together with binder twine. It works. I'm quite scared and I cannot talk—his attention to me, his caring looks and touch—paralyze me, and I cannot meet his eyes. It's me—Derek!—*I'm back*. I'd like to cry, but eighteen year olds don't cry. I'd like to hug the young man who rescued me—have him hold me in his arms for a while—but eighteen year old males don't do these things. What do they do? They stare ahead with unseeing eyes and heave the bales of straw. I can only hope the overflow of tears will not escape and betray me. Later my attacker apologizes. I understand his motivation and the pressure of his sexual needs—yet although the whole affair was a violation—I feel no anger—amazingly, I hope he is not angry with me. He explains that he was carried away, that my youthful attractiveness overcame him. His friends apologize for him also, and transfer him to another work crew. Over the next few days—I still cannot seem to meet the eyes of my fellow workers and I know this disturbs them. Eventually one of the older P.O.W.'s puts his arm around my shoulders; and this pains me to the point of dissociation. Gently he explains the whole matter to me, and how he'd heard it was partially my fault. I feel strange, a little disoriented, and I hope his arm around me and the caring warmth of his body, and the tone of his voice, will last forever, whether I'm *here* or not. It seemed that whenever the Movie Director had completed his sequences, he left, and I came off the stage to be incoherent ME. I never did report the incident, as the P.O.W. would have been in deep trouble, and I could never have stuttered my explanation to those investigating into any form that they would comprehend.

I left the wartime memories behind, and came back to the prairies in the current *"now"* of Yorkton. Throughout this period of escapades in the lack lustre trucking business, Little Boy Wild took off on spiritual quests in long remote walks across the prairies. *He was driven to this, and these changes in his identity were quite beyond his comprehension.* The silence of prairie breezes and their companionship, the hot sun and the springy turf would cause him to leap and run swiftly like a deer, with all the strength and joy of living. Gophers would sit up and watch as we leapt over their holes, while those immediately in front whistled and squeaked, waving farewell with short yellow tails. In these walks we'd review our problems and gain perspective. The Movie Director never came to these meetings, only appearing in order to direct certain scenes, which contained danger, illegalities, fast action and reckless abandon.

Back at the trucking office there were people and problems. They embraced a different value system than mine, and it was money that determined their thoughts and actions. It was not a prime motivator for me, as I lived in other worlds which had much more to offer; and which I sensed, even while being dragged into the whirlpool of materialism, were more real than the apparent real world all about me.

The office next door to ours was rented to an architect who did a considerable amount of drafting, so he required peace and quiet. He was middle aged, an affable type with infinite patience. A number of times, he would pop his head around the door and say, "Boys? Boys, a little quieter, please?" And smiling, he'd leave.

He was referring to the banging and sharp knocks on his wall that came from our scrapping and wrestling while we waited around the office for calls to come in on our dispatch hook-up. Meanwhile, across the road in the CPR parking lot, our trucks lazed in the sun accruing interest and overdue payments. One peaceful afternoon Rex and I and our part time helper were wrestling when, suddenly Rex flipped me, and I catapulted across the width of the room with such force, that when I hit the plaster board partition that separated us from the architect's office, I went right through it and landed underneath the architect's drawing board. I crawled out from among his many rolled up plans to meet his angry face.

"Well, well," he said, "So, this time you finally made it all the way through! I've been expecting this!" He headed for the door. "That's it! That's it!' and he stormed away, leaving me among the plasterboard wreckage. I looked under the drawing board through the gaping hole right into our own office to find two bright-eyed, grinning red faces peering at me. They were only slightly tinged with apprehension. The Movie Director had completed his sequence, and disappeared.

"You all right?" enquired Rex.

"Yeah I'm okay, but I expect some action soon. I bet we're told to get out forthwith!"

I crawled back through the hole and we all collapsed into a damp, sweating, heaving, laughing heap of total irresponsibility. Almost hysterical, tears streamed down our faces.

"That's it! That's it!" I mimicked the hapless architect, and away we went into paroxysms of helpless laughter. I will never forget that poor innocent man's expression as I looked up at him from beneath his drawing board. He was really too nice a person to have been subjected to that ordeal, and for a twenty-two-year old I should have known better. As predicted a short time later we were formally requested to repair the damages and vacate the premises by the weekend. To this we agreed and shook hands on it.

"I'm sorry boys," said our landlord, "but it has gone too far this time. It just isn't done, you know, it just isn't done."

Somehow those words had a familiar ring to them. If I could only get the director to change the script or my role in it, everything would be fine, but he was adamant, smiling vague encouragement from the background of my consciousness. So we cleared all our junk out, had the office wall repaired by a contracting company and the room professionally redecorated. As a final touch we cleaned and waxed the floor to a rich red glow of shining perfection. This was achieved in the polishing stage by using each other as polishers. We would alternate, one picking up the other's legs like a wheelbarrow. The polishing one would pack a pile of rags under his chest, so that as he was whirled around and rushed up and down, the floor received a beautiful shine. In our enthusiasm however, my head struck the new plasterboard as I swirled by.

"Stop!" I yelled at Rex. "Let's quit while we're ahead!" And we did.

Chapter Sixteen

My continued quest for myself always leads me back in time. Even though I'm in my early twenties and learning much in Canada; in quiet times my thoughts always go back to the way I was emotionally conditioned as a child. *I have come to recognise that the real me is Little Boy Wild*; whom I much later learned was *identified by the term the "REAL SELF."* This is the Wild Boy who lives with the animals and communes with the cosmos, a spiritual creature of innocence and remarkable beauty. Always his greatest need was to be loved and held, and to be able to love and to hold, without blacking out or dissociating to the point of psychosis. *His "UNREAL SELF" we learned,* was the self that had to carry on, thus enabling life to go forward; *THIS SELF handled matters* of education, finance and the things the Humans do. As for the Movie Director and the Preacher, We still haven't figured them out yet! *A part of Wild Boy's mental development goes back to age twelve.* We're in the middle of the German Blitz, and our front door has been blown open so many times it doesn't close properly any more. Shrapnel from exploded shells fall like steel rain—a tinkling melody on the tiled roofs. Far and wide, searchlights scan the night skies. We listen to the endless throb of enemy bombers; we recognise the note of their engines only too well. We have gone to bed in the house tonight. The Anderson steel bomb shelter in the back yard contains a foot of water and is a very last resort for us, but I've placed my caged white mice in there on a ledge for safety. There has been a lull in the activity. The all-clear has sounded. We sleep again. Now the temporary quiet is shattered with the pounding of anti-aircraft guns. Already bombs are screaming earthward. Belatedly the air raid sirens raise the ghostly wail that prickles the hair on my neck. Explosions rock the house and our entire block. We run from our rooms in order to go to the ground floor where we will get some protection under the dining room table which is quite substantial and may hold up under fall of debris if the house gets other than a direct hit. SHE is at the head of the stairs. I'm trying to put my underpants on. Sister stands frozen in fear, not for herself, but for me. Even as the bombs scream down, she is unable to move. She is helpless while she witnesses the hell within our house.

"Look at that bloody swine trying to get dressed!" she snarls, and swishes the cane about me with unparalleled viciousness. I can't get my leg into the pant hole. I fall into a naked cowering heap protecting my head, each blow a scarlet flash that will match the welt it raises.

Blat! Blat! Blat Blat! The anti-aircraft guns bark. Our windows rattle and shake. *SHE* stands on the stairs swishing her cane, narrowing our chances of survival as we scuttle past her and hurtle toward some form of shelter downstairs. She is the creator of pain and hell inside our home; while outside, the enemy have that mandate. We lie on blankets under the dining table where I writhe in hot scarlet agony. The scream of falling bombs is relentless. The German aircraft are painting the destruction of London with huge flaming brushes. For me it's the same old story; they get you inside, they get you outside, they get you coming, they get you going. There is no escape from the torment and the pain, except in the secret meadows of my mind. Oh God, this one can't miss! It has to hit us... Our Father who art in heaven, hallowed be thy name... Wwhhmmmp! It missed... Wwwhmmmp! there's another... Thy will be done on earth as it is in heaven ... Crash! Blam! Blam! Blam! Blam! the guns shake our foundations... The bombs whistle and scream like demons escaping from hell... Give us this day our daily ... Bbwwhmmmp! Bbwwommmp!... The others have been clinging to each other in a heap. I have to stay apart because my own pain is aflame to the touch of even a blanket, and I mustn't cry aloud or, even now, further lashings will occur. In these moments when death is almost certain, SHE flings herself over the others to protect them. We are pounded all night, but in the light of morning the throb of enemy engines has left the sky. The all-clear sirens sound a tentative and unsure single note in the distance. Others copy it. Now ours sounds. SHE crawls out and we follow. Already SHE has her cane standing by.

It's time to go to school again, if it is still standing, and we won't know that until we arrive. Our classes in any case, will be held in the underground shelters as surprise daytime attacks are common now. Month after month, day after day as the blitz continues, we have the full reality upon us that tomorrow may never come. Any moment of any day can be our last. Land mines sail down on silken parachutes in the moonlight to level half a city block, red tracer bullets thread the night skies.

My school friends and I dare each other to run across the humps in the fields and roadways where time bombs are cordoned off. We climb over the ropes and play king-of-the-castle. We cross our fingers that the bomb is a dud, and the longer we stay on top of the mound, the higher in esteem we are held by the others in our group. These delayed action bombs usually detonate within twelve hours of falling, some wait a whole day and others never explode at all. We're not the only kids that play this dangerous game: a boy was killed last week about a mile from here. He stayed too long. Over on the hill are fresh flowers marking the grassy mounds of new graves where my school chums lie in their final resting places. Trauma counselling had yet to be invented, and in any case it would not apply to me – because I'm not really here anyway.

There is another empty seat in our class today. Occasionally my eyes wander to the vacant chair and I see all the animated beauty of boyhood, the sparkling eyes, the infectious smile, the careless grace of limbs in motion. All are lost beneath the wet sod. But I find solace and delight in the new weeds and vegetation, the tiny blue Birdseye flowers that grow back over the ugly bomb scars. Never have the woodlands beckoned with such soothing allure. I clasp the bluebells in joy! Life! Life! Here is the creek. There is the crimson-throated emerald stickleback; he knows nothing of death from the sky. Hello squirrels! Hi chaffinches! Hello yellowhammers!

The yellowhammers are singing their traditional song: "A little bit of bread and no cheeeeze! A little bit of bread and no cheeeeze" I go to school. For me there is neither bread nor cheese, and perhaps only a small bottle of milk. There is little money at our home these days. Occasionally another kid will share a sandwich with me if he is full.

"Are you not eating today, Derek?"

"No sir. I'm n-n-n-not h-h-h-hungry s-s-sir!" I blush with guilt and shame. I cannot fool my classmates; they can see my eyes fastened on their food with the longing of the hungry. They know I don't have any lunch. Sometimes there is a bottle of milk left over but I cannot pay for it.

The teacher asks, "Who wants milk? There's just one left."

One of the boys pays for it—a penny—and gives it to me.

"Th-th-thank you." I hold my eyes down as the others in the class watch me, and I drain the bottle as though it has no bottom.

There is a school medical today. The doctor and the nurse line us up—boys only in this room—and we are inspected for fleas and lice. Next we are "examined"—a traumatic experience for me. Most of the other boy's testicles are becoming heavy and more fully descended. Some even have a little pubic hair, and all of them seem to have penises that are fatter and longer than mine.

"Hey! Derek!" calls a tall kid, you ain't never gonna screw nothin' with that! He points and grins hugely.

I blush. "Fuck you!" I retort.

For answer he cups his hands around his precious organs, and gently squeezes them till his face lights up, and with half closed eyes, his lips part to reveal his yellow teeth. He may be horny, but he looks like a roughed up sewer rat to me.

"Derek don't have much of a cock, and he ain't got no balls at all!" says another kid with a snicker.

"Yeah, t'ain't no bigger than one of 'is caterpillars," quips another.

I am, for my age, underdeveloped. I suppose since my brain is artificially retarded, my sex organs are too. The latter are probably very wise, for if they did put in an appearance they would be beaten, so they play it safe and stay out of sight.

I am prodded and poked and listened to by the doctor. He feels around my scrotum, frowns makes a note and then dismisses me coldly as though I'm a factory reject. I'm a reject all right! He doesn't have to impress that on me. I dress and flee to the playground. It's all over—I have no fleas, no lice, and no balls!

But my eyes have to be tested again; it has been decided that I may need a change of lenses. SHE has greeted the doctor and now I'm in his hands. The tests commence. A metal frame is up against my head and the doctor instructs me to tell him when a red dot appears and on which side it is.

"It's on the left, now the right, still on the right, it's left now...

SHE cuts in. "Make up your mind! First you say it's left and then you say it's on the right! Which side is it on?" She has not understood the ongoing process or its methodology.

The doctor, ignoring her outburst asks, "Where is it now?"

"It's on the right."

"You don't know your left from your right! When are you going to make up your mind? I didn't bring you here for this!"

Softly the doctor asks me, "Where is the red spot now?" I see it clearly on the left, but I say "Right," and point with my left hand. He moves the red dot on my left eye. "Are you sure it's on the right?"

"Yes," I confirm with considerable fear. I feel his rising temper and impatience now, but I must keep HER happy and that requires the opposite of what the doctor wants. I get my usual dizzy sensation. It's an unsolvable problem and I'm split in two by fear. Now a third element enters: if I give incorrect information to the doctor, it will affect the prescription he gives me for glasses. I will not be able to see.

"All right you may both sit down now."

We can ill afford to replace these glasses if they have the wrong formula. There is no help and I disappear inside for a while. I see my friend the brown mouse. He has long whiskers and his eyes are full of things to do. I touch his exquisitely formed ears and gently smooth his velvet fur...

SHE cuffs me on the ear. "You're not even listening to me, you bloody swine! Can't you do anything right?" Mechanically I follow her into the street, but I escape almost immediately into my own land again. The brown mouse tells me that tomorrow is another day.

My brother Rex, his friends and I play war games; we are bombers.

"Target in sight!" I call. I'm the bomber squadron leader. We are Heinkle bombers, our arms are spread and we are loaded with rocks. Two nights ago several homes in our area were destroyed, and others badly damaged with most of the windows blown out. Now our bomber crews have to complete the job—especially as one home has a large greenhouse. We run across the pasture next to the target, leap over a horse's head and neck that's been completely blown from its body. Those eyes! My God, that's the soft velvet bluish nose I stroked but yesterday by the gate! And there is the foal!

He used to run before the wind, his little tail flying. We stop and peer at him, his milky white teeth are showing and his clouded eyes have a look of pathetic innocence. Although the dew has hardly left the grass, the first flies are out and they run over the masses of congealed blood.

We arise to the task at hand. It doesn't matter anyway—death will rain on all of us again tonight. Everything gets destroyed. Animals are blown apart in the fields, some cows are bloated and others are matted with gore, their insides lying twisted and raw on the grass. The crows are feeding on them. They pull pieces of intestines out but cannot break them off. The magpies have picked out the eyes before sun-up. I think they eat the eyes first because they don't want to be watched by the victim while they eat the rest of him. Nine of us are in formation as we reach the green house.

"Bombs away!" I shout in exhilaration, and in we go. We take out every remaining pane of glass, and the tinkling of their falling mixed with the vicious crack of rocks hitting wood is pure music to my ears. Now we reload. This is the house where the lady heard the strange whistling noise, and as no alert had been sounded, went out-side to see what it was. She was blown to pieces. Now we are reloaded and attack the house. It still has a few windows with unbroken glass left on one side. A head appears from an upper window. A man shouts. We did not anticipate this, but we are already committed. We aim directly at his window, and just as he pushes the window frame down to latch it, the glass explodes around him. He gives a hoarse type of scream, and now we bolt up the road. I stop for a brief moment to talk to the little dead foal and to caress his soft brown ear. Tears well up within me, and then I join the others.

Now the lust for destruction is fully upon me, and I stride with reckless glee and seek another target. There it is! A home with five quarts of milk in glass bottles standing tall and white on a red polished door-step—everyone has a red polished doorstep!—And I see nine pins. A straight concrete path leads to the front door-step: I see a bowling lane! The door opens, a woman appears in her night gown, and even as she stoops to pick up the milk, a large boulder is already rumbling down that lane. It has a deep ominous note, and on hearing it she looks up. STRIKE! Oh, the beauty of exploding milk and glass! The fragments seem to be frozen in space, even as they fly about her horrified and incredulous face. She screams. The whole doorstep and hallway is a flood of milk and splintered glass. We laugh so much that it saps our energy, and we can barely run all the rest of the way to school.

We are the bombers and *we're having fun, or is it excitement? Or what is that release I feel after the deed is done? Is it because it helps me to BE? Does this terrible destruction enable me to FEEL?* All these scenes unfold in startling clarity in a *slow motion* world. The business of finding fresh milk bottle pins all set up for our bowling becomes a new sport. We find different ways of going to school, just to look for new lanes, because they've begun snatching the milk into their houses before we get there. One lady has just picked up her quart milk bottle. She turns, pauses, and looks fully at me. I feel deprived and cheated—no time or point in rolling a rock—I'll go direct. What flawless precision! CRASH! She is left open-mouthed holding the top of her milk bottle. Then come the slow motion sequences; time slows down—first she is scared, her eyes widen, now she drops the neck of the bottle into the milky mess at her feet, now she is angry, and WE laugh at her as we take to our wings, and time speeds up again.

"Derek, were you throwing that rock at the woman or the milk bottle?"

"The bottle, of course," I replied to whoever from within me was asking the question.

"But she was holding it. Isn't that the same as aiming at her?" I spoke out loud.

"No, because there was not time, and it was a crack job of hitting a specialized target. I would never aim to hit her."

"But suppose you had hit her in the face?"

"That couldn't happen. Of course, if she had moved .... But they never move. They are almost stopped, you know, because everything goes super slow ..."

After a while we have to desist because too many people know me by sight. There are the bombs by night, and me by day, *and the destruction I wreak gives me the feeling of power, of asserting myself as a real life creature, before I disappear inside.*

Now I see a house that I hate, or is it the people? *And why?* It has the usual highly polished doorstep and beyond the oaken door is a shiny waxed hallway. Right where the passageway turns is a full length plate glass mirror. I can see all this from the sidewalk. A tall privet hedge hides me. I can hear the people—THEM—clinking tea cups and chattering, laughing. I select a huge rounded boulder, and down the pathway it rumbles. Its note changes as it jumps and bounds over the lip of the tile doorstep and continues down the passage inside the house. Something about that shiny oak floor is just too, too perfect. *Now they will feel my rock, like an extension of me,* and they will understand the lie that they live… CRASH! The huge splintering explosion of shattering plate glass fills me with something like rapture – like listening to the Warsaw Concerto….. .

I'm in my slow motion mode now… moonlight… bombers… love… yearning… hopelessness… dead foals… the concerto rises… Terrible screams pierce the hot afternoon. They see me, and I watch their faces fill with shock and horror—with recognition of me –they now know me by sight –I must escape –now!

I run swiftly to a field, clamber over the fence and race for the creek. The melody repeats itself and I hear it playing until the Hawthorne boughs conceal me. No matter what happens during the frightening nights, by day the sun still shines, and the chaffinches call. I strip and the cool water embraces me. Cold water is the only embrace I ever receive. Overhead the skylarks sing as they always have. They know nothing of plate glass and destruction. Gradually the disturbed feeling ebbs from me.

On the lush green bank I lie and recall the concerto of another day. I see the young pianist in the apple orchard. He is in formal attire. A grand piano stands on the grass under the trees and as I join the crowd, the musician smiles at me. I watch him with a strange intensity. It's the Warsaw Concerto and I am on each note. I rise in rapture and cascade through the rippling magic of his long fingers. He feels my searching and I am wholly captured in his melody and he plays my soul through his; and there are just the apple blossoms, the green leaves, and his youthful beauty pouring out the life force of his being. I am playing… we both are playing….Other faces turn to look at me following his gaze, and then it is ending, it is over. They surge forward to congratulate him as he rises. His eyes meet mine but the crowd surrounds him. I skip away through the enchanted orchard, taking his music with me.

A yellow wagtail flashes his plumage at the creek edge. I lie still among the soft grass and buttercups, watching the changing light patterns on the shadow-dappled waters. The wagtail is incredibly beautiful at this close range. I feel that I belong in his world. I would never harm him. But things of beauty in my other world connected with the Humans I reach out to destroy. *Why do I feel so alive when destructive things happen? Why the wild elation as I watch myself in action?*

Now as I follow the creek riding the concerto in my mind, I see a brown water vole.

"Hi Voley!" I call. "How are you today?" He drops a leaf on which he was nibbling and submerges his fur into the ripples. I climb up the steep bank to the road and the bridge. I'm almost home. Sometimes I wish I were a water vole or a yellow wagtail.

For there are some moments that should stay blanked out forever—but unbidden, they surface from the hidden pool of hurt to the light of understanding. They say Dad will be home tonight. Every other two to three weeks or so, he drops in, and when he does, the pressure is off. I escape to the real fields and woodland—they are, after all —my only sanity. But tonight my father is happy jovial and inebriated. The storm hits with predictable suddenness. We hear the usual terrible screaming accusations and fighting from below, and it alarms us all. SHE hurls pots and pans—he roars at her—china crashes into the pandemonium. For one nine year old tomorrow will be a cruel, cruel day.

For some reason unfathomable to me, SHE moves my sister and me from bed to bed and room to room at least once a night—I think this happens when my father is home —SHE is like a cat moving her young from one den to another. She carries my sister—I don't get carried—a snarl suffices to move me, and I land up sleeping with my father. At least he is friendly, but my relationship with him is one of awe and fear. His giant hand and arm encircle my small frame as he engulfs me, breathing the foul alcohol smell on me. He usually falls asleep quickly and I try to escape his clutch and the excessive heat which builds up. I cannot sleep till I wiggle free and sometimes I'm recaptured just as the fresh air hits my face. But tonight he is different... like my private tutor in college; this has not happened before...

"No Dad! No!" I whine plaintively—"It won't go in. It's too big, you're hurting me!" I am tearful. Its length is then placed between my thighs, and I disappear until the strange wet pulsations flood me.

"She'll be furious—she'll say I wet the bed! I'll tell HER!" I panic. I do not want to recall what is said, but it subsides me, only to surface later as an echo ...I'll kill you... I'll kill you... Tomorrow he will go, and SHE will cloud my hours.

Chapter Seventeen

Six months after Rex and I had started up our trucking enterprise in Yorkton, we had somehow arrived at the brilliant economic decision that we needed another truck. We had no recognizable cash flow from the Dodge, but we became convinced that if we had a larger truck available it would equate with larger assignments. So we bought a big red two-ton Chevy and had a large flat deck built on it. Again it was financed this time through GMAC; but since we couldn't afford two sets of license plates, we ran both trucks on the set we had bought for the Dodge. One plate went on the front of the Chevy and the other on the back of the Dodge, and then we'd switch them around. Sometimes though, we would get mixed up and park them side by side, each with its single plate on the front bearing their identical numbers.

The local RCMP would say, "Boys, do you have to park 'em side by side like that?" They knew what we were doing, but they never insisted on us correcting the situation and even tipped us off when the highways traffic inspector was in town.

"Keep 'em out of sight for a few days boys, will you?" We did.

About this time we won a contract with His Majesty's Post Office Department to pick up the mail twice daily from the red postal boxes all over Yorkton and deliver it to the post office. This was not exactly a "win," as we had not the remotest concept of cost analysis and hadn't a clue in the world as to what we were doing. We rose early in the morning for the mail run because each box had to be cleared at the time marked on it. Sometimes if the snow was too deep or we were in too much of a hurry we'd leave a box a day or two to make it worthwhile. A couple of times we dropped one of the box keys into a snow bank and never found it again. At other times the boxes would not open no matter how we wiggled the keys. Probably there was too much ice in the locks, and we'd never heard of methyl hydrate. So one day we shocked the Post Master by arriving back at the Post Office with five of the mailboxes that wouldn't open, piled on the back of the truck. The entire department was thrown into an anxiety crisis at such sacrilege. The Post Master looked extraordinarily grim.

"Never in the history of the Yorkton Post Office has any contractor done this!"

He waved an arm at our uprooted mailboxes. "It just isn't done, it just isn't done!" Shaking his head, he walked away. After emptying the boxes we loaded them back on the truck, and in order to avoid panic in the community, hustled them back to their accustomed places. We envisioned regular mailers staring blankly at the emptied spaces so recently occupied by those red symbols of authority and security. How could they ever trust the Post Office again? Each day after a hard day's work of hauling sundry items around town, we took the heavy canvas mail bags into our office. Before folding them neatly for the next day's rounds, I would shake each bag vigorously to make sure there were no letters stuck inside. One evening as I shook a particular bag, a whole packet of mail that had been trapped in a corner flipped out, hit the wall behind the door and fell with a solid splash into our piss bucket which was one quarter full.

Rex and I looked at each other in horror, and then curled up with laughter. Before we could recover and rescue that bunch of mail, the phone rang.

"Yes sir! We'll be right there," I said. "Quick Rex let's go! It's a job! We can make enough money to buy supper!" So off we went in the truck and the mail never crossed our minds again until we returned from the job.

"Oh God!" I exclaimed," "Rex the f-f-f-fuckin' mail, it's... its f-f-frozen solid!"

Sure enough those fat envelopes had frozen standing vertically just as they had fallen into the piss bucket. I could make out that most of them were destined for General Motors Acceptance Corporation in Regina, and most of it came from S & H Motors Limited of Yorkton, the local Chevy dealer. There was other mail of a private nature as well. We tried to release them gently, but they tended to tear as the yellow ice was quite solid.

"Put it on the hot plate Rex," I instructed. "That'll do it."

Rex placed the bucket on the burner and clicked it on. Just then the phone rang. It was an immediate job, groceries to be delivered. With nary a glance at the red glow beneath the frozen mail bucket we left the hot plate on and away we went again.

We just plumb forgot about it. We weren't gone long, but on our return when we opened the office door, a cloud of pissy steam assailed our nostrils.

"Oh, Lord!" I exclaimed, "The fuckin' mail… it's… it's c-c-ccooked!"

We turned the hot plate off and examined the damage. What was left was a thick packet of finance contracts and cheques, for amounts varying from $675 to $2700. They were a pulpy, mashed, stinking mess. How could we explain this to the Post Master?

Or, how could we go to the local Chevy dealer and after a few niceties, thwaap that soggy pulp in front of him and explain ourselves?

"Sir…" we would say, "First we froze your cheques and contracts in a bucket of piss, then we boiled them in the same aromatic liquid… and … and here are the remains. Perhaps you might care to rewrite them before we pop them into the mail?"

On top of that, the dealership was miffed that we had bought the new unit in Regina and not from them in our home town of Yorkton. So it was a "lose-lose" situation. We were splitting our sides with hilarity, but the cold hard image of prison cell bars slowly penetrated our consciousness. We were now appalled. There was of course only one thing to do. Having thoroughly dried it out we drove that mail to a remote spot, lit a good fire, and burnt every shred of cheque and contract, and pulverized the black ash until nothing remained. I told Rex that the mail had been the victim of an Act of God and we went our way with clear consciences. After that whenever Rex and I saw someone putting mail trustingly into a box, we'd look at each other and howl.

"If they only knew, they'd have a conniption fit" I said to Rex excitedly. "Just supposing an Act of God grabs their mail and boils it in a bucket of piss? You know he does move in mysterious ways!"

Some days we'd start off on our mail run and find we'd forgotten the mail bags. Then we'd just throw the mail in through the open window of the truck where it would pile up on the floor, slide under the seat and eventually overflow around the gas and clutch pedals where it got soggy and somewhat discoloured with mud and oil. We'd arrive at the post office, open the door, and the mail would cascade partially onto the loading dock, but mostly onto the ground. The helpers would rush about, grabbing boxes, and we'd pick the letters up by the armful, crushed, creased, many with smeared ink, and heave them into the boxes. Naturally some that slipped under the truck seat were late being processed. We found some Christmas mail wedged under the seat when we cleaned the cab the following summer. Not that mail delivery has improved much today, but at least in those days the post office had a valid excuse for damaged and delayed mail—us!

Reliance Transfer cheques were distrusted. They all knew we struggled along; but one day with sufficient funds on hand, we issued a cheque to cover service work on the big two-ton Chevy at the G.M. dealer. When we dropped over to pick up the unit our cheque was rejected and I said, "Well we'll take the truck anyway, as far as we are concerned, the cheque is legal tender, and more than enough money is on deposit in that account to cover it."

The accountant smiled with a somewhat smug, superior air, as though about to spring a trap—which he did, except he didn't know how to trap a wolverine. He held our truck keys up, and they glinted like irresistible bait under the naked bulb—I'm afraid that won't be possible as we have your keys!" His eyes shone with triumph from behind his glassed-in box as he sprang the trap... and all this over twelve dollars!!

I looked him in the eye and holding up our spare keys said, "With us—ALL things are possible, and we are leaving, here is your cheque."

As we headed for our unit he rushed out shouting, "Don't open that door!" Mechanics heads went up, and an electric atmosphere charged the whole place with disturbing currents. "Jump in Rex!" I commanded—he got the message and leaped up quickly locking the door when he was in.

"Open that door!" I shouted to the mechanics with superb angry resonance that made sparrows fly around in the rafters. "We're comin' through—NOW!" I locked myself in as a mechanic sprang up on the running board. By this time the general manager and president were in the shop. I backed the unit up in a business-like manner, then slamming her into bull low, leaning on the horn, I powered forward at that wide over head door. The big red Chevy would have her first demolition job. The wolverine with bared fangs was going to bust the trap. Somehow they sensed that I was coming through, and they also knew the cost of that big overhead door. Mechanics scattered—people shouted —"He won't stop, he's coming through—Holy Fuck!!"

"Open up, open up, quick!" the manager yelled. The door was rising—hardly fast enough—we just cleared it by scraping the clearance lights on the cab as we shot into the street. We were fortunate indeed that no vehicles or pedestrians were passing at the time. "Wow," said Rex, "You really were going to demolish that door."

I was still steaming, "You're damn right; no fuckin' weasel-faced accountant is going to stop me. He tried to trap us! The SOB!" I exploded with unaccustomed fury. Later on I went into the local card and gift shop and found an ideal, colourful card that said, "What's all this fuss and feathers about?—Let's make up," and it pictured two roosters surrounded by feathers. I couldn't find one depicting a huge broken overhead door, and that was that.

Their cheque went through okay and later on, two weeks down the road I called for our other set of keys. Everyone was most polite smiling and respectful, but I still didn't have the heart to tell them about their General Motors mail, and what we did with it that time—they'd never understand. It just isn't done!!

One fine summer evening while we were hauling coal, Rex leaned on his shovel and said casually, "Derek, aren't you reading the ten o'clock news tonight?"

"My God!" I yelled, remembering that only a new trainee was on the control console. "I forgot!" Hurtling into a truck, I screamed off to the CJGX studio. It was 9:55pm when I leaped into the teletype room. I grabbed a huge roll of news off the teletype machine, chopped it up into sheets in sequence of importance, and stepped into the studio in the nick of time, much to the relief of my young associate at the console.

In beautifully enunciated tones, I launched into the news. All was well... or was it? Whereas the main studio was normally dark and empty, tonight it was brilliantly lit and filled with people. Our station manager was escorting a little guided tour through the mysteries of radio and its workings. I saw their shocked faces and pointing fingers, and I dared not meet the manager's eyes. Only my reflection in the control room window came back to me with any force, and I could see that only the whites of my eyes and the white tips of my teeth showed through the thick black coal dust. I could see little pink rivulets of sweat beginning to slide down the sides of my jaws as I suppressed a huge urge to laugh, and plunged on into the national news.

"You see, it's not always like this," I explained lamely to the visitors afterwards. "It's just that… that ... well, tonight ..."

"Yes Derek, we understand," the manager interjected smoothly and diverted the visitors away from me. Upon reflection I decided that they were really fortunate as at least I had my pants on. Most things seemed to happen to me when I had no clothes on at all, so this was a refreshing change.

One day while the old Chevy truck was still hauling coal, the newer two-ton Chevy had been hauling sugar. Then Zap! Right out of the blue, along came a call from the Swift Canadian Company.

"We'd like to try out your service."

"When would you like us to start? I asked.

"Right away and if you work out okay we'll give you the contract on a permanent basis." Wow! Hauling beef for Swift Canadian! We'd be in the big time, a steady account, a regular cheque, we'd eat, buy warm gloves, pay for our gas.

"Yes sir. We'll be right over," I said with confidence and trying to sound like an effective executive. As I replaced the phone on the hook Rex said, "And just how in hell are we going to do that with one unit on coal and one on sugar, and only one part time helper apart from you and me?"

"Leave it to me!" I commanded. "You go haul sugar. Leave the beef to me!" And away I went, feet fairly flying down the steps and up the street.

"Okay Derek you've got to round up a truck in five minutes and start hauling meat. How are you going to do it?" I always spoke out loud to myself. 'Well good old brain maybe I can pull it off!'

"How?"

"Well okay creative artist and movie maker what do I do now?"

But I needn't have worried. The Movie Director already had the cameras rolling. The Ford dealer was two blocks up the street. I ran the first block and a half, then slowed up to catch my breath, and then slowly, thoughtfully and with great nonchalance, as if I had all the time in the world, entered the truck lot. I worked my way over to the truck of my choice, kicked its tires—the supreme test for any vehicle—and studied its long, flat wood deck. It was exactly what I needed. I peered underneath, and when I emerged there was a bright faced smiling salesman.

"You like her, eh?" He grinned broadly. "She's real good. Here, let me start her up for you." We raised the hood and peered with knowing intelligence at the oil soaked motor as it shook and coughed on its mountings.

"Mmm-hmm," I murmured.

"Why don't you take her round the block? Try her out? You're Reliance Transfer aren't you?"

I nodded. "Okay I'll give her a try," I said with super causal tones. "She might fit in with what we need right now." Of course I meant *right now!* I climbed in and within moments was hurtling—we never drove a truck anywhere, we hurtled—I was hurtling up to Swift Canadian's plant. No plates, no insurance, just guts and hope. Swift's manager was impressed with our promptness.

"Sure didn't take you long to get here." he commented.

The voice in my head said, "Oh God if you only knew!"

They loaded the unit up with beef and pork carcasses, and after picking up my bills of lading, away I went in high spirits to make deliveries. I rationalized that the Ford dealer would want me to give his truck a good workout under actual working conditions. Then in fairly busy traffic in downtown Yorkton where road paving was not quite complete, I drove over a manhole cover that was sticking up five inches above the surrounding gravel. There was a splintering crash and an awful dragging sound. Horns honked, brakes squealed, a woman in the car next to me screamed. I jammed on the brakes and stepped down. Unbeknownst to me the flat deck had not been bolted down to the truck frame, and when I hit the manhole cover that flat wood deck just simply flipped off the frame and now there was meat everywhere!

The woman beside me in the opposing lane was sitting behind her wheel, weeping, a huge side of beef lying across the hood of her green Chevy and the windshield was smeared with white beef fat. She was trying to say something to me, but it went right by me. Beef and pork was scattered across the intersection.

I ran to a phone booth to call Rex at the sugar warehouse. "Rex! Drop everything! Quick!"

"What's up?" he asked in alarm.

"I got fuckin' beef all over the street!"

"Where are you?" He sounded a little panicked.

"I'm downtown! You'll know where to find me when you see all the confusion down here!"

Meanwhile the RCMP had arrived to divert traffic. They were wearing discreet grins. "Boys, how do you do it?" They gestured in helplessness.

"I don't know officer, it just happens," I said. My mind flashed back to Tim saying, "The same types of things will keep on happening to you, but on a bigger scale unless you change..."

In order to reload, everything that was still on the deck had to be removed, so that the deck could be replaced on the frame. When Rex arrived we got to work unloading the rest of the meat, then we put the flat deck squarely back on the frame and sweated those beef carcasses and sides of pork back onto it. The RCMP went on their way and traffic resumed its normal flow.

"Rex, we can't deliver the beef looking like this!" There were chips of tar and gravel encrusted in the white beef fat. "They'll see it!"

Since our office had no water supply and we still had no home base—because we slept when and where we could—we had nowhere to wash the meat off. What to do?

"I know," I cried, "Let's take it down to York Lake!" It was already 4:00 p.m. Poor Rex's head was spinning.

"Where'd you get this truck? Won't they want it back! I got a half loaded sugar truck I have to finish up!" he exclaimed.

"To hell with the sugar!" I yelled. "Let's go!"

We drove the four miles to the lake on a dusty gravel road, taking deep potholes cautiously, while I filled Rex in on what had transpired. Whipping the truck around by the edge of the lake I backed her up to the water. Almost at the edge one wheel hit a large rock and the whole shebang—deck, meat and all—flipped up neatly and unloaded itself among the thistles, grass and rocks, with about half a dozen meat slabs falling with huge splashes directly into the water. We climbed out and surveyed the damage.

"Well..." I said, "Might as well go to work. A quick wash down and she'll be as good as new. We may as well strip off to stay cool. I need a swim anyway."

So, naked as we were born, we scrubbed, washed and struggled with those greasy beef sides. They did not come clean. The tar coated gravel chips had to be picked out with a screw driver—a long, long process.

"We're getting nowhere fast," Rex despaired, sizing the situation up quite accurately. Then suddenly he yelled, "Cripes!" and pointed.

"What?" I exclaimed in alarm. I followed his finger. The beef had a green film on it! We'd failed to notice the green algae in the water, and now in addition to tar, gravel, dust, thistle prickles, grass blades and sand, there was an awful green algae film to contend with. In naked wrath we wrestled and swore under the hot sun, slippery with beef fat, weak from hunger, and aware of disaster coming up on three fronts; a deserted half loaded sugar truck, a truck we had borrowed and not returned, and a load of pork and beef surrounding us in appalling state and already attracting flies.

"Let's have a little rest and think this thing through," suggested Rex, relaxing on a chunk of pork half in and half out of the water. I subsided in straddled fashion over a side of beef at the water's edge. It was good to rest and the sun was hot. The meat was quite yielding, slippery and warm. We relaxed. I suppose it was inevitable—and certainly quite beyond our control, but just then our joy sticks rose to the occasion with throbbing hurt—standing up to complain of recent neglect. At the same time a guy in a blue Ford drove up and stepped out. He surveyed the scene with a most peculiar expression on his face. His mouth opened, but he just couldn't seem to find anything to say. His eyes were large with amazement. For there we sat with powerful erections, primed for action, looking up at him with innocent inquiring expressions.

Finally he found his voice. "How come you guys are runnin' around naked?" he asked. I tried to formulate a logical, plausible explanation. It refused to come.

"Well, it's like this…" said Rex. "Oh fuck! What do you think we're doing." he lashed out with a tinge of anger that dropped his penis to half mast.

"Well I'm sure it ain't very sanitary to sit with your bare arses on that meat like that," said the blue Ford guy. We pursued him up the slope as he made for his car, raining rocks on his departing form. He left in a spray of gravel and we hurled a few more rocks after his car for good measure.

Catching my breath, I turned to look at my brother. "How come you're runnin' around naked?" I asked him. It was all that was needed to bring our spirits back up. It triggered gales of laughter that left us helpless and at the mercy of the flies.

"Maybe the merchants won't mind," I rationalized. "They cut the fat off anyway." We reloaded the whole mess—algae, thistles and all—to complete our deliveries around town. We dare not even hope for the Swift contract now. How could we explain what could possibly happen to a load of meat between point A and point B to make it look the way it did right now? As expected, complaints about the condition of the meat poured into Swift Canadian, and finally they called us.

"Just a moment," said Rex, "I'll let you talk to the manager." And with that he passed the phone to me with a delighted grin.

It seems that the Swift Canadian people understood about the gravel, as word had travelled, but where, they wanted to know, did the green algae come from in downtown Yorkton?"

"Well, sir, it's hard to explain," I said. "It may take time…" And it did.

I returned the truck to the Ford dealer who had already put the whole matter into the hands of the RCMP. But they had assured him that they doubted that our intention was to steal the truck. Later we were called to the RCMP station to explain. They had also received a vague report about two young men committing perverted acts with huge slabs of beef down at York Lake. The Mounties on duty already knew us, and as our explanation like others in the past was related with such forthrightness and honesty, they were overcome with hysterical laughter.

"Look you guys, get out of here! And keep out of trouble will you, at least until next time?" Looking back I think we must have made their day at times. I wondered what they put in their reports.

Somehow the whole affair with Swift blew over, and we even got a trickle of business from them on a regular basis. But it came to an end one day when they asked us to haul turkeys in from the surrounding district to their plant in Melville. On the first trip I went with the buyer; we loaded the turkeys and returned to the plant. All went well.

However, Swift had no idea of the license plate problem that this turkey haul entailed for us. We had only local plates for in-city deliveries, and we required different plates to haul machinery, and still different ones to haul farm produce to the city from country points. As much of our work was done at night, we used to cruise the beer parlours and check the trucks parked outside. We knew certain truckers would never miss their plates overnight, as we also knew who they were shacking up with, and when they would get going in the morning. On some occasions when we returned from a run, the truck we had borrowed the plates from had gone; then we simply left them on the ground in the snow where the truck had been parked. Obviously, they had just "fallen off."

On our last trip for Swift Canadian we rounded up a license plate in record time off a unit in the Pepsi Cola yard. It was forty below. We swept into the countryside through the bitterly cold night with the Northern Lights casting their flickering patterns across the skies for hundreds of miles, while we raced from farm to farm collecting the turkeys. When we were fully loaded we hurtled through the night to unload at the Swift plant in Melville. We had made it in record time.

The man came out to inspect the cargo. It was very quiet in the back. "They ain't making much noise," he said. "Are they all right?" His voice rose with concern.

"Sure," I replied blithely. "It's night and th-th-they're just sl-sl-slsleeping that's all."

We walked around the truck to look at the turkeys. Their heads were pushed out through the crates, but they were very, very still and quite silent.

"These turkeys ain't just sl-sl-sleeping," he exclaimed. "They're fuckin' frozen to death—you dumb bastards!"

We peered closely at them, and sure enough, every last one of them was frozen stiff.

"Well at least they're fresh frozen." Lamely I tried to point out the advantages, but the receivers just shook their heads. We were quite beyond them.

"Didn't you have a tarp or something to cover them with?" they asked.

"They've got f-f-f-feathers, haven't they ...?" I replied.

The buyer cut me off. "Haven't you heard of wind chill? You froze the damn things at about a hundred degrees below zero! Their heads are so brittle they'll snap off. How can we bleed them?" We learned about wind chill factors for the very first time. We hurtled back to the Pepsi yard. Too tired to screw the plates back on their unit, we simply threw them over the fence where they landed in the snow. We returned to our office to sleep.

It was shortly after the turkey episode that Rex and I graduated to a board and room situation with a fine couple who had two very pleasant daughters. They lived in wartime housing, one in a row of almost identical homes. They served good food, and we had clean clothes for a change and regular baths. In fact we looked quite respectable. But we had returned to hauling coal in order to eat! Quite late one night the two of us came in dog tired from shovelling coal. As the bathroom was on the main floor right next to the back door, we were able to tiptoe into the house without disturbing anyone and start running a steaming tub for our baths. Both of us dropped all our clothes in a heap on the floor. Rex climbed into the tub, while I began to clean my teeth. Just then a voice called from upstairs. "Who's there?"

I opened the bathroom door a crack. "Did you say something?" I questioned.

"Yes... Who's there?" said the voice."

"It's just us," I replied. "We'll be as quiet as possible."

Rex was shedding coal dust grime and beginning to look pink again. "Who is us?" called the voice.

"You have to be kidding!" I replied. "Good night!" I closed the bathroom door.

"What's wrong?" asked Rex, sensing my concern.

"They're asking who we are," I explained with incredulity. We both looked around, and then at each other. Was it possible? Could it be that we had the wrong house?

"Check our bedroom," Rex said. So, naked as I was, I padded down the passageway to where our bedroom should have been. It was. But it had been turned into a sewing room and our bed was gone.

We heard footsteps on the stairs. A light snapped on. A harsh male voice asked, "Just what is going on here?" His wife, in curlers, was starting down the stairs behind him. I just padded past them as they looked down over the banister in amazement.

"It's okay," I announced. "We'll be gone right away. We got the wrong house that's all!" So we grabbed our dirty clothes and fled naked from the house and across the sub zero snow banks to find the right one—two doors down. Now it was my turn to have a bath, this time in the right house, and this time, our bed was in the right room. I lay back dead tired while we rehashed the whole affair with gleeful laughter.

"But why did they have to have the same kind of tooth brush as mine?" I asked Rex, as I began to see the funny side of it. "And it was blue too!"

Right then – a flashback. Little Boy Wild recoiled from the memory. I'm in the bathroom – I'm ten years old, and I'm attempting to put the cap on a tube of tooth paste. In order to make the threads match up, I turn the cap anti-clockwise for a couple of turns. SHE is watching.

"Here! Give that to me you swine! You're screwing it on backwards! You never could do anything right," she snarls, as she snatches it out of my hands. At the same time SHE does the identical thing that I was doing – she turns the cap backwards for a couple of turns till the threads clicked. I made the terrible mistake of bringing this to her attention.

"You're doing exactly the same thing that I was doing – you turned the cap backwards until the threads matched up! That's what I was doing!"

"Don't you tell me what I was doing, you bloody swine." Her face contorts, and the beating that followed was as fierce as any I can remember. It is so serene when I flee to *"The meadows of my mind"* – it is so pastoral, and

217

the tranquility is so alluring that I may never come back. How many times a day, or a week – or a month do we turn caps on tubes? These ghostly "cap memories" are a lifetime inheritance, and one of the many silent screams that we endure. "I hope they don't call the RCMP – I just couldn't stand another session of explaining," said Rex.

Each morning I opened up the radio station and took the 6.00am shift until someone else took over – after lunch. In the meantime Rex picked up the mail and cruised looking for odd trucking jobs, like delivering groceries. There were many complaints about our service. We'd lay the groceries cartons flat on the truck floor, but when we hit potholes and bumps in the roads, the groceries danced about in mid-air like a juggling act, and always came down into different cartons. If there were odd grocery items lying on the floor, we'd pick them up and tuck them into cartons which had smaller quantities. People rarely received what they had ordered, and for some reason they insisted on getting whole eggs in their boxes – not raw scrambled ones!

I lay awake some nights, long after Rex had fallen asleep. Where to now Derek? I go back a few years to explore and possibly find myself. I'm fourteen years old.

School is no longer for me. I have to find a job and contribute money to the household for my upkeep. My final marks are dismal, and I enter the outside world as a "Cull." I feel pain and some envy in the loss of friends who are going into higher education. The whole world is opening up for them, while my path lies through a fog. Soon I'll be fifteen. Outside the birds are calling to me. The sun drenched-landscape beckons to me. I must run the pine-scented trails in the woodland, feel the hot sun caressing my skin, build a raft, sail down a river; I just have to vanish in the mist of the distant hills to seek an unnamed something.

I make one last valiant attempt to upgrade my education by enrolling in night school mathematics. This is a mixed age group and I am the youngest here. On these priceless summer nights I battle with logarithms. No one has yet explained what a logarithm is, or why I should need one in everyday life, or what they do, and my work in this class proves that I have not the remotest concept of anything relating to logarithms.

These are nights of torture. I know the instructor has written me off as a "Cull"—the old familiar pattern. When he does come by my desk, he is at a loss for words that will convey to me the basics that everyone else has grasped immediately. Everything the instructor says needs refining for me, and there is just not enough time. Math numbs me with its own grey paralysis, so as always I fall behind and enter my own world.

The final four weeks I skip classes and flee to the shelter of the woodland. It's summer and every flower is smiling at me, the warm scented breezes ruffle my hair in a friendly caress. The birds singing their liquid songs of happiness are my only reality in an unreal world. *Or am I only real in their world and not in mine?* Who would trade the touch and sight of a fuzzy owlet in its nest for a logarithm? Not I! Who would exchange a soft meadow pathway yellow with pollen and humming with bee songs for engines, smoke and concrete? Certainly not I!

I must find a job as a farm labourer, and that will get me away from HER. I can make a reasonable living, and I'll be fed. I'll still have time to disappear into the trackless purple hills in search of my own world—the one that bridges the two that WE now live in.

Meantime back in Yorkton I come out of my reverie and touch the current reality. Two of the announcers from CJGX, Earl Le Page and Don Slade, and one of the copy writers, Don's wife Gloria, had found new jobs with radio station CJOC in Lethbridge, Alberta and the old station didn't seem quite the same anymore.

"Let's go to Edmonton, Alberta!" suggested Rex.

"Edmonton?" I queried.

"Yes Edmonton, we need a total change."

"What about the trucks?"

"We'll sell 'em!" I said.

"Okay," said Rex. As we cleaned things up in the little office, one of our last acts was to throw a tarp over the remains of the hide-a-bed sofa, and bear its torn carcass to the dump. It was a wreck. Along with other activities it had been slept on for quite a while, but it had also been exposed to a lot of wrestling and levering with powerful legs. The fabric was tired of hanging on. We still had paid only twenty dollars on it. I think the kind manager of the Hudson's Bay Company in Yorkton must have written it off the books somehow. Rex stayed behind to sell the trucks, but even then, if they fetched fair market value, it would still leave us well in debt.

I left Yorkton penniless except for bus fare to Edmonton, and a few shabby articles of clothing in a beat up suitcase. Rex was to follow later.

Edmonton! You thriving capital city of Alberta—here WE come!

Chapter Eighteen

In Edmonton I arranged to stay in an old rooming house—a large white building where we housed with several other young guys for about seven dollars a week. There were three floors, and the landlady was a pleasant and helpful young woman. She had a cute little boy whom I christened 'the mouse'. The house was just off Jasper Avenue on 108th street, adjacent to a vacant lot, which still had tall big old trees on it. It was there that the boys who had cars, those who could afford them that is—parked them. Almost immediately I obtained a job with CFRN radio as a radio time salesman —selling commercials. I was not exactly enamored of this job, but it did feed me and keep a roof over my head; but we needed money to get rid of the debts left behind at Yorkton, and also money to answer the pressing need for some form of personal transportation. When summer came I felt trapped in the heat of the city, paved roads, traffic, people and noise. It meant that Little Boy Wild would rebel sometime soon, big time, and I wondered what form it might take.

Then one day a bright idea came to me that would increase my income. Having been the farm service director at CJGX, I approached the non-commercial radio station CKUA owned and operated by Alberta Government Telephones at that time and suggested to their management that I sign them on the air one hour earlier, and run two farm programs for them each day. We came to agreement on this, and I was pleased to negotiate this for a larger figure than my current pay for a full eight hours day at CFRN. Things were looking up!

Earlier—knowing that I would have to keep this extra job hidden from CFRN management, I chose another name to operate under so as to not be identified on the air. I took my brother's name—Rex. It was short and easy to handle and sounded okay. Then on the spur of the moment letting

221

my fingers do the walking through the Yellow Pages I chose the surname Allison—after the famous GM Detroit-Allison truck transmission! Now I have it – I'm Rex Allison – your new radio farm service director at CKUA. Believe me—it's really quite something to listen for Derek, or Rex,—or Kurtis or Allison. Interestingly enough the Bank of Commerce on 101st Street and Jasper never thought it strange I deposited both pay cheques in my account there. Not that it helped the NSF problem, as money did little to alleviate the demand upon it. Now the stage was truly set for a movie – what did the director have in mind?—As usual he was non-committal and just passed me the script, which of course I never had to read—because it just happened. First of all I did somewhat enjoy the respectability of being on sales for CFRN —trundling around in the old street cars, especially when I crossed to south Edmonton over the 109th Street High Level Bridge often with a train crossing at the same time. It was quite a feeling to see the water flowing so far below, as the North Saskatchewan River flowed north-east. Being in the farm service end of things for CKUA brought me into contact with many wonderful people in the Alberta Department of Agriculture—among them I recall Ed Swindlehurst, who gave me a great deal of help and encouragement.

In those days—Robert Goulet—now of television, radio and recording fame, was still an obscure radio announcer with me at CKUA. He put in long hard hours of voice practice out in the main studio, singing like he would burst. This slim attractive youth with blue smiling eyes and dark hair, was indeed destined for greatness as I now look back through the passage of time.

It was while at CKUA that I was approached by a couple of young Norwegian fellows visiting the station. They wanted to launch a Scandinavian program on a weekly basis, and this was arranged successfully. We became good friends and found we were kindred spirits.

From that point on, Svein the younger Norwegian and I, spent almost every weekend and holiday escaping 110 miles North West of Edmonton in the wild Whitecourt country where the Athabasca and McLeod Rivers meet to flow northward. This was virgin forest, well before paved roads and oil discoveries. It was grizzly country. Bears were everywhere.

Having no car of my own at that time, I frequently borrowed the CKUA station wagon on weekends under the pretence of interviewing farmers for program material, and this was of course essential research. Sometimes in our explorations of the area we got confused as to which side of the river we were on, and one night we were grossly inconsiderate, and roused the old ferryman to take us across the fast flowing Athabasca River as late as 1:30 A.M. Poor guy.

In order to wake him, we shouted across the swift burbling current, and honked our horns. But only silence replied. Then Svein opened up with several rounds from his Winchester rifle high through the trees above the old man's cabin while I honked the horn. Bwaackk!! Crack!! Two more shots were fired at his long johns strung out high on a line over his little garden and a couple of rounds hit his tin chimneystack. Results came at last with cursing and lantern waving and shouting; he finally acknowledged our presence as well as our excessive demand on his services. It was an old cable ferry and the ferryman rightfully asked us some weekends whether we would finally make our minds up as to which side of the river we wanted to be on as he would like some rest.

We placated him with several 12% Calgary Stock Ales which we always carried. If there was one thing that CKUA government wagon was famous for in the area, it was its incredible Calgary Stock Ale dispensing ability. It was an instant refreshment wagon. Memories crowded in on me of Tim, so far away. Tim's voice echoed… "Things like this will still happen on a bigger and grander scale… if you don't change!" Change to what? I questioned the movie fiend. "You're scripted—do your thing!" was his command, and I realized how deeply I was in bondage to him—his orders were my involuntary actions.

Svein and I always returned to the wilderness where the rivers met. In early spring at break up time, when the great ice floes broke up on the McLeod River, we would watch them flow around a small island, and with deep booming crunching roars, pile up on a log jam in the narrow channel. Just then, watching the ice floes go by, an idea struck me —my script unfolded—"Let's ride the ice floes down the river and jump off just before they hit the jam!"

Svein lit up. "Let's go!"

I loved my kindred spirits. They never analyzed or reasoned, but just fell in with the script. So as not to get wet we stripped off just leaving our socks on to absorb the ice shock, walked up around the island, and then moved cautiously out across the moving ice floes. We'd select a large one, sometimes two, and then dance on it. Often the floes would divide into smaller ones that could not support our weight, and then we'd dash for a larger floe, which in turn would crack due to our weight and the force of our landing on it. It was the enthralling skill of not dropping into the deep water between the floes that excited us. It was the thrill of disembarking before the big floes hit the ice jam. Boom! crunch-ch, crunch-ch, that made it all worth while. Later with bodies almost blue with the cold, we dressed and listened to the crashing drum beats of spring while we shivered and revelled in the warmth of the car heater.

Years later we realized what a ridiculous and dangerous sport this had been. The ice could have cut off our legs, ground our torsos in two, or forced us under the icy water to drown and be thrown up on the log jam, where no doubt our eyes would have made a tasty treat for the crows.

In the summertime we would wear only shorts with a sheath knife strapped to our belts, tie on our runners, and walk into the Athabasca River until the current caught us, and drifted us effortlessly downstream. We'd find huge grizzly tracks fresh in the wet mud on the river banks. We could hear or even smell the bears at times in close proximity. Once when a grizzly cub appeared at the river's edge where we'd planned to go ashore, figuring Mama to be not far away, we took off with rapidity into the deep current to flow around a bend in the river. Only then did we feel safe to go ashore for berries. Sometimes we'd find a little sandy cove and rest in the sun—talk, plan, drink from the clear little creeks and just plain live. We fed our insatiable curiosity on all things we saw, often enraptured by scenic moments that became sacred. Death by being mauled by a grizzly was certainly a possibility.

But not so long ago there were less noble ways to die. As we lay in the sand, a sudden glinting of *the water ripples triggered a picture that was etched into memory and the whole scene played back.*

I'm in England again: I'm about 13 years old and a prisoner under HER constant watch. We're in the back garden and she will not allow me to leave for the woodland where I want to be with my animals; and that surging call will not be quelled by a Human, even my mother.

"Why can't I go?" I keep asking her in a plaintive note which has a certain monotonous frequency. I suppose I'm whining, but the insistent urge to be with my birds and rabbits is undeniably strong. It's my life force and my whole world of sanity. SHE is performing some dress making alterations and is in deep concentration.

"You have no reason not to let me go!" I state with some vehemence. "You just sit there revelling in your power while you suck on those mints looking self righteous!" There, I've got it out of my system. Unexpectedly and with deadly precision, she leapt up while snatching the large dress cutting scissors. The flash in her hand is like a dagger; her face contorts in a snarl of hatred as I hurl myself into escape mode and flee upstairs to the nearest bedroom. SHE pursues me.

Her screams of "I'll kill you! I'll kill you, you bloody swine," add wings to my feet as her voice reaches a hysterical pitch. In the nick of time I slam the door, forcing my foot against it and throw the full force of my light frame against the door. She screams with rage from the other side.

"I'll kill you, you swine, I'll kill you!" Then she hacks at the door panels again and again. I hear the wood splintering and it terrifies me. If she ever broke through the door or forced it open, there would be blood everywhere. Mine. But soon she tires, calms down and leaves. But I stay with my foot against the bottom of the door for about fifteen minutes longer. She may creep back as she exercises certain cunning in these situations. I should have fled to the woodland in the first place. Much later she returns with the bamboo cane to thrash me.

"Wait till your father hears about this," she shouts.

As usual – *I dissociate and disappear inside myself.* She can't reach me in here. I'll survey the damage later. When it's all over the hopelessness sucks at me, and I rock back and forth immersed in scarlet welts. I emit only a low moaning sound. Night comes and it is followed by morning with bird song rising into the blue sky. I'm now fully awake. I'm soaking wet and stinking. Another bed wetting, what's new? Do I dissociate now or when SHE arrives on the scene? Nothingness is so, so peaceful.

Back on the Athabasca River – Svein saw, but did not question the tears on my cheeks as I rose to go for a dip. Time and watches had no place in our lives, only the rotation of the Earth in relation to the sun gave direction to our days; and so it was that only later did we fully realize the disadvantage to launching one's self to the whims of a strong river current for a mile or so. It was that one has to swim, wade or walk all the way back upstream, as there is no trail alongside the river. This was wilderness and we were idealists carefree under the sun, and by star light dreamy with unfathomable quests. Little Boy Wild was in his perfect element – right here. When Svein and I returned to the city a shadow seemed to fall on us. Freedom departed, the manacles of civilization clicked their locks and we were tugged at like lost logs in the river currents. We knew that we had to return. Civilization imposed a type of prison reality; it was like being penned in –rather like being in a big prison, where one could walk around with apparent freedom that was only illusory in nature.

Things were going well at CFRN—I actually made the odd sale, but I was quite apprehensive of Mac Holmes, the CFRN Farm Service Director. He did not know that I ran things in the farm department over at CKUA under the name of Rex Allison. Sometimes I'd see him at the Alberta Department of Agriculture, and always managed to avoid him. He was a little gruff, but a good guy at heart and I liked him. He would probably have been my ally had he been given the opportunity. Then one day the inevitable happened. It was an agricultural livestock show and sale at a small country town on the weekend—a hot summer day. I was speaking with a group of agricultural officials, when who should walk up—but Mac!!

"I'd like you to meet Mac Holmes from CFRN Rex, he's their farm man," a government official introduced us.

Mac looked at me, after all, he knew me well, as my desk was next to his at CFRN where I was on sales. The official continued with his introduction, "Mac—I'd like you to meet Rex Allison—he's doing the farm shows for CKUA."

Everyone was smiling and relaxed up to that point. Mac's head came up—"He's not Rex—he's Derek, he's on sales with my station CFRN!

"No Mac—you must be mistaken," an official cut in "I've been working with Rex here for some time, he's with CKUA and doing a great job!"

Oh WOW!—Derek—Rex—whoever you are—at least you're not

naked—yet, unless you get tarred and feathered. Confusion reigned supremely until I came to everyone's rescue and attempted to resolve the discomfort everyone felt. I felt fine—but they had pigeon holes they put things and people into, and suddenly I didn't seem to fit properly. I gave Mac one of my cards but I knew he was thinking loyally of CFRN and their image. It didn't take long.

On the Monday morning I was called into the management office and told to make up my mind as to which station I wanted to be associated with—a very fair proposition. So with a clear mind I resigned and devoted my time to CKUA and other pursuits with a lot of extra time on my hands.

During this period, a personal car was out of the question until one day I devised a plan for not one automobile—but two, maybe three or more! Then my friends would have cars too, all for free! In those days, Spruce Grove, just 18 miles west on the Jasper highway out of Edmonton—was a little town—rather sleepy. They had a General Motors dealership there and I decided to visit this car lot.

I hitchhiked out to this car dealer with a close friend by the name of Al. He was a young dark eyed hellion of about my own age. I forget how we first teamed up, but he was always game for getting a free meal, swiping a car, or whatever else might have to be done in the survival game. He was of muscular build, stronger than me and a lot less vocal than I, but he had a good head for planning. Upon arrival we inspected the used ones we might want and having selected a grey Plymouth and a black Chevy we were all set—of course we didn't have more than coffee money on us at any time, and certainly no money in the bank. On top of that no finance company would look at us. About this time the proprietor came out.

"Can I interest you fellows in a car today?" he smiled with nice even teeth.

"Well," I slowly grinned at him, pushing my cap back so that the full innocence of my countenance would set the pace—"Maybe not one—perhaps two!" The owner's face lit up a little. "Tell you what we have in mind," I said, "Al and I have a little used car lot just off Jasper and 108th street, and we were thinking that you don't have much buyer traffic going by your used units, so maybe we'd take a couple of them in and sell 'em for you, and then come back for two more and so on, so we'd both make a little money."

I turned away to let the idea float around for a moment or two, while I looked at the two cars in question for a more critical inspection. The car lot we had of course, was not owned by us, and was none other than the vacant lot next to the rooming house where the other boys parked their heaps. The idea took root. The proprietor whose name we never did know, just marked down where the cars would be, gave us the price he wanted for them, said he'd start off with two—and away we went!!! No plates, no registration, no valid driver licenses and no money. He did absolutely no investigation, although I believe I did reveal my CKUA connection and he recognised my voice. So we drove back in high glee to our base at the empty lot. We parked them with their noses facing the road; put a sale sign on them, and that was it.

The owner of the cars said he'd check once in a while to see how we were doing when he was in town. When after a while he did show up, we told him the reaction so far was that we had expressions of interest but the prospective buyers had thought the vehicles were a little over priced. But—in the meantime each of us had a car. The only difficulty was that we were always running out of gas. Al was just about to buy three more gallons with our last bit of cash which we needed for food.

"Hold it," I said. Al flashed me one of his smiles that lit up his face.

"Alright!" He exclaimed, "What do you have in mind?" His eyes were bright with anticipation.

"We," I said, "Are not buying any more gas—we're going to buy us some rubber tubing—from here on we siphon, like I used to siphon off the British Army trucks during the war when I found them parked around… I used to clean those big Army trucks right out." And that is exactly what we did, we siphoned gas mainly by night and kept those cars running. One evening I ran out of gas right outside the Odeon cinema on Jasper Avenue. My girl Rose to whom I was engaged said, "What will you do?" She was so innocent and so beautiful!

"Simple—just sit tight." I said. Leaping out of the car I grabbed a five gallon can from the trunk, and right there with everyone going by I boldly siphoned off five gallons from the car in front, and got the old bus going again. Only one problem—the car went, but so did Rose—the other way. She was quite shocked. But desperate situations call for desperate measures. I was deeply saddened by her departure, but I always found someone inside of me at times like these quoting "Necessity is the mother of invention!" Okay – so we're mobile again, tomorrow is another day.

In the meantime Al and I took a homestead out at Rocky Rapids by Drayton Valley, the now famous oilfield. This was a government plan that said in essence, that if certain improvements were made in a specified time – we had the land free! Rex always insisted that the place was called Rocky Rabbits and the name stuck. We needed wire, fence posts, tools, saws, posthole augers, pliers, and seemingly endless items for which we had no money, other than my radio station cheque, which didn't go very far. I was however, undaunted. When I was not broadcasting at CKUA, and when Al was free, we headed for the surrounding farms and simply took what we needed from their yards in broad daylight or by night. We'd simply knock on the door to see if anyone was at home, if not we'd help ourselves without being greedy—taking older items if they were in duplicate around the shop. If someone did come to the door, we'd ask for directions to somewhere in the area. In this way we got all the tools and wire needed. I suppose we had degenerated into thieves, but it didn't come home to us that way—we felt convinced that 'Where there's a will there's a way.'

We were supposed to put in improvements of a certain dollar value in our land, and take up permanent residence there. Upon qualification, the land would then be ours —clear title. However, the homestead project never really got off the ground. Although we had accumulated tools and supplies, and our intentions were good, other matters often took over. In my case – Little Boy Wild made it his priority to tryst with the animals in the timeless summer solstice. I really had no choice.

The other side of this coin was the thirsty demand for gasoline that the cars and civilization thrust upon us. One night I was siphoning gas and making a real mess, in fact my ineptness that evening was almost embarrassing. I was emptying the tanks of a big truck at 108th and Jasper Avenue when the shadow of the law was cast over the evening. My best grey flannel suit was soaked in gasoline all down the front, when suddenly Al gave a low whistle indicating the cop on the beat was coming up. Our plan was that he was to stand by and give the all clear whistle when the cop was gone. I learned later that Al had gone home when he saw him approaching. This left me between the numerous huge wheels and axles under the truck. That cop looked all over the lot, and finally left. I lay low for another half hour, hiding like a hunted animal. I feared that the cop might be standing quietly in the fence shadows waiting for me to creep out. In vain I waited for Al's all clear whistle—but he was already home, snoring safely in his bed. That was the last time we ever siphoned gas. The very next morning I went out and "bought" a pump. We would do it properly—in bulk—from here on we would pump it. Strolling into a hardware store on 97th street in Edmonton, I asked for a pump, and found the right one for $27.50.

"Anything else sir?" the proprietor asked in a pleasant tone.

"No, that's all for today," I said,—thereby indicating future business tomorrow.

"That'll be $27.50 sir!"

"Oh—that's a charge—charge it to the Bar 7 Ranches at Rocky Rabbits will you, they have a centralized controlled buying and accounting system."

"Yes sir. Thank you sir! Just initial this please—good day!"

Bearing my prize away I headed next for the welding shop and had a bracket specially made for the rear door of the Plymouth, so that the pump would not jiggle and wiggle around. Good old Bar 7 Ranch! It paid our bills – at least the urgent ones. Then with four five gallon drums on the floor in the rear of the car, and two spares in front, it was easy to angle park, reach out of the window to remove the gas caps, shove in the hose and PUMP. We worked the side streets and helped ourselves. Al would drive and I would pump. There were however certain technicalities to overcome. Like, when one is angle parked, in order to reach the gas cap, one must not go fully into the curb or the gas cap is out of reach. Therefore one must brake, which gives tell-tale red lights, so we had the brake lights put on a separate switch, so that no lights showed, and if someone came by we could roll gently and silently forward to the curb and sit there.

One cold night we had to pretend we were making out with each other, as a cop on the beat became a little leery. He stood in front of the car watching us under the indistinct illumination of the street lights. So in order to make it authentic and to allay suspicion of our true activities; Al suddenly said "Kiss me, we have to make out we got the "hots" for each other!" So we kissed and caressed each other while writhing around, the windows were steamy anyway so the cop could see no detail. Not a sensation without pleasure, but it lacked the innocent beauty of the tender adolescent messing around that I once had with Tim. Finally, the peace officer moved on and we moved our nefarious operation to another beat. We supplied all of our friends with gas, at a fair discounted price, and continued to run our two cars out to the homestead and on other adventures and picnics. In reality we were thieves, apart from running around without license plates, insurance and whatever, but survival is adapting to the environment.

We did survive, but one time Al was in a high speed RCMP chase. Apparently they got on his tail outside of town somewhere on Highway 16 west, and being kind of curious about the lack of plates, pursued him in to Jasper Place. Luckily he had relatives there, and as he turned up their road he was able to sweep to a halt in their garage, and had closed the doors before the cops caught up and swept by in a cloud of dust and gravel. Al was sweating. The RCMP had gone. He'd shaken them this time, but it was too close.

I met Al later and we went for a good feed of ham and eggs at the "Ham'n Egger." This restaurant was new, and the girl in charge could not make change. We'd eat our fill, have pie and whipped cream and coffee afterwards, give her a ten dollar bill and we'd get the ten dollar bill plus change as though we'd given her a twenty. It was amazing. We'd eat there free, again and again and receive change for a twenty. The restaurant only lasted about nine months in business, and we were quite miffed at no longer having free ham and eggs when they finally locked their doors.

At this point the Movie Director and I had a dream. I also had visions—of several thousand acres of land in the Peace country. I could see men falling trees; Don Slade, my young announcer sidekick, carving out our air strip with a brand new D8 Caterpillar. There would be George Wilson on another D8 Cat clearing his home site, and the whole operation would be a cooperative. I, of course, would run the ranching operation.

Just how do you get a herd underway? We decided we would have to rustle some good livestock from southern Alberta and take them north. No one would ever find them up in the bush country. We would try to alter the brands, or pick the calves up before branding time. So it was that I took to studying Herefords of good breeding; we only needed a few heifer calves and one bull calf from another ranch .... My visions had an insatiable appetite for cash. Just what is this 'break-even' point they talk about?

Desperately hungry one day we walked into the Massey-Harris farm equipment showrooms with an idea to price out a used tractor. While looking at some of the new ones we were asked what we had in mind. I alluded to somewhat vast tracts of land in the Peace River country, and envisioned a possible three tractors, two combines and various sundry items like a manure spreader. Massey-Harris was overwhelmed; it must have been quite an enquiry, a mighty big order if they landed it.

"You will have lunch with us won't you?" I heard a voice say, as I squinted at the figures and gazed off into space doing complex mental calculations.

"Pardon me? Oh yes!—Al, do we have time to have lunch with these gentlemen?" Al nodded. "Yes," I replied, "We'd be delighted to join you." Food! Food! Beautiful strength giving food!—I love you. We ate and ate. As Al said afterwards—"The last piece of equipment you need is a manure spreader."

"Yes," I met his gaze guilelessly, "Of course that's why it was last on the list!" That excellent meal we had with the Massey people was really something compared to what we usually existed on at the Eagle Cafe. The Eagle was a dim, dingy restaurant at 108th St and Jasper Avenue around the corner from our base. They served a 35 cent hamburger, and we used to weasel coffee and dessert along with it by being super nice to the girls. In reality of course they just felt sorry for us, it had nothing to do with us being the studs we imagined we were! We made eyes at them or tweaked them, and we got a good feed for 35 cents. True you had to brush cockroaches off the table; as well as other odd little creatures who joined us at meal time from within the adjoining woodwork.

The trouble was, even then, after we'd gotten a good feed for 35 cents neither of us had the 35 cents to pay for it. So I'd write one of my famous rubber cheques. The Chinese restaurateur would flip.

"No teck, no teck! No teck! Your teck no good—bounce—no!" This would cause a stir if others were in the restaurant, he'd really scream. Sometimes he'd ask us if we had money before we sat down. We told him we'd report him to the food and health department for making his burgers out of 50% cockroach meat. It really tasted like what you'd think a cockroach tasted like. Strange meat with lots of filler, served on a pale, tired damp bun. We got him trained to the point where he would allow us a charge account for the dubious roach burgers—he was a good type. We even paid him sometimes.

Perhaps it was a blessing in disguise that at this time we completely lost interest in the homestead deal. To top it off we learned that we had not properly identified our land by correct location—we were two miles out and over from where we should have been. It was time to move on, time for a change of pace.

At the same time the owner of the two cars at Spruce Grove; after a whole year suddenly requested their return in twenty-four hours. It was just as well, because the owner of the lot where we parked our units told us to get them off once and for all. We had also taken to parking them on the streets with the sale signs on them at various parking meters. Our car lot was on the street anywhere we wanted it, but it was costing nickels and dimes—our roach burger money, so it had to come to a stop.

We zapped the two units over to a local Pontiac Buick dealership on Jasper, and asked the mechanic to turn the odometers back to about 25,000 miles each, to bring them into line with what the mileage was when we picked them up, allowing for some small running around. He objected to this and at first outright refused.

"We don't and won't do things like that." he stated with some dismay at our request.

"Look," I replied in lowered voice, "We won't say anything about what we know about odometers being turned back and your used car lot operations—ever." His eyes widened, "Do I make myself clear? It's for the Bar 7 Ranch at Rocky Rabbits," I smiled at him. He got the message and did it free of charge. It's not quite the type of thing you write up on a work order with several copies!

The proprietor at Spruce Grove received the cars back all cleaned up, gassed up, waxed, shiny, and the engines had been steam cleaned; and when he checked the odometers he was quite pleased, and his reserve began to fade—or was it latent hostility?

"Heard you fellers was running them cars all over—anyway, they're back now. You tried." So that was that.

Al decided to move to Saskatchewan with his girl, where they finally married and became fine responsible people, raising kids and paying taxes. Rex married a girl of Swedish origin; she had blue come-hither eyes and a slow beautiful smile. They settled down in Edmonton.

Svein and I took a wild trip to the twin river country, and raised hell for about four days. This was an experience where we alternated between inebriation and the more sober quest for direction in our lives. In between times we had rifle target practice and explored the river country. The whole process seemed to distil our thoughts into a course of action. I had already taken leave of CKUA, and planned to head for Lethbridge in Southern Alberta to join my old friends from CJGX. They now worked with radio station CJOC in that city. What a reunion we'd have—Earl Lepage, irrepressible George Wilson, married and raising a family; Don Slade and Gloria and others! We would surely party around the clock!

There was a happy reunion at CJOC, and I was hired for the news department, but not before Svein and I had planned a long trip to the far north. We would explore the Yukon by canoe, run a trap line, and live it up. Svein and Arne then returned to their family in Edmonton, and I settled into the routine of the radio station newsroom with my fun partner George Wilson. What a smile that guy had.

There was one little incident that the Movie Director staged that is worthy of mention. It happened because Don Slade and a couple of other announcers including myself had decided to go pheasant shooting. We had to get an early start and I arrived at Don's place about 4:45AM. But although I knocked and rang the bell there was no reply. So I sneaked around the house looking into windows until I found their bedroom. There was impish Don and cute Gloria snuggled up like a couple of squirrels. The window was slightly ajar so I opened it wider; then pointing the shotgun, that heavy double-barrelled job skyward, I fired both barrels while screaming with diabolical abandon. They came up out of bed like they were on springs, while I ran around to the front door to be ushered in.

Meanwhile the whole neighbourhood was awake too. The noise from the shotgun blast had hit the sides of the houses echoing and re-echoing, making it far worse that it really was for a quiet conventional upper class residential area. In no time at all people were on the sidewalk talking and looking. RCMP cruisers were cruising. It was just not possible to get into Don's car while carrying the shotguns for about an hour. *But I felt better. There was action and excitement.* Things were happening and the RCMP, my "good friends," were on the prowl. There were minor complications though—when I had let go with both barrels, I had not thought of the roof overhang and it received severe damage. More money to lay out. Now I would not eat for a week or more, or maybe I'd have to sell my gun.

Later I got to thinking about the Yukon and my proposed trip with Svein. We wanted to explore remote regions, travel down almost unknown rivers, and live wild adventures while filming our entire trip. We hoped to get unusual wildlife footage and to write a book about our experiences. But those two years without some girls would be tough, unless we became involved with some Aboriginal women. (Our youthful ignorance and lack of respect for First Nations people in those days was quite pathetic.)

"We takum injun squaw, make good moose hide moccasins, chew skins very soft," said Svein.

"Yeh!" I rejoined, "Injun squaws chew us, make us soft, make us much happy —Hey! Let's take our girls with us, teach 'em to fish, shoot, trap, and make camp, cook *and* look after the babies. "

Our present girls said "NO WAY!"—They wanted a mortgage, kids, dances and parties. So I advertised for a wife in the Calgary Albertan morning newspaper. It was a nice large display ad:

OPPORTUNITY!
If You Are a Young Woman

with common sense and personality between the ages of 19 and 25—desiring marriage—adventure and excitement, then here is a lifetime proposition. If you possess these qualities such an opportunity might be yours.

A 3 to 4 year journey through Canada's Northland with enterprising young Canadian of 25 years—plus subsequent world wide travel is the object of this venture.

Those Interested Write Box 642
Albertan

Chapter Nineteen

The advertisement for a wife drew numerous responses; which was quite unexpected and overwhelmed me. There was even a particularly threatening letter from a farmer, who was very much against his daughter joining me on the expedition. He knew she had written a long letter and had also conversed with me on the telephone. He was also fearful of an almost instant elopement. What had I started? Other letters were scented and flowery. One was humorous—it suggested that large, medium and small sizes were available, including a super giant economy package, and would I please specify size required. Many had photographs which included their children. I had a hard job looking after myself, without additionally trying to handle a woman and three kids in a canoe with a pile of bear meat! Then I received a letter which later set Southern Alberta on fire! In part it read…"and although we do not conform to your requirements, we understand you'll be travelling through an area where a great fire hazard exists. Would you like to represent Nu-Swift Ltd. of England, and sell fire extinguishers along the way ...?"

Communication went back and forth and it seemed like a profitable idea. Svein and I would delay the north trip and make some money first. We needed photographic equipment and many other items, like rifles, binoculars, special clothing, and a raft of other needs which we recognised as we planned.

I discussed the whole project with Tom McLaren—a young engineer at CJOC Lethbridge who had recently married, and invited him to join me as a partner. We put a down payment on two Ford panel wagons with his positive up-front money and my vague know-how. For the next year we had fun, hardships and adventures in learning how to sell NU-SWIFT fire extinguishers—the Worlds' Fastest.

We packed in our jobs at the radio station and launched into the un-known. We read the Nu-Swift sales manual avidly to learn the basics of how to SELL, and were introduced to AIDA the magic fairy—AIDA being the acronym for Attention, Interest, Desire and Action, the prime ingredi-ents for any sale or meeting of the minds. Everywhere we went, she helped us. On the technical end of things, we'd inspect all the fire equipment in a prospect's building before we made a sales approach, which allowed us to know ahead of time which units were faulty.

A Ford dealer in Medicine Hat, Alberta, was working on his books when I walked into his inner sanctum after a brief knock. I was well pre-pared—it should be pointed out that we always carried a can of Esso Extra gas and a screw driver, along with our demonstration model fire extinguish-ers. The prospect looked up from his paper work, whereupon I introduced myself and my mission.

"Not interested, we got all the fire equipment we need." He turned back to his paper work. Okay AIDA—do your stuff. 'A'—attention, cap-ture his attention! I approached his desk where his expensive sports coat hung regally over the back of a beautiful chair. Quickly I poured gas all over the collar and shoulders. Ahh! He looked up, I had his attention. IN-TEREST—get him interested! I had his interest the moment I struck the match—his coat became a sheet of flame—Zzzaaapp—the high powered atomized mist spray of carbon tetrachloride under CO2 pressure had the flame out in one second.

Only the vapour burns in the initial ignition, and one hopes the extin-guisher will work. Not a hair on his coat was singed. DESIRE—he prob-ably had the desire to kill me or at least throw me bodily out. ACTION—he swiftly rose to his feet—he was quite tall—and came round the desk to inspect his coat. It was perfect. I introduced myself and found out that he was the president of the company. He was so impressed that he invited me on a tour of his entire establishment, and to make recommendations for improvement.

We had previously given all the fire extinguishers an inspection and were well aware of which ones were solidly corroded or not operating, and I gave these units immediate attention. It was impressive and I landed some good business—the biggest sale to date. Thank you AIDA—you sweet fairy of success!

One summer evening when AIDA had done her magic in romantic circles, my girl and I were parked in the hills above the main highway leading into Lethbridge, where the road cuts deeply into the coulee. It was an idyllic summer night, soft, with caressing shy breezes that sprang up and were lost moments later. At one point during this AIDA interlude, I stepped out of the car to relieve myself and standing beside the wagon, I stretched luxuriously in the late sunlight, digging my bare toes sensuously into the soft dry grass.

As I viewed the cars directly below streaming into Lethbridge, the wagon suddenly lurched forward and took off down the slope. Oh horrors! Help! Help! Stop! Oh God stop that wagon! As it was related to me later by one of the radio station executives as he drove into town that evening.

"Something caught my eye—then I saw this naked figure with his hair flying, come leaping down the slope pursuing his car."

Luckily the vehicle came to a stop by a large rock. Boy! Was that girl ever mad and shaken up. She insisted that we dress and go straight home. As I did her bidding, I soberly reflected—Derek you haven't changed much, here you are again in an almost impossible situation without your pants on. Tim—you were right! Strange things happened when I took girls out in the wagon. Like the time I headed for Park Lake gaily chatting, when the whole world blacked itself out. One moment we were driving along in the sunlight and the next moment after a slight lurch as we pulled further over to allow another car to pass—blackness, absolute inky blackness.

"What happened? Where are we?" a scared female voice expressed my own unspoken questions.

"I think we're under water," I replied. "I don't know how deep yet, wish I could see, God is it ever dark!"

For a moment we sat there while I held her hand.

"Damn! We're going to get wet feet if we stay in here," I exclaimed, "Let's climb into the back and see if the rear door will open."

We climbed over the fire extinguisher cartons, and heaved on the door which seemed less dark than the windshield. It yielded slowly with much struggling, and water burst in along with some sunlight. It rushed and gurgled around us, and then we were peering up at the road where anxious passers by were looking into the black depths, watching the huge bubbles and glump, glumping sounds as air escaped from the submerged unit. We partially swam and then struggled through the water and black mud up the bank. That put a damper on the whole day's outing. She was too shy to strip off and dry in the hot sun, I offered to dry her things by spreading them on the bushes, but she looked sort of grim. I felt fine, wet, but glowing with exhilaration.

But women get upset about runaway cars, and vehicles leaping off the road into deep water, it was little adventures like this that brightened my day. Eventually the wagon was winched out like a mouse by its tail and was none the worse for wear after going through the shop for a check over and cleaning.

Our spiritual progress was put to the test by another girl I trysted with at Park Lake, she turned the whole evening into a religious meeting. The vehicle gave us no trouble, the problem was inside the wagon. According to her I had to accept Jesus before I could kiss her, but in those days He just wasn't on my mind—sort of, not a top priority, other more pressing things of an earthly nature were thrusting for expression.

"Have you been saved Derek?"

I looked deeply into her eyes, "From what?" I asked with feigned innocence toying with her blouse buttons.

"You know—have you found Jesus?" she asked pulling away from my embrace.

"I didn't know he was lost," I exclaimed, recalling a smart remark I'd heard around somewhere. She looked pityingly at me. We never dated again.

One day we were selling fire extinguishers in the "dry" (No liquor) little town of Cardston, Alberta where a famous Mormon Temple stands—of course for those in the know—the town was far from being dry. A crowd of townsfolk and farmers along with a few First Nations people gathered on the street corner to watch our famous fire extinguisher demonstration. My sleek blue Ford wagon was shining and clean. I raised the hood, poured a pint of gas over the motor while giving the usual sales spiel. The crowd gathered close in, full of excitement. They had never seen anything like this before. I flicked a match under the hood. BOPP! PWOOF! The usual explosive sound and flames, but—something else—an explosion that blew the top off the battery. The crowd surged back like wheat swaying before the summer wind. ZAPP!—out went the fire. Now the crowd looked at each other, themselves, and us, with fear and uncertainty in their eyes—something was alarming them. They were totally spooked! Oh! My! Before our wide and amazed eyes, one farmer's shirt began to disintegrate like remote controlled magic—holes appeared like live things in shirts, coats and pants and people screamed and felt burned, which they were – with acid! They fled in all directions. It looked worse than if they were being attacked by a bunch of hornets. They ran to get water and to get hosed down. The battery had exploded and thrown acid over the whole crowd—this could be an ugly one. I slammed the hood shut.

"Let's get out of here Tom, before they decide to lynch us or something."

There must have been enough of the battery left or the vehicle would never have started. We fled—all the way down to Manyberries, Etzikom, and Nemiscam in the dry southern Alberta border country. The area was climatically truly dry. As we travelled we chuckled and wondered what would happen as a result of this fiasco and if anyone had been really hurt.

Our Fords gave us endless trouble, the doors on Tom's van just would not stay closed no matter how many times the dealership tightened the screws; so Tom had them spot welded shut all of our first summer, and climbed in and out of the window on the driver's side. It raised a lot of questions and was certainly not a good commercial for Ford. My vehicle came to a stop one day when we were both returning to Lethbridge in our respective wagons. I searched high and low for the problem, and when Tom finally came up to find me peering under the hood, he had a strange little smile on his face. He helped me check under the hood too, but finally he said, "Come on back to my van – I've got something to show you." I did, and when he opened the rear door, there was *my gas tank* lying in the back. It had apparently dropped off on the highway and he had almost run over it before recognising it for what it was. Sure enough – here I was – stranded with no fuel or fuel tank! We had a huge laughing session. We ached! It was shortly after this that due to the usual desperate money shortage, that our vans were seized by the finance company for non-payment. Never had the finance company's repossession crew had such willing help to assist them in any way possible! Tom had experienced engine problems and had the engine head and other parts in a heap on the floor in our shop. These, we helped them load, and then we assisted them in the hitching up of the vans to the tow trucks. We gave a loud cheer as those units gathered speed and left our lives forever. We celebrated with a steak supper and apple pie, which we could ill afford, and then went in quest of new forms of transportation. In a week's time, somehow we must have been convincing –we had wheels again! Mine was a blue Buick "Roadmaster" with four portholes on the front fenders, and Tom acquired a green Buick "Super" –it had three port-holes. Sales went well in the border country, especially during the combining season. The farmers would not stop their combine harvesters for anyone; nor would they talk while the sun was still shining. BUT—they were afraid of fire—they all had hair raising fire stories. We found the only way to get their attention was to set fire to their machines as they came by—thanks AIDA—you magic fairy, yes —that gets their ATTENTION, INTEREST, DESIRE and ACTION in swift succession!

There was always a bunch of straw around the engine, packed in here and there, and with one match—poof! It ignites. But before it can creep away—SPLAT! It's out, a very impressive demonstration. We mounted the extinguishers right on their combines, and were often told to go up to the house for a cheque and also install a couple in the barn. We rarely took orders. We loaded up our wagons, demonstrated them in action, and installed them on the spot. There was a lot of truth in the old saying 'you can't do business from an empty wagon'.

In our travels food was a matter of feast or famine. Many a time we were fed sumptuously by the farmers, but at other times it was a matter of no money and sheer hunger. But there were ways to survive, and they left tell-tale tracks! One day at the garage where our vehicles were serviced, the mechanic was checking the left front wheel of my Buick, he couldn't figure out why the left hub cap was exposed to so much heat that it had turned black.

"No bearing ever ran that hot," he murmured, frowning.

"Oh! That's all right," I explained, blushing. "Y-y-y-y-you see, it's my frying pan—I c-c-c-cook f-f-fish in my hubcaps."

His mouth fell open and his face became serious. He gave me one of those strange looks where the eyes narrow and they take another closer, more intense look. He shook his head as he walked away – for him it was the living end!

"Fries fish in his fuckin' hub caps!" But it was my mode of survival. I'd fish for pike in super hungry times for my breakfast and supper out at Park Lake just north of Lethbridge, and then cook them in the left front hubcap. The right hubcap was my plate. I even had two spare cooking units mounted on the rear wheels I'd never used, except for making tea. Maybe I'd fry mushrooms one day, and cook an extra vegetable.

But our urge to achieve financial success was shadowed with unusual problems. One day we made a decision to take on an exclusive dealership for a special chemical compound that would do magical things for anyone who drove a car or truck. An American, complete with Cadillac and a big cigar, worked on us on and off for several days before "awarding" us the franchise. The magic that had captured our imagination was a yucky white pasty substance that was put into automobile tires, and when a puncture occurred—it automatically sealed it and one kept going. It never had to be fixed. Think of all the money one could save!

The local service station that we dealt with set up a huge display, and Tom and I stood by—all smiles and enthusiasm. We gave a demonstration with our sales talk and had a wheel set up to demonstrate the effectiveness of this product We pounded nails into it, the tire hissed mightily under all the extra air pressure we had put in—and then after a few turns—magic! It was sealed.

Everyone was impressed and the cash register kept ringing with that sweet music that told us we'd have steak for supper that night. There were a number of sceptics, and to these we gave very special attention. We would personally put the guck into his tires and for good measure—just to make his eyes pop a bit I'd pound a good sized nail into one of his front tires. They would almost swallow their cigarettes in horror, but we told them to drive while it was still hissing. They did—and it worked. We sold more and more of it. I placed another order with our U.S. supplier. One morning we showed up at the "Guck Stand"—all smiles and rosy cheeks, just itching to pound some nails into a customer's tire. Upon greeting us, our friend the service station manager looked unusually grim.

"Seems like there's a couple of guys looking for you—both of them are pretty fuckin' mad, one of 'em says he's gonna have your balls," he was looking at me.

"B-b-b-but why? ..." I stammered.

"Well," our service station friend continued—"You know those holes you pounded into his rubber? (In fact this guy had three holes in one front tire alone). "It seems the seals came unstuck—that Guck is drying out! He had one hell of a flat out on the highway."

"Oh my God! Tom!" I exclaimed in horror, "We'll have to quit—that stuff has something wrong with it!"

But the real crunch was not the Guck, it was good bye steaks and baby beef livers—I'd have to catch pike at Park Lake and fry them in my hubcaps again. Tom fully agreed we'd have to quit, and our service station man had already taken the display down and it was all packed into a box.

"There she is boys—throw her in your truck—don't want none of that around here no more!"

Over the next several days we were stopped by a number of people—all mad as hornets. A big rancher saw me in the restaurant one morning—he was having steak and eggs, and I was down to toast and coffee ... .

"You!" he roared in recognition. He glared at me from under his huge Stetson —"That fuckin' tire stuff you and your partner sold me—I'm gonna have your balls!" He came around from his table to my booth, towering over me. I stood up. I couldn't even force a smile.

"You know" I said, nervously licking my lips, "Seems like everyone's after 'em these days—what makes 'em so special?" This flat attempt at humour riled him.

"I'll tell you what—smart ass!"—His eyes were not to be fooled with.

"Sir" I cut in, "As soon as you're through breakfast—we'll go down to the service station and fix everything up—okay?"

His face brightened and he became more considerate, I rallied, and tried to explain, "Sir—it seems that the little sticky animals in the guck don't want to stick together anymore and we have had a few complaints..."

"Sticky animals? It's the nails you and your partner hammered into my tires—the cord is busted, they need vulcanizing for Chris' sake!"

"We didn't know this would happen and we've discontinued the sale of that product now." I lamely explained.

"Well okay then—I'll see you down there about nine o'clock," he was still glowering when he returned to his table. My stomach was so tight that if I could have afforded scrambled eggs I would have re-scrambled them almost immediately.

Thus the great restitution program began. Some of the customers were happy with a vulcanizing job, but others were fierce and with hostility pressed their vantage for new rubber at our expense. It increased our charge account in a big way. Our debt mounted ever higher, seven tires and fifteen vulcanizing jobs.

One of the final touches to crown this fiasco was the arrival in customs of $3000.00 of Magic Tire Guck. We refused it, and it was returned to its point of origin in the U.S.A.

A few days later I got a fearsome earful of threats about sheriffs, warrants, small debts courts and extradition—I hung the phone up on the Magic Guck salesman—while he was still screaming about ethics and honour. Seeing Tom's concerned face and skipping the whole explanation I said, "Tom! It's not *extra*dition that we want—it's *extra* cash! and some good products!"

The epilogue to this whole affair which had run me ragged and totally stressed out, was that **WE** took off for a few days. We had to hide and recuperate among the wild deserted foothills. Little Boy Wild had had enough with the UNREAL SELF piling up debt, starving, trying to make ends meet; and always there seemed to be a car payment due, or rent on the shop or a shipment coming in. He wanted a clean break.

"To hell with it!" he exclaimed. He was totally freaked by the whole situation; and it was *not* just a question of me relinquishing control. He took over completely; it was not the first time, and certainly not the last. Without another word he charged a tank of gas, filled up a couple of spare five gallon containers, and headed for the foothills. I merely tagged along.

I knew he was heading for lynx country, and for the clear creeks full of cut throat trout, he wanted to be with the deer and the black bears and much more. Above all, he wanted to lose himself in starlit wilderness magic. Within two hours we were deep into the wilds surrounded by beautiful whispering trees. He parked by a protective grove which opened up on a small meadow. Below, a hidden creek was rushing. Almost as soon as he heard it, his breathing became slow and deep. He had arrived. It was one of his idyllic settings.

"We're here!" He smiled at me, but he was in no mood for talking.

He made up his bed in the back of the Buick, and as it was only about 6.00pm, he stripped and lay on a blanket in the warm sun. He lay on his belly watching the meadow and creek below for signs of life, and to his utter delight he saw a lynx. He'd been here before and knew the trails and his animals. He also knew it had to be pretty wild for a lynx to be in sight. His stomach rumbled and all he had on board were a few cans of beans, some peanuts and a chocolate bar. He shared the nuts with an inquisitive squirrel and finished up the chocolate. Returning to the blanket he took a long drink of water from his bottle. He then curled up, and as he did so, rocked back and forth as tears trickled to escape down his cheeks.

"Keelematu, Keelematu, Keelematu," He wailed in a low voice.

Then great racking sobs consumed him for about seven minutes. It was his friend the perky squirrel who sounded the alarm and began scolding. This was sufficient for his survival mechanisms to come into full alert, and dashing a hand across his eyes he sat up and saw the bear in the lower meadow. It was a grizzly. It seemed not to acknowledge his presence and gave no sign of awareness. The grizzly was just passing through his own territory, but Wild Boy knew that it had pin-pointed his location and what type of animal he was. The grizzly was at the top of the food chain, he was the king of all he surveyed, and it was Little Boy Wild who had to be fully aware of all the dangers involved. Despite this, seeing the bear relaxed him more completely and he felt no fear. Humans would not be here and had no reason to be here, for this was not the killing season. Wild Boy was a lone Spirit Creature and only partially Human. He was surrounded by his friends, the animals and birds, and spent hours just *"being."* He did not have to think about deadlines and debts that became due; it was simply not his world. When the first star twinkled, he cleaned up his gear and retreated to his vehicle. Had the grizzly smelled the peanuts and chocolate? It might check him out. A young male human pre-stuffed with peanuts and chocolate makes a good meal! He always thought of a meal from the bear's viewpoint!

Somewhere around midnight, slow warm breezes wafted across the meadow, and the blazing constellations of a trillion worlds above him brought Little Boy Wild out to merge with the night. He wore nothing, not even his knife or runners. He thought of the grizzly but became lost in awe of the night sky. So much did he merge with starlight and shadows that *he became what they were*. In all his twenty five summers he had never before become a pure thought form moving with such grace and power; it seemed that energy entered him and empowered his whole being from some place beyond his present level of consciousness. His feet lightly touched the green turf, and he could see the sleeping flower forms as they moved in dance with the merest whispers of the night breeze. Wild Boy revelled in his night magic so much, that he wished that the exquisite feelings he experienced when the night sky embraced him, would go outside of time and be an eternal "Now."

"I am a child of light," he mused aloud as he traveled the stars of Orion's Belt, "And my Father is the *Father of Lights** – and I'm not supposed to hide my light!" He recalled this from some evangelical preacher who ran a big meeting out on the prairies from within a huge tent. He was not able to forget it. He wondered how it had became so etched in his mind; but then he remembered the preacher told him personally to go out at night with a powerful flashlight, and "look for darkness." At twenty two years old – Little Boy Wild had done just that – and the darkness had fled before him.

He discovered that this "making darkness flee" could be physical – but, more importantly for him – it could reside within his mind where thoughts became reality. The light of Jesus within him could dismiss demonic powers! He heard again the preacher's powerful voice, 'Let there be light!' –

---

* Father of Lights. King James Bible. James 1.17

and out of all of this, he often imaged himself as a "Child of Light." He had proved again and again – even in the blackest of darkness – that he could radiate this light from within himself, to a level of intensity and brightness where the powers of darkness, as well as the darkness itself could not possibly exist!

He lay on a small grassy hummock gazing into the heavens, and thought of all the poor humans in the cities who never saw stars as he did, because the stars were obliterated by lights of their own making, and this caused them to be blind in more ways than one. They had the brightness of man, but he had lights of the cosmos. Night insects called to each other, an occasional bat winged over, and shooting stars added wonderment to joy. But, slowly a night chill came up, and he arose to return to his vehicle for warmth and sleep. Sometimes his Five Star Woods down filled sleeping bag was too hot, but he could always pull it partially off. Tonight it warmed him quickly, and before sleeping he merged his life force with a brilliant star, where, deeply in touch with his inner self, he allowed his ecstatic release to drift into dreams where love was real.

Sunlight awoke Little Boy Wild with a gentle warm and loving touch. His limbs responded to stretching with a delicious feeling of relaxed power. His powerful morning tumescence was quenched in the icy creek where he washed up, before stepping into the discoveries of another day. Scanning the meadow he ran lightly back to the vehicle. Next was breakfast. He was easily able to catch half a dozen cut throat trout. Scurrying back to camp he soon had blue wood smoke drifting through the trees. He balanced one of the Buick hub caps between a few rocks and gave it a splash of water, frizzling the cleaned trout but briefly, before devouring them in a manner perhaps more like an animal, than that which his appearance portrayed. Wild Boy felt the new energy flow into his system. "The whole universe is the exchanging of energies," he murmured.

For the next two days he occupied himself with dreaming, questing, fishing and sleeping. It seemed that each night he sought out the same bright star in order to merge himself with the night sky. He thought of the space between each breath, the space between his heart beats and the spaces between consciousness and the twilight of sleep. He also went far back into the nightingale's perfect song, like he had done when he was with

248

Tim in the honeysuckle cabin, and again thought of exploring between the notes in the event that one was missing. But they had always been perfect. Perhaps there are other gaps, not between notes of a song, but between levels of consciousness, which would lead to the parallel worlds that he knew must exist. It then occurred to him that he had a space between each of his thoughts. So what was in the space? This sent him into a world of speculation. This surely must be part of the great quest!

Reality raised its head when Wild Boy saw the flat front tire. His own vehicle had become a victim of the Tire Guck scam. He passed control back to me but briefly, and we did agree that we had to head back to civilization. I felt stronger, and I knew *Little Boy Wild had done what he had to do in order to be HE and reinforce his identity*. It was on the way back when a second tire flattened while we drove through the ranch land that it got to him because he knew we had no second spare available. It brought his brain to a halt and in today's jargon – he freaked out big time!

He got out of the vehicle, shed his clothing, and rolled on the ground, finally lying very still. I thought he was going into one of his "Keelematu" type sessions. But he didn't care to move. He just lay there as though in a trance. Ants explored him and flies crawled on him, but he did not move. The sun got hot, and later he rose to take a drink from his flask. I thought we had agreed to go back and carry on selling fire extinguishers. At this rate we would not get home tonight, and this was our fifth day out. I became concerned. It seemed that he had gotten to such a high tension level by knowing that we had to return, plus all the pain from the past which kept re-emerging, that even his rolling around and Keelematu wailing could not handle it. So what would? Maybe he had to get in touch with himself. Sure enough, he rose with a smile of anticipation. He was driven by extreme tension, and in a low husky voice, Wild Boy proclaimed aloud, *"I'm in here somewhere! Why am I here? What is this place? How did I get here?* My only connection between me and my outside world is *this.*" He ran across a sand dune caressing himself enabling him to be *he,* and also in contact with reality. When the moment came to spurt his insanity to the wind, he spotted a huge fuzzy brown bumble bee atop a thistle. The bee was so engrossed in loading pollen it must have wondered what had happened.

"Hit!" exclaimed Wild Boy. He watched the creamed up bee buzzing and struggling as he tried to clean the madness off his fuzzy body, but he just could not fly.

"I remember now!" Wild One suddenly shouted. According to all the rules of aeronautical engineering, the bee is not supposed to be able to fly. But he does anyway! He does not know that he cannot fly! He just does! *If he can – I CAN!* He laughed in exultation at having rediscovered this fact. He went back to the bee, treated it to warm yellow shower and placed it on a purple thistle blossom to dry off. After a few minutes in the hot sun the bee revved up its motors and took off.

"You, you d-d-don't m-m-mind if I'm a b-b-bbee for a while do you?" Wild Boy spoke in a plaintive tone. "I'm supposed to be a total emotional write-off, but this mind-set has as powerful a grip on me as the supposed laws of flying have on my bee! He flies, and *SO CAN I.*" he shouted.

I knew now he had seen an inner strength whereby he could handle what we had to do. We got the tire fixed at a local ranch, and went on our joyful way to join our fire extinguisher team. I did wonder what the outside world of *"Normal"* people would think if they really knew how weird we *were*, and *are*; remembering of course that Wild Boy and I are one and the same!

One of my best salesmen was a mouse—an electric motor mouse. He deserved an award. He sold thousands of dollars worth of fire fighting equipment for me. He was a sort of Jesus mouse too—because he even died for me—inside an electric motor! When an old widow bought an extinguisher, she told that she would never again rely on her well, pump, or hose to fight a fire. During the last fire an electric motor burnt out, and had ignited papers nearby. With the power gone she was helpless, and the fire had been started by a mouse which somehow got inside the motor. Wow! Now I could handle that famous sales objection to buying a fire extinguisher—because they always said "we have a well and a hose... we don't need it."

My face would register understanding and serious shock—"Did you not hear about Widow Moshanski's fire? Burnt her home right to the ground,"... I swallowed, and looked sadly down almost overcome with emotion; "She had a well, a pump, and a good hose—but do you know what?" I exclaimed my voice rising in horror, feeling heat and seeing flames all round—"It was a m-m-mouse! A m-m-mouse in the electric motor that ran the pump, that not only started the fire in the first place, but also killed the power—so, no water! Now, you've got mice haven't you?" I questioned, cooling off the emotion.

There, my case was made, everyone who had a mouse needed a fire extinguisher, and the logic was inescapable. There were mice everywhere.

"Yes— and it's m-m-m-mouse proof," I stammered, patting the red extinguisher, my voice expressing finality. Then bringing things back on track again I'd ask, "Where do you want your units installed? I had visions of squeaking all the way to the bank, that mouse story was a real winner. Now if only I could say MOUSE rather than m-m-m-mouse, I'd have it made!

Others would say "Ain't no mice around here—we got damn good cats."

I'd hold up my hand, like a policeman stopping traffic.

"Did you hear about old Charlie's cat?" I'd ask them—"That big old red bugger that got its fur on fire?—ran to the barn, got in the straw, bingo, she went up like wow! Mind you, if they had put a couple of extinguishers in the barn they could have caught it right there."

"Yeh, but it don't happen too often..." The prospective buyer sat down.

"It only has to happen once," I stated, and so it went, never a dull moment, though we had some bright scorching ones at times as we laid demonstration fires and valiantly fought most of them down with our equipment. It could be truly said that we blazed a trail across the west.

Chapter Twenty

*E*ventually I flew to England on an old Trans-Canada Airlines North Star four engine prop plane to negotiate our taking over the exclusive Nu-Swift extinguisher franchise for all of Canada, and to somehow bypass our present supplier who in essence at that time was doing nothing for us of a constructive nature. In this I succeeded and returned within ten days with the document on my inside pocket feeling very much like a successful international businessman. At age twenty-six this was a good feeling.

Finally we had some real supplies coming in—pouring in would be the better way to describe it, and they were shipped to us at a price that would allow us a decent profit. Now to get the sales rolling into high gear! Oh disaster! Why visit me at a time like this? An economic problem arose. The farmers could not sell their wheat. The market was practically non-existent, and therefore our big sales had dried up overnight. Moreover the farmers could not pay us what they owed us, and didn't order or buy our products in the former quantity.

As Tom suggested—"Maybe they can't get their wheat to market because we're using most of the trains to haul fire equipment!"

This might almost be true. The products were arriving in quantity. It seemed that every train from the East or the West unloaded great blocks of wooden crates containing our fire extinguishers on the Lethbridge railroad platform. We had stopped the orders, but we discovered that everything for many months ahead had already been shipped. We had stopped the flow from England but the pipeline was full! It all emptied out at Lethbridge, and we didn't have a cent to buy it, or to clear it through customs. Indeed it was hard to find money for coffee and a piece of apple pie. The shipments blocked the railroad platforms where they were stacked ten feet high, and there was no where else to put them. We could not pay the freight to clear it out of the station, and Canadian Pacific pleaded with us to clear it all out so they could operate. Thus—the great quest for money began. Of course the banks wouldn't look at us; we had difficulty in cashing even a five dollar cheque.

"Who has money—Tom?" I asked.

It was a top level executive brain storming session held in our tiny shop as we sat on a couple of packing crates. I was desperate, but we did succeed as a result of a massive financial canvass of the local community, in getting directed to a source of financing at 1.5% per month, which was quite a bit back in 1954. We now owed $20,000 in sundry debts, and had a load factor on top of that for storage and interest each month on the still outstanding 100% balance which was secured by the equipment. The outlook was bleak and winter would soon be upon us. Tom returned to Radio Station CJOC, or perhaps it was the new television station. I'm sure Tom's loyal and understanding wife Alice must have heaved a sigh of relief that the whole financial fiasco had come to an end. We closed out the fire extinguisher business and dead broke (what's new?) I headed for Calgary, the cow and oil city, to look for a job. Having arrived in Calgary amid the snow and bitter cold sub zero weather of winter 1954, I made Midnapore my operating base—in those days a little settlement just on the southern extremities of the city. All that winter I slept in the '52 Buick Roadmaster under the Fish Creek Bridge. When I did have the money for a cup of coffee, I'd empty the sugar bowl and fill my pockets with the little cubes when no one was looking. Later I would eat—sugar, with water from the creek. Gas was unobtainable on credit as I had no job, so I fell back on the rubber tube and siphoned what was needed. That Buick got seven miles to the gallon!

Then suddenly one day my eye spotted an advertisement from a management consulting firm in the United States who were seeking an Alberta representative. It turned out that the present agent had been promoted to management and was relocating in the U.S. Away I went for an interview. First I was turned down over the phone due to age —only twenty-six, and to lack of experience. Secondly I was refused when I drove over to the interviewer's home the following day where a haphazard form of interview took place. I lacked the polish, maturity, poise and bearing that he was seeking for this executive selling position. But I did get a brochure about the company, and I read and reread that literature so as to basically understand what a management consultant does for the companies it works with. I liked the idea. It had an aura of professionalism, integrity and legitimacy—and I needed all three of these in good measure right now. I wanted that job! I had to have cash flow. My job would be to interview the owners or presidents of a wide variety of businesses and offer our services. Firstly, I would arrange for a business analyst to come in and run a complete survey of the company and make specific recommendations for improvement. Then following him, the management engineers would arrive and actually implement the changes.

Rex, my brother, at this time was running a truck, hauling flour for George Weston Ltd. between Edmonton and Calgary. He always stayed at the old Calgary Brewing Hotel, the Empire on East Ninth Street. When he came in the next day I borrowed enough money to call the western offices of the U.S. consulting company in San Francisco and Chicago... then I called them up and explained that I wanted that position with their company. They too refused on the basis of my age and immaturity—apart from going over the head of their new regional manager. I comforted myself with "Oh well, I tried."

It was on those occasions when we were with Rex at the Empire that we reminisced on some of the disasters we had participated in as youngsters. "Remember that boat we sank?" Rex asked, as he chortled and sipped on his beer. Oh Yes! How could we ever forget that! We recalled that it was a lovely blue sky sunny day, when on the edge of the woods bordering the lake, we saw, some twenty feet below us – a dad with his two kids and some of their friends. They were about to launch a superbly crafted model sail boat of about three feet in length. Their exuberance and excitement had them dancing with anticipation. But somehow, the flawless blue hull, the white sails and the meticulous detailing – everything to scale – ropes, winches and all – struck us the "wrong" way. Was it the boat? Or was it, in retrospect, the joy and love I saw expressed between the father and his sons? Suddenly my feelings and emotions swung wildly out of control. I went into my destruction mode.

"Let's sink the fucker!" I had exclaimed. "It's the German battleship "BISMARK," and we are HMS.HOOD and the aircraft carrier HMS.WAR-

255

SPITE! Rex ignited, and without a second thought we amassed enough rocks of varying size to make a small "ammo" pile. The group below us, immersed in small talk and lost in admiration of this beautiful craft – were totally unprepared for the first rocks which splashed near the boat. We now had our target's range. Rex chortled with a peculiarly helpless sound that assured me of his full and devastating support. HMS.HOOD will never let me down. This was our expertise – throwing rocks destructively. The next batch of rocks scored direct hits breaking the masts, and down came her sails amid screams of alarm, surprise and rising anger. It all happened so quickly. Rex lobbed a big one which crushed her polished deck, and she keeled over on her starboard side, next, one of my rocks split her hull and she started to sink. We had direct access to our target because when the first rocks hit –the group had drawn back in shock, except for the Dad and his two young sons. Now other adults ran to the scene. The younger boy was screaming, he had been hit someplace and had fallen to his knees and was doubled over, his hands wrapped around his head. Someone swept him up and he was carried away. The other kids had fled out of range along the water's edge. There was loud shouting, huge panic and anger. We took one last look at that craft of flawless beauty, now a pathetic mess with a gaping hole in her hull – the battleship "BISMARK" had been sunk. *How many more times do I have to ask myself – Why do I feel so alive when destructive things happen? Why do I experience such feelings of wild elation as I watch myself in action? Why must I inflict pain?*

"There they are!" a deep male voice roared. We have been seen, but as they give chase we out-distance them quite easily, and we know the trails in these woods so well that we have no difficulty in fleeing to our refuge in the undergrowth alongside a field of ripening oats. We lie low for a while until the sounds of pursuit have died away; but we also lie low a little longer just in case one of our pursuers is cunning and hiding in silence to catch us when we do appear. Later, when we decided to go home, we caught sight of police combing the area which panicked us, and we holed up like foxes for a long time. Rex and I looked at each other – we now both feel terrible about this, which is unusual. We know that we should never have committed this terrible act of wanton destruction. A cloud of guilt and regret came over us. We discussed the nice clean cut, well dressed kids – more than one of them had been hit, though none seriously – perhaps just a bruise or two, a few cuts and a good shaking up, and this had come about mainly because I had lobbed a few extra rocks at them even after the boat was destroyed.

"I had the distinct impression that you deliberately aimed at that little dark haired kid in the blue shirt when he looked up in our direction," Rex charged me.

"Well – yes and no," I admitted. "He was just in the way of a rock that was intended for the "BISMARK," and I just couldn't help it, it was already in motion when he moved into its path." But Rex didn't buy my explanation, and it didn't match up with the deadly accuracy we shared in these exploits. This was not fun; it had gone way beyond our usual boundaries for raising hell, into weird territories of uncontrolled emotion. Human life was at stake, and I had denied the terrible truth – *I had intended to hit him, and I did.* I was lying to myself. Rex had perceived this and was silent. He looked unusually subdued. Why did I want to hurt this harmless little kid? What had he done to me? It was then that *I saw myself – outside of myself,* curled over, gasping, and walking away down a bushy trail. Tears streamed down my face as I cried, not for the boat, but for that neat little dark haired kid, who was probably only about seven years old. He could easily have been killed by the rock that struck him on the side of his head. I kept seeing his face – it would haunt me forever – I had smashed his excited laughter into a mask of screaming terror. I sobbed brokenly and rolled around among the ferns, terrible pains racked me from deep inside. "No! No! – I love you! I don't know why I did it. I didn't mean to kill you! I love you!" I screamed. I found myself holding his limp body in my arms; his long dark lashes partially hid his incredibly blue eyes – which were vacant and staring. They held my gaze. I moaned and rocked while I clasped him tightly to me. Blood soaked my shirt. I kissed his satin cheek, tasting his blood on my lips, all the while I loudly cried, "No! No! You can't be dead." Again I looked at him – but in wonderment – what a perfect young creature he had been, so warm, so beautiful. His tanned legs were spattered with blood, and when I scanned his face in death, his innocent expression ripped me apart. I screamed in anguish, a horrible sound that surprised even me, and then *I disappeared "inside," I never wanted to come back – ever.* A short while later reality emerged. Rex was looking down at me. "He's not dead, he's just cut, bruised and badly shaken up," he said, with a catch in his voice. I arose from my agony, and without meeting his eyes, we slowly trekked home. We never spoke of the affair ever again –until now.

Back again in the Empire Hotel days with Rex, an abrupt change occurred a few days later in the matter of me being associated with the management consulting firm.

It was late evening when an unidentified car cautiously crept through the frozen snow with its tires making the usual scrunching sounds. It approached my abode under the Fish Creek Bridge. I was boiling water in one of the Buick hubcaps over a bright fire in order to make some tea. Was this the sheriff? It could be, as both the sheriff and GMAC wanted that Buick. I grabbed the 30.30 Winchester just in case it was trouble. What if it were the RCMP? It would be a tough situation meeting a Mountie. Me with a loaded gun, and despite my macho image I was not *that* brave, so why am ready to use the rifle I'm holding? Long ago I'd learned as a Boy Scout to Be Prepared. I was!

Seconds later, I recognised the car as belonging to the regional manager of the consulting company. There I stood in my parka, rifle in hand, beside the fire. I greeted him while standing my weapon against the Buick. He eyed me strangely while explaining that both management in the U.S. and Canada had discussed me over the phone, and had decided to hire me because of what they described as my 'colossal gall.'

"Anyone who goes about it like you have so far is worth a try," the manager stated with doubt clouds lurking behind his features and apprehension in his eyes. It was 35 degrees below zero, and there was only one flat rock to sit on, so I agreed to meet him under more civilized conditions on the following day.

Hooray!! Finally the position was mine. I even had an expense account—I'd be able to eat, and even buy gas instead of stealing it—maybe I'd make a car payment and get the repossession boys off my tail. I was youngest man the company had ever hired, and within two years I became one of their most successful. They said I was 'motivated'—perhaps that meant that I no longer had to take a white shirt out of its wrapper at 35 below zero when I woke up in the frosted car at 6:30 A.M. to put that icy cloth against my warm skin. It meant not having to light a small fire under the oil pan of the Buick to thaw my motor so it would crank over with the help of some ether. Within two years I became district manager for Western Canada, the North-western United States, Alaska, the Yukon and the North West Territories.

It was touch and go on car payments for a while, but I managed to elude the sheriff and the finance repossession boys with daring strategies, and by camping out in wheat and oat fields surrounded by bush. Once when I was visiting Rex and having supper, the finance company rep knocked on the door, formally asked me for the keys, and then went back to his office to get someone to drive the Buick back to their "seizure compound." I swallowed a few more lumps of supper, got my spare keys, cranked up that old Buick and sped into the countryside. The finance men returned in a matter of a few minutes, and looked in stunned amazement at the empty space that my car had occupied just minutes before. Rex had a really good laugh, said he couldn't help them and went in to finish supper. Was it because I was so deranged that I got in the scrapes that I did? No, I concluded with the aid of my movie director, it's just a film after all, and soon I'd return to my normal everyday life... which *WAS* the film! Is there no escape? *How do I get de-scripted?* Well—they never did seize that car, and eventually the payments became current.

On the job itself I quickly found that these successful businessmen were smooth, articulate, quick thinking, intelligent, and way better educated than I. Indeed one of my first calls acted like a dose of laxative.

"Mr. Brown will see you now," the beautifully groomed blond secretary stated in soft tones, and suddenly when the heavy door swung open there was my prospective client. The door clicked shut behind me like the lock on a trap. There was nowhere to run; my eyes darted to the windows. I felt and looked like a trapped animal. He glanced up —"Come in boy, come on in, I won't throw you out, you don't have to be scared."

It was as though he had extended his hand to pet a shy rabbit. Wow—what a start to an executive selling interview that I was supposed to be conducting. Hang in there Wild Boy, you can escape to the forest and the chipmunks later. I stepped forward through the deep broadloom. The prospect was friendly and reassuring. I did not make a sale but I got the experience of my first interview.

But in another building as I waded through thick carpeting surrounded by rich walnut, as the secretary led the way to the CEO's office, my courage failed and I fled downstairs, jumped in the Buick and drove back to the creek in a blind bewildering panic without knowing why. Now as I write about this – I recall!! Amazing!! It was the way the beautiful secretary looked at me – she thought I was what she saw! When really I had suddenly become Little Boy Wild, in a hostile situation with a beautiful woman – terror! No trees and animals – more terror, and that meant run, either to the real wilds, or to *"the meadows of my mind,"* where I felt at home. Oh! coyotes and jack rabbits I love you —I'd feel better, a lot better, if offices had birds flying around, wild roses blooming, creek music, breezes, the odd black bear or cougar wandering through—then I could relax. Maybe this was IT—maybe I was through—forever.

I paced up and down the creek bank talking with the squirrels until noon. No. I must face it. I must learn how to handle the humans. *I must do the thing I fear most.* No one had hurt me yet, and I must hang on to that basic pay and the expense account. What was I scared of? People! People scared me. There were so many of them. They talked and laughed, and I wondered what they thought about, and what made them tick. I understood what the animals said and how they lived – but Humans were somehow different.

I'd bath three times a week in the winter at the Empire Hotel when Rex came in with his truck, and after supper—courtesy George Weston Ltd—we'd sit and drink beer with the whores in the beer parlour below. They'd sometimes drop into our room for a beer as we wandered around in just our shorts or with a bath towel draped around us—real nice girls—we never used them, nor did we look down on them, and I'm sure they wouldn't have charged us a penny. In any case I was plagued with intimacy problems and although I put on a good show and spoke of female escapades, they were mostly from my imagination.

About this time I graduated from the Fish Creek Bridge to a little green shack, one of a series of so called cabins behind a motel in east Calgary. It was just an empty cabin except for an old iron bed with a rusty bedspring, a gas stove for heat and a cold water tap. Of course there was the inevitable galvanized bucket in the corner by the door. This was stepping up to a new level of luxury—especially in sub zero weather. I had heat, and my Woods sleeping bag, all down filled, kept me snug and comfortable. However, it was hardly the type of base or accommodation befitting an employee of one of North America's more prestigious consulting companies!

One day an executive of the firm flew in from the States to work with me on the job for a few days. All went well until we ran out of a certain business form, and when I mentioned I had some at home in a carton and would bring them on the morrow he said, "Tell you what, let's go over to your place for a while and then I'll take some of the forms back with me to the hotel and turn in for the night." Oh no! I thought. Let's not and say we did. I swung the Roadmaster into the muddy driveway. We wallowed through pot holes and suddenly I saw the whole scene through his eyes.

There was the shabby cabin with peeling green paint. Grimy half-naked kids were running around amongst the garbage, scrap metal, junk, rags, and old tires, and as I pulled up to the door, a big bony brute of a hound was copulating with a Heinz 57 cur on the pathway. Other wild-looking part malamute type dogs lay around waiting their turn. Two cabins down a drunken woman was screaming, and kids were squealing.

"I'll be right out," I said, hoping he'd stay in the Buick. But—he didn't. He came in and just stood in the doorway and looked. I hadn't emptied the piss bucket in several days, and as I had nothing to lose at this point I took the opportunity to heave the contents outside, drenching the panting straining dogs on the doorstep. The bed stood bare and rusty in the middle of the floor where the tiles were peeling. The water tap dripped. There was not a proper chair to sit on other than a stack of Calgary Heralds.

Reynolds was silent as I picked up the forms we needed. Then we both stepped outside where a grimy kid with green sliming nose, stood in a muddy puddle throwing gravel chips at the panting dogs. Little wisps of steam rose from the entranceway now as the warm sun evaporated the urine into the atmosphere.

We returned in silence to the Palliser Hotel and there amid sumptuous luxury and decor we discussed our business plans for the next day over superb roast prime ribs of beef. I enjoyed the enormous contrast. Reynolds explained, while looking strangely at me, that the company would expect me to vacate the cabin and locate more fitting quarters in line with the company image, to which I agreed. So I checked out of the cabin and returned to the Fish Creek Bridge—at least it was clean and uncluttered.

There was no point in taking a suite or room as I was travelling a lot and would not be there to use it, and using a hotel room every night was too expensive. So I returned to living in the Buick, as the company paid no expenses while I was at home base in Calgary. They did not get rid of me. I was producing too many top quality contracts for that. I made good money, but almost every cent went towards paying off the debts of the defunct fire extinguisher business. As a result an $18,000 a year income in 1954 still left me destitute and sleeping in the car. It was all going to paying of the defunct fire extinguisher company debts. With this cash flow, and no debt, I could have bought a beautiful home—they sold for $20,000 to $25,000 in choice locations in both Calgary and Edmonton.

In spite of all the psychological conditioning in dealing with the Humans, Little Boy Wild remained wild in his total perspective. He was still quite happy so long as we shared daylight working hours equally. In the morning I endeavoured to obtain contracts for the consulting company, and for the rest of the day Wild Boy roamed the surrounding hills and ranch country. He usually explored the back country and creeks, communing with the coyotes and birds and just *being.* It was an Eden of delight to revel in the sunlight with creek water burbling around his ankles, while the whole bird chorus of summer echoed through the poplars and alders.

The consulting company somehow suspected, or knew that we were not working full time, and apparently had put a "tail" on *us* to see how *we* spent the average day! We discovered this one summer afternoon when we had parked the Buick down by the creek, and had wandered up-stream for about a half a mile – when like a coyote, we sensed danger. It was then that we saw two Humans following us somewhat surreptitiously. They were dressed in "city" type clothes and obviously had a mission. Quickly, Little Boy Wild "went to ground" off a tiny island where another creek joined the bigger one. He was mostly submerged in the water and reeds, and on peeking out, he found that these intruders into his paradise were two young men, who now sat on the creek bank almost directly opposite him. They were making notes, and discussing where he could have disappeared to! We wondered after they had left, if this were their first assignment on us, and laughed when we imagined what they put in their reports! The consulting company had no remote concept of the fact that Wild Boy basically thought and acted like a coyote trying to adapt to the city environment. This was *their* world – this was the domain of the Humans. None of them knew me or cared about us, except in terms of our dollar value to them. Wild Boy cared about different things – like the coyote pups in their lairs up the valley, their parents nuzzling in playful frolic before he left to go hunting. We cared about the mountain blue birds of spring, the tree swallows and the scarlet tanagers of summer. *Our very balance of mind depended on all of these elements.* Season by season we drew strength from them and melded it with starlight. To celebrate the celestial music of the night skies was to be *accepted* by the universe – *we belonged.*

Chapter Twenty One

So it was that I ventured into the Human's territory each day to achieve what had to be achieved in the shortest possible time—and then I fled back to my hidden haunts with the winds, the creek and the calls of the wild. I got the signed pieces of paper the Humans wanted, and they sent me coloured slips of signed paper that satisfied those who made claims upon it. There was the "unreal Derek" who unwillingly conducted business matters—and Little Boy Wild who ran in naked abandon among the secret hills with his wild friends. I sometimes wondered – can WE ever be one? Or will WE forever go our separate ways? Money has no real meaning for us. Our currency is one of colour, of scent, of motion and ethereal feelings among the trees when Orion glints in the night sky. My values—seemingly without value to the Humans—embrace a dimension that is far from their commercial activities. For how could one exchange the look and feel of a baby red squirrel in one's hands, or trade the leaping elation one experiences upon reaching the alpine meadows? What would one buy with such priceless living art? From the foothills I hear the distant din and roar of machines and construction, commerce in motion, the sound of humans and their money. From my grassy flower strewn hill I gaze west to the far off snow-capped mountains. Nearby wild roses send their own special messages. I inhale the pure morning air, and fleet of foot, I follow the wind into the Elysian meadows for today's special adventure.

It came to me through the twilight of an evening that I was handling interviews and even board meetings with high power executives—beautifully.

"You must be improving Derek," I stated loudly to myself. Indeed it was now comparatively rare for me to trip up in my speech. These days in my sales work I fielded questions and confirmed interpretations with skill, ease, and quiet confidence. I realized that the old stuttering bugaboo was largely behind me!

In the over-all picture it would appear that I had triumphed. I had gained humanity and the "Rat Race!" I produced volumes of contracts for the consulting company, but the Movie Director said, "Things are going too well, kick over the traces! Do your own thing." On top of that, Alaska called me. Was it the flower strewn alpine meadows or snowy mountain peaks as yet unexplored? Or was it the huge Kodiak bears and the legend of the land itself? Adventure called and called, until finally I responded with that surging tremor that the wild geese must feel in the early spring as they wing northward for the breeding season. I requested permission from management at our San Francisco office to work in Alaska for a while. This was denied. "You stay in Alberta, Derek. We handle Alaska from our Seattle office," they said. No sooner had I hung up the phone when the old entrepreneurial spirit sprang up in me. In my mind's eye I saw the old wood buildings in Skagway, and I thrilled to see the fearsome Kodiaks root out the marmots. How can one deny a destiny so rich in uncertainty? How can one kill the instinct that it as intermingled with the north as the Northern Lights? Every dazzling display of its starry northern splendour seemed to correlate in a magnetic way to the surges of my heart-pounding frenzy. My heart leapt and sang as it always did when the skeins of geese honked on their journey northward. How many times had I flown with them, riding high and remote on their song of spring?

"Hey! Wild Boy! Are you still there?"

"Yes" he replied, "and I'm wondering if I'm a wild goose or a suicidal lemming!"

It was some two and a half years before this, that in our usual weird semi-wild state that *we* had met a lovely young woman whom I'm sure couldn't make head or tail of *us*. But despite this, it was destined for us to be married. The year was 1955. She had no remote concept of the depth of debt that surrounded me at that time, nor could she know *which* Derek she married! And I wasn't sure which one of *us* married her, but by 1956 our first son had emerged to play a role in our lives. It would be a hard thing to explain my different entities to my wife, or anyone else for that matter, because I didn't have a clear picture of them myself! Maybe I'd find myself living permanently in *"the meadows of my mind"* with the rabbits.

Right now though, I sensed a great deal of business to be transacted. As the plane touched down in Ketchikan, all the excitement of new places and experiences possessed me, but there was also a feeling of fear and apprehension, I having proceeded with what I was specifically told *not* to do; and one simply does not act this way with a major consulting company operating in several countries! But the scent of the white-capped seas – the colourful seiners and trollers rocking at their moorings, and my beautiful screaming gulls – all welcomed me! Within four days I had the town of Ketchikan under control, and with a briefcase full of contracts, I strode into the local gun shop.

If I were going to be poking around in the wilderness and exploring Kodiak bear country, I wanted an equalizer to bail me out if trouble should occur, whether it had brown fur, two legs or four! So it was here that I bought my first Smith and Wesson .44 magnum revolver with the long 8-3/8" barrel. To this I added a gun belt and several boxes of ammunition and as there were no permits required, I planned a day or two of target shooting deep in the bush some place. In no time at all I'd rented a four wheel drive unit and headed deep into the forest. I blasted away at targets till I was reasonably accurate and almost deaf. That gun could 'BOP' and roar with a fury that I loved!

Next I discovered beautiful town of Sitka, again with the enchanting allure of the sea as it rolled against the captivating shoreline; it influenced me greatly, and I knew I'd have to leave the prairies and return to the sea permanently sometime in the future. Next I visited Juneau – the capital city, and it was here that I bought a unique necklace and bracelet of carved ivory animals. These exquisite little arctic foxes, whales and seals were alternated with squares of darker mastodon ivory. Things were going so well business-wise that I put these expensive little trinkets on my expense account. How could they say no? On the other hand how could I explain the S&W .44 magnum revolver I had put on the expense account last week? This was possibly my ideal life style. If we could balance the Human requirements demanded by raising a family, paying off debts, and live partially wild with the animals, be it in Alaska or elsewhere – would I be a balanced being? And of some significance – would my wife stay with me?

I had been in Alaska against instructions for more than two weeks, so I decided to call our divisional office in San Francisco. Soon my face and ears were red from the chewing out I received. But I quickly had them eating out of my hand so to speak, when I gave them details of the lucrative bunch of contracts I had acquired, and later when they processed my expense accounts, I heard nary a word about the ivory necklace or the gun! Additionally, I was then assigned Alaska as one of my territories. When I later returned to Canada by air, the .44 magnum was stuffed into my belt with the long barrel nudging me in sensitive areas. The ammunition weighed heavily in my raincoat which was nonchalantly slung over my left arm, with a great deal of pressure to hold it there! In those days there were no squeakers or personal searches, or a swat team would have been brought in! Of course I was guilty of illegally smuggling firearms too, but that did not disturb me in the least. When we arrived home, Little Boy Wild surrendered the tiny ivory animals to my wife. She was alien to him, and he shied from contact with her. He had kept the necklace and bracelet in his pocket while we cleared customs; and I had previously warned him that under no circumstance was he to talk to anyone in his own language, regardless of his tension level. But as he explained afterwards, as long as he could feel the little animals in his hand, it left him quite calm, thus allowing me to do the talking!

These days the primary question was about the Movie Director. Was he now dismissed to lower worlds, or was he still in our same world and had I risen to another? Maybe it was all part of the master plan where as I travelled up the spiral of consciousness, where truths that were true on one level, are only relatively true to what is known on another? As an unloved child we never stopped hurting – the need for love supersedes all other needs. Our heart goes out to all those abused kids who do not have a strip of woodland or a meadow to which to flee from hurt and danger, as they try to escape from perhaps far worse situations than any we have experienced. Arthur Janov's beautiful wording encapsulates the feeling:*

"It is that moment of icy, cosmic loneliness – the bitterest of all epiphanies. It is the time he is beginning to discover that he is not loved for what he is, and will not be."

So far we have lived through an unending futile attempt to compensate for parental love that neither my mother nor father was capable of giving. At this stage of life, I no longer see through a glass darkly – but truly face to face. *I have been engaged in a lifetime of unreal symbolic behavior!*

HERE IS WHERE THIS WRITING PAUSED FOR A PERIOD OF ABOUT FOURTEEN YEARS!! – Yes! A pause like this is a mere "blip" of time in this parenthesis in eternity! Was it really true that the way we are *"Scripted"* as children continues to exert an unconscious influence of the decisions we make throughout life? Little Boy Wild and I have come a long way, but we are sure of this – *we must go forward to unlock the past, or is it really that we have to go back, to unlock the future?*

"Okay Wild Boy – Derek and whoever – tell us what happened!"

"Well – we pick up from where we were still with the management consulting company, and carry on with our adventures. If anything our understanding becomes more profound, and the psychological issues stand out more clearly with far more depth, and we are beginning to recognise our multiple selves. There were rollicking adventures, laughter and tears all the way, as *WE* carried on our journey of discovery! *Tim was right when he said – "Anything can happen – and probably will!"*

---

* The Primal Scream. Arthur Janov. 1970.

Chapter Twenty Two

Iran into a friend at the Seattle Airport one day while passing through to Alaska, and he introduced me to the Robert Palmer Corporation out of Santa Barbara, California; he was selling sales and management training programs and the commission was great. Better than that, the whole concept had none of the nerve racking situations we had in the consulting business with presidents of corporations. I had been feeling fairly close to a nervous breakdown for a while now due to the continuous relentless pressure for performance. Keeping up my own sales production while acquiring and training sales personnel in the field, and running the whole six-ring circus was taking its toll. Far worse than that, Little Boy Wild was hurting badly and was drowning in neglect. Previously when I was not in management there were times when I could go adventuring with him, but this had come to a halt. *Sooner or later I knew that he would have to "take over."*

So I quit the consulting business and engaged in the sale of personnel training programs to corporations. I was quite successful; even more so, because Little Boy Wild was able to spend a lot more time running utterly wild with me in the thickly flowered alpine meadows. When he heard the bleating picas and the whistling marmots, he reached an ecstatic level of mind that was beautiful to see – we merged at times like this – I felt what He felt. This was his world, his animals, and *HE* and *THEY* were as one.

At the time I sold the packaged training programs, my family and I were renting a home in North Vancouver. Rentals homes were hard to find, but I did find a home for sale in our desired location close to the Canyon Heights Elementary School. We had no money to buy a home, and the house in the location of our choice had been on the market for quite a while; so I approached the realtor with a rental proposition. The answer was yes, but only up to that point where a sale was imminent. Fair enough. But the day came about a year and a half later when the place was sold. We had 30 days to vacate the property, and cash flow was practically non-existent. In fact I kept the Valiant Wagon going by visiting lovers lanes on weekends to pick up beer bottles. Those refund monies kept the car going in gas and it was a lot safer than resorting to my siphoning techniques of the old days. But, I simply had not sold enough products. Little Boy Wild loved Stanley Park, the trees, the hidden dells with the squirrels and racoons, and he so dominated the "sales Derek" with his "escapes," meaning "living with the animals," that few sales could be made. Wild Boy was afraid both of the bustling city environment, and the humans. It was a deadly combination. It raised his tension levels to a degree that was beyond being just "dangerous" – to states of dissociation that accounted for many, many lost hours.

As the phone was about to be cut off, I arrived at the BC Tel office on a wet Tuesday morning to see what I could do about the overdue bill. They were closed as I was too early; but right next to them was a second hand store, so I spent time peering through the steamy windows. On a small table not far from the door was a series of little red books called "The Secret of the Ages" by Robert Collier, written I found out a little later, in 1927! Something about those books fascinated me, and when the owner arrived I asked him what he wanted for them.

He looked me up and down and said "How much cash do you have on you?" My face fell, it sounded like it might be a lot of money.

"I only have a dollar!" I explained. "I can't even pay my phone bill; I was waiting for BC Tel to open in hopes that I could persuade them not to cut our phone off.

"Let's see that dollar," he said. I passed it to him, my eyes passing from the books to him and back and forth.

"Sold!" he exclaimed. I was most grateful and scooped them into my little Valiant Wagon. Just one glance told me this was an oasis. I ignored the telephone company and drove far up onto a power line surrounded by dense forest in order to be alone. Maybe these secret books held a key for me. It monsooned, absolutely torrential rain, and I stayed all day and read those books. They were of the 'positive thinking genre' and really said that whatever the mind can conceive and believe, will happen. So I had to make things happen! I usually did, but mostly to the consternation of others. First things first, where do you want to build your new home? Not rent? No – build! I was able to find a building lot higher up, close to Canyon Heights Elementary School. The realtors in North Vancouver wanted $5000.00 for it (This was quite a few years back of course!) Today it would sell for about $250,000.

"Okay I'll take it" I said. I didn't even have enough cash for a cup of coffee! "I'd like to put $700.00 down and pay the balance in 30 days. This was okay with them; I signed the papers and gave them (at that time) a worthless cheque. I warned the realtor not to put the cheque through for 7 days and then put it through very gently in case it got scared! All okay. Now all I had to do was round up $700.00 fast.

Sales of course were the answer and my self esteem and power had risen tremendously. So far the "Secret of the Ages" was working. My whole attitude changed, after all, was I not the owner of a beautiful building lot and just about to build my custom home? I felt positively affluent and it rubbed off. Quickly I made several sales; the commissions would amount to more than $900.00. I mailed them by the fastest method to Santa Barbara and back came my commission cheque in a few days. It actually arrived on the day that the realtor was to put my dubious cheque through. It cleared and all was well. The phone worked. We even bought groceries. We ate. The kids were quite pleased.

This had taken eight days out of our 30 before we must vacate our rental home. Now I need the balance of the $5000.00 some $4300.00 and it was payable in 19 or 20 days! I knew I could never make enough money in the time available. So what to do? Read the "Secret of Ages" and get worked up again! Big time! While I was so engaged I met a nice young Aussie contractor. I explained to him exactly where I was at.

"No problem" he said. "I'll give the realtor the balance of your building lot money tomorrow, and then you choose your home design and we'll get a high ratio mortgage to package the whole thing. The following week the lot was paid off ahead of time; bulldozers and clearing machines prepared the site, and exactly 3 weeks after being told to vacate our rental home, we started to pour concrete. It actually took almost another month past our vacate date before we could move in. As it turned out, the buyers of the rental home were quite okay with us staying another month. So it was that we moved into our lovely new home with a big fireplace, nice broadloom carpeting and the works in record time. But all was not well.

Little Boy Wild wanted to move back to the Province of Alberta. He still had severe dissociating problems, and sales got hit amidships. So eventually we sold the home and moved. We would continue with the sales of training programs in Alberta. The slower pace, along with the wilderness close by, took most of the immediate pressure off Wild Boy. We succeeded in our endeavours. Some clients were so impressed with my sales know-how and ability, that they requested that I actually train their sales persons – so I wound up in the consulting business again.

Success followed success, so I branched out from sales training to management seminars for all levels of management. The only problem at the start was that I knew too little about it! But I still designed, wrote, organized, sold and ran seminars for corporations. The big break came when I was holding a training session at an inn located in Calgary, Alberta. I knew that two quite prestigious, world class consulting firms were also running management training seminars on our same meeting room level and I was most curious to see what they were teaching.

At lunch break I sneaked into their meeting rooms, and one glance told me I knew next to nothing about effective management training or human relations! Quickly I took one each of the hand out materials they were working on, from the side tables. First I stole study materials from one meeting room and then from the other. There was no security or locked doors as there frequently are today. While I was in the second room a hotel staff member asked me how it was going. Great! I told him! Then I carried on taking the hand out materials.

In the back of the various articles in these study sheets was a bibliography of management books with authors. This matched up to what I had seen on their chalk boards and displays. In no time at all I built my own management library stocked with books like The Practice of Management by Peter Drucker and other Drucker books, what a guy! The Human Side of Enterprise, Management by Objectives, books on Job Enrichment, Motivation, Communication and other fields also lined my shelves Wow! What a huge advance! This allowed me to design a quite different approach to work shop sessions. Then I acquired films on these subjects and merged them into my training sessions. One thing I now fully know, the teacher really learns! You're going to be grilled by the executives you are teaching. These are people with university educations running multi-million dollar corporations; I told myself "You'd better know what you are doing!" I did, and became a most sought after speaker and trainer in my chosen field.

I also had the benefit of having worked with a major U.S. management consulting firm and had seen first hand that systems of management fail, when all persons connected with an enterprise are not working as a team. So I wrote a book and developed my own system that I named *"Management Through Commitment"* or MTC Process. It involved everyone, and eliminated the gross errors in the philosophy that you send out middle managers or sales people to get "Fixed." I started at the top with the CEO along with key management and reached agreement on the required commitment and organizational climate needed. If we all agreed to proceed with the program on that basis, we would work with successive levels of training throughout the whole enterprise. It worked.

After one especially powerful session a lady executive came up to me and asked, "Where did you get your PhD? You were wonderful!"

To which I replied, "I have no PhD, but I do have the highly acclaimed EPE in Management."

"Oh!" She gushed, as she went on her way. A young manager standing by us had heard the encounter and said, "Oh! Come on Derek! Cut the crap, what in hell's name is an EPE?" I laughed out loud.

"Why, its Enthusiasm and Practical Experience, what else could it be?" We both laughed about the matter. He had gained a lot and was very impressed.

My feedbacks from the seminars were excellent at every level. How could I tell them that my formal education was limited primarily to a small village elementary school in England, where we basically learned reading, writing and arithmetic, the three "Rs" as they call them? Furthermore, what would they say, or do, if they found out that I had no real higher education, and had a multiple personality problem, now known as Dissociative Identity Disorder, and that Little Boy Wild was taking more than fifty per cent of my time as an emotionally retarded rebel, running wild and naked with the animals in the alpine meadows? I laugh to even think about it! However, this never came up, and I was invited on several occasions to lecture at a most prestigious management school, as well as at a couple of universities.

Looking back on the days when I sold training programs, I can now see how our two lives ran parallel to each other. Wild Boy was usually in the dominant position. He just *had* to explore remote wilderness areas to live with the birds, the pica and the elk – with total disregard for pressing financial matters. *He was driven, and it was quite beyond his power to take control or do otherwise.* Few people can envision, much less comprehend a personality change where in this case, Little Boy Wild takes control and I have to tag along. At times I found myself far out in the mountain valleys, and wondered why I was there and where I was going. The "Unreal" Derek's life, including his family – intruded into consciousness once in a while as though from another world. The *"Observer"* seemed to look at both of us, but did not lend weight in favour of a course of action for Little Boy Wild or me! *No, you can't take back control at will!* He just *had* to commune with the coyotes, deer, squirrels, martens, and butterflies; nor could he acknowledge that we were responsible for supplying a family with its needs.

People still ask:

"Why did you not take back control and act responsibly? Your behaviour under the circumstances was grossly reprehensible!"

"Yes, you are absolutely right!" I reply. "But there *were* and *are* powerful psychic forces at work that override the will, change personality, and produce psycho-sexual activity in addition to psychosis; and questions about mental stability arise. Thank God for the sanity of the animals in the forest, at least we understand each other!"

Early one summer We discovered a coyote lair, she was out catching ground squirrels so we had all four of the pups to play with. We were amazed as we approached them with the Leicaflex camera that they just stood and looked at us. One little coyote had the late afternoon sun behind him illuminating his ears to a beautiful pink. Wild Boy slowly picked him up for snuggling and love session, kissed him and petted him. He could never forget the sensation of this little coyote's world being transmitted to him. Wild Boy said it made him feel like a coyote! The other three who had not gone into the hole just studied us. We knew their mother would be back with food shortly so we put him down and slowly withdrew. Wild One also experimented with other coyotes. When he saw a single one not too far from us, he deliberately sent out messages of death and man and guns and aggression. Part of the time they seemed to react and turned to run, but was this just because they caught his scent? He tried this telepathic communication a number of times and could come to no definitive answer.

Generally as he moved through the wilds his thoughts were far from aggression, *for was HE not the hills, the forests and creeks, the animals and the cosmos itself?* Therefore, the coyotes and he were as one. They flowed through his time frame inside this total immersion, as though the coyote were a fish and he was the water! *All were contained in him!* It was self sustaining. As Little Boy Wild has said many times on his rambles, *"I am the mountains, I am the marmots, and I am even all the Humans. It is as if all creation was within me and I was the fabric or substance or molecular energy field in which "ALL" exists!"*

Back in the world of Humans and commerce, a Norwegian manufacturer was turning out an excellent array of small polyethylene boats and we decided to manufacture them in Canada and distribute these craft throughout North America. Of course we had no money; at least not enough to really float an enterprise of the size required. But that was beside the point. I liked to think that lack of money was never a problem, or was I just dreaming?

Did I discuss this move with Little Boy Wild? Yes and no! He did know that boats meant water and lakes and travel into wilderness areas, so he was not too concerned. But he was still quite upset about a situation we had run into, while on a mountain valley trip the previous week. It occurred while I was looking for a camping spot that was accessible for the vehicle I was driving, and as I scanned the land to my right that was fringed with deep forest, I saw a young fellow with a pack walking toward the trees.

"That's great!" said Wild Boy. "Why don't we walk over to see if we can make a camp together, then we won't be so lonely?"

So I walked over, and yes, he was looking for a safe camp site and we agreed that I bring the car over and help to set things up. He was quite a handsome youngster of about twenty summers, and was overwhelmed with the opportunity of having some company. Of course he didn't know that I was Wild Boy too! We were both clad in short cord pants, mine navy blue and his khaki. Our legs were equally tanned and muscular so it appeared that he too must be quite a hiker.

Little Boy Wild and he hit it off big time, and I was phased into the background of consciousness. Rob could not take his eyes off Wild Boy while they gathered some firewood and rocks to make a small fireplace, and Wild One could not help but notice the intense way Rob's concentrated gaze at his thighs and shorts made him tingle and stir. When Little Boy Wild met Rob's eyes they were alight and dancing with the pleasure of their closeness. As discussion arose by the fire while they boiled water, Rob said he had been dumped by his group of about eight others, and that they were on their way up the Alaska Highway to Juneau. Rob was not very clear as he tried to explain why he was "dumped." But between the lines I read that certain disagreements had come about between him and others in the group, and it was mainly due to Rob's overtures to those to whom he was attracted.

Strangely it was I who took over control as the night progressed. We made soup, the chill evening air came on, and eventually the stars shone with such brilliance, it was as if this were their very first night! Wild Boy had fully taken in the raw need that Rob was expressing with such eloquence in his body language. His whole lean presence and questing eyes portrayed his undisguised yearning for physical contact. Every time their eyes met Little Boy Wild's heart hammered and skipped a beat or two. He had the perfect set up; a live youngster of about his own age and there was no question about their mutual attraction.

It was almost time to turn in, and also too cold to stay by the dying fire. The stars reached down and seemed to touch us. Then to our mutual surprise as we stood there, I began a discourse on the creation of the universe. It was prompted by the stars no doubt; and surprisingly, of all things, I launched into an introduction to the Lord Jesus Christ! So the Preacher is still with me? Shortly after we retired to our respective tents, it was quite apparent Wild Boy was really freaked out over the fact that I had intervened. He was extremely tense and totally frustrated and I felt his needs as deeply as my own.

Again and again he exclaimed, "This is what I wanted, this is what I need! Rob needs me and I need him, how on earth could you bring Jesus in at this point?"

"I didn't, it must have been the Preacher." I explained.

He pounded his pillow, tossed and turned and eventually sobbed himself to sleep. Owls hooted. The stars followed their courses and the giant firs slowly moving in the night wind towered over our tents almost as protective entities who understood. They sighed softly. "There is nothing new under the sun......All is vanity."

The next morning we rose early and got some coffee going. Rob wanted to stay with Little Boy Wild for the day, and gazed longingly at him. They both imaged a lazy sun-drenched day, just the two of them entwined in mutual need, surrounded by the bird songs of summer. Their intimate chuckles and laughter would rise through the firs and across the clearing, as they achieved their satiating releases. By now, Wild Boy's tension level was so dangerously high, that it meant that he would be totally reckless, without any regard to the outcome of this encounter.

I intervened and envisioned my three young sons at home anxiously awaiting my arrival, as they anticipated a trip to a lake or nearby river. Wild Boy urged that we stay with Rob. He was explosive in his urgency to consummate their feeling for one another. But in the end we parted. Rob sadly continued his way to Alaska, and I headed for home some two hundred miles or so to the north. Little Boy Wild was deeply saddened and terribly hurt by the whole affair, so he retreated far inside himself leaving control to me. It was like having a part of me withering or dying inside somewhere.

I was rewarded by my kid's enthusiastic shouts and smiles of greeting. After supper we rolled and wrestled on the lawn and had some wonderful fun. Each of these kids was quite precious in their individuality. I felt like a male coyote returning to the lair with food. How often had I watched their joyful reunions, the kissing and nuzzling? My own marital situation was such that we were not close at this time as I had too many financial problems to keep things running smoothly; which in turn placed extra stress on Wild Boy, as he had no natural outlet for his pressures. It seemed that he felt much more alive and safe with a Rob-type situation. Little Boy Wild of course being the Real Derek, whose total upbringing and conditioning were such, that female contact meant pain and dissociation. It is a wonder that we had ever married. Years later a friend said, "Well Derek, your wife didn't leave you!" and I had to admit that this was quite strong validation for her, as she valiantly struggled to raise the kids a great deal of the time without me, and always without sufficient funds. It was a wonder that she survived the mental stress of our situation, especially when one compared it to other "normal people" in normal households, and the way they ran their lives. Of course she had no understanding of *our primary duality,* and at that time I certainly could not identify either my mental modes or behaviour.

Although I had always anticipated that these weekends at home would be rejuvenating and uplifting in nature, they were often terribly depressing. I reaped the rejection and anger of all that we had sown in our struggles, and these situations, although bad, were created by us, whether we wanted to own up to it or not. It was psychologically destructive, and it reduced me to "vacancy," at the time of my leaving. When I say "vacancy" I mean moving in a robotic, lifeless, drained manner. I was totally depressed, and only the opportunity to shake it off, was to engage in manic activity on a new sales target. *The more I worked – the less I felt.* At this time it seemed that Little Boy Wild and I had receded to nothingness. We were light headed, disoriented, and were so mentally disabled that it was not possible to work or plan or even think, and this I knew would last for several days. It came back to the same position when as a child I came to a dead end. It was the "cornered rat trauma" all over again. Wild Boy deeply regretted the decision to leave Rob, when they could have gifted each other with fun, acceptance, and lots of laughter, which would have been so healing.

"Why did we come home to this?" he asked, and stated, "This is unnatural, it is torture." Our only way out of this hurt and rejection was to go into the wilds, lie by a creek, gaze into the blue and do absolutely nothing. This however, created new tensions for I was aware that we would have to catch up some time. It was always a battle to live somehow, or jump into the "River of No Return." To make matters worse and to increase the level of tension was the fact that no one knew, or cared one iota whether I lived or died, except perhaps the kids. I suspected that psychiatrists had only *formulas* and *drugs* to keep people like me under control and manageable. Further, I speculated that they would label *"our reality"* as *"hallucinations,"* our situation being beyond their personal range of experiences or training. But my primary fear would be that Little Boy Wild would leap into the "River of No Return" and be swept away.

I pursued the Norwegian polyethylene boat manufacturing idea, but the rights had been already granted to a new plant in Montreal. My only alternative was to go for the sale of them as a manufacture's agent and distributor. I launched a company by the name of Western Watercraft Ltd, and the die was cast! Yes, we set up dealers and did all the things we could do as a one man outfit with no money. Additionally, we handled several brands of outboard motors and a host of boating accessories. During this period of high activity and cash flow I also acquired several building lots on the Sunshine Coast of BC. I was more than a little concerned about the accounting aspect. We had no book keeper and floundered horribly. One person can only do so much! The day of reckoning had to come! *When will I finally learn – as you sow, so you shall reap?**

---

* King James Bible.Galations.6. 7

Chapter Twenty Three

One bright day my entire "Empire" began to collapse. Like cascading dominos, all my financial dreams fell into oblivion. First the boating business under the name of Western Watercraft Ltd sank. We sold small boats from 8ft to about 14ft, mainly for fishing on lakes. Oh yes! We had canoes too. Prior to handling the beautiful Grumman and Alumacraft aluminum units, we had a polyethylene molded canoe about 8ft long. Not a serious craft, but certainly a fun unit for the kids at the lake. It came in colors of red, blue, yellow and of all colors, black! We wanted to promote these little canoes fast to pick up some extra cash to handle the eternal demands for money. As always, bills came in bunches and cheques were very shy about putting in an appearance!

Then an idea came, why not sell these little canoes by the carload as an automotive sales promotion. Buy a Ford—get a free canoe! Inasmuch that we were the manufacturer's agents, we had the necessary margin to work with. One Ford dealer was particularly flamboyant and aggressive in his marketing, so we approached him with our marketing idea. He loved it! He ignited right away.

"We'll take two carloads!" he exclaimed.

"Well," I cautioned, "Why don't we start with one carload (about 100 units) and if it catches on like we expect, we'll supply the other carload on short notice."

He was a good fellow and wrote a cheque immediately for one carload. Wow! We were elated. We even cleaned up a small overdraft and went out for a steak supper. The fabulous "Give away" canoes arrived as per schedule, and the day after delivery we drove by the car lots. Oh! What a blaze of color, stretching around the entire perimeter of the dealership. On the roof of every Ford vehicle, our proud little canoes dominated the landscape as they painted pictures of a new car for the holidays and fun on the water. It surely must be irresistible, especially with summer coming up. But why are there always "buts" with these things that look so good?

Every night the staff had to remove these canoes so they would not paddle off by themselves in the dark of night. It's very easy to heist a unit like these. This was a lot of work and the staff grumbled about the chore of storing them every night and hauling them out in the morning. But far worse than this, was the problem of prevailing winds in the area, and the unforeseen accumulation of gritty, sandy particles which now coated the roofs of the Fords. So when they lazily slid the canoes off the roof tops, rather than lifting them off, the scratching and damage that they inflicted to the pristine paint work, gave one a very sick feeling in the stomach. Not that it was noticed for about a week, and then the horrible truth became evident. Most of the roofs would have to be repainted or at least be given a good cut-paste wax job. This must have been quite a financial blow for the Ford dealer, what with labor, materials and manpower involved and we were sorry to hear about this fiasco. It seems that they had to sell the canoes below cost to staff and customers in order to get rid of them. On the other hand maybe they needed a good tax write off? One never knows!

Meantime our colorful molded polyethylene boats for distribution in Alberta arrived in quantity. BUT—Oh yes! Another of those *"buts,"* these boats were not the heavy duty, heavy weight samples that we had tried out on the lakes and rivers prior to ordering, and about which we were so enthused. They were lighter and their molded sides were quite obviously warped. It also altered their handling characteristics among the waves, especially the white caps. They were not a pretty sight. Then complaints started coming in on the 12ft units. Where the rowlocks for the oars were formed, the plastic was splitting from the strain of rowing. What next? Of course there is always a *"next"*—like night following day! And I worked night and day disposing of the failed units, and sold the last of the colorful canoes too.

Another catastrophe occurred when a large outfit in the Province of Saskatchewan outfit ordered two carloads of assorted craft, and upon arrival suddenly decided not to proceed with the matter. In order to save de-murrage on the rail cars, they unloaded them in huge piles in the melting snow of spring on a deserted rail spur out on the prairie, without telling us! Fortunately not one craft was missing. Only after the manufacturer asked for his cheque did we follow up and find out what had occurred. It took two weeks to go there and rectify the situation, which I did by first loading, trailer load after trailer load to a wash up place, and when they looked clean and like new, I wholesaled them out at a price that no one could refuse! What more could happen? Well – the fabulous Shakespeare Wondercraft arrived in quantity from South Carolina, and that diesel freight truck idled on our lot for hours while I worked to come up with a certified cheque for about $22,000.00. This was only achieved through my bank on the basis of a personal guarantee; a small disaster in itself, inasmuch as it bypassed our limited liability status. I sold the units, but at that time they had technical material problems which had severe repercussions for us. So after a year and a half of struggle and expense, I was in the hole about $15,000. We retained our home, but never again would I give a personal guarantee as the head of a limited company. I was an entrepreneur that had failed. But I had not failed to try!

How did Little Boy Wild react to all of this? He became somewhat depressed. He viewed the loss of direction and the financial disaster as a personal assault. He had been neglected whilst I poured my energy in the new enterprise. I went back to Dr. Janov's "The Primal Revolution"* to look into the mirror of reality. On page 166 I found:

"Give a depressive a new outlet, a new project, or a chance to go shopping, and all of his inner directed pressure now pours out in manic activity. He will literally throw himself into his work. He will be "happy" for those moments when his work will make him happy. What has really happened is that he has found an outlet for tension, an outlet that hides the Primal sadness. To become well, the neurotic must reach into his past to retrieve the present".

It was now well past time for Little Boy Wild to take over completely, and I knew he would head off into the mountains. Just like that! He rounded

---

* The Primal Revolution –Arthur Janov. 1972.

up a few travel items, thrust them into his pack, and it was only then that the "freedom" feeling really hit him. The whole responsible world of the Humans, finance, and deadlines rolled away. He breathed deeply. It took four and a half hours to reach his heavily wooded tract of solitude, blue birds and water. The early summer sun was warm, and every tree called out to him. He watched the young beavers at their idyllic dam site, listened to the flickers calling, and in the hotter sun of mid-afternoon he followed the wafts of scent from the wild roses. They seemed to have special meaning for him, and as he walked the flower strewn grassy areas he teased the grasshoppers in various ways. Next he stopped to watch the huge fuzzy bumblebees at work, and while he was thusly occupied, in the background of his mind he was working on the rose scent and why it haunted him in such a special way.

An unknown boy's face had been picturing in Wild Boy's mind for some weeks now, a somewhat fuzzy picture that was associated with roses. Now it came fully into focus with brilliance and clarity, as he watched some coyote pups play in a little secluded valley. He sat at the base of a graceful silver birch. I ached to watch the tears slowly mark their way down his tanned cheeks. He went into his rocking motions, meaning that his mind had gone into his *"all is lost"* mode.

"What are you looking at?" I asked him, although I knew from the distant look in his eyes that he had gone far into his past.

"It's playing like a movie" he said, and sniffing he wiped his nose on the back of his hand. "I'm about seven years old and playing alone by the tennis courts at that place called the "Club" where we lived at that time. The Boy sees me; he's fourteen coming on fifteen. His name is Jason and I know him by sight fairly well. He's always hounding me to go exploring the grounds of the old deserted house next door with him. Also in a conspiracy with me, he recently hid me in the cottage where he lives close by. Maybe his dad is the gardener or something. He wants me to see his female caregiver, whoever she is, give him a bath in the tin tub before the fire on Friday night. I do, but I don't know why I'm here. It's uncomfortable behind this old sofa in the corner. It smells damp and moldy. She soaps him all over and rinses him. Then she lathers his privates with predictable results, he is after all, nearly fifteen. Finally without any pretence she grasps him and in a few rapid strokes achieves her purpose to Jason's extreme delight. I just gaze at Jason's parted lips and glazed blue eyes without any remote cognizance of what has occurred, while she rubs the lather that leapt up, all over her face. Jason tells me over and over again about what happened with much animation and excitement. I just don't know what it's all about.

However, Jason is very different today. He chases me and I'm swiftly captured by the rose bushes. He is powerful compared to me at half his age, he rips off my shirt with one hand, I hear it tearing, while with the other he shakes me out of my shorts. I scream, and scream again. I then vanish "inside" under the onslaught of his thrusting. The pain is excruciating. My face is pressed into the rose petals. I love the scent of roses and the feel of the velvety, moist earth.

Finally it is over, and I dress while Jason disappears among the beech trees. Then I run back into the Club. There is a man in a brown hat sitting on the lower step. He looks at me with a sickly, knowing smirk. He has seen the whole thing. I run inside. I can tell no one. I run to my room down the cold passageway and fall asleep. I'm awaked by HER entering. I sit up on the bed and it reveals my torn shirt.

"You little swine—what did you do to your shirt?" she screams at me. Then I get shaken up and in the ensuing struggle the shirt tears some more.

"Well—you can wear it you swine, that'll teach you. You're not getting another one!" Of course I cannot tell her of the sodomy among the rose bushes. Besides, I do not have the words for what was done to me. I'm still in lots of pain. She stamps off in righteous indignation.

When Jason approaches me the next day I scream my loudest. But he came up to me and put his arm around my shoulders to calm me down, and I trust his persuasion enough to go adventuring with him through the broken fence. There are several slats that can be pushed to one side, allowing us to squeeze through one by one. We're going to explore this overgrown weed patch which used to be a garden. It is scary, I have difficulty walking, and we see a strange calico cat with one blue eye and the other green. It scampered by us in a panic, maybe it has kittens somewhere nearby. We walk the garden and peer into the dirty windows of the lonely old house. Jason keeps looking at me in a certain way, and eventually we lie together in the hot sun among the long grass. I know from what I see in Jason's eyes, and the rise in his shorts, what he has on his mind.

"No, no!" he exclaimed, seeing my face crumple up and eyes starting to tear. Then for about half of the afternoon having shed our clothes, he slowly and patiently coached me in the art of fellatio, obviously a one sided affair. It was impossible for my small mouth to accommodate him. However, despite aching jaws and occasionally retching, in one way or another I was able to meet his needs. Of course Friday nights for him were already taken care of, and although I had become quite adept at avoiding him, I intermittently became his sex slave for most of my seventh summer.

He would put his arm around me and say, "Let's go see the calico cat," and I would even say, "Yes, let's go and watch your calico cat throw up!" and then we'd break into huge bouts of laughing. Afterwards he would put his arm around me, I really liked it. He even said it was like him having a little brother. It gave me a warm feeling. Sometimes he'd put his arm around me three times in one afternoon, and I could tolerate a great deal of trauma in exchange for some close snuggling afterwards. He never did sodomize me again, and one day he disappeared. I never saw him around so he must have moved away. Strangely, it was a sort of routine that I missed. It left an empty space inside of me. I missed his breath taking releases, but most of all I missed his strong hot touch when he gripped me. Finally I would relax into his arms. Once he even kissed my cheek with a bashful sort of smile. There are times when life can be beautiful."

Little Boy Wild stopped his rocking back and forth motions beneath the green cover of the birch the same moment that a flicker called loudly and quite close by. In the next few seconds he observed her feeding three little flickers in a tree hole. He was utterly entranced. He became a young flicker, he imitated their excited feeding calls, and then she was gone. The three bright eyed heads with scarlet caps disappeared inside. He called moments like this "Woodland Magic," and it seemed to feed his insatiable appetite for beautiful scenes. He stored them flawlessly in his mind, and once told me that if ever he were imprisoned or captured by an enemy, he could go for a thousand different walks while in captivity, and merge with that world of wild ducks, bluebirds and squirrels, not to mention his rabbits! They would never be able to understand why he had that happy far away look on his face. They would probably write him off as 'not the sharpest knife in the rack' so to speak.

Wild Boy sat under his flicker tree which was a tall black poplar. A furry reddish brown caterpillar crawled up his leg over his fuzzy gold hairs, and when it reached his thigh, he picked it up and placed it on a blue flower, all the while assuring it of a wonderful life ahead. He was too warm, and after lazily removing his clothes he walked to the edge of the small lake where he paddled, splashed around, and after a short swim returned to sprawl under the flicker tree. She had just left, and he heard the soft murmuring of her babies inside.

He dreamed while he dried off, and enjoyed the hot touch of the sun, then, gradually he mentally fogged out of all reality. Little Boy Wild had lived for twenty seven summers, and this was a familiar trail into his half dream-like state. He was fully aware of all his surroundings amid the chorus of bird songs, and deeply yearned for the close reality of Human touch. He was heavy and aching with raw need and his tension level was extremely high. It dominated his hypnotic fog. He looked on the inside screen of his mind seeking his young friend. This sensitive boy was in his early twenties, and he never did know where he came from, or why. He had a smile that instantly bonded with Wild Boy's innermost core of being, but he was never sure if his friend was solid, alive and real – or just in his imagination. Little Boy Wild fully relaxed as he gazed into the boy's intense eyes, and it was then his young friend melted into him as he slowly caressed him from head to toe. When these sequences occurred, it was as if Wild Boy were split totally in two, the other half of him being the lonesome kid, who continued his intimate touching until Little Boy Wild was so gripped with electrifying tension that he would know it was time to surrender. He recklessly threw his head back into a bed of wild violets, and in utter bliss, clung to his friend as they merged into an indescribable ecstasy of escape.

Almost two hours had lapsed while he lay entwined in the fusion of love that the needful boy had imparted to him. It was an aura of intimacy that melded sky, woods, flowers and their raw needs. It was also a closeness that Wild Boy found was not possible with female Humans, as they were equated with hatred, physical and emotional damage along with extreme pain; and even worse, the blackness following dissociation.

Little Boy Wild was oblivious to everything but the beauty of *his being in touch with himself, and experiencing his body as a reality rather than a shadow-like replica of himself.* This sharing of their love essence was so absorbing, that neither of them saw the flickers come and go. Repeatedly they fed their babies; the sunlight kissed the young one's scarlet caps, and their cries filled the clearing with calls of hunger. Although Little Boy Wild was lost among the scent of the purple violets, it only took a few big spots of rain to return him from the swirling dream fog of consciousness. But it was the louder call of the male flicker that called him to action. Under the branches of the flicker tree, he slowly came back into the *"now"* of reality, as suddenly a great gust of wind whipped the branches. He had not noticed the clouds coming up, and then with equal suddenness he abdicated his control and *I* took over. Quickly I ran to the lake, washed up and swam around. It lifted the last of the mental fog that had engulfed us. I had no time to dry off, so I dressed while the baby flickers were having another feed. I was in a panic. "Oh God! How long had I been away? What was I supposed to do? What if a grizzly had come up on me? What do the Humans want? Wow! That rain is coming down in buckets." My heart was racing.

"Keelematu! Keelematu!" cried Wild Boy.

"Yes of course you can come with me." I replied. Now that the high levels of tension had been dissipated, the world began to look more real again, you know—normal. We had supper in the canyon, where pure water raged down from the mountain heights to fill the lakes below. There is something calming about "normal" Humans doing their routine thing and having a full stomach, we sat in the twilight sipping hot coffee while watching for the first stars to appear. It filled us with anticipation of the coming night adventures. I have yet to find a camping site in the forest somewhere, I'll have to pitch my tent too. On the other hand I may sleep in my vehicle tonight. Everything is soaking wet from the heavy rain and I have a sensible dry place to sleep in—my truck! It was a done deal. To heck with tenting!

"Hey! Little Boy Wild, are you alright?" I asked, while snuggling under our down sleeping bag.

"Okay I guess," he murmured.

"Well, you don't sound alright, what's up?" I asked.

"Sometimes I get weird feelings, and I can't seem to breathe right when I think of bed time stories."

He squirmed around a bit while he sniffed. Then he began to breathe rapidly and began shaking at the same time.

"I'll try to tell you, it came to me last night …. NO!" A small terrified gasp escaped him. I squeezed my pillow tight and held him.

"Its bed time, and my brother, in his room, always gets a bed time story about owls and funny things that make him laugh. Tonight I ask if SHE will tell me a story too; she agrees and asks what kind of a story I'd like. I simply said I didn't know.

"Well – how about the story of the little princes being murdered in the tower?" (I believe she was alluding to King Henry's kids that were killed because of squabbles regarding succession to the throne).

"Okay," I said, wondering what this weird story might be about. I listen, wide eyed with a mixture of awe and horror as the story proceeds.

"What is suffocation?" I stammered a question, "And how did they suffocate them?" I ask in all innocence. For answer her face changed.

"Like this," she said picking up my pillow and placing it on my face with light pressure. Then as I move the pillow slightly to one side, I get a shocking glimpse of her livid, contorted face. I feel a sudden stab of fear – this story has gone horribly wrong! At that same moment she forces the pillow down on my face with huge force. I cannot breathe. I try to scream but there is no air. I struggle and thrash around; this is not a situation where I can "disappear inside," and I get a wave of blackness. Then in extreme desperation I fold my legs up to my chin and kick hard with all my remaining seven year old strength. They strike her fully in the breasts throwing her back. I suck air fast. She throws the pillow at me and leaves the room after snapping the light off.

I will never ask for a bed time story again. I stay awake as long as I can. Will she come back to kill me? When? Will I die? I don't want to die…. . .I cry and cry and cry until sleep comes to rescue me, and it takes over as it always does. In the light of morning when I awake, the full horror of last night hits me. I delight in breathing. Suddenly I hear HER coming down the passageway, the door opens and she is smiling. *A smile from my mother is like a kiss of death!*

As she approaches, I scream the most piercing screams I'm capable of; so loud that father comes part way down the passage to see what is going on. *I see myself outside of myself.*

"She's trying to kill me!" I scream, "She's trying to kill me!" I go totally to pieces. Father does not believe me.

"It's alright," she says, "I think he was having a nightmare or something."

Father is satisfied. I have to dress now. She will come back soon with a breakfast tray. She keeps me in isolation. Older brother and my new young brother are in the light, color, warmth and normalcy of the living room – off limits to me. When my breakfast or any meal is left with me, I always taste it, cautiously at first. Poisoning is also a possibility, but the worst so far is rancid butter. I did not eat it in case it was masking some other flavor – even at age seven I understand some of these things. When she looked at me this morning, it was with a weird, knowing type of probe, as if she sought to find out if I really knew what happened last night.

I know! I know! I know! An icy wave grips me and I opt out to *"the meadows of my mind."*

"Little Boy Wild," I said softly. "It's okay, it's okay," But he continued to shake. He was wet with tears and his nose was running. It's good for you to remember these scenes; but they can never happen again, you're grown up."

"But there's more!" He gave a muffled shriek. His small fist struck out. "It's about pins!"

"Tell me! Tell me and let's get rid of it," I almost demanded.

"It's about Chicken Little too, an' I keep hurting – I don't want a bath. I don't want a bath!"

"Okay – first things first, what about the pins?" I said in a tone that sounded like we had to get to the bottom of all of this.

"Well diaper time is bad. It's trauma time and for some reason an unforgettable phrase keeps coming to mind: *"This is the cause of all the trouble!"* It keeps repeating itself; *"This is the cause of all the trouble!"* She says this when she's changing my diaper. She purses her lips, and with a horrible look, she jabs me on the shaft of my small penis. I scream and thrash about. "Hold still you little swine." She cuffs me about the ears. At last the diaper is on. I'm frequently stabbed and become rigid when she starts the changing routine. I tense myself against the inevitable prick of the safety pin; *I can also see myself lying on the table.* She slaps me if I cry out. Thank God she hasn't noticed I've already wet myself with fright. Wild Boy turned over and sighed in a tone of resignation, as if there were no other course but to accept his fate, but he did have the courage to carry on between sniffing and small cries.

"Bath times are always bad. What will she do this time? Is this going to be the end? Chicken Little was right, the sky is falling! The sky *IS* falling. Several times when I'm being bathed in the big tin tub on the mahogany table, SHE has laid me back in the water, but not for the purpose of rinsing my hair. She holds me under the water with her hand on my face till I'm choking. That's when the blackness approaches. *The sky is falling!* I kick violently making the water whoosh all over the table and floor. She pulls me up and is furious. I splutter and choke and spray water everywhere. She screams at me while slapping me around. I'm not supposed to struggle while she attempts to drown me. Softly Chicken Little keeps whispering, "The sky is falling.....truly the sky is falling!" *It is.*

Wild Boy blew his nose and wiped his eyes clear of tears. Outside the stars were showing, and branches from the fir that we had snuggled under in the truck, brushed the roof whenever a strong gust of wind came up. Of course we always heard skitters of little feet as mice explored the strange metal creature that had invaded their world. I held Little Boy Wild tight as I encircled my snuggle pillow with my arms. He breathed a half sob, and dissolved into dream as did I.

Early morning sunlight and bird activity roused us, and we greeted the morning with much anticipation at upcoming adventures. We planned on climbing a trail to several lakes that had that wonderful turquoise hue, and maybe stay with the wild sheep for a few days. Wild Boy wanted to see the new lambs, but I doubted very much that he would be able to catch one for a snuggling session. We often scanned the terrain for grizzlies as we had no means of defense at that time. Later I always carried a loaded Smith & Wesson .44 magnum revolver, in a very low profile inconspicuous way, and always with an empty chamber under the hammer. In all my years in the wilderness I never had an occasion to use that weapon for destructive purposes, although one time I did have to destroy part of a wild dog pack that were chasing an exhausted deer, and I wondered if it had survived. Little Boy Wild was totally in his element among the turquoise lakes, and was thrilled to see the mountain sheep and lambs. He was happy just to be himself. It was in the way he moved, and in his eyes, I could see that the whole wilderness and he had became one. In sunlight he said, *"I am the sheep, the lambs and the mountains beyond,"* and by starlight he breathed, *"I am the summer breeze, the owls and the spirit of the animals."*

Chapter Twenty Four

$f$ollowing the Western Watercraft financial disaster, I was completing a consulting assignment in Lac La Biche, Alberta; it was in the depths of winter, and one morning when I came out to start the IHC Travel-all, I got to thinking. It was 50 degrees below zero or thereabouts, and as I climbed into the truck and dropped onto the seat, I hurt my tailbone so badly that I felt the pain all day. That seat felt like a block of frozen concrete!

"Rats!!" I yelled in a stab of red hot pain, what am I doing here? Why am I suffering like this?" I resolved to go out and live on the west coast of British Columbia; I never wanted to suffer like this again! So the wheels were set in motion. The home in Edmonton was sold. We already had several lots in a development that had a magnificent view up the Sechelt Inlet on the Sunshine Coast, and we planned to live in a rental property while our new home was under construction.

On the business and cash flow side, some interesting things were happening! Oh no! Oh Yes! I had several government contracts for management consulting work with the Indian Affairs Branch which amounted to about $25,000, so I was not too concerned about cash flow matters as the house went into the construction phases. But one fine day, when the sun was shining brightly and all was well with my world, I found a letter in the mail that forecast the gathering storm! The government had decided not to proceed with the project in which I was involved. Already I had committed time, research, plans and materials to this contract, and now, WOW!! All had come back to square one. Another engineering firm had already proceeded with advance plans too, and they were out some $100,000. But my little contract had to pay for this part of the home construction and keep us going. Where was the cash going to come from? There was little doubt that we were headed for bankruptcy. ***Little Boy Wild was knocked clean out***

295

of orbit. We were out in the forest that bordered the inlet and he rebelled violently.

"Why?" he screamed. "It's the Humans again! We don't need them!" He seemed not to understand dollars, but the facts were that I had a wife and three sons, and we were in the middle of a somewhat major financial disaster. Perhaps he chose not to, but he was certainly privy to all of our communications, and knew what was going on.

It was Wild Boy who drove to the nearest tract of local wilderness that he could locate that day, and, turning off down a narrow winding trail toward the ocean, he parked under a flowering dogwood tree. He turned off the engine, and all was silent, apart from the gentle breeze that moved the white dogwood flowers, and the early hum of bees among the blossoms. As soon as he stepped onto the soft turf and inhaled the essence of the morning he changed. He was in absolute control. Carrying his camera he lightly ran down the trail, now partially overrun by bramble bushes, until, in a clearing he came across an old broken down moss covered cabin.

In the hot morning sun he shed his scant clothing and knelt by a single purple flower; he licked the dew from its petals and leaves, and as the sun was not at the right angle for a picture, he had time on his hands. He crawled around among the grass and then rose to check out the cabin. His eyes had a wild glint, almost defiant. He was still slim and muscular and was always completely tanned. He could not fully grasp the feeling of entrapment that I had created. His whole mode of thinking took on a desperate bent, as though he contemplated leaping over a precipice. But just then, he heard the tree swallows, and a distant woodpecker working away on a tree. He visibly relaxed. This was his home; he was in control, and surrounded by his friends. He spread his arms to the sky as if to embrace the whole wild natural world and smiled. It illuminated his face in a special way that never occurred when he was with the Humans. A bee winged its way across the clearing and joined others in a patch of white clover.

Little Boy Wild lay spread-eagled on the grass; and very softly hummed his bluebird song. This was his Garden of Eden in an eternal realm. Then falling further back into a deeper form of consciousness, he dreamed of dimensions other than the one he was in. It seemed that he could float among the Dogwood tree blossoms, and seeing a huge fuzzy bee, he wanted to ride on its back to a hidden hive somewhere in the dense brush. He lay there looking skyward, and felt as though he was the entire world that he could see, and that all creation moved within him.

It came to him slowly at first, that every time the breeze dropped, something was not quite right. Whereas it had caused the bushes to gently rustle while it was blowing, when the breeze stopped, the bushes still had a faint rustle that could not be accounted for. He kept observing the breeze phenomenon, and finally he arose, strode over to a pile of rotting 4x8 planks, picked one up and heaved it into the bushes right where the gentle rustling had come from. From the other side of the dense brush, the bush exploded! A huge female black bear with two cubs came hurtling out. The cubs fled up the nearest tree and big furious Mama came charging around the cabin, her teeth popping while she woofed. All hell broke lose.

"God!" exclaimed Wild Boy "Is she ever mad!"

Naked and unprotected, survival made him try to climb a thin little tree that was not ready to be climbed. Even as he struggled upward he knew how ineffectual this defence was. Suddenly, his little rescue tree swung toward the rotted cabin roof and dropped him right through it. He felt his skin bruise and rusty nails cut into him. On the floor inside the cabin he lay stunned for a few moments, and then he scrambled to his feet. His eyes were wide with fright and his heart was pounding. Next he felt for his testicles, they were still both intact, but his eye glasses were not, and he made a quick mental note to return and get them later. In the meantime, among all the noise of splintering rotted wood and his shouting, the big black had retreated a little, but was not too far away as her cubs were still up the tree.

Wild Boy came out of the cabin, snatched up his camera and clothing; then in desperate haste he fled swiftly back up the trail. He was a good runner and it seemed only a matter of moments before he was standing beside his truck, he had the door open in case the bear should show up. Next he surveyed the damage to himself. First he removed the cobwebs and moss still clinging to him including a couple of sow bugs, and then caught sight of himself in the mirror. He saw a stranger. He was shocked. Blood ran down from his right ear and across his face. There was a cut on his left thigh that was still bleeding down his leg, and he was crusted with dirt. His top lip was cut and bloodied his front teeth. He was such an apparition that he even scared himself. He had blood on his hands, and as he leaned across the front seat to find a rag underneath it, he froze and was jolted into a series of especially hurtful scenes.

He cried out – an animalistic throaty sound. Then he began to cry. It shook him through and through. Maybe it was from the bear encounter or the recalled memory or the combination of the two that elicited such a reaction He withdrew from the truck, slammed the door and crawled under the flowering dogwood tree. His sobs continued to shake him. He ignored the ants as they checked him out, and it was at this point I decided to step in.

Very softly I called "Wild Boy, Wild Boy, are you alright?" His serious young face, streaked with blood looked up at me. He was in bad shape and he was suffering both physically and mentally.

"It's the rooks in the elm trees, it's HIM!" he gasped. "I felt as if a scene from the past was being repeated the moment I leaned over the front seat. It was so real and what made it more so, was that nail gash so close to my rear end." Little Boy Wild smeared his tears and shiny mucous across the dried blood tracks on his face. Even in this mess he had an endearing innocent quality about him that encompassed his whole being. He leaned back against the dogwood trunk, and after a deep breath he gave a shiver that shook him from head to toe as he ventured into his story:

"I'm sixteen and wandering around Devonshire in the west country of England. It's quite late in the summer and soon with autumn and winter approaching, I'll have to find a job in order to eat and put a roof over my head. There is a village about two miles ahead. My total possessions are in a small back pack that I'm wearing. A car draws alongside me and a pleasant looking older man asks if I'd like a lift to the village ahead. I acquiesce, being tired and weak from hunger. I have not eaten for days other than some dandelion leaves and clover flowers. I get in and settle back while he makes small talk.

"Oh!" he says, "I just have to go up to the church to a see a friend for a few minutes, you don't mind do you?" I, of course, have no objection as he pulls up a narrow overgrown lane lined with beech trees. We stop by the church but there is no one there. Even the church itself looks wild and deserted.

"He'll probably be along in a few minutes," he says while smiling at me. The Rooks are cawing loudly and fluttering among the elms, and we talk about bird watching.

"Come over closer and you'll see them better," he said. I can see the rooks quite well from where I am, but he is so nice and insistent as he opens his window, that I move over and sit on his lap to obtain a better view. We both watch the rooks. His arms are about my waist, and it's not an unpleasant feeling for one who is starved for warm touching. Then I feel his erection pressing into me, and I look at him.

"It happens," he says, in a matter of fact tone. I slide off him to my own seat. Whereupon he fully exposes himself to me and asks me to do the same; after some minutes of cajoling I'm persuaded for various reasons to do likewise. I seem to be under some kind of hypnotic foggy spell. In a short while he holds me in his hands, and I feel very good. But – how could I allow this to happen? I do have an excessively high tolerance level for the intolerable. But I'm sixteen! Not seven or eight or even ten years old! I step from the car in a type of mental fog trying to pull my pants up, but he has already come around from the other side and is standing behind me.

"Lean over!" he commands. His face is flushed and his eyes wild. I'm pushed over the front seat as I obey, and he fully exposes my body for the upcoming trauma. I half turn and get a flash of mad, depraved sexual hunger on a rampage. His genitalia are much bigger than mine in every way, and his eyes are – terrible! I scream as he grips me. He makes several horrific thrusts as he forces entry. *I disappear inside, but my screams remain.* Why does a fairly strong young sixteen year old, even weak from hunger, not turn and punch him in the face or kick him in the groin? Or resist in any way? Why am I so obedient and so submissive? I simply do not know! I just obey. Is it my imprinting? What followed was one of the most brutal acts of sodomy that I had ever experienced. *I saw ME outside of myself observing the scene.* Every thrust was accompanied by a high pitched helpless scream. When he was through, I turned once to look into his glittering eyes and red face, I hitch up my pants and run like the wind through the willows. It's a narrow trail if a trail at all and the willows whip my face as I run; but I disregard all of this. It could be something more terrible awaits me if I'm captured. My back pack has been left behind. I have no blanket and no ground sheet to protect me from the damp earth, and no book to read.

"Come back!" he shouts, "You won't get away! Come back!"

Why use the words "You won't get away?" I run faster. I must use the skills of my red fox friends, the survival methods they use when pursued by the hounds. I do have friends out here in the woodland. But right now it would be comforting even to talk to a rabbit. In any case upon reflection, I knew he could never match my speed in any way. I ask myself again and yet again – how could this have happened?

Dusk is approaching and finally I take refuge under a thick conifer tree, its branches are low to the ground and bushy. Exhausted, I fall asleep. The pain tortures me all night and the cold penetrates me as I now have no blanket. I know I'm damaged and that I need a doctor or a hospital. But I cannot approach the Humans about this terrible affair. They would never understand, and I'm an inconvenience anyway. On top of that I have little or no money, and as we well know, none of them can be trusted. It is too, too unthinkable to contact them. I may have to jump into the "River of No Return." In the cold light of morning, I discard my multicoloured under-shorts, mostly red, and carefully wash up in a nearby stream. I hurt as I walk. I just hope I have no seepage.

Hunger, weakness and trauma assault me to the point of collapse, and in sheer desperation I knock on the door of a bed and breakfast place. When the big oak door opens, I see the effect of my appearance on her face. Shock and horror followed by curiosity. Then she accepts me. Hot baking smells surround her. I can only imagine what she saw expressed in my face: wide eyed fright, desperation, pain, fear and panic – a half wild creature poised for flight, but pleading for food in order to live.

"Wh-wh-what food can I buy for one sh-sh-shilling and six pence" I stammer while holding out the money.

"Come in and we'll get you some breakfast!"

I wolf down hot porridge and toast and a couple of muffins along with really hot tea. I feel like I might live after all. While I ate, two of the staff members kept looking at me strangely. They had never seen an animal quite like me. I blushed. I always blushed easily anyway. When I leave I hope there is no red smudge on the chair. There is not.

Outside in the warm sun I leave the village, and cut across the downs among the hills so as to avoid any human contact. It's also possible that my perpetrator is out looking for me. Perhaps he wants to silence me. I walk more swiftly ignoring the pain, I need time to heal, and eventually I bask in the late summer sun. The healing warmth embraces my entire body, and along with rabbits playing and birds singing, I return to a level of what is, for me, normalcy. I wave to a red fox as he goes by and fall asleep among the daisies. I spent four days resting up in a remote little woodland dell by a creek, until the pain from the terrible encounter had subsided. By then I could slowly walk without the awful pain at every step. *I'm sixteen*. This was the very last act of sodomy I was ever subjected to, or *allowed,* if that is the correct word. Later, due to my programming or whatever, I unconsciously attracted circumstances which would invite my past to be repeated. I still have no love, no holding, no touching, no caring and no embracing. I generally distrust all female Humans – they are tarnished with my mother experiences, which include fear, extreme pain and possible death. As for male contacts, they are surely equal in pain and torment, and this combined hurtful imprinting can haunt human relationships for a lifetime."

When Little Boy Wild was through with his story which had been interspersed with some writhing and weird sounds, he crawled out from under the Dogwood tree and stood tall.

"Hey Wild Boy, you just have to get cleaned up," I said, "If the Humans come across you, anything can happen and probably will."

But to my surprise, he retained control, and humming his "Bluebird" song, he started the truck and went back up to the road where he branched off on a power line. Before he had gone even one kilometre, a creek crossed under the road in a steel culvert. He stopped, and still unclothed from his latest escapade, made his way down to the creek bed on the rocks. The culvert water would act like a powerful cold shower. It was icy cold. But when he had gently cleaned up the crusted blood and dried himself off in the sun, almost all of his old self returned. He dressed, we explored, chatted with the squirrels and watched some deer; but Wild Boy did not relinquish control to me until quite late in the afternoon, and only then, when I assured him that we could always escape and go to live with the animals, forever if need be. Upon returning to my family, I know I'll have difficulty in explaining just what *I* or *we* have been doing. No doubt they will ask questions about our appearance as I was supposed to be out "working" and earning money.

"You look like you just had a scrap with a cougar or something – what happened?" one of the boys asked. I mumbled something about tripping up on the edge of a ravine and being trapped by some brambles. In reality, wild scenes of cabins, black bears, blood and fury raced through my mind, plus the reliving of the last sodomy. Immediate family members would not, or could not grasp an understanding of my dual life and what it was all about, apart from commenting upon occasion that I'm *"weird" or "strange." I don't think that anyone ever really suspected that I ran two lives.* They just saw *me,* and never met Little Boy Wild, the phantom whose world was one of uncontrolled emotions.

On looking back through the haze of time I now realize that I have been split into at least two major entities, from as far back as when I was about six years old. *Only recently was I able to recognise my two main lives running parallel to each other.* I now know these as the *"Real"* and the *"Unreal selves."* All those years that I handled what the Humans wanted, I was enabling Little Boy Wild to live with his animals in the forest. Not that I had much say in the matter, for when he'd had enough of the false human world — he just took over. I never was able to manoeuvre myself into a position to explain any of these psychological convolutions to my family, because I could not face the consequences of acknowledging my mental deficiencies. They, being a matter of such deep reality, that were they exposed, our worlds would be in collision – and it could be that I would never recover. *WE* would lose control, and be at the mercy of the human's standard realities. An unthinkable consequence! Indeed! Most people think that the whole matter can be handled by an admonition to "Smarten up!"

The new home was being built. Cash flow and contracts had dried up. There was little management consulting work to do locally; in Vancouver yes – but that entailed hotels and expenses. The only local job available was for a dog catcher, and that had no appeal for me whatsoever! Meantime I supervised the home construction, while the cloud of financial doom swept toward me like fingers of rain clouds across a lake.

One day, I discovered in the Vancouver Sun, an advertisement for life insurance sales persons. Oh no! Has it come down to this? Yes it had. I needed cash flow fast on a consistent basis. So for a short time I became associated with a major American life insurance company – a very large and successful outfit. They trained me in Chicago, licensed me in Toronto and put me to work in Chemainus, BC – a town now famous world wide for its murals; they are incredible and beautifully portrayed. However, back then it was a sawmill town.

Our manager checked us into a fancy hotel which we had to pay for. I had no cash at all, and my gas guzzling IHC truck would soon come to a shuddering stop if I didn't ply my trade of old and use the siphon tube to keep it going. The pressure was on. One had to sell policies, or owe the hotel and starve. We were instructed to give our canned sales pitch all day and half the night. As long as there was light on in a house – even at 11.00pm we had to knock on the door!

When a door opened I would start my presentation with, "Good evening! I believe this will interest you also, for only a few pennies a week we are giving a one thousand two hundred dollar life insurance policy." The last door I banged on one evening really did me in. A poor little old silver haired lady of about 75 years showed up in her night gown.

"Good evening! I believe this will interest you also…." I could see that she could have no possible use for my offering, but rules are rules and one cannot deviate from them or our explicit instructions. When the agony was over, I returned to my truck in the thick fog. It was 11.20pm and I had only made one small sale. I believe we were paid a commission of $2.50 per policy and one had to sell at least 25 policies a day to survive!

I asked myself, "What has my world come to? My family needs groceries, my truck needs gas, I need supper and I owe the hotel. I was overly tired and hungry. I collapsed into tears. I pictured my wife and three kids sitting in our new home by the fire. What do I do now? How did I get into all of this? And to crown everything off, I had several bills coming in ranging from $4000 to $10,000 on the house contract, and the bank was not too impressed with my earning ability.

On top of all this stress, *if, Little Boy Wild took over permanently,* and well he might under these conditions, what would really happen? He may decide that we go and live with the animals in the forest and that would be the end of everything. Suppose he really did take control and not relinquish it? I re-ran the question again and again. Deep down I feared that I might become Wild Boy one hundred percent. *Would this then mean that I would become real?* Difficult times lay ahead and any further shocks to our psychological system could trigger *my* demise. *He is mentally damaged, emotionally retarded and whatever his age,* he would be running my 35 year old body.

Somehow I made it back home, with no money. My marriage had always been somewhat rocky due to circumstances that I unwittingly created. But my wife was wonderful with the kids and in addition to being an excellent chef; she ran a tight ship at home. We both loved our kids but we had difficulty with each other, as could only be expected with my background. In reality, she did not deserve to be involved in this relationship. My struggles with intimacy and bizarre mental states were something that she could not devote time to understanding as she raised the three boys, not knowing where the next grocery cheque might come from. Commission sales did not reliably produce an even cash flow, or a successful marriage, at least not in the early days. It was then that I looked at my own insurance policy. It was with a major life company that specialized in term insurance policies, and espoused the philosophy of "Buy term and invest the difference." So on my return to Vancouver I arranged a contract with them –and became one of their top producers for many years. But right now – there was considerable financial turbulence to go through. I could not bring the cash flow up fast enough to service the massive debt accumulating against the home property. One day on arriving home, I dropped a bombshell by announcing with somewhat casual mien, that we would have to declare personal bankruptcy.

This created a storm of hurricane force on the emotional scale. The extreme rejection of all that I had put into fruition, struck *us* with unparalleled fury, and the destruction so ravaged Little Boy Wild that he totally spaced out. Animals here we come! Our home was not fit to live in. The black looks and uncivil terse monologues that occurred increased the wall of rejection to an intolerable degree. A black pall of despair and anger gripped our home. On top of that was the guilt of knowing that I had created the whole scenario, although that was never my intent. I loaded the truck with some clothing, survival items and the necessary sale kits and fled across the water to Vancouver Island. The bankruptcy proceedings were underway and I planned to return to conclude whatever the Humans wanted.

In the meantime Little Boy Wild landed on one of the off shore Islands. It was he who had been in control ever since we left home. There were no "Good Byes" when we had left, we had just departed, and now he was alone among the ferns in the wilderness. While he was exploring he found a tiny secluded dip, like a miniature valley. It was dense with ferns and a red deer took off as he descended.

"Stay little friend," he invited. He pushed deeper into the fern jungle until he came to a small grass clearing, and it was here that he divested some hot clothing and lay down to fall into a deep sleep. Ravens calling from close by awoke him a short time later, and the whole horrible cascade of despair and pain descended on him again. He squirmed around in the grass, writhing with pain from the memories of the past 48 hours as they burned into his consciousness. His brain was a whirl of desperate plans and mixed up ideas. Should he make a complete break and leave for Australia and start a new life? No, there were the three boys, and he loved each of them dearly.

Wild Boy's psychic pain had risen very sharply. It beat into him unrelentingly. No interactive release of tension would handle this. It was bigger than both of them.

"How does one escape from interminable pain?" he asked me. "One can physically run away, but our problems run away with us. Or one can dissociate and opt out while the main performance is running, but how long can one stay dissociated? Periods of several minutes to several hours *we* are both familiar with, but this is a major psychic catastrophe. Surely if we stay dissociated for too long, it is far too risky, as I would have to make the irrecoverable decision to enter the "River of No Return," and that could result in the equivalent of a prison term, with well educated psychiatrists and psycho- pharmacologists, which would surely be a recipe for living death."

I interrupted him just as his facial expression changed to that of an innocent eight year old kid. He closed his eyes, his mouth was partially open – and I sensed the pain in his eerie silent screams.

"What do you see right now, Wild Boy? You were going to say something," I encouraged.

He sat up in the fern hollow and studied a green beetle that had crawled onto his foot. It too, was discovering a new world, and when it struggled into Wild Boy's leg fuzz and started to tickle he placed it on a leaf. He looked up and a light breeze ruffled his hair.

"It all started one afternoon …. ." A frown of concentration came to his brow.

"I was crying and had been doing so for about an hour I guess. Every time I tried to stop, the crying carried on, except with greater intensity as if it had a life of its own. It was no doubt fed by a circular track where void meets void endlessly. My weeping came out like a story sobbed aloud, like a script for pain performed to an utterly indifferent audience. SHE came in the room.

"You know this isn't any good, you crying like this all the time. You have to stop, you're always crying." I feel confused. She sat on a chair. "Come here you poor little thing." I dropped to my knees, my head in her lap, still weeping. She cradled me, stroking my hair with all the warmth and softness I had never received in my whole eight years on earth. I opened like a sun flower soaking up the sun. This was for me the ultimate exposure to a rare intimacy of touching and a possible turn in the tide to love. Little Boy Wild's body suddenly jerked and he fell among the buttercups, his voice powered up with loud helpless desperation. His fists clenched.

He screamed, "But it got worse!" Tears streamed down his cheeks. He tried to maintain coherency as he relived the scene.

"I got so loud and my sobs took on such deep racking shakes, it nearly wrenched me apart! I couldn't handle the great surges of pain as they shook me. The unrelenting beatings, the repeated sodomies, HER attempts to kill me, they all kept flashing by, only to push me further out of control. Now the overwhelming shakes toss me about, I scream, a long despairing note of hurt – then – SHE threw me to the floor where I collapsed into a quivering moaning heap.

"Well," she said, her face contorting. "If you're going to keep on crying anyway, I'll give you something to cry about you swine! I'll give you cry!"

Her bamboo cane, always close at hand, swished its first burst of pain, a message of orchestrated flaming red colors, mixed with great flashes of brilliant white. The baton caused my screams to rise to a crescendo, as only a soloist can play when riding a void to nowhere. This beating carried on for longer than usual, non-stop for about two whole minutes, which is a very long time. I thought she would not stop venting her fury until I was dead. I writhed and screamed the whole time. The sounds etched the afternoon as they rose higher and higher with all the terrible desperation and helplessness a child can only utter while he is being beaten to death. Suddenly it was over. The door slammed. I'm alone again, but not quite. I have the great wheals of blazing pain throbbing over my entire body. I lose consciousness, but I think it's because I'm so tired and have to sleep."

Little Boy Wild tumbled into the grass among a profusion of small blue flowers. Quickly he curled up, fetal tight, while emitting an eerie sound. It came from his throat, other-worldly and unnatural. It then turned into long stretched out moans as he rocked himself into nothingness. Then he lay very still. Minutes passed, and only the gentle rise and fall of his little blue shirt told me that he was still there. Time passed.

"Hey Wild Boy," I whispered. "We have each other, and I will never leave you, *we have each other and the animals.* He stirred. Slowly his face became animated again.

"Oh! I was thinking about my "River of No Return," he said with a frown. Then rising, he gifted me with a quick smile. Some minutes passed while he stood there, the sun touched his gold streaked hair, and illuminated the finer gold hairs on his arms.

"Afterwards," he continued, "I went out into the vegetable garden to complete a weeding task. I sniffed. I was still shaking and in shock. In addition I was making strange sounds like a wounded animal. Crawling into this overgrown weed forest, I curled up very small and silently cried. But just then through the fence, a small friendly female voice said, "Derek! Are you alright?" I nodded, giving her a quick glance. She was Rene, our neighbour's little girl who was about my own age.

"Are you sure you're alright?" she even indicated that if not, her mother would bring help. The implications terrified me. She wanted me to climb the fence now while I was still alive, and assured me they would protect me. However, if this plan of theirs did not work out, and I was returned, I knew that SHE would stab me to death or kill me in some other way after I had gone to sleep that very night.

"Yes, I'm okay," My lips were trembling. I must not look at her. Even

307

now I'm almost paralyzed by her concern. She cares. Someone cares! But Rene especially cares. She knows I'm here. I'm in here somewhere, *but I cannot accept her caring concern. It destroys me. It blacks me out!* If I did go over the fence into Rene's home – I would collapse into this blackness inside of me where I cannot find myself. Kindness, love and caring – are supposed to calm me, and I should "open up" and smile, because it's friendly, but I feel exactly the opposite – *I freeze,* cold shudders shake me, and I dissociate and hide "inside." I only feel warm and safe in the *"meadows of my mind,"* and snuggling with a warm furry rabbit, is for me – an unequalled state of bliss.

For the second time Little Boy Wild burrowed into the clover scent, just leaving his small tanned legs exposed. A few minutes later he emerged to lay on his back, watching the fleecy clouds move slowly by. He smiled and softly began to sing his bluebird song:

"Somewhere over the rainbow, Bluebirds fly, Birds fly, over the rainbow, why then, Oh why can't I?" His small tremulous voice was almost lost among the bee hum and bird songs. Then his image faded, faded away like the gathering dusk as it covers the flowers of summer. I was alone again.

Back in the fern hollow, in my heart I hugged Wild Boy, for he was explaining how this definitive Primal scene, deeper than any he had ever experienced before, was a parallel to our current needs and emotional devastation. However, he did *not* return control to me, and following a snack and a long drink of water, ran through the ferns with his right hand held high as if he were holding a spear and was out on a hunt. But soon he tired, and stripped by a shallow grassy pool where he could just immerse himself. The water was tepid and after refreshing himself, he lay in the longer grass till the moon rose. Time stretched. Night birds called. The stars filled themselves in as darkness fell, and still he lay there. Bats emerged for nightly feeding, and an owl hooted its thrilling note from deep in the night woods. In the distance he could hear the waves crashing on the beaches. It was music, punctuated with the squeak of bats. He merged himself with the night, for the fern nest in which he lay was a needful trysting place, and all he needed was to feel a warm kiss on his cheek to quell his star mist passion. *Slowly, Little Boy Wild split in two, so that he could be held, touched and loved.* The magic of the moon shadows highlighted his body, and cast an aura of warm beauty over his solitude. Crickets called, and shooting stars fell through the cosmos, until finally he relaxed in a fusion of love. He curled up his body for warmth and fell asleep in abject wonder. The tall ferns guarded him throughout the night, and in the early dawn a deer placed its wet nose on his thigh. He stirred but slept on.

When the sun began to rise, it revealed mist in the hollows. Ravens called one to another. He knew their distinctive vocabulary, and when one called with notes like a double phone ring, he replied, "I'm not taking any calls today!" He struggled somewhat stiffly to his feet, yawned, stretched luxuriously and then went in search of his clothes by the pool. He was cold, but by night he had snuggled so deep in the fern base, that he had not been awakened by shivering. He returned control to me unexpectedly and only then because hunger was gnawing at him with cutting realism.

"Before we rustle up some breakfast – Little Boy Wild – tell me more about this "split" that you experience – why is it so real?" I asked.

"Oh! That!" He gave a shy chuckle. "I'm not sure that I can explain it, but I'll try. You see – when *"need"* engulfs me – the need to be touched, and loved, I have to go back far *inside* myself, because there is never anyone in the real, solid, *outside* world, with which to share this joy and beauty of feeling. One day, while I was in this "twilight state," a young fellow of about my age appeared on my internal screen. He had an almost shy, tentative approach, and a warm smile, and his eyes – dark blue under a mop of gold hair, were open, loving, and questing – but behind them, I sensed a great sadness that touched me deeply. They expressed his raw need of me, and further, it was as if upon my recognition of his desire, that he took control of me. He already seemed to know of my need for *him,* which I now could not disguise. I know it sounds strange, but that first time, and all the times that followed, *it is at this point that the "split" occurs.* His smile melts into me, and the caress of his eyes, touches the core of my being. He is exquisitely sensitive to our every nuance of touch and feeling, and I do give him total control of me." Wild Boy winced and looked shyly at me, blushing at voicing his most intimate thoughts. "These sequences are critical to my survival – *they prove that I exist.* I don't have to touch myself with the point of a penknife blade to see if I'm still *"here."* However, I've also found these liaisons to be highly addictive – *but, it gives Me to Me, and I feel – and when I feel, then I am! I'm here! And it's beautiful. I'm needed, and I am loved – and I can feel! It also gives me identity. I become substantial, and not a mere thought form in motion.* I haven't seen **him** for a while now, but another lonely kid has taken his place. Does this make sense?" He smiled, even though his face was pained as he glanced at me for support; for he had exposed himself in such an aura of boyish innocence, that he felt unsure and vulnerable.

"What will make sense," I said, wanting to get out of any analytical questions at this time, "Is for us to get some grub – now!" I found the truck deep in the brush where I had left it, and we located a café in the village for a much needed topping up of our energy reserves. Once this was over I decided to do some work and pick up some life insurance contracts. It was necessary, and Wild Boy partially understood that living with the animals had to be supported by some cash flow.

On returning to the mainland the bankruptcy procedures demanded that I surrender all real property. Credit cards were already relinquished, and our home was sold, but we were allowed to retain our furniture. They seized the Toyota Land Cruiser, even though it was my only means of making a living, something I understood afterwards should not have been done. We rented a small property and somehow we survived, and this was the only time in my thirty odd years in Canada that I ever requested something from the government treasury. We needed groceries badly. Three young growing boys eat! But when I visited the local Human Resources office, they looked upon me with extreme suspicion when I told them my story. Amazingly – they assumed that being a "businessman" I must have stocks and bonds and other investments!! How clueless could they be? We were bankrupt, broke, up the creek without a paddle. I realized later that I was far too bright looking, articulate and neatly dressed to qualify for assistance. Had I gone in with dirty jeans and shirt, a face with three days of unshaven stubble, bleary blood shot eyes; and preferably reeking of beer and smoke at 9.00am – that would have qualified me right away! I explained that I was going to Vancouver Island on a sales trip and would be returning in about a week's time. When all was said and done they issued a cheque for $90.00 to pay rent, buy groceries, get to Vancouver Island, pay living expenses, and get back again! That was that! So we bought groceries and ate. But I had no vehicle and could not operate. I was still fully employed and capable of producing good cash flow as a life agent. I was not just "hoping" to find some work while sitting around smoking a pack and a half of cigarettes a day. I am a non-smoker and always have been. All I needed was a small stop gap of funds to get going again, and that would not take long; in reality about three weeks at the outside. Of course I could not leave without cash and bankruptcy whether one realizes it or not, takes a psychological toll on one, so that logical planning is not possible. One cannot request credit. It was almost like being a leper in the old days, where they would have to tinkle a little bell as they walked the streets, while proclaiming "Unclean! Unclean! Unclean!" My call between the tinkling of bells would be "Bankrupt! Bankrupt! Bankrupt."

Chapter Twenty Five

It was a strange and disconnected feeling, that of having a good position which could quickly develop good cash flow, but having no means of transportation. For about a week we lazed around in the forest, in a haze of turmoil and indecision. Black bears roamed through, and ravens called. Wild Boy was in charge, and lying among the grass on the banks of a fast flowing creek, we re-read "The Primal Scream," by Arthur Janov.

Little Boy Wild still wanted answers to his previous questions in regard to the "split," and here, Wild Boy is not talking about *"our split,"* but rather his *"internal split"* which enables him to interact with his friend both physically and mentally. I knew he would expose his innermost core to me in this intimate search for himself, because he was fearlessly honest, and hid nothing from us in his quest for the truth.

It seemed that we were swinging from one disaster to another, and typically this generated huge amounts of extra tension. It was then, as always, that Little Boy Wild was eager to liaise with his lonesome friend, which he did – simply by imaging his face. He was mesmerized by the beauty of this boy's smile; his open face expressed such unreserved hunger for contact and love that it haunted him. The boy would appear through a curtain in the fabric of Wild Boy's consciousness, and step into our oasis of safety. He knew that ours was a place where no Humans could exist, and that here in this solitude, his yearning for touching and understanding could be appeased.

Wild Boy frowned and murmured, *"So why am I driven beyond my control to tryst with him?"* His empathy had become even stronger when he discovered that this boy, for most his life, had *also* been inundated in a sea of hate and rejection, and this made him want to more deeply share that hurt. These were euphoric periods of appeasing emotional hunger. Now,

313

in trembling anticipation, his friend stands quietly before him in mute appeal, smiling, face to face, and in the silence of their need, Little Boy Wild released himself to the boy's exquisite touch. They were enraptured. The tremor in his voice as the boy spoke softly to him; and the innocence of their searching hands was a concerto of tenderness and love. There is total fusion, and they become lost for hours in the fog of consciousness.

There were times when Little Boy Wild lay so still after the peak of their encounters; that small birds would alight and hop around on his chest and tummy. They made little "chipping" sounds, and were unafraid of him, even when he moved and opened his eyes, and looked directly into theirs. It more fully merged him with his animal world, and effused him with a joy of oneness that extended beyond their seclusion under the trees, all the way back into the mists of time. Later, our tryst is broken by the whisper of reality, and once again we are alone in a hostile world.

It was then that I loudly exclaimed, "Little Boy Wild, you are one, weird, sick, psycho kid! Don't you realize that normal people do not have sexual relationships with *"unreal"* people? – not that you are normal in *any* way – like your friend – you're just a twisted lonely kid, lost in deep space between a questionable reality – and your own dreams!"

"Perhaps," Wild Boy responded. "But for me, my friend is very real, *how could I not absorb him and yield to his needs?* He is a mirror image of me." Wild Boy looked up at me, there were tears in his eyes and I saw that he was resigned to his situation.

"Is this not better than dying?" he questioned. "Where else could I find such a close friend? Without this needful interaction – I am *"not,"* and I want to *"be,"* for this is life.

How else could I "achieve" myself without him? And how else in his search for love could he sustain HIS life and being? We need each other – in order for us to grow and journey into our futures. Without it, *he* may well drop into his *own* "River of No Return." Little Boy Wild's impassioned reply to my charge that he is a sexually sick psycho kid – caused my chest to writhe in pain – we both were wounded. We shed tears for each other, for his friends in the "split," for all the torment we had endured – but mostly, for our tragic loneliness in our fearless search for self. Wild Boy had thoughts that made even he uncomfortable, and later he asked if he was gay and in denial, and if it were in the imagery of his mind, rather than in reality, was it the same thing?

He paraphrased Dr. Arthur Janov, in "The Primal Scream,"

"The neurotic often is classed as being very sexy, whereas in reality it is not sex that he is experiencing at all, he is merely feeling the discharge of tension. Sex as in a love relationship does not exist for him. His tension always rises again, and that is why the practicing gay also must turn trick after trick and can never be satisfied."

Maybe gays are, or are not, neurotic – that was beyond his experience to know. However, the gay life style simply did not exist in the world of Little Boy Wild, because apart from disease, drugs and the emotional pain, it would also involve the male humans in a way that would surely drive him into his "River of No Return." True – Wild Boy's only partners were *within* him, living in the other worlds he had created, and it was these secret trysts that enabled him to maintain his mental equilibrium. This was despite the fact that *I* was married with a wife and three kids. *We* just could not understand how one person can live two lives, and be involved in real and unreal relationships at the same time. *Especially as Little Boy Wild is "real" –and in an "unreal" relationship, and I –Derek, am supposed to be the "unreal" self, and I'm in a "real" relationship!*

"Little Boy Wild," I asked in a serious tone, "How long can you escape in this manner from the everyday world of reality? When will you stop running away and hiding inside yourself?" I simultaneously felt his surge of hurt and torment, which should not have surprised me – *"we" being "one."* "It's possible that your friend will not always be there for you, and what will you do then?"

"I hope he has a twin – if not, I will be in a black void," he sadly replied. "However, I know that another lonesome kid will find me Derek, they always do – but, do you think it's possible that when they don't come back, you know, when they disappear – *that they have never left, and are now a part of us?*" He laughed, "Maybe we should hold a party – for all of us! And – speaking of black voids, we still have no answer for that Bavarian incident – *that one, shut us down completely.*

Little Boy Wild was referring to a European trip where we stayed with some of Svein's friends. They lived in a beautiful old heritage home close

315

to the Swiss border. We were saying our Good Byes, when the wife of our host reached out and hugged Wild Boy and me. As we hugged – a cold blackness of panic and terror struck us. Svein, who was facing me over her shoulder, said afterward – much to my horror – "I hope never to see your face again when you are hugged. It was terrible to witness." I had difficulty in explaining my feelings of dizziness to our hosts. I was ready to faint. "And no, Wild Boy, I have no answer for that yet. It is still in a captive dimension."

In the here and now – I looked at Little Boy Wild where he sat among the daisies, and as I could not reply to his question I remained silent. It had always seemed to me that he had a phantom-like quality about him, and now, as we lay beneath a squirrel tree, he vanished into a deep sleep of emotional exhaustion, leaving me to attend to the human affairs, which I did – about two hours later. Squirrels flicked their tails and flowed after each other among the trees – and another idyllic day began to merge with eventide.

We returned to civilization, and a few days later, a tiny parcel arrived in the mail at the post office. It was mysterious because I could not buy anything and had not done so. Upon opening it up, we found a lovely Seiko watch with a leather wrist band.

The wheels in my mind began to turn; what if I swapped the watch for an older car, a really old car? Where had the watch come from? It turned out that I had won some sort of sales contest and the insurance company had sent me my prize! I was always winning prizes and trips to wonderful places, and the fact that they had a contest running had nothing to do with my production. Contest or no, I was always a top producer with very happy clients.

I walked down to the Gulf Oil station. They had a few dubious pieces of tired transportation lying around, so I chatted with the owner, dutifully rang my little "bankruptcy bell," and made a deal on an old Rambler car. It was a straight swap, a clear title transaction. The engine ran like a Rolex watch, but the rest of it seemed a little dubious – mechanically speaking! But a car is a car. I tanked up my Rolls and went home, proudly displaying my new acquisition. It was greeted without enthusiasm. So I loaded a few things on board, and with a small commission cheque I'd received, took off for the Island.

Now for some sales, let's get that cash flow going! But wait, what was that cloud of steam doing rising from the front of my new Rolls? I discovered that every time I traversed the hills going north, the cooling system overheated. It leaked badly. Yes! Big time! I came to know every accessible creek and puddle of water between Nanaimo and Port Hardy. I would park that rusty steaming chunk of steel, grab a plastic bag, and run back and forth until its thirst was quenched. Another unique problem it had was the manual transmission. It had a very high ratio top gear, good for economy, but great for stalling if changed up prematurely. Anyway, it was my new home. I could sleep in it too.

Oh little Rambler, we'll have some good times together! Some bad ones too! We parked in a small wild campsite along side the Nimpkish River surrounded by the rain forest. It had a strong tendency to rain above the fiftieth parallel, which is of course a gross understatement! I worked successfully each day and the contracts piled up. I planned to drop my sales off at the insurance office in Vancouver once a week late on the Friday and visit the home base on the Sunshine Coast over the week ends. There, I would see the kids, take a short course in depression and rejection, leave some cash, and head back to Vancouver Island.

Meantime I lived on bread and peanut butter with raspberry jam. I slept in my sleeping bag, curled up in the back seat of the Rolls Rambler. It was very damp. But the real problem was that the Rambler leaked. I don't mean just from the radiator, I mean inside, somewhere around the windshield. The floor in front was absolutely water proof. So each morning the water flowed into my shoes as my feet reached for the pedals. I solved this inconvenience by decreasing the integrity of the floor with a rusty old spike. I punched a generous supply of drain holes through it. Problem solved. Dry feet!

It was a cold day in December, rainy, with the rivers running high, not the best time to schedule my water baptism, but that's the way it was! I made no bones about the fact that I frequented the churches so that I could eat occasionally. After the service some even served up little sandwiches! But the Holy Spirit was opening up new levels of understanding for me. I loved that ***Proverbs 3.5 "Trust in the Lord with all thine heart, lean not to thine own understanding, acknowledge the Lord in all thy ways, and He shall direct thy paths!"*** For me these words were the ultimate confirmation of listening to "The still small voice within!" In that verse, I heard verification about running my life by intuition, and not by logic. There's more to this Bible stuff than meets the unspiritual eye! Maybe the intuition frequency was the Holy Spirit's frequency. Yikes!

I had already had my cold morning shave and dip in the Nimpkish River, and had forgotten all about the small group from our church, along with the Pastor, who was due to arrive at 8:00am. I was prepared by this act of baptism to reveal before the Humans that I believed in the Lord Jesus Christ. Then, I heard the hum of motors and the entourage from the church came into the grassy campsite. Wow!

I greeted them and we all eyed the deep swift flowing river. In the trees above on the higher branches were a couple of bald eagles, and ravens called from across the river. I was in my swim suit and after a few preliminaries the pastor and I entered the water. I was taller than he, and he was on the outside in the deeper water. Then just as I was about to be dunked, someone said, "Derek, your watch!" To which I replied with a surprised look, "Oh! It's a Rolex! Good for 100 meters!" and at that moment I went under. I had bought the Rolex some years before and had kept it as the ultimate emergency cash generator for security purposes, and after the baptism I thought – what a lovely commercial for Rolex! I thought the pastor might get swept away, so I was prepared to swim after him and drag him to the river bank, but the Lord was with him and we went ashore. I hurried to the Rambler. Boy! Was I cold! Two dips within half an hour, now for some hot coffee! But the Church people wanted to pray and do stuff like that. I don't think they realized I had slept in my damp Rambler and already had bathed in the icy river that morning. I stood with my teeth chattering and shivered uncontrollably for a few minutes or so before someone observed that I was in distress!

Then we went for coffee. I needed breakfast but had to settle for coffee only, due to lack of funds. While sipping up the heavily sugared coffee I tackled the complex internal problem of which one of us got baptized. Was it Little Boy Wild? I think not! So it must have been ***me,*** so half of me is sort of heathen and the other half is kind of holy. I had the same problem when I got married, but I had since figured that out. My wife married *me,* the *"Unreal Self"* and Wild Boy was just thrown in for good measure, or was it for bad measure?" From far back in time an echo comes to mind, *"You're an unreal psycho!"* Was this really true? No! I was just "different," and anyway, why *should* I be like the Humans?

Now another problem arose when it was time to go home. I could drive down the Island to Courtenay, making stops to water the thirsty beast, but I had no money to pay for the ferry across the Straits of Georgia to Vancouver first thing in the morning. Arriving in Courtenay at about 9.45pm the evening before my departure, I was desperate for cash. I had a lovely Gerber hunting knife with a huge blade, so I figured I may be able to sell it in one of the pubs. This didn't work out. I was as out of place trying to sell that knife as my Rambler would be, were it parked in the courtyard of Buckingham Palace. Okay, Problem Remover, what are you going to do now? Little Boy Wild wanted to flee into the bush, hole up and sleep, but that would not solve the cash problem. I spied a service station that was still open. It was 10:20pm. I walked in the front door. The lone attendant was half asleep behind the cash register, his cap pulled over his eyes. I stood there, he didn't move.

"Hey man! I need some cash, fast, right now!" I said in half frightened tone. At the same time I brandished my flashing Gerber hunting knife, meaning to show it to him and borrow some money on it. Wow! Did he wake up in a hurry, *and the world went into slow motion for me,* as it usually did under circumstances like these. He jumped, pushed his cap back, and I saw his eyes widen as I held the knife toward him.

"No, No!" I exclaimed seeing his serious concern. After all it was late at night, and a typical robbery would stage like this. "I just wanted to see if you could help me out, sorry if I alarmed you." I explained my situation to him. He was a nice older guy, of about sixty years of age, and the whole affair ended with him loaning me fifty dollars till next Monday. I heaved a huge sigh of relief, and I'm sure my benefactor did too! It was Wild Boy who then drove and headed for a piece of wild bush land on the power line. I never felt good parking under power lines, supposing one broke? Supposing all that power sent weird frequencies through the car roof and warped my brain even further? Anything can happen in our world, and usually did.

Dawn broke. Quickly I found a deep puddle on the graveled roadway. I stripped and stood with my sponge sopping up the water, and in no time I had the equivalent of a shower, shampoo, and shave. I slipped into clean socks, shorts and shirt, and I looked as usual, as though I had just blown $65.00 on a hotel room. Many times over the years I found that all I needed was a clean rain puddle to wash up in, especially if no creek were available. So I was then able to cross on the ferry and all was well. Before I returned to the Island, I had the leak in the radiator fixed, replaced the saggy springs, had an oil change and lube, and even squandered some cash on seat covers to hide the stains and "yuk" on the seats which had come with the car at no extra cost.

A month or two later the same situation came up. It was Friday afternoon. My ferry crossing was scheduled for the next morning, and here I was again with no cash. This time it was as usual – a somewhat desperate situation. I walked into a large sporting goods store and asked for the owner. I explained that I had a business proposition for him, and would like to outline it in the privacy of his office. He called his wife in too.

No sooner had he closed the door when I said, "My problem is that I need money and have no way of obtaining cash or credit due to my recent bankruptcy." I paused.

"But I have my Smith & Wesson .44 Magnum revolver." I yanked the beautifully crafted nickel plated gun out of my belt, shook the chambers free of the live cartridges letting them fall into my hand, and passed the gun to him in the correct fashion. *Eeeeek! Why do I have these surges of wild delight when I go into my slow motion mode?* Is it the reaction that people have to a possibly dangerous situation? Or is it that wide eyed look and the frightened expression on their faces? *Is THIS what enables me to FEEL?*

Oh my God! What's going to happen next? Am I just a "crazy case" looking for trouble? Maybe it was my polite manner and British accent that allayed their major fears. I'll never know, but this could have gotten completely out of hand and the police could have been involved. The gun was registered. But I had no authority to carry it, certainly not in my belt fully loaded. As it worked out, Al was a great guy with his heart in the right place. He loaned me a hundred dollars and I was on my way. When I paid him back on the following Monday we had a really good laugh over some wonderful coffee. There *are* some nice Humans around!

Then, one night Little Boy Wild had a rather serious "time scene" of recollection. It was after we had called on a number of businesses to enquire about group insurance coverage. This last sales call of the day was on a wood cabinet and kitchen cupboards type of manufacturing operation with all the saw dust and wood smells that usual permeate these shops. After we were through and had returned to the car, Wild Boy took complete control and drove to a far more remote camping site than our usual one. I knew he was in trouble and suffering. He began to shake while he was driving, and spoke in short staccato sentences in his own unique language, as tears streamed down his face. I remained silent. He finally pulled the Rambler in under some thick bushes. I was thankful I didn't have to be concerned about the car body or the paint job. The vehicle hit a stump and stopped abruptly.

I knew from the way he parked that he was hiding and didn't want to be found. It was not a time to communicate. He simply threw himself into the grass, curled up in the fetal position and moaned "Keelematu! Keelematu!" while he rocked back and forth. I never did know just what Wild Boy's cry of "Keelematu" meant, but it appeared to be a general cry of despair and pain in his secret language.

After a while, before going down to the creek he shed his clothing, and something about the way he discarded it told me that for him, it was like divesting himself of the Humans. It reminded me of a cat with rear paws that are wet. It is a distinctive type of shake that says "Get that water off me!" I briefly smiled at the analogy. Now, standing at the water's edge he spoke to the trees, he embraced one, and then caressed some yellow flowers before entering the water. When he came up the bank to the level of the Rambler, he threw an old blanket down, took out his 'Leaves of Grass' book and stretched out on his stomach to read. He was already drying off in the evening sun and a little while later he arose and got a can of sardines from the car. After opening them he poured off the fishy oil into the vegetation, ate the entire contents and went back to his book.

He was totally unaware that he was being watched. The trees and bush surrounded him almost completely. Suddenly, he decided to get up for a different book, he had not risen fully to his feet, when the tree nearest him about 15 feet away, rocked from side to side and a large black bear appeared, the low bushes springing back as he came forward. Wild Boy had just reached his full height.

"Yhaaaa, Yhaaaaa" he yelled and raised his arms to increase his height, simultaneously, being only steps away from the Rambler he opened its door. The bear had stopped when he yelled, and the car seemed to intimidate him a bit. Wild Boy blasted the horn and that bear took off in a hurry, crashing through the bushes until all was quiet again. It must have been studying him for a while, calculating the risks and trying to determine if he were a big fish or some other creature. It had been attracted by the sardine oil. On second thought, knowing the scenting power that all bears have, I really have no doubt that it knew it was a human pre-stuffed with sardines. What bait! A very substantial evening meal was in the offing. Little Boy Wild was shaken up, he realized that had he not gotten up to get that other book, the bear could have taken him in about 2.5 seconds. Black bears are predatory and opportunistic in nature, and in similar type situations there are cases where the black bear simply stood on his prize, ripped off an arm and began eating. In still other cases they prefer to start with the organ meats, heart and liver and so forth. To make things easier, this one didn't have to be skinned!

"It's been a rough day" I said, "And this tops it off! Do you want to talk about things like we do? I know you're sort of freaked out about something. Let's start with the wood working shop." Wild Boy turned his head from side to side, as though trying to grasp where to start. He knew he had had a narrow escape, and was now almost weakened into getting things off his chest.

"That hot sawdust and wood took me back to elementary school. I'm nine or ten years old now. This is our wood working class and we make small articles or cut out plywood animals with our fretsaws. Mr.Cox is our teacher. He's a serious faced kind of person with a small moustache. He rarely smiles, but I like him because every now and then he gives me booklets about Jesus. I love these little gospels complete with pictures, some are even in color. On several occasions I have not waited to be given one, but I have sought him out at recess or after hours to make my request for further reading.

Three times now he has locked the door behind me when I entered, and on each of these occasions has used me sexually. Several of the boys have warned me about Mr.Cox but I didn't believe them, after all, he gave me Jesus booklets. One time some kids caught me leaving the wood working shop rather rapidly in tears.

"We told you so! We told you!" they exclaimed excitedly, but with some genuine concern. The fourth and final assault happened during one recess when I was retained to do some cleaning up. I was pushed into a small storage room and brutally sodomized. He did it in a cold powerful way that was devoid of any human warmth and feeling. When the boys returned to class, tears were still streaming down my face. I tried to restrain them, but finally I broke down and sobbed openly without any attempt to hide my hurt. This is always an embarrassing situation for the other boys; it makes them feel very uncomfortable and when I tried to use the fretsaw, my body movements brought on huge waves of pain.

"Derek!" Mr.Cox called out. "If you can't stop your sniveling, you may go home!"

So I did just that, but if only I could have had an excuse for HER. Of course I arrived home too early with my tear-stained face.

"You've been misbehaving in school again, haven't you?" SHE screamed.

"Yes—but it..."I replied.

"Get upstairs you swine," she interrupted. This was followed by the second thrashing with the bamboo cane that day. I curled up small on my bed, a hot ball of pain with no way *"OUT." There is no way out.* It goes on and on and on. I fall into my usual rocking back and forth motions as I rhythmically moan.

"On and on and on." It keeps my mind blank. I just do not want to think or remember. *I want Blank...I want OUT!*

"You can stop that noise up there or I'll give you something to moan about you bloody swine!" The threat hangs darkly in the air. I dissociate and fall asleep.

The Cox situation cleared up, when an enquiry was launched into his behavior some weeks later. I was called into a meeting, where some of the other boy's parents were convening with the head master. I was questioned a number of times about what had been done to me by Mr.Cox, but each time I tried to formulate a reply, I'd look at the black forbidding face of the head master, the horrified expressions of the parents, the cold blue eyed innocent look of Mr.Cox – *and it seemed that I was on trial.* I denied that anything had ever occurred! I lied again and again. The parents looked at me with disapproval, but I felt a deadly threat from Mr.Cox that truly terrified me. I was told to leave the meeting. We had a new woodworking teacher shortly after.

Back by the Rolls Rambler, Little Boy Wild lay back among the grasses, it was his usual position for contemplation. He looked almost pleadingly at me while he frowned.

"When is the right time to enter the River of No Return?" he asked. "Is it when you come to a dead-end severing point? Is it the finale to the "Cornered Rat Syndrome?" which surely must come about because the rat dies inside, he just succumbs, gives up, disappears" He fell silent. I felt that some answer would come to him; I hoped so for I was stumped. He started suddenly at a noise in the bush, still feeling nervous about the bear encounter which could have answered his question once and for all.

A short time later as he watched the sun cast longer shadows, he again asked me. "When does one decide to pull down the curtain of nothingness? Is it decided for us, falling silently as a great gift of love and compassion? Or is it... Mercy falling as the gentle rain from heaven?... And is this what they call catatonic psychosis? *I'm not here anymore.* Maybe this really is the final adventure where the currents of hopelessness float me down the 'River of No Return.' What would happen to me then? Would Little Boy Wild live happily ever after?" He leapt to his feet and started to prepare for nightfall. Of one thing I was certain, that black bear would be close in around the car come dusk because of all the fresh sardine smells. Wild Boy passed control back to me, mainly because he was too mentally worn out from the excitement of the day to make a decision of any sort. I was grateful, so I tidied things up, washed in the creek, cleaned my teeth and generally sorted out the tasks for the morrow. I planned to immediately drive to our usual camping place with which we were familiar. There were bears there too, but no food smells of any type. Not even on our clothes! We had survived another day – survived the silent screams, and shed more hurt by re-living it. Just beyond the forest edge, Little Boy Wild heard the roar of waves from the ocean, and it relaxed him into a dream state – perchance to even visit other worlds.

Chapter Twenty Six

*E*ventually the cash situation improved and I created a large client base in the area that I worked. So rather than continue to sleep in the damp Rolls Rambler I decided to find a small travel trailer. I located one in a local paper which belonged to the owners of the trailer park which was primarily comprised of mobile homes. I checked the trailer out. It was parked close to their garage on their own home lot. They wanted $2200.00 for it. It was older but solid, and to me a real palace compared to the ancient Rambler. Of course, being bankrupt, no financing was available to me from any source. After I viewed the trailer I made my offer.

"I'll pay you $2400.00 for it in four equal monthly payments starting with $600.00 cash right now. But, it will have to stay parked in its present location as my vehicle could not possibly tow it." I explained. To this offer they agreed because the security factors were so high. The whole purchase worked out okay. I had really made them an offer they could not refuse. So I moved into the luxury of space, heat and comfort. It had a power hook up, but no sewer line. The regular grey water drainage I could handle myself and haul it away or even just let it drain among the rain rivulets. But what does one do when nature calls at quite unexpected times? (I thought you'd never ask!) Well, it's like this; you've probably never heard of S&S bags before? (Squat and Splat!) Also known as white plastic Kitchen Catchers? They make ideal containers to handle these situations. One seals it up right after, and the trailer blows clear with fresh air almost immediately. End of story!

Oh No! Not quite—hold on there! At the back of the trailer was a wide 8 inch ledge that was positioned over the storage compartments, and it was on this ledge that I "stored" my used S&S bags. Once or twice I ran short of bags and had to use a few twice over which made them about twice as heavy. Then once a week I'd drop them in a dumpster in town somewhere.

One summer evening having just completed an S&S procedure, the trailer park owners small yappy poodle type animal by the name of Lucy came by to check out the tantalizing smells that wafted with the breeze. I thought I had heard scratching and scrabbling sounds at the back of the trailer, and as I opened the door to investigate, that beastly little poodle creature of theirs dashed triumphantly by me with a fresh hot bag of "you know what" in its jaws. With its head held high it proudly trotted up the pathway right into their lovely home and started to rip the bag apart on the luxurious broadloom carpeting. I had pursued it right up to the front door, thinking I might rescue that "doggy bag." But when it saw me coming, it jumped up and dashed around the living room with the torn bag in its mouth, while the contents dropped and smeared everywhere. Finally, it jumped up onto their white sofa and I was privy to watch it start its delectable meal. In a terrible panic I fled back to my trailer.

"Wild Boy! Why do these things happen?" I asked in a fierce whisper.

Just then we heard shouts and high pitched screams coming from the house. So I quickly gathered the balance of the S&S bags and put them in the trunk of the Rolls Rambler. Then as I spotted Lucy's owners coming down the pathway, I quietly closed the trailer door, only to emerge a few moments later, yawning and stretching like I'd been napping and had come out to see what all the noise was about. I expressed equal horror and surprise at their terrible experience, and we all wondered where Lucy could have gotten that stinking mess from.

First thing in the morning as I headed out I was determined to unload those Lucy Bags fast. Just a few kilometers out I saw a muddy logging-type road coming up on the right hand side, so I pulled up and parked. Blue wood smoke was rising through the trees and as no human habitation was anywhere in the area, I assumed it was a Forestry Department project to burn up debris after logging, and it was still smoking from the day before. I opened the trunk. What a stink! I'm sure that smells go right through plastic somehow. So Little Boy Wild lined up all nine of them for launching. They had a nice heft to them, especially those with a double load; and as he whirled them around his head, I was struck by the beauty of his form. The early sunlight shone on his brow and he was for me, just like David in the Bible as he faced up to Goliath. Then one after another in rapid succession he whirled them like he was using a super powerful slingshot. All nine of them rained down among the trees and smoke. He aimed toward the smoke hoping the bags would land on a fire and burn.

"Bombs away!" he gleefully exclaimed with a wicked glint in his eyes. I was quite sure that Goliath had been slain, and I was very relieved to have disposed of those incriminating Lucy Bags. But wait! What were those horrified screams, cries and shouts of surprise and consternation about?

Oh no! Oh yes! David alias Wild Boy in his fight to the death with the giant had hurled the whole works down on what now seemed to be a small tree planter's camp. They were probably innocently frying up eggs and bacon over their fires when it suddenly rained shit bags from heaven. Plastic tears when dropped from a height with a weight in it, and at least two of them were carrying a double load. Who or what got hit? Almost immediately the roar of pick-up truck engines rent the air. Wild Boy gave a cry of excitement as he leapt into the Rambler.

"Let's get the hell out of here!" he exclaimed. We did. We just could not face up to any explanations or apologies. Indeed, what *CAN* one say? The car leapt forward and we merged with a stream of workers driving to their shifts at the mill. Saved! We drove towards town with a certain decorum and feel of accomplishment. Not a bad start to the morning. Little Boy Wild laughed a lot all day, and the laughter curled us up even more when we thought of "Manna" falling from heaven! Or as Wild Boy stated in a rare somber moment later that day, "Shit happens!"

It was during the nineteen seventies, when autos had bumper stickers proclaiming various messages, that I saw a number of car bumpers claiming – "I'm a King's Kid," and upon investigating I found that it originated with Harold Hill's books, one of which was named, "How to Live Like a King's Kid!" This guy Hill was super-real and filled with the Holy Spirit. He lived the word of God in reality and good things happened all around him. Of course the term "King's Kids" is based on the Bible, and I quote, *"As many as are led by the Spirit of God, they are the sons of God."* I read all of Harold Hill's books and put his theme of *"Living like a Son of God"* into everyday practice. (Lucy bags excluded!) Wow! If God be with you –

who can be against you? IT worked just as the Good Book and Harold Hill said it would, and I became more successful in what I did, day by day!

We were well into our bankruptcy period, and things were still lean and somewhat tough. Brad – my second son would be redundant in his present employment in about two weeks, and he was hoping to run into another job, what with pressures of car payments and etcetera. Then one evening an opportunity came up to practice the King's Kid principles. It was totally unexpected. Brad was relating stories to us from logging camps up north.

His face was a study in amusement as he related his story.

"And then Pete goes down to this big fir and cranks up his chainsaw and starts in. It's the last tree he'll take down before lunch. We hear a steady drone for a short while and then we hear him shouting. Then there was this erratic high speed engine noise of a chain saw running at high speed with no load on it, more shouts, and the saw then begins to bite in again, a real work noise. Then there was more shoutin' and the free running high speed motor noise, so we went down to see what the hell all the fuss was about.

"Hey Pete! What's up? What are you hollerin' for?" I ask him.

"Fuck man! It's a big fuckin' weasel tryin' to get me! Every time I get going that fucker comes down the tree snarling somethin' fierce. He's real pissed off man! I can't get rid of him!"

Just then this furry critter starts climbing down, an' yes, it is pissed off, but it ain't no weasel, it's a fuckin' wolverine! Pete backs off because it looks like it might leap at him.

"Pete! For Chissakes man, that ain't no weasel! Get the fuck out of there, it's a wolverine!" someone shouts.

"What the fuck's a wolverine?" Pete shouts, sounding kind of scared now.

"What's a wolverine" the same voice shouts, "It's that snarlin' fucker that's goin' to rip your balls off if you don't come back up here quick."

"In the meantime" my son continued, "The wolverine took off, it was a scary experience for everyone; on top of that we thought everyone knew what a wolverine was."

I got a kick out of his story, and at the same moment, I had a sudden inspiration, and asked Brad if he believed the King's Kid stories I'd been talking about.

"Yes" he said, "But there is a lot to know—all this Holy Spirit stuff an' that."

"Well," I continued, "Do you really want a new job, right now? You only have about ten days left in your present job."

"I sure do." he replied. He was lying stretched out on a cushioned bench seat in the kitchen eating area while the rest of the family were in the living room.

"Tell you what," I said. "I have a job for you. Just this afternoon the Jones outfit up the inlet—the shake blockers, lost a man from their regular work crew and he has to be replaced. He's hurt his shoulder very badly and can't work and they need a man to be on the early morning plane to make up the full crew. Do you want the job? Because if you do, we have to be at their place (about 10kms away) fast! It's 9:00pm already. Come on King's Kid, let's go – your car or mine?"

Brad stirred himself, amid some derision from the living room, and away we sped in his car to the Jones' place. There was a light on. "I'll go" he said. "Me too," I replied, "I want to see this." He knocked sharply on the door and Mrs. Jones appeared.

"Oh Mrs. Jones"—he sounded almost apologetic; "I was wondering if you had a job opening in your camp?"

"Come on in," she said, "Just this afternoon one of our men injured his shoulder badly and we need someone to go up on the 8:00am plane tomorrow morning!"

Now what you have to appreciate here; is that *I knew nothing of this,* other than what the Holy Spirit had given me through the "Gift of knowledge." I had no remote way of knowing about the injured man and the job opportunity!

"Oh yes," Mrs. Jones said to Brad "We'll be glad to have you but I'm not sure about the early plane, just get there as soon as you can!"

I intervened. "Mrs. Jones—he's a King's Kid and already has a confirmed reservation. He'll be there"

Mrs. Jones looked a little unsure of me and what I had said, and my son tried to explain it away. After working out the pay details, he thanked her and we left.

"I don't have any rain gear and such likes." Brad voiced his concern, "and how about my present boss at the building supply, what will he say?"

"Let's go and see him and get some gear from the store at the same time." I replied.

So we sped to the store manager's home. It was 10:05pm. We had no problem there, he understood and gave Brad the keys to the store instructing him to write up the bill for the personal logging gear he needed, and to sign it, take his gear and return the keys. He was also released by his employer with very best wishes. We entered the store, flicked on the lights, and as we passed the phone I said, "Brad, call the plane base and confirm your 8.00am flight. He was hesitant, but he put in the call. Yes! They had received a cancellation and would be glad to put him on the 8:00am flight! So he booked it, picked out his gear, returned the keys to his boss, and we drove home.

We were greeted with, "And how did the fabulous King's Kids make out?"

"Fine!" said Brad," I got the job at the Jones' and I fly up the inlet on the 8:00am plane tomorrow morning." Of course the whole thing was put down to *coincidence*, but he and I know better than this. The entire gift of knowledge sequence, the injury, the required replacement, obtaining the job, disconnecting from the old position, getting the necessary gear and confirming plane reservations was the Holy Spirit in action. Hooray for we King's Kids!

Another interesting experience came up in that period when I had been discussing *faith* and its application in every day life with some friends. I was pretty sure I had the right picture of what it was all about. But one night at about 2:00am a word came to me, just one single word, *"Casuistry!"* About every hour that word kept repeating in my brain, casuistry, casuistry, casuistry! So when morning finally came, right after breakfast – there it was again! Casuistry!

"Ridiculous!" I exclaimed, "There's no such word!" Oh! But there was! In the dictionary it said, *"Casuistry"* and gave a full explanation, which, when I looked up all the big words that *it* meant – it also said that in relation to *faith,* I didn't know what I was talking about! Well! That blew my mind! The Holy Spirit had torpedoed my interpretation of *"faith"* with

ONE word – *CASUISTRY!* I later read a little book by Oral Roberts, it contained just about everything I would ever need to know about faith, apart from the Bible – in terms I could comprehend. People call experiences like this *"coincidence,"* but I know this is not so. *It is the gift of knowledge through the Holy Spirit.*

Business was good and the cash flow increased in line with the effort expended, and I even had enough money to cross on the ferries without scaring the hell out of innocent citizens. But it was time for Rolls Rambler to go to the crusher where it should have been in the first place. It had already gone through three clutches and the last one had only lasted about two weeks.

Before I had left my trailer base up north, I asked the nice owners of the Lucy creature if they would finance a new vehicle for me, about $12,000 odd. They would have a lien on the vehicle, *and* on the clear title trailer. I offered them the same interest as the finance company would charge, and to this they agreed. So away I went shopping for a car. At the Nissan dealer in North Vancouver, I found a demonstration model Bahama blue Nissan hatch back. I fell in love with it; and although it could never pull my trailer it would be super economical. I listed the extra equipment I required, got the grand total and told them to have it undercoated ready for delivery the following Friday.

"How do you wish to pay for that Sir?" my sales person asked.

"Ah! That is what I want to speak with your sales or general manager about." I said.

The salesman sat with me in the president's office, where I told them I was an undischarged bankrupt and wanted to proceed with the sale.

"How large a down payment are you able to make?" they asked.

To which I replied "One dollar!" Indeed, it was all that I had! "But I'll give you a certified cheque for the balance on delivery next Friday."

So I handed Grant the one dollar bill, we shook hands all round; then I hitch hiked back up north to do the documentation and legal stuff, got the cheque and showed up early Friday to take delivery. All was complete and okay. The little Nissan was a dream compared to the Rambler and I was able to sleep in it with a lot more comfort as it was a hatchback. What happened to the Rambler? I left it at the Rambler dealer in lieu of payment on the last clutch job. Things were looking up.

Little Boy Wild could gaze up through the glass at the star studded skies each night. It was sort of like "living with the animals" as we parked in the wildest places every bed time. He saw grouse, black bears, deer, a couple of weasels and a host of birds; it was very relaxing for him, which was good for me as I had much to do to pay for our new acquisition. The Nissan contract was flawlessly performed to completion and everyone was happy.

About this time Wild Boy ran into some sea otters and they captured his heart. So we decided to buy a canoe and explore the off shore islands and inlets. It was an Alumacraft 18ft camouflage color craft that allowed us to disappear more quickly if need be. There were many logging camps around the inlets and two or three were major operations which meant they would have lots of mobile homes with young families and kids who were ideal insurance prospects. On our first trip through the Quatsino Narrows, we saw several boats moored and thought they must be fishing. We had never heard of tide tables, and had no idea that the Narrows were in full flood boiling towards us. In no time at all I was paddling for my life, desperately, between giant whirlpools. Later, several people who were in the moored boats waiting for the tide to change told me they thought I had been sucked down into the whirlpools because I had vanished. In actual fact I had prayed – yes! I prayed, "Oh God give me the strength to paddle to that shoreline. Save me!" It was quite a struggle, and after I had landed and rested up for a while the water milled around and started to flow the other way—next to no paddling, just guide your canoe through!

One other lesson we learned the hard way was an experience on the way back from one of our inlet expeditions to our base. I wanted to get back to the comfort and warmth of our trailer. At that time we had only the open Alumacraft canoe, and I had ignored the obvious weather signs all around us. We had hardly gotten underway when the wind came up fast, and we were about two kilometers from base in the middle of Rupert Arm with white caps dancing and cascading all around. Suddenly the small 4hp Johnson outboard motor quit running. It was clogged with kelp, and had overheated and seized up. I should have thrown it overboard right then, but I had the hope that it could be repaired. So I resorted to paddling – the waves got higher, spray, mist and rapidly falling dusk kept obscuring the lights from the village where my base lay. The paddle was slippery, and then – horror of horrors! It slipped from my grasp and danced away across the white caps. The canoe angled the wrong way and we shipped a small amount of water. I quickly untied the spare paddle, and chased after the first one – a mistake maybe, but I did retrieve it and thereby still had a spare, but not before I had shipped more water and almost tipped. It was impossible to bail water and paddle like crazy at the same time. The first doubts appeared; can you really make it back? It's almost dark now. I knew the general direction of the village, but my only guide to the nearest shoreline are a few intermittent twinkling lights about a kilometer ahead, and they keep disappearing into the spray. Suppose my canoe is washed ashore the next day? No one knows I'm gone, and no one cares anyway! The sea lice and crabs will pick my bones clean, and some kid fishing from the shore will find my beautiful Alumacraft canoe. End of story! Never have I paddled so hard to get back to base – Little Boy Wild was silent the whole time this fiasco unfolded. It took another 45 minutes before I benefited from the protection of the bay from the higher winds. We arrived. Wild Boy cried out "Keelematu! Keelematu!" and shed some tears of relief. He sniffed and snuffled the whole time I pulled our canoe and gear from the water, and that evening we had a chat over a bowl of hot soup. The questions were – *why did I have to get back now, right now?* What was the hurry? We had no reason whereby we *had* to get back tonight, so why were we out in the middle of Rupert Arm in the dark – riding three foot whitecaps in a high wind and shipping water? We had done this with a dead motor, and had just our guts and stupidity to paddle back with. I had told myself; "You'd better pray boy! Or you ain't never gonna get back – no ways, no how!" Thank you Lord for your guardian angels, they even help dumb characters like me! From then on, I learned to pull up onto an island or a sheltered bay somewhere and wait for the storm to subside. After all, we had our tent, Optimus stove, fuel, canned soup and other grub on board. We had dry clothing in waterproof bags, a Smith & Wesson .44 magnum revolver with lots of ammo, fishing kit, binoculars, camera, a New Testament, first-aid stuff, flash light and spare batteries. We even carried fresh water. Maybe the only thing we did lack was intelligence enough to think and act sensibly! I picked up a lot of good contracts on these trips through sheer hard work and know-how, and most of this occurred when the fallers came in at about 3.30pm. I had to work fast because they went to bed around 8:00pm! All the time I worked, Little Boy Wild was aching to explore the remote shorelines.

During the day Wild Boy basked in the sun and watched the river otters catch salmon and gorge themselves. As he lay scenting the salt air, he kept up a good scan of the kelp beds for his sea otters. He also found a lot of time to read our Bible. But how could he ever forget his uncle Kevin who had arranged his version of "Bible Studies"? We lived with him and his grandmother at that time. Little Boy Wild described the whole scene to me, while with his eyes he followed the swallows of summer as they swooped up insects on the wing.

"I'm about eight years old and we have moved from the "Club place" to my grandmother's home. They lived at 62 Warminster Road, an address that seemed burned into my mind; it was totally demolished by a direct bomb hit during the latter part of the blitz on London. Granny was a gracious lady and accustomed to wealth. She would sit grandly by the log burning fireplace frequently popping chocolates into her mouth with delicate, refined motions. In particular, the little pinkie finger had to be extended "just so," which was for me a mark of aristocracy, the high and the mighty. On her right side was a huge velvet rope that seemed to hang from the ceiling. When she yanked on it, a butler would appear to handle her every whim. Sometimes when she was not there, my older brother and I would pull on the velvet rope just to see the little bald headed man appear as if by magic. It was akin to having Aladdin's Lamp! In addition things happened to me. I always had toilet problems from way back; and the toilets in Granny's time had the tank above the throne by about four feet at least, and the unit was flushed by pulling on a chain which hung down within my reach. I had difficulty in flushing this thing, as I just didn't have the knack of tripping the mechanism – I just sort of pulled on it! This day I pulled and nothing happened, and I had a choice; either you pull and flush it, or you get a good thrashing from HER. As I pulled with all my small eight year old strength, the ball mechanism contacted the ceramic cover above it – and the whole ceramic top came crashing down, striking the back of my head, and

felling me to the floor before it hit the hard tiles, splitting into many pieces. I scrambled to my feet, and had not yet pulled up my pants, and as I stood there, stunned and bleeding from a small cut on my head, help came rushing in to see what the terrible sounds of devastation were all about.

I was pulled out of the small room and fell flat on my face causing blood to spurt from my nose. I had fallen because my pants were trapped around my ankles – the Humans would never take something like that into account. Somehow, I recovered from the reprimands and the thrashing I had earned. So now my future flushing problems had worsened. What do I do when I have to "Go"? Sometimes the chain worked – sometimes it didn't. Usually I had to flush twice, and this was bad!

But there were times that when the urge came, I – an eight year old, did it right there on one of the beautiful Turkish rugs. There were reasons for this that the Humans didn't know about – except my uncle. It was the terrible pain in my rear end when the urge made itself known, that caused me to drop them right then. Many years later I realized that my sphincter muscles had been weakened and stretched to accommodate a typical unit of average thickness and about six inches long. I also knew why my Grandmother exclaimed at times when she almost tripped over one of my "logs," before she picked it up, "Really – in all my life, I have never known a child to pass such big ones!" I suppose other kids were not "reamed out" and made artificially large like I was, and it was this very largeness that also caused the chain pulling problems. "They" just would not go away, and leered back at me when I tried to flush them.

This house had become a house of horrors for me; my uncle Kevin was about seventeen and I became his natural sexual prey. In talking with me about sexual things, I had revealed to him my experiences with Jason that happened when I was seven years old. It may have set the mould for our relationship. A number of times when Kevin asked my brother and me to go up into the dark regions of the attic, I was the only one who accompanied him because of the promise of a Bible reading, and this is what enticed me. There was a lot of junk lying around, and he had set up an old steamer trunk covered with steamship labels as an altar. He had even placed tall white candles on it, our only source of light other than his flashlight which enabled us to come and go."

Wild Boy shifted his position, scanned the kelp beds and explosively laughed when he discovered his sea otters again. Our Zeiss 10x40 binoculars filled his eyes face to face, eye to eye with those furry creatures, the brightness and clarity both enraptured and captured him for almost half and hour. This was his life, living with the animals, and my work enabled him to do just that, so I always planned for us to be in remote areas regardless of the economics involved.

"Oh yes," he smiled. "I was always instructed to stand before the altar and read the pages he had selected. He wore a long black robe, maybe it was his dressing gown, but underneath it he was totally naked. He always commanded me to read out loud, and as I did he removed my clothing. It was cold in the attic and the strange shadows scared me. I was already familiar with the pain of intrusion; it combined with my dissociating in and out. But he did use a lubricant, some kind of greasy stuff. Sometimes he didn't enter me, but greased between my thighs and held me brutally tight until he had finished pulsating.

There was nothing friendly or warm about these incidents. Kevin was just cold, powerful and painful. Nor did he attempt to clean me up afterwards, and his episodes had none of the intimate beauty that I experienced with Jason. Jason at least held me afterwards, and that made it all worth while. He was soft, warm and affectionate. Eventually Kevin would snuff out the candles and we would descend. I seemed to have accepted that sodomy was a part of my life. I had no one to help me, and I had no words to convey any meaning to my experiences, even if I could tell someone."

I was surprised that Little Boy Wild had not gone into his rocking motions and "Keelematu!" exclamations, but he told me he did not feel threatened as he had his friends the sea otters nearby, so he could go into the pain, and then out to the otters for reassurance. It was as if he was in communication with them and had become a sea otter himself, a warm intimate feeling that touched his inner space. It was not uncommon for him to become the creature he was watching; a type of transference wherein he contained the creature and they moved in each other, as one creature, in some strange way. After scanning the horizon for a while, he turned to me.

"Perhaps the worst scene of all was when Kevin got absolutely desperate for sex one day just before we were called for supper. I had failed to fellate him having thrown up all over his dark pants. In a rage he had stripped my shorts off and was in the final strokes of completing his violent release when a voice on the stairs called, "Supper's ready!" Kevin's face was flushed and eyes were particularly wild.

"Say one word about this and I'll kill you." he hissed. "We'll be right down," he shouted. I pulled up my short pants and followed him down to the supper table. The slippery stuff oozed slowly down into my socks; and I was feeling badly hurt and frightened. He knew I was an absolute write off and a loner, and I didn't doubt that he could arrange to kill me in some way. We are seated at the dining room table, and I study the design in the beautiful damask linen tablecloth. The smell of food is wonderful, but I want to throw up, *I want scream, I want to explode, or disappear in someway. I give a long silent scream.*

SHE says, "What's that thing sniveling about? It's always crying about something!"

I looked across at Kevin with tears rolling down my cheeks; his eyes clearly say "I'll kill you, I'll kill you!" The threat was very real. I mumbled something and reached down my leg where it was cold and tickling. I gathered up a handful of the yukky stuff, and smeared it on my short pants. I smelled my hand afterwards and wiped the balance on the table napkin in its silver ring. Later I went up to the room which I shared with my brother, and lying on the bed I cried until I felt the tickle of rabbit whiskers on my cheek, it was so tender and friendly that I fell asleep. My brother sort of knew what was going on, and flatly told me not to go to the attic with Kevin. However, this last brutal incident had occurred in Kevin's room. It could happen anywhere.

Back by the Sea Otters again, I wondered about our ability to go back into time, and about changing the way things were. "I think that is enough for both us for a few days." I replied ruefully. Wild Boy's re-lived pain was beginning to affect me in some way.

"That's also enough of the Humans for one day," I stated, and immediately I knew that Little Boy Wild had taken over. He knew his sea otters were just off shore, he called to the sandpipers, and flexing his nostrils he scented the gentle wash of waves on the sand and rocks below. He gazed into the heavens alive with the lights from an infinite number of worlds. He could not remember the number of starlit nights that he had stood in similar rapture, gazing into the night skies – and one beautiful quote always came to his lips as once again he murmured – ***"In my Father's house are many mansions."***

Wild One felt warm and vibrant as he lay on his sleeping bag, he was content; and to complete his starlit ecstasy, he opened his whole inner being, allowing himself to be lifted to new heights of "oneness." He became the starlight; he rode on the lilting cries of the shore birds, and then softly floated with them into the vistas of dream. A seal barked from somewhere in the bay, its repeated calls blended with the rising moon and the rhythmic lap of the waves as they kissed time and passed into eternity.

Chapter Twenty Seven

There were times during the early insurance days, when although we were working, we were slightly hungry! In one small town, I was fairly sure that someone would pay cash for their first policy premium, and I could use this to eat and to buy gas, and the matter would be taken care of when I turned my sales in at our Vancouver office.

Day one: Yes, I had two sales, cheques only. So I took a drink from the river and made up my bed in the Nissan hatchback while my stomach growled a little. Never mind. Tomorrow is another day. Little Boy Wild gazed up through the glass at the star studded night. He was living wild with the animals, and he was happy though hungry. We slept.

Day two: A mama black bear with two cubs strolled by us in the early morning as we were rising. A good wash up and shave in the river, and we were ready for the day's work. But although three contracts were arranged, they paid by cheques only! So another starry night went by.

Day three: I stroll along the river in the early morning, keeping a watchful eye out for hungry black bears, and there on a sand bar by the river, a bright shiny twenty five cent piece lay in the sand. Wow! What a find! That quarter plus the fifty cents I already had would buy a chocolate bar. I waited for the store to open and savored that bar. It's nice to eat! Two more contracts that day and they both gave me cheques.

Day four: If we don't eat today we'll have to go back to our base, because I know I have at least one can of beans there. I feel light headed and weak. No sales today. Just long rest periods by the river, watching the little black bear cubs play around. Evening is approaching and dusk is falling. I knock on a door and a tall friendly character greets me. He looks like a logger who has just came in from a hard day felling firs in the forest.

"We're just about to have supper, but come on in and grab a bite if you haven't already eaten, and we'll talk about insurance after."

I step inside the warm kitchen dining area; the smell of food makes me drool.

"We're not having much, just a bowl of soup an' that." These are words of life to me!

I thank him. I'm giddy with anticipation. What he calls "just a bowl of soup" is really a big pot of thick venison stew, with potatoes, carrots, onions and big chunks of deer meat. The steam rises in clouds above our bowls. He takes a spoonful and blows on it. I eat. I wolf it down. I have not eaten in four days, and just the thought of that bowl of deer meat and vegetables disappearing in some unforeseen manner before I can eat, freaks me out. Both he and his charming wife are still blowing on their spoons. I am embarrassed because my bowl is totally empty and still very hot—the steam is still rising from the empty bowl and as I watch it, I meet their eyes.

"You'd better fill the boy's bowl up Mom, looks like he's kind of hungry."

I, of course, exclaimed that the venison stew was just super. The next bowl was brimming full and I took my time, occasionally blowing on my spoon. He didn't buy insurance, but when I left I shook his hand warmly and thanked him profusely. What a life-saver, when one eats for the first time in four days it feels very good indeed! Little Boy Wild and I gazed at the stars as we snuggled into our down sleeping bag that night. Our tummy was stuffed with hot venison stew and it sent new life coursing through our system. We slept well all night with just the murmur and `swishy-swishy' sounds of the river singing like a soft lullaby.

On another hungry occasion I was far up an inlet in the kayak when I observed a small cluster of buildings with a small white church among the sparse homesteads. I paddled into this sheltered bay, because churches often have coffee and cookies after the service, and I would eat and survive! So on Sunday morning I showed up ahead of anyone else, and as a gesture of faith in tea and biscuits or whatever, I slipped my remaining cash comprising of a two dollar bill into the damp and ornate collection bag on the wall. I could not buy anything to eat for two dollars anyway; in addition, there was no store in this little settlement. I studied the inside of the Anglican Church with all its trimmings and waited for others to show up. No one did! Finally the minister swished his black robes through the door, and after a few words began the service with me as the only one in attendance. It was an amazing affair, I got the shortened version with no sermon and then I was on my way. No coffee, tea or cookies either. Now what? Hunger assailed me. When the coast was clear I snook back into that church and with apologies for robbing God, slipped my hand into the damp bag to retrieve my two dollar bill – but it was gone! The preacher had taken the money, so now I really was down and out. I knew that God would have forgiven me for borrowing two dollars to feed one of his starving critters. So ignoring the fact that it was Sunday – a day of rest, I started to solicit business. It was a flat and unrewarding day, and I made my last call on a lovely old waterfront home at 5.30pm. I was weakened by hunger and felt down and depressed; but Little Boy Wild had been rather taken with the loons calling. They seemed to have assuaged his hunger somewhat, and he felt comforted when they answered his calls.

The nice fellow who answered the door explained that he was not prepared to talk about insurance until after supper, and had I eaten yet?

"Come on in, sit yourself down and grab a plate. Dig in – we'll talk after!"

What a spread! They lived like kings. Not only did they have fresh home baked rolls, but smoked salmon, oysters, and a stack of little birds the size of quails, perhaps a little bigger, and all roasted to perfection. My plate didn't have sides on it but it should have. After I finished up two birds, they insisted I have two more. Was I that ravenous, and was it that obvious? Is that the way I came across to them – a starving insurance salesman kayaking between the islands? How can one ever repay such kindness? How close to the truth this really was! I had tears in my eyes when I thanked them on leaving.

The very next morning I had success – yes, by cheque! But I was still full of grub from the previous evening, so it didn't matter that much. When I had finished my insurance presentation with this middle aged couple, their son walked in from the basement or somewhere. I was introduced. He was taller than my 6'1" inches and quite heavily built. He wore thick glasses. His Dad said "Michael raises rabbits – he's quite a rabbit farmer."

"Oh!" I exclaimed, "I love bunnies too, what do you do with them all? Do you eat some?" The boy's face changed. He took two steps toward me, grabbed me by the lapels of my jacket, and lifting me clean off the floor, said rather fiercely, "You no eat my bunnies! You no eat my bunnies!"

"Of course not," I said, "I just love to stroke their silky ears as much as you do, how many do you have?"

He hesitated. His Dad said, "It's okay Michael – you can put him down now, he won't hurt your bunnies." So I was placed back on the floor again, where I adjusted my jacket and proceeded to write up the application. Never a dull moment!

Tonight Little Boy Wild sat by the ocean next to his kayak deep in thought, and as the gathering dusk descended, he set up his craft as a wind break alongside him. Some stars appeared among the clouds and a light breeze came up. Next he placed his S&W .44 magnum fully loaded under his pillow, there was always an empty chamber under the hammer of course. He was well prepared in the event a big black bear or some other curious or hungry critter should show up. On one trip when I saw heavy dark fingers of rain trailing across the water in the distance and coming up at a rapid rate, I said, "Wild Boy! You an' me is gonna hole up right here on this cute little island." So we pulled in and brought the kayak up the beach to this lovely protected camp site. A small creek was trickling down to the shoreline, while in the distance were dark trees swaying in the rising wind. But something was not quite right about this beautiful spot. The more I looked out across the ocean towards the dark rain clouds coming in, and then looked back to toward the swaying trees on my island; the more the small hairs on the back of my neck kept rising and tickling with terrifying apprehension. What danger lurked back in those trees—watching me? Why did a quiet internal voice say to me, "Leave now, right now? And don't look back?"

The *logical* part of my mind said, "Nonsense, pitch your tent in that little grove of trees close by and get set up for the evening." Of course, had we arrived earlier we would have explored the island with me carrying the .44 magnum for safety. All the *intuitive* side of my mind said, *"Get out and leave now, I mean NOW!"* I shivered with cold prickles all over, and knowing that these immutable intuition messages *MUST* be obeyed, we launched the kayak and headed downwind with the rain clouds still chasing us.

Shortly after, we located another camping possibility that met with the approval of the intuition frequencies. **Little Boy Wild and I rarely fail to obey intuition,** that which folks call their "gut" feeling. With practice over the years, **acting in obedience to intuition** has no doubt saved my life time and again. It is something that has to be honed or polished by use—like developing an "intuition muscle," until it is an automatic response, and is as, or more powerful than the **logical** side of one's brain. It is the overriding indisputable authority! **Intuition is the primary directive force in which we live, move and have our being!** One must always be tuned to the **"still small voice within" and obey it.** The hardest part is that because it defies all logic, it is too easy to be disobedient! I know that bears and wolves travel between the islands by swimming to these new territories and one can never really know what to expect. So between **intuition,** my trusty .44 magnum and the Angel of the Lord outside my tent, I reckon we're pretty safe! In the meantime I find that ignorance rises exponentially with every new in-sight and acquisition of knowledge that we achieve! Indeed – the more one knows – the more questions arise!

So that night when we snuggled safely down, we nibbled on a choco-late bar. Prior to this we had enjoyed a crunchy peanut butter sandwich with raspberry jam. Any bear within at least half a mile knew about us, and what we were stuffed with! People grossly underestimate how powerful the sense of smell that bears have, and how intelligent they are! Wild One and I have often watched the bears walk on the beaches between the islands at low tide. They make out like they are just exploring and questing for food, but they sure have us cased. They are aware of every move we make, and I'm sure they can smell the residual gun cleaning compound and oil on my 45.70 rifle. We feel that black bears are beautiful creatures, but are oppor-tunists, sneaky and predatory, whereas in comparison, we feel that grizzlies are noble and honest animals!

Wild Boy and I were stalked by a big black at one time on the West Coast. We were checking up on what appeared to be a deserted tree plant-er's camp site, Little Boy Wild had "taken over" and the day was bright with a lovely blue sky and the promise of adventure. He saw the top of a tent and nothing much more and decided to investigate. To the right of the tent and running for many hundreds of yards long, were windrows of logging debris bulldozed up for burning. Being a summer afternoon he thought a stroll would be good for him and maybe he'd meet a few people if it were an active camp. Walking away from the truck to the tent was a distance of some two hundred yards, and when he arrived at the tent he discovered it was just a lone tent left behind for some reason. He sat on the inflatable mattress and began reading a couple of xxx magazines that had been left there – an erotic interlude.

After about ten minutes he became aware of an insistent feeling boring into his brain. *Logic said all was okay. Intuition said, check it out;* the feeling suddenly became so decisive that a cold tremor ran down his back. The feeling screamed aloud—Beware! Beware! In two seconds he stood tall outside the tent.

All looked okay, but he decided to get back to the truck anyway, and as he did so he was walking parallel with the windrow of logging debris which stretched more to his left away from the truck. He made a straight line for his vehicle and it was then that he saw the very top of the rippling shoulder muscles of a large black bear on the other side. They only just showed occasionally as he progressed in a crouch similar to that of a lion stalking prey. Little Boy Wild increased his pace and so did the bear, it was now quite obvious that he was being stalked for the kill. Meantime due to the angle of the windrow moving left away from the truck, it gave Wild Boy the advantage of a lesser distance. He then ran for it with all his might. He had almost reached the vehicle then the bear came round the end of the windrow and charged straight toward him. Wild Boy leapt into his truck, the diesel roared to life as he blasted the horn, and it was then that the big black desisted and turned back the way he had come. Again intuition had won.

The next day Little Boy Wild took over total control quite early in the day. He had been restless the previous night and had trembled with mild shakes. Even when his owl friends called he burrowed deeper into the down and covered his ears, and I knew he was lonely again. He seemed *to look at himself from outside of himself,* like they were walking together, and always the question came back as, *"Who am I? What am I doing here?*

How did I get here? Where am I going to? What on earth am I here for?"
The answers did not come easily.

By late morning the sun was hot and *he wanted to FEEL*, to be caressed by sunlight and go in search of himself. "Au naturel" as usual, he wandered along the sandy beaches delighting in the calls of his sandpipers; they formed a symphony of wave-lapped orchestration along with the gull cries, and just inland the wise old ravens talked one with another. Wild One's eyes had a dreamy questing look and he decided to explore within *to see if he were really here.*

"Am I experiencing a dream image of myself?" he asked.

"No of course not!" he exclaimed, then he ran, picking up speed along the shore line, putting the sandpipers to flight and scaring a great blue heron into slow-winged escape. He did not think about bears, cougars or other possible dangers; he just spread his arms to the sky laughing loudly, and returned to his camp a short time later at a slower pace.

There, he threw himself on the soft turf, puffing as he regained his breath. He was tanned golden brown and was lean mainly from hunger, but his ribs were not prominent.

"There is just the cosmos and me; just the sun, or the stars, and the moon, and me," he said in whimsy. *"But I AM the stars! I AM the sandpipers! I AM the trees! And I AM the wind."* He clapped his hands and sprang to his feet, *"I AM all things, all people, and all the animals* —It's just like Whitman in `Leaves of Grass' – I see it now, but I could never express this to another because as Whitman says:

> "When I undertake to tell the best I find I cannot
> My tongue is ineffectual on its pivots
> My breath will not be obedient to its organs,
> I become a dumb man."

Wild Boy was elated. He stood like a young god in a foreign land, and master of all he surveyed. He effused, "I'm not Dante, who said his vision was greater than his speech was capable of expressing; and I know for myself that spiritual knowledge cannot be communicated from one intellect to another, but must be sought in the spirit of God. But what I do know, is mine, and that which I have experienced, no man can take from me." Little

347

Boy Wild looked at me with such a radiance of countenance that I saw a different creature, young but mature, a cosmic explorer who emanated all the human earth bound qualities of beauty and carnality – but he was undeniably a Spiritual Being.

"Of course I'm not Whitman, or those other famous persons of vision," he said.

"What am I? I'm just a little sandpiper running along the shores of time...... "

I did not comment, as he was fully in control and it was best to leave him when he was in this state of mind. He gazed out across the ocean, his consciousness in rhythm with the waves as they spread along the sand.

"All knowledge is the ocean," he breathed softly. "The thoughts and dreams of man are spread out along these beaches in the time dimension, just like these little waves —some go farther and make inroads and channels in the sand; and these are the insights and deeds of those who tune into the infinite. To others they are mere foolishness."

Little Boy Wild lapsed into a deep reverie as he lay back among the purple vetch. He was quiet and lost in dream thought for about an hour, and when he returned he was thirsty and drank deeply from his water bottle. In the far distance orcas briefly rose and dipped. *"I AM the killer whales and I AM the dolphins."* he murmured.

Then in the late afternoon, being restless, Wild Boy dissipated his loneliness and his tension. He wanted to find himself. In his innermost self he embraced his friend while they touched with exquisite understanding; and as he reached his zenith, he softly whispered, *"I am the star flow of life, and I am a Human."* The core sensations he experienced at that moment with his deepest feelings, put him in touch with himself. This was what he wanted; it was possibly his only genuine connection to his real physical being.

These days though, he often stated with new found assurance, *"I FEEL therefore I AM. I'm here!"* He then smiled in absolute relaxation and joy. He was satiated with feeling and self identity as he returned control to *Me.*

Wild Boy realized that as he traveled, sometimes things could get quite scary, and he felt that with a companion we might be safer – and a lot less lonely. But as always we could never find anyone to share this type of life. We were just "too different" and also *we lived on the cutting edge of reality*. Indeed, if it were not for intuition and obedience to it, we would likely have been lost or killed a dozen times over!

We had a weird experience with wild dogs on one of the off shore islands. Sand martins were nesting and feeding babies in a tall clay type bank; and photo opportunities were in the offing. Thus while engaged with my Leicaflex camera, we spotted in our peripheral vision a movement, which turned out to be a line of about ten dogs coming single file behind a leader along the narrow roadway. At that moment I moved my head to take a better look and get a better grip on the situation for defensive tactics if needed. In one flick of an eyelid there was not a dog in sight. They literally vanished in a blink of an eye to leave us feeling that we must have been mistaken, but for one thing! The last dog in the pack at the rear of the line must have recently joined them, or was less experienced; for a single second, he peeked up from the ditch and disappeared again. It is an eerie experience to recognize that you may be the one who is being hunted! These tactics were in my experience, hunting or attack modes, and there was my vehicle about a hundred paces away.

Slowly, without any hasty movements of a sharp nature, we very casually, with camera in hand, strolled toward the wagon. We had not gone more than fifty paces when the lead dog appeared, a big Doberman, and behind him were the other hounds, all of a substantial build. They came leaping forward at a fast pace, I do not know exactly what their intent was, but it boded no good for me whatever the outcome. I raised my arms and shouted loudly as I ran for the Land Cruiser. My voice was almost lost among the baying and barking as they closed the gap. Then I changed tactics and ran directly toward them as if I were charging them in attack mode, and momentarily this seemed to give them hesitation, enough for me to get safely into the vehicle as they all swirled around in a pandemonium of barking. How many times had I found myself in situations like this where I was not carrying a gun? Too many for real comfort I concluded.

An even scarier situation came up during the salmon berry season on the back end of this same island. I had left the wagon and gone some fifty paces eating berries from each bush as I passed. In one area from under the hollowed out bramble bushes I was stopped short by a most vicious growling, not by one dog but several, and on peering into the darker shadows there was a whole pack of wild dogs lying there. Seeing their shining eyes and hearing their deadly growls raised the hairs on the back of my neck in a big way. However I did not panic and run, but slowly moved away still eating berries as I picked them, until I was in a direct line with the wagon. Again – where is your gun? It is not just a question of being armed; it is knowing how to use a gun with good judgment. That goes for bear spray too, we know of many hikers who carry it – but how many of them are like the young guy who had been killed by a bear and mostly eaten, while clenched in his right hand was the bear spray – he had never learned how to remove the orange safety clip!

Chapter Twenty Eight

*L*ittle Boy Wild always had adventures – although some of them were not quite of this world. One was very special, and pre-dated his serious Bible reading days. We had gone to very remote lake, and planned to stay for about five or six days before returning to see what had to be done in the financial world. The very word 'financial' gave us the shudders! On trips like this it goes without saying that Wild Boy was fully in control, and even if I had attempted to take over I would have been pre-empted. He had been looking out over the lake for most of the morning. The sun was quite hot and he'd been down to the shore for a skinny dip, and now sat watching the myriad of insects and bees in the midday hum of activity. Surrounded by all manner of wild summer flowers and being so many miles away from the Humans put him in a very relaxed state of mind.

Little Boy Wild had found that if he stayed relaxed, not concentrating on anything in particular, and especially with no hint of danger to his person, that he would fall into another state or wave length of consciousness. The long soft grass was as tall as he, with only his head showing above the flowers as he sat in utter surrender to the moment in his natural state. Unconsciously he simply gazed out across the lake. The surface was calm, and there walking on the water, was a very tall being in white robes coming towards him. He did not for one moment associate what he saw with Jesus, and was not at that time involved in so called 'Religion,' so it was an amazing sight. He watched the tall being for about 45 seconds before his logical mind switched frequencies on him, and he was back in his own dimension watching the swallows dip and zip over the cool water, gathering insects for their babies.

He had entered other wave length dimensions before and it fascinated him that he could go somewhere ***"Outside of Time"*** as he called it. It again reinforced his concepts of parallel worlds occupying the same space as we do. He was determined to consciously adjust his wavelengths if possible, but he remembered that he had to relinquish control and go into a deep state of non-thought for the frequencies to shift. The logical mind must not interfere, or in an instant *"Now"* returns, and once more he is back among the flowers.

Several more years went by before Wild Boy again shifted into parallel worlds. It was mid-afternoon as he focused on the distant snow-capped mountains across the straits. There were no white caps to the waves and the tall cedars were still. We were camped in a small logging road cul-de-sac, so that no vehicles could approach from any direction except one, and indeed it was doubtful that any Humans were within miles anyway to disturb him. Of course he was "au naturel," what else?

But on this occasion I specifically asked him why he preferred this state of undress. He was thoughtful for a moment and replied that he was just pure Little Boy Wild and nothing else. He was not contaminated by the Humans who had made his hiking boots and other articles of clothing he wore. He was free and unfettered—just him and the universe as he wandered between dimensions into different wavelengths of consciousness while seeking the essence of life. He always slept that way for the same reason, so that if and when he had the opportunity to *"translate"* himself, he could do so without the fear of grosser foreign molecular elements generating interference. Besides that, he just loved being naked anyway. He explained that it started many years ago because the warmth and hot touch of the sun was the only warmth and touching he had ever received; and he needed it as much as a flower or a tree.

He lay on his tummy and further explained that he liked to think of himself as pure `thought,' and that his thoughts could be translated at the speed of light or faster. He felt he was on firm ground in many of his assertions, but I was not completely sold on all of his theories despite the fact that he claimed, "I was never hampered by higher learning, but maintained an inquisitive mind, so that it was possible to let my intuitive mind receive the answers direct from the cosmos." This boy or man, or both, looked up at me.

"If you put a piece of bone or tissue under an electron microscope," he ventured, "You will find the higher the power used, the more the solids break down into the finest of filaments, and then I suppose into molecules and atoms, and then after that, it becomes pure thought!" I loved to hear him propose ideas no matter how weird. Just then he sensed a horse fly that had been sucking blood from his left thigh, and in one swat he smeared fly and blood into the past.

"I remember now!" he exclaimed. "I think it was Sir James Jeans, a great British physicist and astronomer, and it was he who stated, *"More and more the world begins to look like a great thought!"*

Wild Boy stood up, tall, intense and thoughtful, shading his eyes to take in the scene of the oceans and the distant mountains. The sun had bleached streaks of gold into his hair, and he stretched once again before settling down. About 45 minutes had passed when he suddenly moved and swatted his Rolex. Again he moved and slapped his wrist right across the face of the watch. He stared at it in disbelief, after all, a Rolex is a finely crafted time instrument that simply does not stop and go in an erratic manner.

"What happened?" I asked.

He replied that his watch had stopped for about a whole minute, the hands froze, the sweep second hand did not move, and that is why he "came back."

Between us we got it sorted out. I was pleased that he'd been wearing his watch.

"To come back, you must have been away," I suggested trying to sound helpful.

He kept emphasizing the impossibility for his Rolex's big sweep second hand to stop and then go forward and catch up. Nor would we know until very much later, that his body was on automatic pilot so to speak while he was in this timeless state. It maintained blood pressure, breathing, heart beat and so forth along with a million other complex chemical and molecular processes. *But, Little Boy Wild was not there.* Only when his auto pilot had observed and reported an abnormal function did it alert him, as it would have done were any bodily function out of phase or some danger approaching, like a cougar. At that precise moment when his auto pilot alert came in, so did his logical mind switch into the current frequency.

"I can't believe that I was away from my body. *So where was I?*

My Rolex is perfect so I must have stepped outside of time!"

Wild Boy was standing now and he was excited. He kept checking his Rolex —needlessly of course. It was working because it was "inside time." A light breeze ruffled his hair as he faced the ocean. He was still "here" and he still had his I AM identity. Above all, he could FEEL, and he had the power to assert himself for he was in total control.

When Wild Boy says he can feel, he does not mean a total physical feeling but one that is connected to his psychic core. *It is the REAL ME, as he puts it, and it gives him his "ISness" identity*. At times like this Little Boy Wild was glad to be back `inside time' and the stunning discovery he had made for himself was cause for celebration. He shook the ants off his blanket, put a cushion under his head, swatted a couple of horse flies and decided to read for a while. One of the horse flies was stunned but not dead. It lay buzzing and looked like it might right itself and fly off. So he took off his glasses and angled them to the sun so that a white hot laser beam of light zapped the luckless horse fly. It revved its motor to a very high pitch, blew a gasket and laid smoking, fully cremated.

"That'll fix you, you bastard!" he exclaimed.

"Did you really have to do that? It was just doing what it was designed to do," a small voice inside him said.

He viewed the cremated carcass and tried to get the ants to carry it away but they ignored it. Next he zapped a bluebottle fly from his knee, it was mildly crushed and this too the ants chose to ignore by going in every direction on the compass, until one ant seemed to run into it quite by accident, then other ants came, often two or more of them pulling in the opposite direction to each other, and eventually the fly was ushered into an underground chamber.

Wild Boy could not settle down, it was the same old problem and he was under too much tension to read or do anything. Maybe it was extreme, but it had to be handled before it got to his brain and drove him wilder than he already was. Today he wanted to be absolutely earthy, carnal, devoid of any decency, and be super sensual. He lustfully wanted to recklessly hold and to be held, even by a real Human, until he could explode in one wild anguished release that would further expand the whole universe if such were possible. I assured him that these were human emotions and not remotely linked to spirituality, and were merely a matter of reducing tensions created by his silent screams.

His desperate urges drove him across the little clearing where he found a huge patch of purple thistles in full bloom and alive with huge fuzzy bumblebees. A short while later history repeated itself when with a joyful sound he splatted a clump of bees, some flew off and a couple fell to the ground as they struggled to de-sperm their wings. Wild One squatted over them, something like de-icing the wings of a plane he thought. He left them and returned to his blanket. But now he was calm and once more he became his more beautiful self. But would that mean he would release control back to me this evening?

Wild One examined the afternoon, who else did such crazy things he thought; and was he too far gone from his real self that he might never get back? Possibly he was asking if a line of separation existed that would not permit him to return. I assured him that there is nothing new under the sun and that he was not alone!

If this was the only way he knew of to retain his sanity, and at the same time keep in touch with himself – so be it! *His key was always, "Have I still got me? Am I really still here?* Sometimes I feel that whereas *everyone else has substance and reality, I am only an ethereal wraith-like form* that denies that I am real; especially when I'm with the Humans. They talk, they laugh, they plan and do things like humans do, and this leaves me feeling stunned and lost in the backwater of time."

Yes – he did relinquish control to me that evening, but not before he had launched his second attempt to expand the universe. He lay spread-eagled in the damp grass watching for the first bats to appear, and breathed deeply of the earthy smells of trees and vegetation. Then from beyond the early stars, he slowly enticed the God of Eros to meet with him and his friend. When at last he did arrive on silver wings to embrace our desire, he bathed us in early moonlight, touched us with love magic, and in a final act of mercy, cascaded Eros' fountain down the ecstasy of water music and solitude. Little Boy Wild felt warm, relaxed, and dreamy with pleasure as he gazed out into the galaxies; for him, "night sky dreaming" was pure inspiration, and he opened his consciousness to receive other frequencies from beyond his imagination – allowing them to be scanned by the steward of his mind, and wondering which thought track to follow.

Health wise it had already been confirmed for some time that we had blocked arteries, and were used to angina pains – probably the result of tension accumulated over many years. One day in Vancouver when I had a "weird feeling" relating to my heart, I went to see my cardiologist who it turned out would not be in for a day or two. I was seen by another cardiologist and his bright young intern.

First they took our blood pressure which was about 250 over 165.

"Did you see that pressure?" the senior doctor asked his young intern. "He's going to explode!" Little Boy Wild did not want that intern to be misled, so he turned to him and said, "I can bring it down, is it too high?"

They both looked at him while he went back inside himself to a wonderful river valley he sometimes visited, and spoke to his heart and blood pressure. In moments to their utter amazement it dropped to about 180 over 110. The senior doctor had his intern make a note of this, and just then the phone rang and he excused himself to answer it.

Wild Boy turned to the young intern in order to explain how one can control these things by adjusting one's consciousness; the intern listened attentively, but with some reserve. Wild Boy then went on to explain how it is possible to go "outside of time" and gave him his Rolex story. In addition, he told him that *his current project was to find out where he was when he was not here!* Meantime I had not realized that the senior doctor had finished his phone call and was standing by listening to all of this!

What a wonderful letter he wrote to my own doctor! It contained many scary psychiatric terms, like paranoid, neurotic, schizophrenic, manic depressive, and other weird mental disease terminology. Of special note was the apparent evidence that I was unbalanced, and it all revolved around the Rolex watch incident, and the starting and stopping of time sequences. Following this cardiologist incident, over the next few years I had many similar experiences, but it was not until some *eight years later* when I was in a book shop in Hawaii, that I found out the truth of the matter!

Itzhak Bentov had written a delightful little book called *"Stalking the Wild Pendulum"* sub-titled "On the mechanics of consciousness" and for me it was like water in the desert. On page 71 the chapter was titled *"An experiment with time."*

Upon reading this I found out that our experiences were real, and that we were not just weird or mentally unbalanced, at least not in this matter! It is an experiment that can be performed, but is somewhat limited to those persons having especially good control over their states of consciousness. I quote Itzhak Bentov:

"When a person has been trained by bio-feed-back to produce theta waves or can put himself into a deep meditative state, and at the same time is able to watch the second hand of a clock in front of him, he will be surprised to find that the second hand has come to a stop. It's rather a startling experience, and the natural reaction to it is: "This is impossible!" At that moment, the second hand will accelerate and resume its normal rate. However, if we can get over this reaction and watch with half open eyes the face of the clock, while all the time being in a deep meditative state, then we can keep the hand from moving as long as we wish."

"Wow! Wow! And Eeeeek!" Little Boy Wild exclaimed. He was elated at this discovery, especially as we had never been trained in bio-feed-back, and had no idea what it was about – being just a wild creature of the wilderness.

"We're not alone!" he exclaimed. *"I'm a Theta Boy, I can produce Theta Waves! It's possible to travel within this theta frequency – at the speed of light to anywhere! But I mustn't go faster than light – or I'll be back before I leave – and that is yet another dimension! Do the animals also have access to this frequency? Do they use it?*

This whole enigma set us up for much more advanced research in our own inimitable way that defies logic – of course! Wild Boy often thought of himself as a Richard P. Feynman, the great theoretical physicist. They were poles apart in ability, education and experience, but there was something in the writings of Feynman that he identified with very closely. Perhaps it was the way Feynman walked the streets at night working out problems intuitively, or just because he was such an outrageous character. One of his books "Surely You're Joking Mr. Feynman!" is a great classic. I think Wild Boy grew almost two inches when he found out about the stopping of time, which would serve as a starting point for future explorations. His smile may have indicated for the first time his acquisition of self esteem or a step toward it.

It was in this time period that I had begun to observe changes in our relationship; *Little Boy Wild being the Real Self was taking control more and more often* and I felt that if he really dominated, I would become a background figure of a supportive nature taking care of financial matters and Human concerns – but I also feared that I might disappear. It sounds strange; but will the Unreal Self be dethroned? Or will a merging occur in which it will become a win-win situation and we become a beautifully balanced "Oneness" type of entity?

Wild Boy is absorbed more and more into matters of quantum consciousness, quantum mechanics and also the bridging of quantum theory with so called "Religion," which he prefers to think of as a spiritual relationship. He wishes to have nothing to do with "Churchianity" and religious legalism, dogma and rituals, robes and authoritarian oratory. In fact, Little Boy Wild says that true Christianity is a personal relationship with the Lord Jesus Christ, and that the "church" is really all those Christians who form the body of Christ – wherever they are, and has nothing to do with buildings and church services, and that as individuals, each of us is a temple of the living God.

I even suspect that he will have to be baptized like I was! But I have difficulty in equating Little Boy Wild running wild and free with the animals, and his uncontrolled carnal exploits co-mingling with his declared spiritual values. There are times however when he has difficulty in reaching out to me because he has theoretically died and is unsure whether he is alive or dead. An example of this would be the hand grenade incident. I'll let him explain:

"One day while sitting in an English class at school a terrifying 'over the edge' extreme experience occurred. I'm about *thirteen years old* and it's about 10:30am." Wild Boy looked at me with a reluctant, hesitant expression; he did not want to go into that scene. I felt cold shivers go up and down his back. His face became pained and he started to crouch over as though he might dissociate and go into the fetal position.

"The kid next to me pulls out a shiny hand grenade out of his pocket, it is war time and he could have found it or gotten it anywhere. He's proud of it and passes it to me for a brief look-see. It eyes me like a cobra about to strike. I look into the grenade's bright shine and it holds me in deadly fascination. He sees that I'm terrified of it.

"It's okay," he says. But then he does the unthinkable – *HE PULLS THE PIN!* My mind reels with sudden hurt, and I know the consequences of this move. I've seen enough blood and gore of the wounded and dead; I have visions of heads being blown off as I leap to my feet and hurl my body forward.

"Miss. Elliott, Miss. Elliott a hand grenade!" I scream, "He's got a hand grenade."

Then I seem to black out and fall to the floor. The class is in an uproar, and I'm the cause of it, which is not unusual. I come around and see faces peering at me. Miss. Elliott has confiscated the hand grenade and it is sitting on the front of her desk. Maybe there are de-activated hand grenades, but on the other hand might not this have been a faulty unit? like some of the delayed action time bombs that have fallen in the area. Supposing something inside is just jammed up and it is really still alive and any knock may trigger it? I'm told to go home for the rest of the day."

Little Boy Wild burst into tears and he shook with deep memory sobs that he could not control. He had been pushed to such an extreme 'over the edge' into death and oblivion feeling, that he had difficulty in understanding that he was still in the land of the living. "That 'edge trauma' is so extreme that all I see are the red and yellow flames in the middle of an explosion followed by blackness," he said. He looked unbalanced and totally freaked. He shook his head and cried out while he flexed his tongue to taste the salt of his tears. Again he cried out, a long anguished cry of fright, and fell to the turf. Fortunately we were in the woodland feeding squirrels, so no hurt came to him. But enough memory pain racked his frame that it pushed him into one of his "Keelematu! Keelematu!" sequences. After the grenade incident and having been sent home, he should really have gone to see the rabbits, real live ones in the meadows; but once again he made the mistake of going directly home. SHE with the bamboo cane who dispenses justice was there to greet him. He was experiencing a terrible trauma headache already, and following a short shouting match with her, he simply phased out under the welter of the beating that came upon him. He did not know when she stopped the caning, his body was a sheet of scarlet and white pain in his mind, and probably his body looked that way too.

He just remained *"Inside,"* – very deep inside, and in this state he fell asleep. It was very tempting for him to slip into the "River of No Return" in order to escape the pain. Flower scent was in the air and bluebirds flew back and forth across the river; and all of this was almost too peaceful under the warm glow of sunshine. He just knew it was not the right time for such an irrevocable action, he still had his animals – and for that very reason he did not go.

Coming back into the reality of "NOW," Wild Boy cleaned up his tears and blew his nose, but in breathing he still had a few dry sobs before he was in control again. I should not have pushed him into the grenade sequence, because of the double whammy of HER being involved. He had relived a terrible hurt, but now he needed to be held and loved, and this was not going to be an ideal situation as he was not on loving terms with the Humans.

I had planned a business trip to the Queen Charlotte Islands and I knew this would be good for both us. He would have a healing time. A time to race along the sand and chase his sandpiper friends, and I knew there were deer and eagles everywhere to commune with, apart from the sea creatures, so he would be alright. If anything, right now his furry sea otters would be perfect.

But Wild Boy felt as lonely as he had ever felt, it left him stranded, not quite real and solid, and not entirely a pure thought form, and I knew his extremely high tension level would go to dangerous lengths for him to re-capture life as he wanted it. A warm human touch or a smile of acceptance would ignite him to a level of uncontrolled emotion that would be explosive and totally irresponsible.

He had reached a point where he wanted to kill the pain of need, to kill the torture of not being held, touched and loved. Perhaps the way to kill the pain was to kill himself. But in his very heart of hearts—he knew that he could never leave his beloved animals.

It was about this time that we embraced the high tech advances in telephony and acquired a cell phone. Little Boy Wild was almost stunned with delight, he instantly saw "living with the animals" and creating cash flow for the Humans, as a dual accomplishment. We had good cell coverage in our local areas and parts of Vancouver Island, and this meant that although most of our insurance appointments were scheduled for the evenings, it gave us all day from early morning to be with the birds and animals. Even better, we could move our entire "office" into the wilderness areas, and arrange appointments, medicals and branch office communications from some beautiful tree lined grassy areas by the creeks. On these warm days Wild Boy would immediately adopt his normal "au naturel" state, and merge himself with the soft breezes, as well as the colorful flowers and berries of summer. His heart hammered in ecstasy at the timeless cosmic infusion he experienced. Sometimes he would lie on the flat water worn rocks in the creek allowing the water music to flow over him while he reached for salmon and huckleberries. He savored all of their wild flavors, but he loved the thimbleberries and blackberries best of all. Wild One passed control back to me only for those times when phone calls had to be processed, and it often prompted queries about all the burbling water sounds that the branch office staff could hear, especially on really hot days when he would lean back under a small waterfall. So I usually let Wild Boy handle their questions, which he did with some glee. Head office in the USA commented in the monthly newsletter on our insurance escapades; such as kayaking up the inlets and living among the bears and sea otters, and could not quite equate this idyllic life style with what was known as "work!" You are on holiday all the time, they charged with some envy. But they could not argue with the number of insurance applications that we turned in on returning to civilization. Now there was even more time to dream and explore other modes of consciousness.

There were some occasions when he was in such close proximity to unseen hornet nests, that the hornet guards would buzz him in a not so friendly, dutiful warning. These powerful insects were not to be messed with, being about an inch long. Some had low droning notes that added menace to their presence. But if they persisted in their circular predatory attack mode, especially after a few return swipes with his cap, Little Boy Wild would move further away. If they buzzed him in a clockwise circle – he would use an anti-clockwise direction with his cap, thus increasing the force of the collision. It was while watching his eagles soar high in the blue, that on several occasions as he sprawled his lean brown form among the grass, that a hornet would actually try to haul one of his nipples away! First there would be a gentle almost fuzzy tickle of grappling feet. This was followed by the quick painful grab of the nipple in the hornet's mouth parts. Hornets have quite a pull – something like a helicopter trying to take off with a load, while the load is still chained to the ground! It hurts! Especially when they rev their engine for take off with the prize, and nothing happens! We assumed that the hornet with its excellent eye sight had spied a small pink blob – like a hamburger fragment, and simply swooped down to seize it for the larva back at the nest. He studied their tactics, and saw that a hornet would approach at a very low altitude – like flying under the radar, cut their engine noise to the merest whisper, and then grapple with the prize! A quick light brush of the hand sends them on their way, but it is always an unexpected contact.

I was never stung by any of these hornets, but Little Boy Wild often talked with them, in the same way that he merged his consciousness with so many other creatures. He sometimes tried to figure a way to reduce his size from six foot one to a fraction of an inch, so that he could experience their world while he rode on their backs. He also suspected that he might be fed to their larva, so his real concentration when in this thought mode, was directed to the huge freighter-like fuzzy honey bees, an altogether more friendly experience. Whether he succeeded while he rode them from flower to flower, he was never quite sure. Was it just his imagination? Or had he momentarily changed form? He felt their warm furry vibrating power as he gripped them with his legs in flight. Strangely – they understood. He was accepted, and he loved them for whisking him away to the heavy scent of honey back at the hive – hidden very deep in the darker woodland glades. Sometimes he would find a fuzzy bee in the early morning dew, where it simply had run out of fuel and dropped, as it had no energy to return to the hive. Wild Boy always carried a "first aid honey kit," and upon discovering a downed bee would gently place it on a strong leaf and while he spoke to it, place a few drops of honey close to its mouth parts. Sure enough, the little proboscis or sucking tube would go to work and after a while as it refueled and warmed in the early sun, it eventually revved its engine and winged toward another day of duty.

Little Boy Wild quite naturally found himself with the wild creatures.

He was probably about as wild as they were, to be drawn into the same remote wilderness areas. There was fearlessness in these encounters on the part of both the animals and he, and he never failed to be enraptured by their beauty, whether it was a white tailed deer or a grizzly, or a tiny brown mouse. Certainly they must know him by scent, but this by no means guaranteed his safety where the big carnivores were concerned.

One warm summer morning, Wild Boy was determined to enter his Theta Wave mode of consciousness – to find out "where he was, when he was not here." He had selected for this adventure, a lonely, far out deactivated logging road. It overlooked a large lake and was some miles in length; and what made the morning so perfect was that there were no demands on his time, for at least two days. In this utterly relaxed aura of receptivity in his "au naturel" state – he attained a floating feeling. He was relaxed enough so that his Theta wave mode should kick in. But, a sound came in on his awareness frequency that played havoc with his relaxation. Among the bird calls and the slow breeze from the lake which quietly moved the vegetation, there was an unidentified "Whvrmp – whvrmp – whvrmp" sound. Not loud, but soft, and slow with an occasional squeak. Somehow it was a natural sound. Little Boy Wild lay still on his blanket, and the sound stopped. Then about two minutes later it began again, only this time it was closer. Once again he dismissed it. He ran that sound through all of his memory banks, and came up blank. This start and stop sequence was repeated several times until it stopped – quite close by. Wild Boy opened his eyes, and as he rose, came face to face with a huge black bear. True it was only twenty five feet away, but that is only 1.5 seconds in bear pounce time. The sound he had heard was its massive foot pads on the gravel surface, with occasional pressures of pebbles creating a squeaking noise under its weight. The bear's head was huge; he had rarely seen one of this size. He sprang to his feet and leapt with agility into his truck, while the bear just stood and looked at him. He noted the massively beautiful head again, and only when he fired up the diesel did it move off up into the bush.

This killed any hope of attaining Theta Wave mode, so Little Boy Wild read for a few minutes. But something was not right, and he rose and walked to the rear of his truck, and peeking around, he saw that the bear had indeed gone up into the bush, but had also come out on to the narrow logging road behind him. It now approached the truck on what would have been his blind side. Wild Boy and the big black looked at each – without fear, and it once again confirmed for him that black bears are predatory and opportunistic in nature. As he dressed, he thought that it was fortunate indeed that the bear had viewed the picnic spread with him as the main meal, all laid out ready for eating – with suspicion! One thing for sure, it would have answered once and for all his question of – where am I, when I'm not here! He chuckled. But this Theta Wave boy knew he had to leave the entire area, as this particular bear was not going to give up, so he moved into another area some miles away, but the impact of the danger he had incurred negated any possible Theta frequency that day.

But animals or not, there was the incessant need to love and to be loved, to touch and to be touched, as well as to establish real communication with the Humans. The ache of need is always there, but how does one trust? How does one truly love? What great barrier of emotional pain do we have to go through before we are free to make the connection? The Humans see me, but which ME do they see? Just then a still small voice whispered – *"It matters not. I knew you from before ever the foundations of the world were laid."**

---

* King James Bible. Ephesians 1.4

Chapter Twenty Nine

A short while later we headed out on our annual trip to the Queen Charlotte Islands to serve my insurance clientele. These were my autumnal years – although Little Boy Wild still seems to be of an indeterminate age – but certainly young. It was while cruising across on "The Queen of the North" ferry; our habitual loneliness was stolen in a most delightful way. I was in the ship's dining room reading Maurice Nichol's "The New Man" for probably the fourth or fifth time over the years, when a young man approached me and with his infectious smile, he expressed curiosity about the title of the book. He was about twenty two, slim and tall, with an open face that held the glow of one who is in quest of the great truth. He also held a quiet reserve about him, which held for me the possibility of some deep discussions on various subjects. So for the rest of the trip we immersed ourselves in discussing spiritual matters, all the way from Madam Blavatsky's "The Secret Doctrine," to the Holy Bible. I delighted in his lissome movements, his serious young eyes and blond wavy hair. It was like being with Tim as of old, all over again! We made plans after docking to meet up in a couple of days, which would give me enough time to handle my immediate business affairs. In the meantime, I loaded necessary supplies on board the truck, so that we could avoid civilization for a while. At our next meeting we again surveyed each other to see if our original assessments were as we remembered. They were. At lunchtime we pulled off up a trail lined with tall cedars. Soon a small fire flickered, and we sipped cold beer by the river while waiting for some embers to glow fiery red for our wiener roast. We dined sumptuously and lay back in the grass for a beautiful afternoon of idle talk, and in a more serious vein we discussed the books we'd read. We also had to keep up a smoke screen to fend off blood thirsty insects.

That evening we made camp in a little grassy meadow along side the ocean on an old deserted homestead. We watched the moon rise slowly, causing the broken down cabin to cast long shadows, and we delighted in the warm open trust we had achieved in our relationship. It was relaxed and comfortable. A cool breeze carried the cries of the sea birds, and crashing waves to us, and David added to this by wandering barefoot through the feathery soft grass, playing sad plaintive notes on his flute. I followed his shadow of wild sound. The whole scene was surreal. It was soothing and I loved him for merging twilight magic with my innermost heart. When dream time came he curled up in his sleeping bag among the long grass, while I slept in the comparative luxury of the truck. Brilliant stars dominated the night skies. My world was almost complete.

Then in the early morning just before David awakened, a soft shaft of sunlight beaming through the cedars fell upon him. I found myself enraptured by his face in total repose, exposed and unmarred by hurt, a creature of angelic beauty. We explored and camped for three beautiful days—they felt endless. The weather held, and the sun watched us climb around an old shipwreck. We skinny-dipped in the placid river, fought off huge horse flies and generally merged our sunlit escapades with our life stream experiences. Little Boy Wild ached with an incredible longing every time he met David's open gaze. On his part David regarded me as a sort of guru, a learned one, perhaps wise enough to expand his consciousness, but I could never violate a sacred trust or allow a spiritual quest to be broken by my own sensual emotions. However—Little Boy Wild had found a soul mate! His heart leapt to see David in motion. Above all he yearned to an almost intolerable degree to touch and be touched; to hold and be held in order to merge into one blinding light of love force. But I, the "wise" one, gently restrained him.

My departure from the Islands was scheduled before David's, and I left him with some sadness on a wave crashed beach where the wild strawberries crawled out across the sand from the tree line. Just beyond were hundreds of shells, sand dollars and other ocean treasures. Wild Boy embraced him in a good bye hug which revealed more than he could ever have expressed in words.

Farewell David! You have your life and we have ours. You are just starting out whereas my autumnal years are approaching; and I already understand that which everyone has to find out for themselves—the knowledge that no one in the fourth room can give the key to the second room, to another who is as yet dwelling in the first room. Time is a graveyard of lost souls, and we only truly die, when we forget why we were born into this parenthesis in eternity in the first place!

Several weeks later an unexpected call came from David. Yes—David! In a hesitant, endearing way he said in his rich timbre, "I miss you, I really miss you, are you coming out my way in the near future? I'd love to see you!"

So it was that Little Boy Wild felt his heart leap in wild elation, it pounded with joy to hear David's voice and soft laughter, he remembered his trusting grey eyes and said, "In this whole wide world, is there a feeling more wonderful than that of being needed or missed?" For days he floated on air in euphoric anticipation of our meeting which we had scheduled for one of the more remote off shore islands. Prior to our tryst I had rented a woodsy log waterfront cabin on a quiet bay. It was so secluded that it would seem that we had our own private island.

On meeting at the appointed time we shook hands and hugged each other. David had not changed from what I had remembered, and he exchanged warm smiles with Wild Boy. Both were quite animated in their chatter, and their feelings for each other were fuelled further by their anticipation of being together for a few days. In addition David had revealed to him that for some unknown reason he had not been able to speak for the first few years of his life. Little Boy Wild saw this as a mirror or a window into his own life, and a strong bond instantly meshed between he and David, causing tears to start in their eyes; however they quickly recovered and ran forward to watch the ferry merge into its dock.

After disembarking, we quickly located the cabin snuggled under a giant cedar tree. We had little to do besides unpacking. Then we were able to just roam to explore the beach front and all the surrounding area. In doing so we disturbed several deer and even a few rabbits. The weather held, with no rain in the forecast. All of Wild Boy's beloved sea and shore birds were active, and the fact that he had seen rabbits was the crowning experience of wild seclusion for him. Twilight fell, and we made preparations for a tenderloin steak supper with mushrooms and wine. The late September air held a chill, and we enticed a fire to flicker in the stone fireplace. Oh! The smell of steaks! David's fire illuminated face expressed open delight, and his smile radiated whenever he met Wild Boy's speculative glances.

In fact Little Boy Wild immersed himself so completely in fire, David, and log cabin magic, that I was summarily excluded. *He had definitively "taken over" and I was left alone.* Supper was superb as it can only be to young savages whose appetites had been fueled by much exercise. Afterwards they showered, drying off before the fire, finally squatting in front of it in their shorts and shirts. All lights had been extinguished, and in the flickering fire-lit shadows they began to talk about levels of consciousness. David's eyes sparkled, and they ignited each other with streams of thought forms that connected, and linked into wider frameworks. They even delved into sub-atomic particles. Little Boy Wild attempted to explain Bose Einstein condensates from Danah Zohas' fabulous book "The Quantum Self," but it became so deep that David fell silent.

From time to time Wild Boy stole a searching glance at David's lean form, it was a lingering look and he paused to see what might be coming up. On his part, David rose suddenly to his feet and strode to the bedroom. On return he carried a contraption that he must have had in his pack. Thus was Wild Boy introduced to the smoking of hash. It had a water filter type of deal that removed the more acrid taste when drawing on it. Not being a smoker of anything but wood fire smoke he was taken aback. But they swapped the pipe back and forth. David enthused over the process but Wild Boy was not impressed. So once again David went to his pack and came back looking mysterious.

"I have something here which we can take, but it is a special ceremony, and you must do exactly as I say!"

He pushed the hash outfit to one side. They sat cross legged facing each other.

"We are going on a trip – an LSD trip, everything will be alright, but you must do as I say!" David said this with such intensity and special intimacy as he looked into Wild Boy's eyes, that Wild Boy felt weak all over. He nodded his assent. David placed a "hit" on Wild Boy's tongue and then on his own. They absorbed it while holding each other's hands. But nothing happened, and after a while David concluded that it must be too old.

"I get more kick out of a couple of sips of whiskey than this," Wild Boy stated.

David frowned, concentrating, while Wild Boy unabashedly studied David's fuzzy well muscled legs as he rose once more to go to his pack. On returning he said, "Maybe that stuff was too old. I have some fresh new California stuff." So once again they each had a couple of hits. David wanted to make sure that "something happened."

It did. Even before the new hits had been absorbed, the older ones came up fast on the inside rail, and these were joined by the new ones; it was going to be quite a race. The fire flared up. David's face was flushed and Wild Boy's face expressed confusion mixed with some concern.

"Let's go out and look at the stars," David suggested.

The cool night air hit us refreshingly. Waves softly crashed, and the whole cosmos became part of us. I leaned over the rail with a huge urge to vomit. I did. But now something was disturbing. David had retained his supper and had somehow climbed up on to the cabin roof. He strode with god like power and confidence, and it looked like he would fly off the roof into the ocean beyond. I looked up and repeatedly asked that he come down and join me. For answer, he strode around the roof several times, almost falling through the glass skylight. I envisioned jagged glass slicing David up, blood everywhere. What had gone wrong? He did finally come down and threw up over the railing into the flower beds below as had I. He felt a lot better. But the outside adventure was far from being over. As we stood slightly apart between the tall cedars, I saw David on another planet reaching out to me, and I on mine reaching out to him. The night wind suddenly blew fierce gusts of wind among the tree branches, blowing the stars around.

Next I saw David on a magnificent white steed, it had wings, and for me David became Pegasus Boy. Maybe they had just arrived from that northern constellation. The worlds revolved. One tall thistle close to me sent out dark thoughts of death. I touched David's hand as we stood on a precipice and we leapt, we held on to each other until we stumbled around on the beach just below. Our jump had been all of six feet only. We separated and laughed aloud with the joy of our night adventure. Every star invited us to visit, maybe I could ride with Pegasus Boy and fly star ward. But the cold water on our feet at the water's edge brought us back to a form of reality. Then we chased the little luminous lights as they disappeared and reappeared among the seaweed. Finally we felt refreshed enough from the cool night air that we returned to the cabin.

Once we had cleaned ourselves up, David threw a few more logs into the fire, and they flared up as we settled back into the cushions on the sofa. His eyes were dancing with elation as they both painted their experiences with much excitement and gesticulation. The scope of their discoveries was quite beyond that which they imagined. After some time had passed in silence other than the crackle from the fire, Little Boy Wild arose and knelt before David.

"So Pegasus Boy...." He smiled.

But what he was feeling now in some depth was what David could never feel. The **LSD** had partially removed Little Boy Wild's defense system which had taken a lifetime of unconscious internal effort to build, in order to survive the unspeakable traumas of his past. It was a level of unprecedented psychic pain, and it engulfed him in a desperate agony of need; of what he knew not. Slowly, Wild Boy searched David's face seeking a flicker of acceptance of his condition. Then taking David's lean strong hands in his own, he kissed them with soul wrenching feeling as he clasped them to his face. Then he rested his head on David's lap.

"This is getting very sexy...." His friend said in a quiet voice.

Little Boy Wild was pained to the depths of his being. David rose and lay on the carpet before the fire where he sprawled out carelessly on his back looking up into the log beams. Wild Boy crawled toward him, his face a mask of pain.

David raised his head slightly and queried, "Why do you need me so much?" Fire-lit moments passed. "I can see that I have hurt you in some very terrible way."

His tone was sad, low and concerned. Wild Boy showed torment as he realized that his naked soul was so exposed, he caressed David's lean face, stroked his golden hair and then as one possessed he exclaimed, "We don't want these clothes on!" Wild Boy peeled his off and the flame shadows darkened his tan to an even darker shade. David shed his shorts and Wild

One, unable to undo the buttons of his friend's shirt ripped it off him, revealing the powerful young heart pounding beneath his silken skin.

After a few moments of searching each other's eyes, they scrambled shakily to their feet. A brief smile of venturesome anticipation crossed their faces as they both disappeared into their room. Once on the cool sheets, they both writhed in close engagement with unparalleled urgency. Their whimpering and love laughter, born out of such intense pent up sensations, echoed throughout the cabin. They, both having been sodomized as youngsters, had no desire of this type towards each other. Little Boy Wild gave of himself totally, a rapture of reckless abandon, it took no thought, yet was so tender, so fierce and so utterly unreserved that it ignited them both in their great need to be close to each other, and to share their love and sense of belonging. Just before he fell asleep, it came to Wild Boy that *sex is not something that one person does to another – but a beautiful two-way relationship of giving and receiving.* They fell asleep in each other's arms, while slowly the stars revolved and then faded into the dawn of another day.

Mid-morning sunlight streamed through the windows and Little Boy Wild was no where to be found. David's curly head lay close to mine; his arm was across my waist. We both stirred. The reality of this day slowly came to us. It was ME, and the whole scene was not "right." Slowly we separated and the drama of the star lit fusion faded. David reached into his pack, and, after a few moments, a match flared and the detestable stink of "pot" pervaded the bedroom and beyond. I arose and showered as did he. For a short while we looked at each other appraisingly in silence. The hot strong coffee restored normalcy to the scene, for the present anyway.

After a while, Little Boy Wild cautiously peeked out at David. He exuded a delicious smile of intrigue and wonderment as he took in David's presence. Wild Boy's glances were always caresses of such intensity as to be almost physically felt. Pegasus Boy's eyes widened, and after a pause he slowly took Wild Boy's hand, and rising they embraced each other, an embrace of deeply shared feeling, in that they both needed to confirm that this was reality and not a star misted dream. The impact of this realization came upon them again and again. Wild Boy radiated smiles, *for he had been gifted with the ability to feel something other than pain and rejec-*

tion. He had been held, loved, and delicately touched to the core of his being by a real live human being, of his own sex it was true; but he was accepted totally, and he had returned this beauty of expression with a love he had never felt or projected before, and all of this, in addition to satiating orgasmic rapture. This morning it left him stunned and empty. The aching in his chest was a beautiful pain, a pain of need to be completed. He met David's eyes a number of times with muted eloquence. Eventually Little Boy Wild gave into soft laughter as he gave vent to his feelings. His face was a mask of innocence, need and wonderment, as he reached out for David to embrace him again. They stayed locked until David's eyes glazed over, and at that point they both consummated their bonds in a way which was quite beyond their any wish to control.

To everything there is a season, and a time for every purpose under heaven, a time to embrace and a time to refrain from embracing; even a time to love and a time to part. I played with images of Pegasus Boy rising star ward on his winged steed, naked, powerful and silvered by moonlight as he rose slightly to spur his steed to the worlds beyond. But on parting I had a flash of rude reality. Maybe he was not the angelic being I imagined him to be. Really—was he not just a pot head, a compassionate questing kid I'd accidentally run into? No! He was far more than that. I didn't freeze and dissociate when we hugged. This was a real break through in itself. I loved him for what he was, and what I had become because of him. *I CAN FEEL!* I've been touched, and our feelings regardless of our age differences were stunningly beautiful.

As Little Boy Wild said afterward, "I can always listen to his flute, his soft voice, and look into his lovely gray eyes as he holds me – forever. But – you know I have doubts and concerns, because when we were orally involved – I discovered that what I thought would be absolute heaven, like watching David's eyes when we were thusly engaged, well I don't quite know how to say this, but all the anticipated magic of this peak experience, sort of evaporated. I know he was thrilled and delighted with the orgasmic part, but I felt kind of lost. *It was still him that I wanted, but not in this way.* Maybe this 'being gay' business was just a big lie I had come to believe and accept from sometime long in the past." Wild Boy then got lost in reverie, and I left him to his thoughts.

Just before we headed out from what we now called "Ecstasy Island," I said, "Hey David! You take the rest of this beer; I can't have it loose in the truck." He transferred it to his vehicle, and when he returned he said, "You can take the rest of this!" and he popped a thick wad of LSD hits into my top pocket. He smiled warmly and I thanked him. I found that the best way to say good bye – even in the present, especially after an intimate embrace and soft kiss on the cheek, is to look away. One cannot see anything anyway, and tears will dissolve the outer world as it disappears with the one you have loved. We had no plans to meet again yet, as it depended on our schedules – or did it? Only time would tell.

Chapter Thirty

It is now mid-October in the beautiful and somewhat remote Bella Coola Valley in Northwestern British Columbia. Snow has crowned the surrounding mountains, and will drop to lower levels day by day till the valley has donned its white winter mantle. This is always a cause for concern at this time of year, because even if one does have winter rubber and four-wheel drive, if one is also towing a trailer out over the famous hill with its 19% grades, a good hard packed grippy surface is most desirable.

As usual I've been servicing my insurance clients in the Valley. This takes place primarily in the evenings because the people I want to see are working all day. So during the daylight hours I'm relatively free to explore, which means watching the last of the Grizzlies top up on the salmon before hibernation. Whether the cubs are one or two year olds, their coloring and antics keep me involved – no, enraptured, for hours. September is an excellent month for doing this, and frequently I haunt stretches of the Atnarko River with my video camera and binoculars.

Of course Little Boy Wild always says, ***"I am the river, and I am the grizzlies."*** He embraces this mystical oneness and explores the trails in a trance-like state of wonderment. For him, this is the year's final long wilderness trip to be with his animals, until the geese call on their way north in the spring. More than a decade ago we fell very much in love with the Grizzlies, when on one September day we observed a large sow with two cubs standing on a gravel bar in the Atnarko River. With the late afternoon sun streaming behind them, the light so suffused their fur with halos of golden light, that it held us spellbound, and initiated our resolve always to return season after season to live with our beloved bears.

My 15ft Wilderness Lynx trailer is snugly parked away up by the beaver dams, and on this particular evening while catching up on paper work, I

peeked outside. A chill breeze off the mountains had an edge of snow cold-
ness; it whipped the fall colors into a dancing frenzy sending cold shivers
all over me. I closed the door. The trailer was warm and bright, but the outside scene left me feeling desolate, empty and very alone. Little Boy Wild
had taken in the whole scene. He had not been in control for a while now as
I had been engaged in business affairs and interacting with the Humans. He
was longing for the closeness he had felt with David, it was such intimate
companionship.

He said, "I'd like him to be here just to share the little grizzlies and
walk among the fall colors. If only we could talk and plan some adventure trips; for he really means so much more to me than our psycho-sexual
involvement, as needful and delightful as it was. I think I need him as a
friend." However the last time Wild Boy had seen David—it was their final
meeting, and a somewhat short one. It was David who had severed their
connection at that time, and the words David had spoken were etched into
his memory.

"I don't think we should see each other again, I believe that you may be
dangerous for me." It had taken its toll on David to say it, but he did. Little
Boy Wild's elated face fell. It momentarily stunned him. The old hunted
look overtook his features.

"Why?" he asked in hurt amazement.

David did not look up, but continued to scribble on the table napkin
before him. This was painful for him too. Then Wild Boy began to understand. After a few more words he read between the lines that David thought
him to be a full time practicing gay and the AIDS specter had emerged.
The truth for Little Boy Wild was that this was his one and only experience
of this type, and it had only come about after the massive LSD psychic
devastation.

Apart from an occasional wind gust the night was quiet. I'd already
studied the skies and marveled at all creation. Then, not too far away a wolf
howled, and it imparted to me all the beautiful feelings I live with on my
wilderness trips. Again he howled and I tingled with joy, yet at the same
time was hit with an overwhelming aloneness.

Little Boy Wild was in control and was rummaging in the pockets of
our Goretex jacket, when quite accidentally he felt a little wad of something

in the corner of the top pocket, and on drawing it out, recognized it as the LSD wad that David had poked into his pocket on parting. Wild Boy's mind fogged up. Here was David! Companionship, closeness, touching and feeling – Pegasus Boy! Abruptly he put the whole wad into his mouth. How many hits? Probably 17 or 20 or more, it just didn't matter. To him it was like having David right there with him – only an embrace a way. After a few minutes, I, or the observer stepped into the scene. Common sense has always been in short supply, but here was a possible death defying feat underway, that had been launched by Wild Boy simply because he was hurting and so lonesome.

He was in his *"Silent Scream Mode"* where the psychic pain level peaks to where he screams long and silently. I cannot watch his escaping tears and I know that no psycho-sexual tension release will handle this level of hurt.

But right now I see Little Boy Wild *and* Me! So who am *I*? Or should I say who are *you*? I suppose I'm the observer who watches the whole show and records it. Regardless of identity we must shape this thing up, or we very well may die tonight. Some Human will find our body in a few days or weeks or whatever. I plugged in the tape recorder and did a brief introduction, they may as well know *how* we died, but they would never understand *why* we departed. Not that the Humans cared anyway. I lay on the rear bunk and as the night progressed it was just like the TV ads portrayed in their warnings on drugs – I could actually hear my brain frying! But one cannot call the flight attendant at 50,000ft and say "I'd like to get off now, right now!" As it is, we will not reach the airport (so to speak) until about 9:00am and we may well come in with no expectations of a soft landing!

During the night I came to from time to time, and used this opportunity to change the tapes. They were a real revelation to me, several personalities speaking to each other in different languages, that is, at least three others apart from Wild Boy and me. I appear to be the observer to all these weird interactions. The strange sounds continued in my head until about 9:00am when I "came to," with sudden awareness of where I was.

I peeked outside to be hit by a swirl of wind and snow. It was definitely time to hit the trail, fast. We must leave the valley now! But first some hot coffee and oatmeal with raisins mixed with Red River Cereal.

377

My head is buzzing strangely. What have we done? Why did we do it?

In all of Dr. Arthur Janov's books I'd read, I had always skipped the chapters on drugs as they simply did not remotely apply to me. I don't do drugs! A voice said to me, "Little Boy Wild and Company, you're in denial! Wake up wild creature! You just had about 20 odd hits of LSD simultaneously. You're up that famous creek without a paddle." I'll let Dr. Janov quote from his masterful work—"The Primal Scream."

"I believe that LSD is a reality trip in the sense that it stimulates intense real feelings. But the neurotic does with this reality what he does with reality in general; changes it into something symbolic. There is no doubt that LSD stimulates feelings. The problem with the use of LSD is that it artificially opens up individuals to more reality than they can tolerate within their neurotic systems, resulting in *a daytime nightmare—psychosis*. The defense is there for a reason—to maintain the integrity of the organism. LSD upsets the defense system with the tragic results that LSD users are filling the neuropsychiatric wards across the country. I believe that LSD not only mimes psychosis, but produces a real, though often transient, insanity." Thank you Dr. Janov!

What have I done? If I was screwed up before—what have I now become?

I further quote Dr. Janov: "The person cannot become involved in his paper work for example; the feelings are too strong and immediate. LSD does not allow connections to be made solidly. The drug mitigates the full impact of reality."

So I'm in a state of consciousness where nothing is real…. Or is it? Speaking of paper work, I have a stack of it! So what must I do to channel or control these wild and powerful feelings? Little Boy Wild was a spacey rebel before this LSD affair, so just where will this lead to? My mind reels in a swirling foggy blackness with millions of sparkling lights. It is daytime, so is this the psychosis that Dr.Janov talks about, the daytime nightmares?

Arthur Janov, please: "LSD opens the limbic gate, the cortex is flooded with pain and the person must symbolize heavily." (I see David in the fire light at the cabin and Little Boy Wild symbolizing into exquisite feeling).

The complexity or bizarreness of the symbolism depends on the dosage of the drug and the amount of underlying pain."

"Thank you doctor! Eeeeek!" I'm dangerously overdosed, totally freaked out, and a silent scream of writhing pain. People who have never experienced psychic pain – and we're not talking about a headache, can have no concept of this hurt to identify with, nor of what one will do to alleviate it.

A final comment Dr.Janov please! "One key danger of LSD is that it evokes painful feelings out of their natural sequence of ascension, so that an unsuspecting patient is flooded and cannot integrate his experience. It is the premature liberation of feelings that is the danger. We are now seeing just how dangerous the uncontrolled use of LSD is."

I have yet to drive home. Boy am I freaked! If the RCMP should stop me for some reason, to whom will they be speaking? Little Boy Wild may stutter badly under the pressure. Supposing the constable closely examines our pupils? Are they dilated? And worst of all, suppose I speak to him as one of those individuals who have European accents, and alternate in their dialogue?

Okay Derek! Just drive home sanely and safely. You're kidding of course! You ARE insane at this moment! I put myself in the position of the Humans driving toward me; if only they knew what type of crazy animal is behind the wheel of the vehicle approaching them! However, it is interesting to note from a clinical stand-point that there *IS* a director here running the whole operation. Maybe it's *ME* or is it the *Observer?* Although there is a freaked out madman at the wheel, there is a cool calm entity in control. I think.

Eventually I arrived home without mishap. I thank God for that. Yes, I did pray while that chemical destroyed portions of my mind. No one seemed to notice my spaced- out condition on arrival and my wife was just leaving to visit her sister for a week over in Alberta. Good! I would have the whole place to myself wherein to scream, cry, and roll on the floor or whatever. Psychic pain has to be understood. It is not something that one can address by saying "Smarten up!" It is all encompassing; the entire mind in my case seemed to be operating on multiple frequencies. They took over my brain deeply and continuously whether I was sleeping or awake. There was no escape from this torture.

About 25 letters and bills were in the mail and these I went over; they also included a refund cheque for $1500.00 from some place. I cashed this at the bank, and with fifteen one hundred dollar bills in my back pocket I headed for Vancouver. It was a quest for psychic pain relief. Somewhere, someone had to have a "Fix" for this agony that distorted my world. The stars whirled around with intermittent black void spaces. I was immersed in a sizzling, dizzying type of psychosis that ran 24/7, and *I* was responsible for this. Little Boy Wild rode among the star mists with his friend on the back of the faithful Pegasus. He was "not available for comment."

So just what did I have in mind? Well for one, to kill the pain at any cost; so I sought a "Fix," maybe a needle or whatever, dope or something.

I did check of Dr. Arthur Janov's "The Primal Scream" again, and I quote: "The drug addict is an example of someone who has run out of inner defenses. He is usually one who has cancelled out so much feeling that he is almost dulled out of existence. Because he cannot defend himself as other neurotics do, he develops a relationship with a needle; pain – needle – relief. Remove the needle and there is the pain. The penis serves the same purpose for the homosexual. Both represent relief from tension." Thank you Dr. Janov.

So now we have confirmation – all these years my psycho-sexual escapades have merely been exploding tension from our system; and we cannot blame a testosterone reading of 60 plus which is just about off the scale in medical terminology. We wandered the streets of Vancouver, but as it was early in the day, and we being not "the type" I failed to make a connection. Finally the "Observer" stepped in and directed me homeward with my $1500.00 complete. I think I actually heaved a sigh of relief. Maybe there are guardian angels out there!

We returned to the Sunshine Coast and stayed with my sister and her husband for several days. They accommodated my thrashing around, tears and incoherency with great calm and compassion. We will be forever grateful to them for helping me "land" as it were. I discovered that one way to tolerate psychic pain was to play music on a continuous basis, not rock, but lighter instrumental suites from the great classics without getting too deep.

It focused my mind, giving it direction, and slowed down the kaleidoscope of colors, blacks and voids; I was even able to think occasionally. The overall feeling was that of pouring salve on an open wound which my psyche was. But when the music stopped, the demons came out to play.

It was impossible to do any work with paper or Humans, so I took off in the Landcruiser all the way down to Cabot San Lucas on the tip of the Baja Peninsula in Mexico. The weather was gloriously hot and the travel adventure was a picturesque journey, a world of sand, blue skies and cactus. Little Boy Wild had dismounted from Pegasus at last, and had released him to the star mists, it was an emotional parting. He had stroked the flying horse's glossy powerful neck with both hands, and after looking deep into his eyes, he merged their consciousness, kissed Pegasus' silky blue nose and released him. Both David and his beautiful steed flew beyond Wild Boy's vision, and once more he was earth bound, naked, wild and free. He knew of the dangers that we might encounter in this foreign-type land and was content to share his time with me; if anything, he was in control but had assigned to me the duties pertaining to logistics and security, but really I had just assumed my usual role anyway.

All the way down he seemed to be mesmerized and totally immersed in bird life, insects and flowers. But by night we had to play our music to retain a form of sanity. In retrospect, this whole trip was a dangerous and foolhardy thing to do. Wild Boy was elated with this adventure. However, a lone individual freaked out of his mind, and on the loose is asking for trouble. I was sure that if we had much to do with the locals, it would translate to them with relative ease that I was a wounded zebra limping across the African veldt waiting to be taken down. Sick critters usually meet with an untimely end. Their vulnerability, somewhat veiled from themselves, is an open invitation to the predators. Of course I slept in the Toyota Landcruiser not being able to afford a hotel. A cheap hotel room would be almost the same as red flagging the zebra anyway!

While I stayed in Mexico I always selected a camping place in the desert well before dark. The sun dropped rather suddenly at about 5:15pm and was followed quickly by total darkness without the accustomed evening dusk coming on. I would plot a turnoff to my camping spot within a tenth of a kilometer so I could enter it without being seen by traffic behind or approaching. If lights were coming from either direction I would punch the trip meter, go by my turn and come in for another attempt in the total privacy of darkness. It worked and I was never seen.

So what did we do during the day? Of course Wild Boy had to be far out in the desert alone with the snakes, birds and cactus. As the great surges of psychic pain racked his system he ran wild in his usual nakedness under the hot sun, screaming with abandon while shedding tears to the wind. At other times he would lie in the sand beside the ocean, allowing the rhythm of crashing waves to have the same effect on his brain as had the music; and wherever he found flowers he caressed them and spoke softly to them, as well as to the bees. Little Boy Wild ate little. Sometimes he would read, at others he would lie and dream. He thought of David, and Pegasus too, and often joined them in the star mist of his imagination. He rode high on the wild notes of the shore birds. He laughed as he ran along the water's edge, occasionally dipping in the waves for coolness and delightful splashing sessions. But, the waves still had to crash, ebb, and flow their cosmic rhythms to fend off the pain. One day he asked, "Why do I always have to be alone? Why are there not kindred spirits out there, somewhere, with which to share my joy of living?" Wild Boy is a thinking entity, and often questions himself about his place in the universe. An idea came to him one day from across the sand. Maybe it came from the blue waves whispering on the shoreline.

"Is it just possible," he queried, " That because **all that IS,** dwells within me already, that I experience what God feels like in situations like this, and He is lonely too? I am not God, but he must feel sad, especially when most of his creation does not acknowledge Him or care that He exists. But," he murmured, "He who dwells in the secret place of the most High shall abide under the shadow of the Almighty, and although right now, I'm almost a wiped out LSD freak, I will still say of the Lord, He is my refuge and my fortress, my God; and in him will I trust!"

Wild Boy's spirit flowed through his blood stream in beautiful harmonic synchronicity. It enveloped him, while his heart beat in time with the celestial music emanating from the planets and beyond. *"I AM."* He murmured. Those wonderful starry Mexican nights and soft evening breezes wafted their healing love messages to him. He **WAS** the night, the stars, and the sea scented wind, but none of these dreamy visions ever took precedence over his being as wary in a foreign land, as the bunnies are to the red foxes back home.

We returned to British Columbia in one piece, but a lot of my operating memory banks for day to day matters were missing. Something had pressed the "delete" key too frequently in too many places. Slowly I would have to re-learn the many things that had been deleted in the deadly LSD chemical invasion. Day by day and week by week as I attempted to perform the many tasks I had as a financial and insurance advisor, it became more and more clear that I would have to seek some form of professional help.

Derek! Little Boy Wild! Do you realize how serious this is? What would your faithful clients think or say if they discovered you were a total LSD freak out? Some of them would laugh, but others would take a dim view of my interpretation of fiduciary responsibility.

All attempts to obtain competent professional help failed. Some counselors said, "It's all in your past. Forget it and get on with your life." A psychiatrist at a major hospital seemed to think that psycho pharmacology (drugs) was the answer. When I read about the possible side effects from the prescription, they were so horrendous that I flushed them. I imagined that somewhere below in the labyrinths of twilight, the sewer rats might exhibit strange behavior. Maybe their sex lives would change dramatically. Maybe they would change their molecular structure and become a race of lithium rats, and we would serve them roasted to psychotics for supper! But I already knew the rats were as full of chemicals as we are. I recall reading that the tigers in Viet Nam were attracted to the sound of machine gun fire. There would be fresh meat all over the place, but the tigers ate the Invaders last as they did not decompose as quickly being so full of food preservatives! So now – what next must we do?

For some years I had been familiar with Primal Integration Therapy (P-I-T) and had been in touch with a California group, never imagining that I would finally go to them for help. In P-I-T one works as it were on an internal split screen mode. There is the therapist, and say for example, the current scene in which a seven year old boy is being brutally sodomized. One actually **becomes** in this case Little Boy Wild, reliving all the terrible trauma of a particular incident, and **integrates it** with his current emotionally more mature level of understanding and acceptance. This is assuming that his system can handle the pain of the input, and that the particular scene has been released for absorption in his current state.

The memories will be released from the cerebral cortex storage area, only if the mature being is strong enough to handle it. The resulting benefits are stages of lowered tension plus the physical benefits of stress reduction in the body. If he is not ready to relive and absorb the incident, it will remain encased within, exerting destructive pressures on the organism until the time for release is right. Such incidents may be opened up in a year, or three years or even ten years down the road when the strength is there to handle it. This therapy has also been known as Primal Scream Therapy, but it is more correct to identify it as Primal Integration Therapy which of course originated with Dr. Arthur Janov in his initial book "The Primal Scream," – although screaming may be a part of the process at some time or level, generally the whole concept is ***integration.***

By this time Little Boy Wild and I had reached a level of psychic degradation where it was no longer possible to function. Even the continuous instrumental music input could no longer hold back the waves of trauma. Degrees of psychosis really indicate degrees of pain. When pain reaches its zenith, all reality is blotted out. I did my best to hide it and I had yet to contact my P-I-T outfit in California. Then a few days later I did call them from a phone in a local mall. Just hearing their concerned and understanding tone was enough to trigger the racking, gasping sounds I had been emitting for some weeks, and tears flooded down my cheeks.

"Are you able to drive and function somewhat normally otherwise?" they asked. I assured them that this was so. Usually this institute would not be able to take on anyone for Primal Integration Therapy without an advance booking of some months, but for some unknown reason they had a three week period blocked off on their calendar. Maybe it was reserved for a holiday. Then my call showed up and they recognized the immediate need for treatment and set the wheels in motion. It was a real life saver. I was accepted for therapy and agreed to meet with them in four days. I packed the Landcruiser and headed for the border where the US customs people wanted to know the nature of my business down there. I explained

I was joining a psychiatric group for several weeks in California. But they insisted on knowing more!

"Are you a psychiatrist?" they asked. I had to tell them.

"I'm a patient" I explained.

After a few more questions the customs officer said that he had been in the life insurance business for a short while and fully understood why I needed treatment. He wished me the best of luck and he meant it! I had just turned the key in the ignition when he said, "One more question, do you have any firearms on board?" Eeeek! Now what!

"Yes" I replied, "I always carry my Marlin 45.70 rifle."

"Are you going to do some hunting as well?" he followed up.

"No" I replied, "It's part of my travel gear and it has bailed me out of two or three bad situations over the years without my ever having to resort to its actual use.

Besides, with a 405 grain bullet, it's really a "stopping gun" more than a hunting one. You know – stop a grizzly in its tracks!"

To my amazement he said, "Good for you! Good luck down there!"

If you're not familiar with the 405 grain 45.70 cartridge, it is a big slow moving chunk of lead that stops what has to be stopped. I suppose in hunting it would push the willows aside to wack a moose in the thicket too. It is also an easy handling gun that carries well in a sling when one is far out in the bush filming bears.

All this therapy stuff costs a pack of money. So much was needed that I had to max out my Master and Visa to the hilt to get a handle on the situation; and there were hotels, gas, and meals to pay for yet. So this left me sleeping in the Landcruiser on the way down. We had three nights of hiding out in the bush with the big California jack rabbits. Little Boy Wild calmed right down when he saw the rabbits. He smiled and talked with them in his own language. He was *feeling*. For a while he surveyed the night sky while traveling from one star to another.

"Its okay bunnies, it's okay," He murmured.

On arrival at our destination, I researched the motels for a three week stay and settled in a Comfort Hotel that was bright new and clean, unlike some of the other tired smelly places I'd checked. We were now ready to face whatever had to be faced the following day.

It was while watching TV that first evening that we ran into a movie called "Discovery Passage," I believe, and it was absolutely the *last* type of input we needed. It really was the straw that broke the camel's back! It was all about a bunch of young male society misfits, between the ages of about 17 to 25. They were on a large sailboat bearing the name "Discovery," and this was their last opportunity to learn how to get along with each other and the world outside, and to work as a team before they were released from custody. The alternative was further incarceration for all those who were identified as incorrigible, with further prison terms and hell. Little Boy Wild's eyes filled with tears as he recognized their individual hurts and pain. *It mirrored the traumas of his own childhood.*

One of the crew on board the *"Discovery"* was a seventeen year old boy who always looked down, even when he was spoken to. He had a history of striking out at anyone who came too close to him, especially if they came suddenly upon him. His counselor questioned him for our benefit. He raised his eyes. He was a good looking kid. He frowned and was silent for a moment. Wild Boy gazed through his own sudden tears at the boy's eyes which told him everything. Finally the Discovery Kid looked down, cupped his face in his hands, and shook with sobs.

"All they ever wanted from me was my butt!" he cried out in anguish. "I was just a good fuck! All I ever meant to *anyone* was just a good fuck!" He bowed over racked with sobs and hurt.

Little Boy Wild screamed in anguish and threw himself on the bed, where he pounded the pillows and writhed around striking his head on the head board. It caused him to bleed. Again and again he screamed finally rolling onto the floor and thrashed around hitting the chairs. All the while he emitted terrible half strangled cries of distress. When the Discovery Kid spoke again he hurled himself onto the bed to catch every word that was spoken. He threw his arms open in a wild gesture as if to embrace this kid's hurt. Each glance at his tanned face and tortured eyes was like a knife thrust into Wild Boy. He was beyond containment. Grasping a pillow he hugged it and wailed as if trying to take some of Discovery Boy's hurt onto himself.

"I'll be your friend," He gasped. "You are me, and I love you for all you've been through. Share your pain with me. Hold me! We'll protect each other. I understand!"

But this was to be the night of nights to hit the jackpot of a second trauma. The straw had already been laid on the camel's back to break it; now came the double whammy. Maybe while the camel is down we can finish him off. I was about to click the TV off and had skipped a couple of channels because the sailboat "Discovery" was already heading out to sea; when up came a commercial featuring the famous McDonald's Clown, colorful red nose and all.

Little Boy Wild sat up and looked straight ahead. It was as if he had gone into a type of trance, he stiffened all over, his glazed eyes were fixed and far seeing, and when he spoke it was without any expression. His fists kept clenching and unclenching. His voice was hoarse and broken.

"I've always hated clowns and never knew why. Clowns scare me. I'm nine years old and we've gone to circus on the edge of town. I don't know my care giver. Maybe she is an aunt. We've had a wonderful time on the roundabouts and I even stuffed myself with ice cream, so I know SHE was not around. I enjoyed the circus animals best. Elephants, tigers and performing bears, but the llamas I really love. One little brown one with such large dark eyes looked directly at me. I am spellbound by his beauty. If only I could stroke him for a while and whisper into his silky ears. The animals exit and I run out while my aunt is preoccupied; "I know" I exclaimed, "I'll look around into some of the tents. My little llama must be there somewhere." One tent has a lot of hay in it and smells nice. I go in to explore and there sitting on a hay bale is a clown, all painted up.

"What are you doing in here?" He asks.

I stuttered, "I'm looking for my little brown llama. Maybe I can stroke him." I ventured.

"Well now, let's see if we can find him." He had a pleasant voice but a very scary face. We talked a bit and then he said.

"All right, I think you should meet your little llama, come on –let's go find him!" He took my hand and as we stepped behind some hay bales, to my surprise and horror he dropped my short pants and proceeded to sodomize me; he was greasy but it was still very painful. His breath reeked of onions and he hurt my ribs with his fierce grip. When it was all over, he pulled up his pants and I did likewise. Then I fled from the tent with my shirt still hanging out.

I cried as I ran and looked for the aunt, but it was she who found me. She neatened me up and dragged me by the hand while she gave me a good talking to. I cannot tell her what happened. I have no words for it. Again and again I relive the whole sequence; how could this have happened? If only I could have rescued my little llama we could have run from all this hell to go and live among the distant hills, snuggle down at night and fall asleep under a haystack. But the warm snuggling would be best of all."

Silence then fell upon Little Boy Wild. He toppled sideways on the bed and lay there without a sound for almost fifteen minutes. I thought he had fallen asleep. But no, when he rose he was still in a distant trance mode. He went to the door and inhaled the cool night air, it relaxed his whole body; and when an owl called from across the courtyard he answered it. Both he and the owl called to each other several times. It was clear to me now that he was out of his trance, but still in his other world. He wandered among the trees and flowering bushes, saw the owl take flight, and leaned over to scent a flower before settling into the grass and lying down. He went into a reverie of self examination, sometimes speaking softly to himself, and at others he spoke aloud.

"What do they see in me and my Discovery Kid that make them abuse us the way they do?" he questioned, as he pictured several of them including the clown. Speaking into the night air he continued, "Is it something in our looks? I know I'm not as good looking as the Kid, but maybe there's another clue; can they see and sense that we're unloved stray kids by seeing the pain in our faces? In my case the stutter would increase the vulnerability factor. In addition to this, there is the mystery of what it is all about, what makes them do it, and who is going to do it to us next. This seems to program us from about age six and upwards, at a time when we have no remote idea of sex feelings till wet dreams erotize us at about thirteen years of age more or less. So when we are close to some male, teenage or older, we look from their face to their crotch and back again, wondering if it is going to happen. Also we were far too young to know about sexual arousal, or the feelings involved in the sex act. So do we send signals to them? Or are we just looking for a father? We have also been sodomized enough times to wonder why we submit to this, even when we're 16 or 17. So does the hot urgency of contact make us feel needed? Do we suffer the pain of sodomy solely in exchange for that close holding, and hot embrace?" Wild Boy sat up and brushed a few lurking tears from his eyes. "Take David for example" he continued, "Was it sex that I wanted, or was it his friendship, his love and his caring embrace? Why can't I separate the two, even though they are so closely entwined? Further, is need linked to 'Being' and identity?" There are so many questions and so few ready answers." He lay back in the grass. I had no comforting or definitive suggestions available.

Then – acting as if I did not exist, he arose, yawned, reached out and took the Discovery Kid's hand in his, and in this dream trance they both went back inside. It was so real in motion that he may well have taken a spirit being by the hand. Little Boy Wild smiled in the darkness and hugged his tanned-faced pillow, murmuring something about sharing pain, and fell asleep. The two kids hugged each other a lot that night, and tears flowed freely. Several times before morning Wild Boy's owls called, and each time he stopped breathing to listen. To acknowledge them, he transmitted thoughts of *oneness* to them, for they were also *within him.* His smile deepened as the lonely calls continued; but being among such friends relaxed him more fully. He hugged his Discovery Boy in tight closeness, and entered a deeper sleep.

A shadow of normalcy settled upon us in the morning following a hot shower and a good breakfast. We showed up on time at the Primal Center and were introduced to the principals and therapists who would be working with us. They began by asking a few basic questions, but it was Little Boy Wild who replied to them and in a matter of a few minutes from our introduction, we were in full vomit type posture with forceful wide mouthed "trying to eject something" sounds. Tears of fright and consternation flooded us. "You'd better get him in right away," said one therapist to the other.

Normally when a patient shows up for P-I-T Therapy it can take from several days to many months or longer to break through the defenses in order for the process to go forward. In our case WE arrived with no defenses whatsoever. The LSD had eliminated all defenses. We were raw naked pulsating consciousness; a quivering entity of mass psychic hurt that could possibly, if successful, wend its way to a level of operating functionality. Or, if things did not go well, we might have to launch into the "River of No Return." I believe that catatonic psychosis could well be the conclusion of unsuccessful therapy for us both at this stage, but that would be due to the indisputable fact that we were still under the effects of an extreme overdose of LSD, and nothing to do with Primal Integration Therapy.

Days and days of therapy went by. Evenings were free. Odd wisps and fragments of concepts go by us ....All the King's horses and all the King's men could not put poor Wild Boy together again .... HE HAS TO DO IT HIMSELF!!

What's that? I have to call out for my mother? ....MOTHER? Oh no! You don't invite pain! Who wants to come to the killing scene? How shall we kill him? Stab him with a knife? Suffocate the little swine? Poison him? Or shall we slowly drive him to insanity far within? ....I have a loss of reality today and I ask myself – who am I? What am I doing here? It seems I'm trying to wake from a dream. *Unless I imagine myself to be, I'm not here! Unless I create who I am, I am not.* When I cannot act anymore or imagine myself into being, I may not exist. Is this the rebirth of the Real Self or the capture of Little Boy Wild? I cannot leave home yet, I'm still too young, and I'm held here by a cord of hate and a thread of life.

Terror is unscreamed screams! My whole life has been one long silent scream. *My whole life IS a silent scream!* Wild Boy screamed and collapsed in a heap on the thick corduroy padded mattress; and so the therapy continued. Two weeks have passed. I'm not playing as much music to alleviate the pain, so we are making progress. Several times I have seen light coming from under a door in the screen of my mind. I know I *MUST* open that door. I always scream aloud and withdraw. Why do I not want to go through that door? The only way out is THROUGH! Through what? – through the door and through the pain to freedom! And what is freedom? Is it to be ONE and WHOLE, and not split in two and fragmented?

For some time now Little Boy Wild had been talking with the Touquans. The Touquans speak Touquanese and are of another dimension. They exist in a parallel shadow world operating on a different frequency from us. Wild Boy can apparently converse with them at an elementary level. He has even been coaching me on certain phrases, however their manner of speech does not concern me and I don't intend to start learning now. One day, in the third week of therapy I saw again the crack of light under the door that I greatly fear to open. It was a matter of choice. Go through, or continue to suffer the psychic hurt. I braced myself and involuntarily vented a gigantic Primal Scream and found myself .... .in the land of the Touquans. *It's really something to be suddenly dumped into another frequency of consciousness!*

Imagine, if you will, a high Arctic mountain valley with tall rugged mountain crags. It is silent. The silence is deafening. Above the valley the sky is brilliantly lit with the dancing splendor of the Northern Lights, great rippling flowing curtains of green, red and gold with glorious multi-colors; and right here in front of me are tall "Beings." They are very tall and wear long loose garments of a similar shade of brown to the feathers of an immature bald eagle, except that they have intricate designs woven into them. To one side of me are rows and rows of little cribs stretching almost to infinity. They are very solid looking – like they're made out of rock, all are of a dull brown color, and in each of the cribs is a tiny Human. The Touquans are tall and silent. They have a hooded monk-like quality about them, and their faces are always averted. I see only the side or back of them at any time. I ask questions of them silently and receive silent answers. This does not seem to surprise me, because it's as if I have known this all along, which of course I have, through Wild Boy.

"These are those who are not ready to die as yet," a Touquan answers my question.

"We protect them here. Some never leave till their time on earth is completed. Others like Little Boy Wild, as you call him, may leave at any time by joint agreement between both of you. Wild Boy is under our protection."

"Who holds him here?" I asked.

"He holds himself here. He is under our care so that he does not damage or kill himself. He is not being held here. We are caretakers only. When he has direction and purpose, he will achieve his spiral ascent. He will recognize when he is ready to leave, and will find himself free to go."

"But I have been interacting with Little Boy Wild for years," I ventured, not quite understanding how he can be here with the Touqauns and also with me.

"One might say that this is his base regardless of his age or size," A Touquan replies. "It also is a matter of time adjustment. When he has an expansion of consciousness it leads to an expansion into space. He is involved in both Objective and Subjective space time. When he achieves his spiral and merges his Real Self with his Unreal self, to use your terms, he will be ONE and WHOLE with you, and we will have a spare crib! He never needs to return. He will no longer require our care."

Today I actually spoke with Little Boy Wild at his base—live! He squatted, his back was toward me. He knows only darkness and does not want to cross the chasm over the golden bridge of light anymore than I did coming the other way. He was very young—it was like going back into his mind as a child and speaking to him as the child he no longer was.

"Why did you neglect me for so many decades?" he sobbed. "The only way I could make myself felt was in the making of irrational decisions for you out of pure emotion. I thought you'd notice me, but you didn't even learn from it! You just went on in life and dug deeper holes to fall into—just so that the struggle to get out of them would make you forget your real problem."

"I'm truly sorry," I replied, "But I didn't hear your calls for help; of course I'm the unreal self that was created to take care of things for you while you were away —which was going to be forever if I had not crossed the bridge to get you!"

Wild Boy came back with some justifiable anger. "You left me in isolation for decades! I was used to hurt, loneliness and darkness as well as neglect, so I always went "Inside" to survive, and I've always had to fight for my identity!"

Tears of sadness flowed down my cheeks, "We have always needed each other. Inasmuch that you created me to represent you while you were based with the Touquons, I pose the same question for you, why did you not merge with me long ago?"

A Touquan intervened in both our thought processes. "Neither of you is responsible for neglect, neither did Little Boy Wild create you," he said, addressing me. "We did. But it took decades of learning before either of you could consider coming together."

The Touquan left us to our thoughts. We have made progress, I now have access to Little Boy Wild on a live on-going basis, and the door that

I had so greatly feared to open –remains open. The next day he faced me – and I loved him at every age that he had ever lived. He smiled.

"You know," he said, "Over the decades as you lived your manic behavior and depressions – always a new sales project, always new sales ideas for success, you slowly, out of ignorance and fear, unwittingly tried to kill me! Yes – kill me! I was just a sad frightened little kid. If you ever stopped your manic struggles you would have come face to face with me, but you could not face that reality, so you dug deeper and deeper holes so that your struggle to escape would delay your confrontation.

You walked down streets with big open pits and you deliberately stumbled into them just for the pure struggle of getting out. You wanted to forget – to go blank. You could not hide your pain and sadness, and you could not afford to stop – It just hurt too, too much!"

"I see that now in retrospect," I admitted while shaking with apprehension. The pieces of the jig saw puzzle were falling into place, and I realized then that I had never seen the complete picture of our puzzle on the outside of the box so to speak.

"Neither of us will die if we merge and become one," he assured me, "And I know this is your concern at this time."

The question for me was that Little Boy Wild is almost pure emotion, and he is still capable of forcing decisions that have little logic and enough insanity to destroy both of us. By this I mean a gross lack of emotional maturity. *But Wild Boy has a right to LIVE, a right to BE, a right to be I AM, and a right to wholeness. So be it!* There is an empty crib in the Land of the Touquons. *Little Boy Wild – this is your homecoming! I love you – and your rabbits!*

When all three weeks of therapy were completed, I knew that we had only established a small beach-head into this psycho domain. Little Boy Wild had released himself from the care of the Touquans and was with me; so we headed north back to Canada. He had asked if it were okay to stay a night or so with the big northern California jack rabbits on the way back, and as we had to pull off the highway for the night, our timing was ideal.

It was also a little strange for us when we realized that we were both together, and he was no longer anchored, as it were, in the Touquan frequency, which meant he was now an entity of free choice. We had measured each other up almost with an aura of apprehension; but Wild Boy felt good now that we had branched off to sleep with the rabbits. He gained confidence. Maybe life's decisions would not be made by a hurt and angry kid any more. But it was his smile that told me he was glad to be going home – for good.

When *He* selected our camping place, I knew he had *"taken over,"* – so nothing had changed there! He just walked naked into the dusk of evening; and his manner was as though he were appearing on stage as himself for the first time. The earth was his theatre and stage, and it was alight with a million stars.

"Just the stars and the night sounds," he murmured.

Soon he caught sight of a rabbit scampering. It paused, and he mentally asked it to stop, which it did. He spoke to it in his own language and it started to feed while watching and listening. Other rabbits joined in, and gradually the stars grew brighter. Wild Boy lay on the sandy pathway; the moon started to rise, but he was not cold even though the evening chill was growing. While gazing at the Big Dipper he began to sing his bluebird song. "Somewhere, over the rainbow, where bluebirds fly." So I knew that he was in harmony with his world. The rabbits didn't run, but seemed to pause in their feeding to watch him and to listen. Some even hopped a little closer. He sent love messages to them, and their ear movements told him they had heard.

But when suddenly an owl hooted from high in the trees, he found himself alone again; alone with his song, the rising night wind, and the stars. *"He who overcomes, I will give him the Morning Star,"* he quoted softly in a husky voice. He looked directly at me, his eyes held that distant 'star quest' gaze as he arose and started to trek back to where we had left the truck.

"I am the moon at night, I am Venus and the rising sun, and I am the coyotes!" His voice surged as he heard the coyotes yipping and howling. Their calls echoed across the valley, a lonely musical prelude to the hunt; he could resist no longer and joined in their joyous evening chorus. He sat on a grassy knoll and imagined himself as a golden coyote, an alpha male with his golden mate giving throat to their zest for life and his love for her

and the pups back in the lair. In the truck again, we snuggled into our down bag and briefly watched the moon shadows cast by the trees.

"***This is your homecoming Little Boy Wild,***" I said, smiling at his cosmic halo. We are truly together, I love you and you will never need to leave – ever again!" We both sighed and embracing each other, slipped into another dimension within our dream world.

When morning came I woke to say, "The only way out of pain is through it, not around it and not over it. I can walk another street! I don't have to walk the ones I used to and stumble into the deep holes and struggle to get out. I do not have to achieve identity through struggling to hide my sadness. I am free! We are free! I know that recovery is a process and not an event in Primal Therapy."

I stretched to greet the sunrise and we smiled, "I'm not in therapy... We are in rabbit land!"

"Wild Boy!" I called.

"Yes?" He replied.

"We have to discuss our emerging powers and who does what and when, so that we can now do things we could not do by ourselves alone"

"Yes" said Little Boy Wild, "and I must not go back to that terrible realization that SHE, my mother, had actually killed me! To all intents and purposes that is what she did. I became a separate spirit being in a capsule, which is the same as being dead; I had become disembodied but somehow still attached to you. I know SHE was happy because I was no longer in my eyes, I had gone into hiding. She was pleased that I had become a defective human which she only kept alive for her pleasures of torture. She fed on pain. When I was older, about fourteen, I had become quite strong, and when she attacked me with the bamboo cane I would rip it from her grasp, take her by the wrists and push her into a corner of the room, while I placed one leg across the front of her to prevent her from kicking. Then I would look into her contorted demonic red face while she threatened me, all the while she was spitting at me and viciously snarling. When I did finally release her, she would grab the bamboo cane and attack me like a wild Tasmanian Devil!"

"All that is past now Wild Boy," I said in a serious tone. "We're still what the Humans call neurotic, paranoid, schizoid, psychotic or whatever, but we can work together now."

Wild Boy suddenly winced. "I just remembered that one time she grabbed an iron fire place poker, and in a livid fury screamed at me "Get out of here or I'll split your skull you swine!" and I believe she would have, and that's really bad. But you know, she did have one or two redeeming graces; for one, she was a stickler for good English grammar and correct pronunciation, and that has never left me. In addition, believe it or not, on some occasions at bed time she would talk about God—up there; and I would look at the ceiling lamp-shade and get strange ideas as to what God looked like."

A squirrel noisily checked us out as I addressed Wild One.

"These memories, and worse, will continue to rise out of our consciousness for years to come, how long I don't know, but we no longer need be concerned about them. We know what they are about and we can handle whatever comes up, we are much stronger now".

We threw some peanuts for the squirrel and just then the rich coffee smell perked into the cool morning air. The sun arose as it had for eons, rabbits scampered, and the wheels of time moving forward launched the day into orbit. We decided not to hurry as we had no schedule, and just let the sun slowly warm us while we floated on bird song and the rustle of our friends in the bushes. Little Boy Wild chatted with some wild bees and a short while later we gave thought as to whether we should stay for a while, or take our leave.

Chapter Thirty One

We decided to stay with the Jack Rabbits for one more day before heading north to British Columbia and home. The next morning I cranked up the Optimus stove on the tailgate of the truck, until the noisy blue flame roared aloud that it was ready to perk the coffee. Columbian coffee odors again wafted through the clearing; and a short time later while I sipped the brew, the water boiled for our oatmeal mixture. The sun slowly rose, and Little Boy Wild in navy blue shorts and runners, wandered through the brush to look for rabbits. He was powered by oatmeal and coffee, and probably too much Rogers Golden Syrup for his own good health.

"Wild Boy – what are you trying to tell me?" I asked. For I knew he wanted to say something but was not too sure how to approach it.

"It's about your honeymoon trip," he said. "I could not tell you before, but now we are together I can clear up that mystery."

"What mystery?" I asked.

"About the time you cried and cried and couldn't stop and didn't know why." He smiled.

"Yes I remember that only too well ....but . ." Little Wild Boy looked at me, *"It was ME – not you! I was the one who cried so heart-brokenly.* I felt totally betrayed, disowned... discarded is the right word I think. You who were not even real! You married and made love to a Human female. You "sold out," you left me, your real self, and made a life on your own. I felt as if you had dealt me a death blow. Of course I cried, I was heart-broken, and you had no idea what it was all about and nor could you explain it to your new bride. So now you know!"

"But I wanted kids," I replied. "I had to overcome the fear of the Humans, and more precisely, a female, to try and block out the trauma, pain, and distrust I normally associate with them. I always felt that they enslaved,

397

controlled and dominated the male, who meekly brought home his pay cheque, passed it to her, and then had to ask her permission if he could go out to see a friend or whatever, and even beg for a ten dollar bill out of the money he had earned. In the final analysis, I had always interpreted marriage as an expensive adventure into losing control of one's life."

"I realize that what you just said is true, but not in all cases." said Wild One, "For example, in your case frequently you never *had* a pay cheque to hand over! But I did enjoy seeing the kids come along, all three of them; and no –you did not desert me, we both still ran wild and free!"

We lay under a bush for almost an hour watching the rabbits, and when we rose he said, "Tell me more about this Holy Spirit stuff, you know – like the Kananaskis incident."

"Oh, we were camping out, my wife and the three boys. We had arrived at this nice wild spot on the river among the ranch land and forested areas, the tent had been set up and we headed out by wading through the shallow water of the river, on our way to explore some beaver dams and maybe see the beavers too. It was a walk of about a mile and a half away. The sun was very hot, and our youngest complained about the long walk, but we did see the beavers and had a nice rest before heading back to make up our evening meal.

On approaching our campsite, which was now of course on the opposite side of the river, we heard the roar of water – alot of water rushing very fast. As we came to the riverbank I knew what had happened. The power company had opened up the dam gates and released huge amounts of water. We had casually waded across through the shallows and coolness in the early afternoon, but now it was a swift turbulent raging torrent of some five feet in depth! Now what would we do?

There was an old broken down log bridge over the river at this point, mostly fallen into complete ruin, and only one solid log in the center still remained that could still carry a person. The distance was about 160 feet or approximately 50 or so paces. The only alternative was a walk of about three miles to a bridge, cross over and then walk the 3 miles back, and it would be quite dark by then, and we were ill equipped to handle the situation. After a brief conference we decided to cross the bridge. First I took our miniature dachshund "Pepi" in my arms, relaxed, and picked my way over on the center log, which was just a matter of putting one foot in front of the other, and tried to ignore the roar of the swift foaming water beneath. One slip and we'd be gone – somewhere down stream. This crossing was achieved, and then I had to do the same journey all over again to get back! It was getting to me already. My wife and the two older boys aged seven and four got across by straddling the log and working their way over. All was okay so far. Our youngest boy could not do the straddling thing, being only about two and a half years old. So I hoisted him up to straddle my neck and instructed him to hang on at any cost if I tripped or fell. I assured him we would be alright, but he *must* hang on to something. This is an enormous responsibility, to carry your youngest son on your shoulders way high up over a raging river in the twilight on a single log. So here, Wild Boy – is where you call on a power much greater than yourself. You pray and completely surrender your entire mission to God. It feels like your body is in one dimension and your head is in another. That's the Holy Spirit in action! We crossed safely, with the family on the other side anxiously looking on."

"You forget," he smiled. "I was there too! And yes I do know what you mean now by surrendering to a greater power than either of us! Let's go back and grab another coffee, it'll heat up real quick with the Optimus stove." We did just that, with squirrels occasionally scolding, and big rabbits looking at us while they nibbled.

Once we were back in Canada, all I had to do was catch up on the paper work the Humans wanted and generally do Human types of things; all of which were boring, dead and pointless. But as I observed out loud to Wild Boy – this is what keeps us in wheels and takes us where we want to go, and it also enabled me to support the kids and their dedicated mother.

Often we would look at Humanity passing us by on the street and we would wonder what made them tick. What drives them? What do they live for? Have they ever seen or experienced the star light with a trillion worlds awaiting them? Most of them didn't look very happy, and were mainly dominated by what they owned or were trying to acquire. It came to me that – *men ARE their houses and possessions*, this is what creates their *"I AM" feeling. Without "owning" they are nothing.*"

This realization made Wild Boy and me feel like we were merely visiting from another planet. We would watch their television shows of sickening mental mediocrity, and realized that where you sow mediocrity or inane values without principles; you get this river of bland blind humanity hurrying to nowhere. No wonder they are unhappy!

There is nothing wrong in owning or acquiring, but this is secondary in the sequence of life.

"Seek ye first the Kingdom of God and all these things will be added unto you," quoted Little Boy Wild. "But let's not get too far into this or we'll get to quoting most all of the Bible and the Humans get real freaked out about it."

"Okay, I understand – but let's go somewhere into the wilderness as soon as you've done what has to be done. I want to do my flower thing, you know, lie and dream among the flowers, and drift on the hum of bees, and slip into the gaps in our consciousness and see where it lands us. Other "Realities" lie within these spaces, and we should explore them. There is another thing too. I want to decipher an answer pertaining to another dimension, where upon occasion unseen beings, not of Human configuration, move close by me. *I cannot see them!* But I can *see and hear* the bushes move in the same way that one would see a friend or small animal move the bush as they walk through. It is chillingly eerie when one cannot see anything causing the motion and sound! It is not a breeze or gust of wind. It happens on rare occasions, and it is not something I can forget! I know it sounds weird, but is it possible that beings from another planet already occupy our world? They mean no harm, but simply operate on a frequency which precludes our type of vision, and their mission would be quite alien compared to our caveman quest for owning things, and blandly going through life as out of tune beings, with no cosmic purpose other than fun and inanity – or should that be insanity?"

This was a long speculative dissertation by Wild Boy and I felt good all over just to hear him speak his mind. It was some months before we could finally go into the wilderness, as I had to get financial matters under control – whatever that means, and then we both were ready for a mountain meadow adventure.

The snow capped peaks beckoned us; we envisioned turquoise lakes, very wild alpine meadows with no Humans for miles, and probably no remote possibility of an encounter with them. We were well equipped with supplies and we had one thing in mind – just to enjoy each other's company, to interact, to merge or differ in our viewpoints. It didn't matter in the least what psychiatric label the knowledgeable ones might place on us, that was simply irrelevant. I had already, for some time, had the habit of saying to Little Boy Wild, "Are you alright?" and I always knew from the way he replied by his very tone whether he was, or wasn't. If he sounded neglected or unloved or I had not consulted him on some matter which would affect us both; then we had to have a session in the wilds somewhere. It really meant that he needed to be in control 100% and live his reality; for his was another world apart from mine, uncontaminated by the Humans, where he could step into the cosmos in all innocence – except now I would share his experiences more fully as he was rooted in me and I in him.

Little Boy Wild chuckled, he was happy, and even more so when the mountains began to tower alongside us. Here and there we saw bands of elk grazing, and it reminded us of last year's trek to this region, where we watched a big grizzly chase an elk calf. With incredible power and speed the beautiful little calf had been swiftly overtaken, and as the calf went down we lost them both from view and knew the inevitable had happened. We found our narrow trail as it turned off toward the talus slopes, and in four wheel drive alongside the river we crept up to the alpine meadows. Below us the river veered off to the right and we climbed still higher until we finally found a snug place before the tree line disappeared. I killed the engine and remained silent for several minutes. In the wilderness we never ever slammed a door or made metallic sounds, all we wanted was to simply silently merge into the scenic beauty and wait for the world to move on its course around us. We had achieved a level place to camp which meant that all we had to do was to make up our bed in the canopy.

The fuzzy lined canopy on the Dodge Diesel had no condensation problems, and the windows were equipped with mosquito screens with one side having the additional protection of no-seeum screens. "No-seeums," for the uninitiated, are tiny black biting insects that one feels before one sees, and in the evening and especially the early morning they seem to require blood. But of course we are beautifully equipped for survival in the wilderness.

Little Boy Wild scanned the area when he heard the bleating of the

Picas – little rock rabbits the size of a clenched fist, furry, with rounded ears, and usually with a mouthful of flowers and grasses to make hay for the coming winter. Next he took to the game trails as they meandered through gorgeous blazes of flowers – Indian Paintbrushes and so many other scented flowers of different colors for which he had no names. A fast little creek caused him to stop for a drink, and he looked up at the whistling of the marmots. A small rock slide higher up made him think of bigger animals, maybe it was natural, or was there a grizzly approaching from higher up, or a sheep coming down?

He was already soaking up the sun "au naturel," and he felt the ants exploring him as he lay almost hidden among the taller blossoms. He idly studied the big fuzzy bumble bees, some had pollen bags on their legs, and others were small and fuzzy. There were beetles too, and other unidentified insects and he loved them all. But he could not help thinking of the grizzlies due to the rock movements and his most recent experiences with them when he had been so careless.

He thought of his truck as a safe haven, for it was not uncommon to be awakened by grunting and woofing grizzlies along-side the truck, but even with extreme caution those bears know if one has food on board through their incredible sense of smell. Safety depends on whether the grizzly is hungry or not. If he is stuffed with fish, and he smells fruit like apples or nectarines, a visit is coming up. One is not necessarily safe inside a truck as a grizzly can open up a truck canopy like a sardine can if he really wants something. There are many fascinating stories of grizzly bears and human encounters, and most of them have a chilling effect on us, even though we love and respect all bears. We usually examine grizzly scat to see what they've been eating, and find small bones, along with huge amounts of seeds during the berry season. The sliding windows into the cab from the canopy are always unlocked, so we would be able to wriggle through very quickly to get the engine going in short order if we had to. However the truck alarm system would probably scare them away anyway, as it is of a type that is very loud and sounds like a swat team coming in, with sirens and Braapp! Braapp! Braapp! noises, along with other scary ones. That alarm is with us at night, handy and within reach!

Wild Boy sat up and scanned the alpine meadow, the marmots, and the area where the rocks had fallen, but nothing was cause for alarm. He knew he would be warned by his own receptivity to wavelengths of danger, but even this thought made him pause. How about the time we were rising early to get the video apparatus set up for the morning shoot? What happened on that occasion?

He went into a brief recent recollection"

We had quietly dropped the tailgate of the truck while watching the river from two directions for bears that started to fish early. Next I dropped to the wet turf and started to stuff my shirt into my jeans before cinching up my belt – when – Wow! My peripheral vision picked up a movement to my left, away from the river, and there I was confronted with a beautiful female grizzly with twin two year old cubs. She was 60ft away – about 20 paces which is two bounds or 3 seconds to reach me. I stood in absolute awe of her stunning appearance as she rose on her hind legs, sniffed, shook her head, and "woofed" once. Had I made a move to re-enter the canopy she could have clawed me back in 2 seconds. My pants were not done up and would likely have fallen to my ankles. The passenger door was still locked. The driver door was unlocked but it was on her side.

She had obviously had the advantage of studying me as she entered the clearing with her cubs. She was in complete control and had taken me by surprise and she knew it. So I stood there, although strangely I was not frightened. She dropped on all fours and continued up the trail with her cubs and about a hundred yards further up she began tossing her huge head, swinging it from side to side, all the while snorting. Maybe she was telling the cubs about Humans, but somehow I knew she was just – excuse the language – pissed off with me being in her territory. It would not have taken much for her to turn back and eliminate me.

Why was I so careless? Why did I not scan the forest side, as well as the river before exiting the truck? Why was my alarm system unit not available and within reach, like in my pocket? Why was my Marlin Rifle fully loaded and on safety but lying on top on the aluminum storage boxes? It only takes one thoughtless move out here to end one's life. These situations are terminal, and they do not have to happen.

As for Little Boy Wild, he was so thrilled to watch her; he just projected love thoughts to her. He became a third cub and looked to her for guidance, and as a cub, he trusted his mother to have things under control. He just loved her so much; no other thought came to him, just awe and wonderment. I have little doubt that she felt no threat or fear, or hostility emanating from us or the tide would have turned rapidly.

Later that day a younger female grizzly with two "this years" cubs came within 10ft of the truck which was parked under the low tree branches with its nose pushed into the deeper green brush. Of course I saw what was shaping up as she had to come by me on my side of the river. I retreated inside the truck as she went by, she must have known I was there; the little grizzlies peeked at me through the bushes with bright eyes and inquisitive faces. They stood up and sniffed my video camera on its tripod and eventually followed Mama up the trail and round a bend in the river. Would they accidentally push my whole expensive video rig into the river? The greatest temptation was to get super close footage and go to the camera. I watched the little ones as they stopped to look at the truck before following her, but any move on my part with her cubs so close to me, could have spelled disaster on a furious scale. I just watched them, entranced, until they vanished.

Wild Boy was so absorbed and in tune with his "Infinite Dimension" that he hummed his Bluebird Song all day, usually the lyrics were his own, but that day of the grizzlies his voice had a special quality. Quietly he just stood and took in the total scene; he saw the bears, the trees, and the bald eagles. He heard the slap of the salmon as they leapt above the water and surged upstream to spawn, and *it all became ONE within him.* He somehow encompassed this scenic wonder on several levels of insight; he was the little cub's past, their present and their future. More than that, he felt himself as a pure thought form; he thrilled to capture every single magical heartbeat of this eternity, and held them as treasures to be possessed in a vision of cosmic oneness. He stood tall, breathed deeply and softly murmured, *"The Gods have come to Earth."*

He was deep in recollection and it took a moment or two for him to return to our alpine meadow among the flowers.

As is my habit I said, "Little Boy Wild – are you alright?"

For answer he rose, picked up his blue shorts complete with belt and Gerber blade, and it was then that he saw the ears.

"I'm fine," he said, "But those ears .... ."

Our eyes had picked up just the tips of moving ears, and then a bear head profile and then nothing. Then the ears came closer, and as the grizzly started up the slope, he came fully into view as we went behind trees on the trail in order to return swiftly to the truck if necessary. Maybe that was what had caused the small rock slide. We felt safer close to the truck, but as the bear didn't come up our trail, the temptation was to check and see where he was, however we refrained from doing this. Tree shadows turn into bears or hide bears so effectively that it makes us apprehensive. It was still a lazy beautiful day, so we filmed the Picas and the colorful green and orange lichens on the rocks, watched the eagles soaring and scanned for sheep or goats higher up the mountain. We did not see the grizzly again, which made us a little nervous when food preparation is underway, but we always eliminated food smells from any source and cached them away from camp about two hundred yards up the trail.

It is interesting to note that Little Boy Wild is taking over more and more as our primary personality – after all, he is REAL; will the day come when it is *he* who asks *me,* "Are *you* alright?" Or will we be so balanced in required proportions that we finally become an harmonious whole? Or am I simply the *observer* who watches them both, and who really is the observer, and why?

No doubt there are psychiatrists out there who know exactly where we are; but there really is only one Master Psychiatrist – *He who created me!* He who knew me from before the foundations of the Earth were laid! It was not until several years later that Wild Boy came to fully understand the Bible quotation, "Know ye not that ye are the temple of God?" These words burned slowly into his consciousness until *he viewed all Humans as temples of God.*

Wood smoke, blue and fragrant, rose from our campfire. The flickering fire embers were comforting and Wild Boy's face was a picture of pure contentment. I knew he was listening for his owls to call, so I let him talk aloud to the first stars without interrupting –he would never respond anyway in this type of mood.

"It's about stewardship," he mused. "Stewardship –I am the steward of myself, my resources, and above all, a steward of my mind. I alone, stand at the gate and allow or disallow the types of thoughts and circumstances that I wish to enter. I am accountable to God for my actions and thoughts. But there is one wonderful thing we have learned to do – we can come to the Father in the name of Jesus and discuss our innermost thoughts and feelings; He knows them anyway! Most of the time we stand like a small child with our hands over our eyes saying "You can't see me, you can't see me!" Wild Boy chuckled at the thought he had just expressed.

A log fell further into the fire and flames sprang up for a few moments illuminating his face. He rose and cleaned things up for the night, and then retired to the truck and the comforts of his large down bed. He watched the stars for a while, and then murmured somewhat sleepily, "King David was right – for I am fearfully and wonderfully made; marvelous are thy works and that my soul knoweth right well."

One final oft repeated phrase came to Wild Boy as he yawned, it was a message of beautiful comfort that allowed him to "let go," and utterly relax, ***"Thou wilt keep him in perfect peace whose eyes are stayed on thee, because in thee we trust."*** * He smiled as he slowly reached for his soft snuggle bunny, and caressing its silky ears, he fell asleep with its fuzzy face close to his cheek. After a while his owls called – again and again, but he was too far away to reply.

---

* King James Bible. Isaiah 26. 3.

Chapter Thirty Two

The next morning Little Boy Wild was up with the sunrise. He scouted his camp site and noted that a grizzly had passed close by in the night, although of course he would have heard nothing anyway unless it decided for reasons of hunger to investigate the truck. There were a couple of grizzly prints by his cache of "things that smell like food," including his jeans, but nothing was disturbed. He lit a small wood fire just because it was warm and friendly, and perked his coffee on it too. But all the while, he was thinking about what he had formulated in his mind as – *"Calling things into being."*

He sipped his overly sweet coffee noisily with long slurping sounds. Then speaking softly while avoiding wafts of wood smoke, he said, "So I am the steward of my thoughts and actions, I have to control the words that come out of my mouth, and bring them into obedience to the word of God, which is God's spiritual law. Faith will make prayer work, but prayer won't work without faith!"

He chewed on some trail mix, loving the crunch of nuts and seeds. All around him the world was coming alive; woodpeckers called and tapped, squirrels had their say about him eating the nuts, and bird songs seemed to fill the clearing with sweet trilling clarity as though they were celebrating life itself, which they probably were. But he could not escape his line of thought.

"I'm beginning to sound like a religious freak!" he exclaimed. But escape was impossible because he was a joint heir and creator with Christ, and these matters were central to his purpose in the cosmos.

"When *I AM*" he paused, "I cannot deny that *I AM.*" So he continued his soliloquy all the while watching his surroundings, and just *BEING*.

Little Boy Wild paraphrased his recollection of a great quote from the

Book. "Now faith is the substance of things hoped for, the evidence of things as yet unseen; for by faith were the worlds created when as yet there were none, and were made out of that which does not appear." In other words they were *called into being* by the spoken word. "Greater things than these shall ye do because I go to my Father," Jesus had said, and then he sent us the Comforter – the Holy Spirit to guide us in all things.

In addition to that he said, *"You have not chosen me, I have chosen you!"* And then he ordained us as individual ambassadors for Christ and empowered us with grace. *I am a Son of God because I'm led by the Spirit of God*. I have all authority on Earth and in Heaven through the Holy Spirit in the name of Jesus, to bind or release all power as I am so directed. Wow! Someday this will come fully into focus for me!

Wild Boy stopped to scan the marmots higher up on a rock bluff, as their whistles had interrupted his thread of thought which he spoke out loud into the cool mountain air. He stood tall in his blue shorts, and looked sturdy and capable in his well-cared-for hiking boots. His face had an ex-cited look as once again he filled his coffee mug, splashed in evaporated milk and a big spoon of brown sugar; he knew he had to take to the trail soon, as he was so restless with energy. But right then he changed his mind and dumped his mug, there were things to be seen and experienced, and thinking to be done, and what finer place to meet one's creator – than at the base of a flower blazed snow capped throne of creation?

This heavy duty line of thought he had spoken was no doubt possible because he had read parts of the Book so often by now, that it had become the architect of his life. Death was unthinkable. All he had to do was learn *obedience* to the Word. But just then nature called him up into the bush, and following this inspiring interlude he stripped and washed up, checked out his camera equipment again, and was set for the main adventure of the day. He just could not seem to get enough of the flower-scented air, he kept breathing deeply and it seemed to power him for some type of take-off. He felt that levitation was possible, that gravity could be overcome, however this was not an LSD flash back, or remotely connected with it. It was like flying on spiritual wings through a beautiful frequency of color and sound. He spoke again as he came in for a landing.

"Trust in the Lord with all thine heart, lean not to your own understanding, acknowledge the Lord in all thy ways, and He shall direct thy paths."

His "Landing," was special and necessary. He had been so enthralled with living every second of beauty, that only now with pounding heart, he observed a huge Mama grizzly with two cubs about two years old. She was in the meadow just below him and it appeared that she was digging out ground squirrels. Little Boy Wild was always aware of wind direction like the other animals, and it was in his favor, but he took no chances of having an encounter, and slowly retraced his steps through his flowery meadow so that he had her in sight and was not too far from his truck. As the sun rose higher in the sky the grizzlies disappeared into the bush, and he returned to the immediate proximity of his truck, where he lay "au naturel" to read and to dream.

For safety as a warning of his presence, in the event his scent had not been picked up, he threw another log into the fire. It was also time to 'mark' his territory, and as he was overdue for a good leak he found it a relief to mark his staked out area which included his truck, fireplace and about one third of an acre. He ran out of juice before he could complete the task, and planned to have it done by late afternoon. He refueled on two cans of beer, and chuckled when he was reminded of the time he had cached some beer close to his campsite and the Grizzlies had helped themselves. There were huge teeth marks and crushed cans to prove they enjoyed Old Stock Ale. Little Boy Wild felt strong – there was just all creation and him, and he was made in the image of God.

"In Him we move and have our being," he quoted with a beatific smile.

The ale had given him a 'buzz' and he drifted off into a semi-doze, but a part of him was also tuned to the world outside. Over a period of about an hour and a half, several little blue butterflies landed on him as had two other types; they probably tasted the beer he had spilled over his chest and belly. Although they tickled, he did not stir and shortly after, each butterfly took off. What *did* wake him was a big horsefly – it had a bite that deserved the swat he gave it, and, as was his practice, he removed his eye glasses, angled the sun and smoked the high pitched buzz to silence. He then finished 'marking' his territory. There was something intrinsically satisfying in this act. He established ownership and his scent said 'Come no further –this piece of land is mine!' On the other hand, scent or no scent – grizzly ruled all. In fact his scent may have told the predators that he was full of peanut butter and raspberry jam sandwiches, and all of this was washed down with some good ale! What more could a bear wish for?

But for some reason he could not fathom, *a still small voice within, told him to leave before dark*. He had planned to stay for another day, *but when the voice said to leave, it meant just that, and he had finally learned obedience.* Dousing his fire he cleaned up the site he had created, and searched for any remaining signs of his presence. When he was satisfied, he fired up the diesel and crept down to the lower elevations.

"Okay! Thy will be done – not mine, praise you Lord of all creation!"

Little Boy Wild planned to go down and locate a site somewhere along the river, he would watch the red headed mergansers, study the owls, follow the eagles in flight and maybe find some animal to talk to. The sun would not set for several hours, and just then he found an old deserted cabin on the edge of the river. This was all he needed, a place to walk around and just to *"be,"* without any particular plan. As he lay watching the hay meadow, he saw a cat at some distance, just lying on its back batting grasshoppers and chasing them. It was playful and also fun to watch, but then Wild Boy's reasoning kicked in, he recognized that it would have to be a very big cat to be that size, and half a meadow away, and also – why would a domestic cat be this far out? Then it clicked. It was a beautiful cougar, just playing like a barnyard cat. He watched it play for about twenty minutes, and then it rose, walked to the far end of the meadow, and disappeared into the tree line.

It made him feel good all over, his animals, his friends, even though they might eat him; he still loved them and moved with them. When he was able to see the expression in their eyes, were he close enough – *he became them,* in a level of consciousness that was quite separate from his, and then after, he had to come back to himself; it was a transfer between dimensions that totally altered his own body and thought. It had a different time element, and often after an individual experience, he would watch the entire scene and feel all things and all creatures move through him, and he seemed to be in a *"now"* dimension that encompassed the past and the present. Sometimes he felt very sad after these sequences. He would become small and innocent like a cougar kit, and curl up into a little lost bundle, while something inside of him wailed "Keelematu! Keelematu!" After a while he would become himself, and a current reality reigned. Usually he had tears to wipe away, and the old longing came upon him for companionship with his own kind, but he was not too sure what his kind was. In the end he would become so lost that he had to seek the North Star – or an anchor of some type, or he would be swept away and drown in turmoil and utter confusion. The only stabilizing factor he could locate time and time again when desolation struck him amidships, was to return to He who said "He who overcomes, I will give him the Morning Star."

Little Boy Wild has always considered his altered states of conscious-ness as being "Realities," and considers the "Human's" small "peep-hole" of vision into their narrow band of experience – that of being awake, dream-ing, and sleeping, as a sad grasp of even the smallest band of the cosmic wonder available to us. When Wild Boy sings his "Rainbow Song" – as he calls it, he views every spectrum of color in the rainbow as an equivalent interpretation of frequencies in consciousness; including the emotional, mental, intuitive, and the Theta wave components. Every current electronic marvel of color reproduction – speaks of color gradations in millions of colors, and Little Boy Wild sees his mind as having the same gradations in levels of perception into consciousness. *There are no barriers to our understanding or perception – other than the ones that we are taught, in-herit, erect, or refuse to break down – so why not walk boldly through?*

When one does not belong to the Humans and is not really a separate animal, what is one? One becomes a wanderer between worlds, yet with-out the strength and ability to build trust relationships in the one in which he belonged? Eventually Little Boy Wild did find Christian friends in his church. It was a wonderful break-through. But he was still not immune to silent screams, and occasionally writhed with sudden psychic pain.

A few wonderful days passed, and Wild Boy thought it would almost be okay to meet a "Human" and talk, but he was so far out that none of these creatures came his way. What he desired most was to have a compan-ion who could meet him where he was at, and discuss his dimensions, chal-lenge his concepts, and to scintillate their mutual facets of understanding off each other. He wanted a friend with whom he could interact, one who would enjoy a campfire, and delight in watching the stars while riding the winds of cosmic thought to where others may not have been – but all he landed up with was a baby squirrel! On a trail close by his campsite while he was collecting grizzly hairs off a grizzly bear scratching tree, he saw a little red squirrel fall from high up in a big fir to the soft forest floor. It lay very still, and as he carefully picked it up in his cupped hands, it slowly became less stunned. Little Boy Wild had a friend he could talk to, so he took it back to the truck and settled it into a soft blanket. It lay curled up; sometimes it opened its bright eyes, but not very wide. Wild Boy went to his trail mix bag and sorted out some nuts and then lay down beside his squirrel. He whispered little comforting sounds as he stroked its soft fur, and caressed it in tiny short strokes like a mama squirrel licking its young. He nuzzled its fur with his nose and mouth and breathed on it. After a while it looked at him, sat up, and of all things began cleaning itself. It was not at all afraid and Little Boy Wild surrounded it with love waves. Then, while it was washing its own exquisite little face with one paw behind a tiny ear – it lost its balance and keeled over.

Wild One was delighted and his heart pounded with excitement, but when his little friend nibbled on a nut, he knew it was about time to return it to its tree; this baby squirrel still needed its mother to teach it the ways of the forest and how to watch out for the martens – their mortal enemies. He gently picked it up and walked back up the trail to its fir tree, and placed it on the trunk where it clung with tiny claws. At that precise moment, a big, tall, almost black long legged grizzly came up the bank from the river, and Wild Boy slowly made his way back to the truck behind a screen of firs and cedars. He stayed in relative safety, and after a while strolled back to the squirrel tree. He had seen the grizzly take the opposite direction earlier and felt safe, even though he knew it could scent him, but when he reached his tree, there was no sign of his little friend and he had to assume it had climbed up, or its mother had come down to its calls. He would never know – but it really made his afternoon.

Evening was coming on, and as he was light of heart, he opened up some beer and made his evening meal on the Optimus stove, consisting of a dehydrated package of chicken and noodles and for dessert he finish up his bananas. All of this was topped off with coffee, and afterward, he strolled in the hay meadow while he softly sang his Bluebird Song.

"Somewhere over the rainbow –where bluebirds fly…."

Kingfishers gave their harsh little cries, a few frogs croaked, crickets called and some mosquitoes desperate for blood found him to be rather attractive. He also heard his wary red headed mergansers take flight. Something had disturbed them, but he felt safe by just keeping in touch with the wild noises and sights around him.

In the meantime where was I? Wild Boy had been in control for such a long time that I had not felt any need to require him to return control to me. It was simply not necessary to do so. *Is this the melding where we become one? YES!* It came to us with the impact of a fresh birth, real and utterly beautiful!

I AM Little Boy Wild! I AM the Real Self – the little Derek who was not supposed to be alive! It still seemed that when it came down to doing the stuff the Humans required of us, Big Derek – the Unreal Self, due to his experience in Human matters, simply acted in this subordinate role. So this was why *I – Wild Boy*, did not have to return control to the now lesser and unreal self, who was blended into my personality –And, *I was living with the animals!*

We did not want to return to civilization as yet and spent several more days reminiscing, during which time we saw the long-legged black grizzly on several occasions. I would have to get back fairly soon to step up production of insurance contracts in order to clean up the accumulating bills that piled up while I was away.

I reminisce on how WE have changed – or have we? Having always been a top producer of insurance contracts, my wife and I had been awarded trips to Mexico, Hawaii, Bermuda, Montserrat, Antigua, and Monte Carlo as well as the USA. We had also traveled on non-corporate holidays to Costa Rica and to Mazatlan in Mexico. I particularly liked Mazatlan, because out in the ocean within sight of our hotel was Rabbit Island, and Deer Island, and as soon as a couple of days had slipped by, Little Boy Wild and I went to explore Deer Island. From our shoreline, the green of the island looked much like the green grassy downs of England, but on arrival we discovered they were massive growths of thorn bushes. Each day we hired a boat to take us across and arranged for the return trips, so as to be picked up just before the supper hour. On approaching Deer Island we leaned over the side to search the water for marine life, and were rewarded by seeing giant Manta Rays cruising gracefully beneath us. As soon as Wild Boy touched the warm sand, *he achieved himself.* He had left the humans behind and this still changed him in many ways. He carried a linen bag with four cans of beer, a towel, his binoculars, a note book and pen, and his small KJV New Testament. He wore old runners and his swim suit. His shirt was packed in the bag.

I – the supposed lesser and subordinate Derek, wonder when *our* perspectives will change, and when will it be Little Boy Wild who is reporting what I am doing. Or – will we meld into one solid entity under one authoritative *I?* Because right now, although we work well together – maybe this is the best that it will ever get to be!!

Each day it was our routine to cross over to Deer Island, and in the early morning Wild Boy was entirely alone. A few Mexican fishermen had summer abodes on the island, but he saw little of them. Wild boy followed the coast line, shed his swim suit, and made a base close to some tall rock formations. Day after day he followed this routine. He wondered what the hawks fed on as they drifted on the hot air currents, and discovered that they lived on the ground squirrels and snakes. Some days were spent on the inner trails, and this is where he found the wild goats; while on other days he just wandered along the shoreline without a care in the world. All the while it felt as if his heart was keeping in tune with a rainbow of celestial music. It permeated his whole being with sacred knowledge from another realm and in a language few Humans would ever comprehend.

But this dedication to exploring Deer Island from early morning while carrying a bag, and then returning in late afternoon with the bag, piqued the curiosity of the local police who were always battling illegal drug activity. One morning when he had landed and was half way to his playground, he heard the rotors of a helicopter approaching, and as any normal animal would, he climbed up a bank and crawled under a thick bush to hide until the intruder had gone, but it kept cruising closer and lower looking for him; at this point Wild Boy clawed like a fox and dug a shallow depression in the soft sandy soil, so that he was partially covered. He curled up as small as possible and then pulled the tall yellow grass over him until he was totally hidden. At one point he could see their faces and binoculars, but they failed to locate him, and must have wondered where he disappeared to. One moment they saw him in a clearing, and the next moment as they approached he had disappeared. Not unlike a fox!

"Hey Little Boy Wild – they're looking for you!" I laughed.

Did they really think I brought back packages of drugs? I suppose anything is possible. With the helicopter gone he resumed his usual shoreline walk to his target destination. There were Oyster Catchers with long yellow beaks, and in the myriad of little tidal pools were all manner of marine life including some tiny brilliant electric blue fish. All day long, day after day, he had his own private island and beach. Rarely did anyone come this far as they were snorkeling and swimming close to the usual boat mooring site. Wild Boy explored, drank beer and read his Bible. Sometimes he would walk up and down the sandy beaches clutching his little black book and reading aloud. When he was tired he lay and napped or wrote notes on his thoughts.

But, he was not alone! While scanning for hawks and snakes higher up on the thorny bluff one day, he was surprised to see two Mexican police Officers keeping him under surveillance from one direction. He later saw three on a hill behind him, and then one stood up quite close by where he had been hiding in the long grass! Little Boy Wild stood tall and naked, a can of beer in one hand and his Bible in the other. Both he and the police looked at each other as they came out of hiding, and then the police pretended they were looking for something along the shoreline, but he knew he was their target and they had come up empty handed.

While he waited for his boat to pick him up that day, he joined some Mexican kids and their Dads. The little ones were stunning the bright green hornets as they flew by, and while in this stunned state they would tie a short nylon fish line around them; so that when the hornets recovered, the kids would fly them like kites – except these were self propelled kites! Wild Boy swapped his strong ale for some less powerful Mexican beer and partook of some roasted meat which was probably raccoon.

When the boat picked him up, the man in charge could well have been a policeman –he made no pretence, and asked him outright what he was carrying in the bag, and he showed them his four empty beer cans and personal items. He was again checked before he entered his hotel premises by uniformed Mexican Police, but I believe they already had received a report on this weird guy who ran around reading his Bible and drinking beer. They were even amused when he spoke to them about how he hid from their police helicopter. Their eyes twinkled and they got a kick out of the whole thing, especially when he explained – as only Little Boy Wild could – not being Human, that he had been hunted by this huge noisy creature, and he had gone underground like a fox until the danger had passed. The pure innocence of his expression and the sincerity of his explanation must have made their day! Of course, each day that I returned I had all kinds of adventures to relate to the family, who had for the most part, simply basked in the sun on the beach, and sipped tall drinks. How tame can it get? Why not talk with a Manta Ray, fly a green hornet, eat raccoon meat, be under police surveillance, guzzle beer and read your Bible in au naturel state under the tropical sun?

Back in Grizzly country again: The following morning, after having flown from star to star the previous night in the heart of all creation, ***I arose as my own major personality, Little Boy Wild,*** to greet the morning sunlight. Just looking at the sky at dawn was exciting – because one morning when I awake, I'm sure the celestial bodies that I see will be totally different from where I view them now. Is this the view from Venus? There, to the west on that blue planet is where I used to live, on earth with the Humans. I feel a touch of sadness. When will the Humans finally discover who they are, and recognize the powers that have been gifted them? Mostly they think they are just their bodies. They paint, preen or muscle up and beautify them when they're alive, and have them preserved, embalmed or even cryogenically frozen when they're dead; and then mark their graves with monuments to their egocentric ignorance, and even steal prime real estate locations from the living to commit this last indecent act. Who really cares anyway? No one on Earth, apart from a few close relatives who will not be around much longer; so short is our time.

Wild Boy said, "Let's pack up, say good bye to the grizzlies and hit the trail. We'll have some breakfast with the Humans in the valley, and meet a few more of the "Living Dead," who think they are alive." As we headed out, hunger pangs and stomach rumblings confirmed how hungry we were. Little Boy Wild still retained his "other world" state of mind. I sensed his excitement, and saw the star dreams in his eyes. Alongside of us, a family of red headed mergansers came into view, bobbing in the swift river current, and this one little scene, instantly captured and unified his current vision of, *"All that is, is within me – I am!"* He smiled. He knew his *real* discovery of the universe was fully underway, and that as a Christian he was *in* the world but not *of* it.

Along the narrow talus trail, we unexpectedly met three young grizzlies fishing in a deep pool – probably three year olds, still together. I thought there were only two, until the third one finally scented me and took off to the other side of the river. All three just looked at us. I had of course killed the engine, and all one could hear was the ripple and swirl of the fast river current. We spent about ten minutes just appreciating that whole magical sequence. Finally we moved slowly forward along the rocky base of the slopes, and the young grizzlies disappeared into the thick brush.

In the civilized world of "normal" people, at this time in life my wife and I had moved to the North Okanagan Valley, in central British Columbia to the small city of Vernon. It was surrounded by ranch land, wineries, orchards, wilderness, lakes and rivers – all of which were highly agreeable to me – Little Boy Wild.

But now and then I still experience serious sequences that are totally beyond my control. One comes to mind when our kids – now in their forties, along with their in-laws went on a fishing trip up to one of the many lakes with cabin accommodation.

That evening we were all gathered around a super fire where we barbequed our steaks, and prior to this I had been in a discussion with my older boy's Dutch father-in-law about the war (WW2), that is, rehashing the memories. While we were stuffing on steaks and beans, I suddenly stiffened, my breathing became harsh and noisy so that the others looked up to see if perhaps I was having a heart attack, but this was not the case. I remained stiffened, tears streamed down my face. My steak and beans plate took the vertical position spilling the food by the fire. My cutlery clinked onto some rocks, while I looked from one person to another in desperation, and then broke down into sobs.

I was viewing the campfire situation as a dream –my inside reality had suddenly switched to the roar of enemy planes, and bombs exploding among the bark of anti-aircraft guns. I left my body by the fire, and leapt into the brush screaming. I rolled around while the powerful search lights sought out the bombers.

"Keelematu! Keelematu!" I screamed. I was on the way back home from seeing a friend and now had taken to the ditch. It was difficult to determine where the next bomb would fall, they whistled in such close proximity, I buried my face in the earth and wet grass, and it seemed the noise had driven me out of my body. Wild One as a youngster was not sure if he were alive or dead as he viewed his slight form lying in the ditch. What does a small boy do when he has no more tears to cry, no more screams left to scream? He vanishes inside, deep inside where the bombs, guns and Humans cannot reach him. But later he feels his heart still beating, he is wet with ditch water from head to toe, and this does not bode well for him when he does arrive home because SHE ..... .

The noise has stopped, and he feels the warmth of a hot campfire – someone is pressing a cup of hot coffee into his hands, he is no longer small, and is surrounded by strangers, who are concerned about him. Slowly I sip the hot coffee – now I remember who they are. But they regard me somewhat warily, and no one wants to discuss what happened, they just talk about current affairs and this tends to isolate me. I feel utterly alone – while surrounded by my family.

So based on this I am careful not to get too involved in discussions of war, and try to avoid dialogue on child abuse and brutality, but only if it gets too lengthy, and perhaps too personal it may push me into a fetal "Keelematu" situation. I am still learning!

Earlier I spoke of the havoc that brutal child abuse can create in the body with tensions and turmoil, and in 1999, with no heart attack, I acquired six bypasses one morning. This delighted us as we had to cut all normal activity, and spend some three months recuperating, which meant for that we would be in the wilderness somewhere with the animals! Now six years later all is still well, and we have plenty of trips into the wild.

Life keeps unfolding in so many levels of consciousness that I know it will never end! Little Boy Wild and I are still in transition – and *the whole infinite Universe is within us, as we are in it!* And the only limits to our understanding are the limits we place upon ourselves. Viewing all that is below us, and behind us, it seems that we have ascended our "Everest," and the view from the peak is breath-taking. Where do we go from here? There must be some great work that has been set for us to complete while we are still here on Earth, or why else would we have been designed and prepared for it in this manner? I believe that life is just starting at this peak of our "Everest."

I believe that our images of the hereafter may only be revealed when we achieve a level of Christ consciousness beyond the fourth dimension. This *"Now"* that we are in, will then disappear – because the *"World to come"* has arrived! And will this be that time when we knock on the door of heaven – and I hear God ask, "Who is there?" *And finally I no longer reply, "It's Derek," but "THOU ART!" "Come in – there never was space for you AND me! For we are ONE!!"*

Epilogue

Well! – One small boy has shared some of his adventures, and there must be many hundreds of others that I have not recorded. But this is life as Little Boy Wild and I lived it. It took almost a lifetime for us to become *ONE – sort of !* We make no excuses or apologies for all that occurred, we simply did the best we could and struggled, phoenix-like, from the ashes of childhood pain and oblivion, to a world of imperfect normalcy. We were *gifted* pain and psychic torture, to become a tempered entity of extraordinary resilience and strength. We could never have been empowered to help others with such insight and acceptance, had we not traveled this path. We now see with eyes that know the unknowable, and understand that which others can only approach as unexplored frontiers.

A number of people have asked "What happened to the characters you interacted with throughout the book?" Okay – I'll do a quick summary!

Tim, I lost track of. Someone said he had gone overseas and others seemed to think he had been killed in a truck accident in the West-Country.

The nice farm folks at Lemberg, Saskatchewan all passed on in due course as they were in their middle years when I was still about twenty.

My good friend Bill Liska of radio fame in Yorkton went home in the late nineties, and George Wilson, my side kick in radio at CJGX was for many years with the CBC and eventually retired in the Caribou country of British Columbia – we still visit and have good times.

Oh! And Don Slade and Gloria live in Calgary, Alberta. When I last saw him he was still in radio – just for the fun of it!

Tom McLaren of our fire extinguisher period became the owner of a Cable company distributing television programming. Alice, his wife, is a devout Christian, as is Tom, and involved in many activities. She forgave me long ago for slyly teaching her blue budgie bird some rather beautifully articulated words that were unfit for a Christian household.

Svein Madsen of long ago adventures on the McLeod and Athabasca Rivers retired to the Victoria area of BC, after a long and successful business in marine diesels and supplies.

My brother Rex after a lifetime of commercial ventures and struggling went the way he would want to go in 2004. The ranchland he acquired, now falls into the middle of a huge ski and recreation development with land values sky rocketing. His family will prosper.

BROTHER – the nemesis of my childhood has become a close friend over many years now. We really enjoy each other's company and have traveled widely together.

My sister Shendra, following the loss of her cinematographer husband Collin, continues with their pioneering work in film documentaries. He was an explorer, sailor and adventurer. Shendra also had stuttering problems, having been born into a very traumatic childhood. In later years she learned that several attempts were made to kill her in the womb. She fully understands, accepts, and has also long ago forgiven those involved, for they "knew not what they did," or why. Her life has been, and is, dedicated to teaching and encouraging growth in others.

"SHE" – mother, and my father, passed on in due course, remembered and fully forgiven.

My loyal and industrious wife is still with me, doting over the grandchildren and generally enjoying life. Yes! She still thinks I'm *STRANGE!!*

How about my three sons? They are all quite successful. The older boy is in the general insurance business, and is busy raising his two sons. The second boy is managing a large mill operation with a major forestry company, and the youngest one is a professional geological engineer, as is his wife. We have six grandchildren, and nowhere in our family or theirs has anyone ever been touched by the child abuse factors with which I was raised – if that is the right word! Perhaps I should say "razed."

Of course *Little Boy Wild is ME,* but I get a lot of input from Big Derek – the Unreal Self, as we move toward our goals. *We* still both talk to each other, and it is relaxed and friendly like old friends which we are. In addition to this, at times we sin – simply meaning that we have are living contrary to the will of God. This is quite human, and we have learned that empowered by His grace, we can return to Him. *Speaking of Humans – Little Boy Wild IS Human — his Creator told him so!*

We no longer have to create disastrous situations in order to *FEEL*. We still live on the cutting edge as it were, but the scenes that we generate are humorous – not tragic. I now feel that perhaps I know why pyromaniacs have to burn things down. At that point of explosion, fire or other created disaster, they reclaim their identity. They *find* themselves for just a brief while. *They become alive and actually feel – they become themselves,* and it is a beautiful feeling of birth and release, before they fall back into their normal dulled-out-of-existence type of life. This is a life that passes them by, and they watch it from their shadowed retreat. Setting fires is not simply a way of "getting attention" as is so often claimed. It *is* a desperate attempt to be fully alive, to *feel,* to *BE* and to *live* – even to love and be loved. There must be multitudes of unrecognized silent screams and psychic agony between those fiery acts.

As usual, every autumn we visit the grizzlies in the wilderness during the salmon runs, and just *"live."* Sometimes I still have a "Keelematu" sequence, but when I project light as a spiritual Son of God, all darkness disappears. It is spiritual law. *This really is the beginning!!*

I have shared our experiences through the pain and hatred, that both *you* and *we* have endured, and have recorded it here because it is genuine, colorful, funny, extraordinarily honest, and one long period of growth in the hope *that others will realize that they are not alone!* Little Boy Wild, and the now lesser, "Big Derek," will pray for you in faith and love, for your obedience to the Word of God!

ISBN 141207920-9

9 781412 079204